wonderful women by the sea

the new press international fiction series

Tahar Ben Jelloun	*Corruption*
Hector Bianciottti	*What the Night Tells the Day*
Bruno Bontempelli	*The Traveler's Tree*
Patrick Chamoiseau	*Creole Folktales*
Marguerite Duras	*The North China Lover*
Tibor Fischer	*Under the Frog*
Tibor Fischer	*The Thought Gang*
Romesh Gunesekera	*Reef*
Aldulrazak Gurnah	*Admiring Silence*
Aldulrazak Gurnah	*Paradise*
Mark Kharitonov	*Lines of Fate*
Jaan Kross	*Professor Martens' Departure*
Jaan Kross	*The Czar's Madman*
Adriaan van Dis	*My Father's War*
Antoine Volodine	*Naming the Jungle*

monika fagerholm

wonderful women by the sea

a novel

translated from the swedish
by joan tate

the new press
new york

Library of Congress Catalog Card Number 96-72012
ISBN 1-56584-338-x

First published in Swedish in 1994 by Söderström & C:O
Förlag AB, Helsinki
Published in the United States by The New Press, New York
Distributed by W.W. Norton & Company, Inc., New York

Established in 1990 as a major alternative to the large commercial publishing houses, The New Press is a nonprofit American book publisher. The Press is operated editorially in the public interest, rather than for private gain; it is committed to publishing, in innovative ways, works of educational, cultural, and community value that, despite their intellectual merits, might not normally be commercially viable. The New Press's editorial offices are located at the City University of New York.

Book design by Ann Antoshak

Production management by Kim Waymer

Printed in the United States of America
9 8 7 6 5 4 3 2 1

Much gratitude for valuable information to
Kristin W. and Merete, Pirr,
and enormously so to Henrika,
to whom this
book is dedicated.

“I have heard the mermaids singing each to each.
I do not think that they will sing to me.”

I

isabella, mermaid

One time Kayus was throwing balls at the mermaids at the amusement park. Each mermaid lay or sat on a green shelf above the pool. The shelf gave way and swung down whenever the ball scored a direct hit on the pink board below the shelf. The mermaid screamed, fell, and landed in the shallow water, which was barely higher than her knees. Again and again Kayus aimed at the same spot on the board. Again and again Isabella fell, again and again she screamed, the same brief shrill scream, which was not beautiful but certainly not inaudible, a scream that began to haunt Kayus so that it reverberated in his head all the time, even when he was not at the amusement park.

Then one evening, after the park had closed, he waited for Isabella at the staff entrance.

In this and similar versions Isabella and Kayus told Thomas their story—the story that Isabella was a mermaid Kayus had brought back from among the mermaids at the amusement park.

"Wasn't it awful sitting there waiting for someone to make a hit?"

"Weren't you cold?"

Thomas asked all kinds of questions. He was dangling between them, one hand in Isabella's, the other in Kayus's, and was being swung over prickly plants and over stones in the forest. Isabella would smile, Kayus would smile, and they would look at each other over Thomas's head.

Isabella said that it was original to have a mermaid for a mother. She said it was more fun to fall off a shelf than to wait around for someone to throw the ball and hit the pink board under the shelf.

But Isabella left the scream behind at the amusement park. That hadn't been her own, she told him, she had learned it when they trained her. The people who ran the amusement park had wanted the mermaids to sound a particular way when they screamed and fell off the shelf and landed in the pool below. In order to scream the right way, she mustn't breathe too deeply, because otherwise the sound wasn't as loud and piercing as it had to be. And the scream had to be forced out between half-open, always smiling, lips. Isabella laughed when she described the way. Isabella's own laugh, Isabella's own voice, were both different. Her laugh tumbled out everywhere, reproduced itself through all the days of summer, and floated out over months, years. Time, in general.

In winter they live in a third-floor city apartment above a square courtyard. It is a new building, so Thomas is one of the first generation of children in the courtyard. They have two rooms, a kitchen, and a balcony. One of the rooms is Thomas's, and his window faces the street. He often stands at the window to watch the people waiting at the bus stop below. The other room is the living room, where Isabella and Kayus sleep on a pullout sofa bed. That room is also where they keep the record player, mounted on a stool next to Isabella's dressing table with its triple mirrors, which they call the wing mirror because the outer mirrors can be moved like wings. In the bathroom is the tub where Isabella and Kayus bathe together. They move the record player as close to the bathroom as they can, pour some Fenjal bath foam into the water, put on a record they like, and get in. Then they have a bath, and jazz roars through the pipes in the building until deep into the night.

In the living room is the balcony door, which Isabella opens.

"Want to go?" asks Thomas.

Isabella says yes. Isabella nods.

Isabella turns around and blows smoke in Thomas's face.

Thomas loves having smoke blown in his face.

"Come on, Thomas," says Isabella. "Let's go. To the mermaids, out into the world."

Then they close the door and go back inside. The game is over. Time to cook or clean or do something else until Kayus comes home.

In winter they live in a third-floor city apartment above a square courtyard.

In summer they live in a summer paradise.

At first they live in a small gray cottage, which they paint red so that it becomes the red cottage. Isabella pulls Thomas along the forest road in a box on wheels. Thomas is small and fits into the box for a long time, until he is seven. When they get to the white villa, Isabella stops on the path and says that she's never seen anything so lovely.

They move from the red cottage to the white villa. The rooms on the ground floor are furnished with antiques and there's a regular attic with partitions, and that room becomes Isabella's studio.

"This will be my studio, Thomas," says Isabella the first time they go into the attic, then quite empty, the only room in the white villa that is not furnished. "We'll do all kinds of things here, Thomas. I love empty spaces. You can fill empty spaces." She says nothing for a moment, trying to think of something really good. "With all kinds of things," she says then. "Whatever you like, Thomas. Doesn't that get your imagination going?"

Thomas and Isabella paint the walls pale green and carry in two mattresses, a low chest of drawers, and magazines.

The glassed-in veranda on the ground floor is Kayus's. He keeps his summer library there, and his new transistor radio, a Helvar Rita de Luxe. Kayus listens to all the radio programs, though mostly when they play jazz.

The big room is big. They call the far corner the reading corner; it holds a white table with an oil lamp on it, a white bookcase, and three wooden chairs. The shelves behind the glass doors of the bookcase are empty, but magazines lie on the table. Sometimes Isabella sits in the reading corner, just so that that part of the room can also be said to be in use.

She lights the lamp with her cigarette lighter, although it is the middle of the day and sunlight is pouring in through all four of the tall windows. She taps a cigarette out of the pack, picks up a magazine, and opens it on her lap. She lights her cigarette and calls to Thomas to bring her an ashtray. The next moment she stretches and puts the magazine back on the table, gets up and walks over to the sideboard to look at herself in the mirror made up of little tiles that reflects her face in many bits and pieces. She blows smoke at herself in the mirror. She fishes a lipstick out of the makeup case she keeps below the mirror, twists it open, and paints her lips. Isabella's summer lipstick is pink, always pink, for no other shade goes so well with tanned skin and yellow clothes. She smiles and straightens a few strands of her thick dark hair—quite unnecessarily, since Isabella's hair is always at its best, whether it's neat or unkempt. Then she is satisfied. Isabella is always satisfied when she looks at herself in mirrors.

She stubs out her cigarette and turns to the audience of whom she has by now become very much aware.

And she says, "Come on, Thomas. Let's go out and figure out how to have some fun."

isabella's studio

" . . . and that's how I became a brunette," says Isabella to Thomas in Isabella's studio in the attic in the white villa, that summer when they stay there nearly the whole time and tell each other secrets to pass the time. "It's a secret, Thomas. Now I've told you. You mustn't tell anyone. Promise."

"I promise," says Thomas drowsily. He remembers the promise for a long time. But he forgets the story about how she became a brunette almost as soon as Isabella tells it. Perhaps he isn't listening.

But that's what it's like. When you're right there, in the same studio, it's easy to let your mind drift and pretend to be absorbed in Donald Duck comics even if you can hardly read. Actually it's possible not to listen at all, even though you say "Yes, yes, yes" while Isabella's voice blends with the rain persistently battering against the windowpane. Over your head it sounds like machine guns.

1962. A wet beginning to the summer.

Thomas is lying on a mattress at one end of the room.

Isabella is lying on a mattress at the other end.

"Do you remember her?"

Isabella holds up a magazine and points at a picture. A woman in a fountain, the water coming up to her thighs and spurting all around her. She is fully dressed. Her wet clothes stick to her body so that her curves are revealed all the more clearly and her nipples and her navel show darkly through the wet material. She looks happy. She is laughing, her mouth large and wide open.

"She was one of the mermaids, Thomas. Now she's gone out into the world. That's the most famous fountain in the world. It's called Fontana di Trevi. That's where she is now. In the middle of *la dolce vita*."

"What's that?" says Thomas.

"The good life." Isabella braces her legs against the wall above her mattress.

"What's that?" Thomas braces his legs against the wall above his mattress.

Isabella tosses the magazine, and it lands in a corner. She

drums her heels against the wall in time to the rain. Then she pauses in her drumming and says, "Hey, Thomas. Do we really have to ask that kind of stuff?"

"No," says Thomas.

Of course not.

When you're there, there are a thousand better things to do than ask silly questions.

Then there is a honk that makes itself heard above the rain. Thomas runs to the window. "Look, Isabella. Come and look!"

A big white car is tearing along the forest track, straight into their summer paradise.

the angel family

They call them the Angel family. The Angel family call to each other outside their newly built wooden house up on the hill. They call to each other in American. They speak this language so insistently that once, outside the Johanssons' sauna, after the Angel family has just been picked up by the Lindberghs' boat to go to a party on an island on the other side of the sound in the real archipelago by the open sea, May Johansson feels compelled to point out that they are probably every bit as Swedish as we are. She does not put into words what can be heard in her voice: The Angel family thinks it is superior to the others.

Thomas is trying out a few sentences. He is practicing his pronunciation. One day, when the younger Angel daughter is using a stick to dig in the mud on the shore of May Johansson's inlet, splattering brown sludge all over and around herself, he goes up to her and says, "How do you do? Do you speak English?" She stops, flings the stick far away into the reeds, and says something that ends with *you idiot*. Thomas turns around and goes away, scarlet to the tips of his ears. Suddenly he stops and listens. No. It cannot be the echo of his own steps. He looks back. She's following him.

"My name's Thomas," says Thomas.

"Renée," says Renée.

They walk on, deep into the forest. They go on walking, she close behind him all the time. Just before he gets to the hornet's nest, which he does not notice until it is too late and he steps right into it, he turns around again and sees that she has disappeared.

They call them the Angel family. Before anyone knows the Angel family, everyone has heard Mr. Angel talking about his *white angel from over there*. The white angel, that is the car the family drive along the track one day, one of those first wet summers when Kayus and Isabella and Thomas live in the white villa.

Mrs. Angel often comes walking down the hill that summer, wearing white slacks, a white sweater, and a white scarf tied around her head, a basket on her arm. She walks down to the beach and stops at the jetty. Sometimes the Lindberghs come for her in their shiny mahogany speedboat. Once Mrs. Angel asks May Johansson if she can borrow Johansson's rowboat. (It is not until the following summer that the Angels acquire a little boat of their own, with a 5-HP outboard engine mounted in the stern, and two summers later Mr. Angel buys a second-hand 18-HP Evinrude.) May Johansson says she would be very welcome to it but she herself needs it to get to the floating shop. Mrs. Angel walks back to the hill. From the nearby beach, where, protected by blankets, she lies in the sun, Isabella calls out that Mrs. Angel can borrow the white villa's rowboat if she likes, and Mrs. Angel says thanks and turns back.

In the evening Mr. Angel comes down to the beach and stamps on the Johanssons' ramshackle wooden jetty and says that since they own that strip of the beach jointly, the Angels and the Johanssons, before next summer they must get together, dig deep into their packets, and shell out the necessary money to build a fine sturdy breakwater. They must also test for water in the subsoil and have a real well dug, one that won't run dry in the middle of the summer. There has to be enough water to wash the car in August.

They call them the Angel family. That is because of the car, the white angel from far away across the ocean. They bought it in America, in Washington, D.C., where Mr. Angel worked for an electrical firm and where the Angel family lived for at least a year. To bring a car like that into the country tax free, says Huotari, who spends occasional weekends and his vacation at his fisherman's cottage on an island just across from the summer paradise, a real Chevrolet Chevelle, you have to have lived abroad for over a year.

They call them the Angel family. That is not their name. They have an ordinary last name, a name like anyone else.

They are Gabriel Angel, Rosa Angel, Nina Angel, and Renée Angel, who even then has the wildest hair, the most vividly orange T-shirt, and the freshest mouth.

"The future is electric," says Gabriel Angel, smiling.

"Better living through electricity," says Gabriel Angel, smiling.

"You must come and see our place sometime. Our little summer place. And next summer we'll put in electricity—there and all over this summer paradise," says Gabriel Angel, smiling and spreading his hands in front of Jazz Kayus and Isabella Mermaid, who are off for a walk in the forest with their son Thomas, seven years old, whose most noticeable feat so far consists of having seven different kinds of allergies—and they are discovering still more. It is a week or two before he puts his foot into that rotten tree stump where the hornets have their nest.

But so far there has been no going to the house on the hill this summer. Only an occasional glance, in passing. You really don't want to go without a good reason. You have a feeling that you'd be a nuisance, in the way you can be a nuisance to people busy living the good life. And it's not just because you want to be polite that you hesitate to disturb them; it's also because it would probably make you miserable to see how deep some people are into the good life, while you yourself are trying to do the best you can in a more remote backwater, where the sun does not shine so brightly, and the fun is not quite so clearly fun. Like, for instance, sharing the cost of the grilled sausages to celebrate Midsummer at the Johanssons, for May Johansson says the Johanssons are a poor family with a lot of mouths to feed, and they cannot possibly think of *living it up* and *burning their candle at both ends* like some people.

Mr. and Mrs. Angel are often taken to parties at the Lindberghs' on the other side of the bay or to the homes of unknown people who live out on the islands in the real archipelago by the open sea, where Isabella has never even been.

But at other times, if the evenings or the days seem too long, the Angel family drives away in the car.

"We're restless people," says Gabriel "Gabby" Angel, smiling, and his eyes rest on beautiful Isabella Mermaid. She smiles back. "So are we," she wants to say, but Thomas squeezes her hand hard because a large spider is walking along the ground, heading straight for him, and this summer he does not yet particularly like spiders. Kayus squeezes Isabella's other hand: a sign of understanding. At this time they have several signs of that kind, Jazz Kayus and Isabella Mermaid—gestures, looks, smiles, certain words, snatches of music.

"If you listen to jazz long enough and learn to understand it, perhaps you'll learn to love it just as much as I do," says Jazz Kayus, and he means it, and this summer it is still possible to love a certain kind of music because you understand it.

"Mmm, I think so, too," says Isabella Mermaid, trying to hum with the music. And she means what she says; every single word.

Mrs. Angel comes walking across the yard of the white villa carrying a small measuring cup. A plastic Mickey Mouse measuring cup. It is the very end of the summer, and Marilyn Monroe has been dead for two weeks. When Mrs. Angel comes into the kitchen of the white villa and says that she is going to bake a cake, but she forgot to buy flour, and Mrs. Johansson would not get her a two-pound bag from the floating shop because it weighs too much, and it so happens that on this very day May Johansson has promised both Maggi and Erkki Johansson that they can go with her, and the rowing will be hard work . . . and Mrs. Angel stands at the center of the dark-blue kitchen floor saying all that, then she falls silent, wriggling her fingers meaningfully for a moment, so that without a word Isabella realizes that she is imitating May

Johansson's prattle. Isabella says that sure, she has flour, but the measuring cup isn't big enough to hold the amount needed for a cake. Then Mrs. Angel gives a smile that Thomas has seen only on his mother, Isabella Mermaid, when they talk about the mermaids and the good life, and Mrs. Angel replies, "Of course, and I suppose I could have asked Gabby to go get me some, too, but the thing is, I never bake cakes, and when I do, I use a mix," and her hands twirl in the air like a whisk, then she laughs again and comes and sits at the table and says that her name is Rosa.

"If I've got an American accent that's because we came back in the spring after three years in Washington, D.C. Marilyn Monroe is dead. Have you heard?"

"Marilyn Monroe," says Isabella, laughing the heartless laugh of brunettes.

"Marilyn Monroe," says Rosa, laughing the heartless laugh of brunettes.

When they are together, they are *almost* like Elizabeth Taylor and Jacqueline Kennedy.

They are together for two hours.

Before she leaves the white villa, Mrs. Angel says, "You must come up to our place and see what it's like, Isabella. Some day soon."

And again, as she stands in the doorway, "I was thinking. How lucky that you're here. I thought I wouldn't survive in this summer paradise. How lucky," says Rosa Angel as she leaves the white villa, "that this is a summer paradise after all, with civilized people in it."

Rosa Angel leaves the Mickey Mouse cup behind on the table. Thomas just stares. He wants to take it and squirrel it away, hide it and save it.

After Rosa Angel came to the white villa, Thomas feels that he has been touched by something greater and more beautiful, something from the beyond. So far his only comparable experience happened a long time ago, at the amusement park. And he does not remember much of that except for what Isabella has told him, and that isn't quite the same thing.

Once, at the amusement park, all the hysterical women were crowding around all the other places while Isabella and her son Thomas were standing near the candy booth. Suddenly Paul Anka has appeared from nowhere, breathless, red in the face, as only someone who has run from thousands of women fans can look.

"Here you are, son," Paul Anka said, handing Thomas a stick of cotton candy. Pink. Thomas remembers colors. Paul Anka chose a yellow one.

"What did he say?" Thomas asked.

"He said, 'Here you are, son,' " Isabella translated.

They went home and told Jazz Kayus everything, and he chuckled at the idea of Paul Anka, a charmer without any musical talent. Then he laughed some more, as if at a lot of nonsense, but not really condescendingly, since Thomas and Isabella were pretty excited, and did not want to spoil their mood by knowing more than they did. Later, when the newspapers reported that Paul Anka had stood at the window of his hotel and thrown down all his clothes, one garment after another, for the thousands gathered on the pavement below, Isabella said what was it to have a piece of Paul Anka's underpants when you'd met him Live, as in this recording—with is it Bill Evans?—which Kayus put on the turntable before saying to Isabella, hopefully, happily, and optimistically, "If you listen hard enough and learn to understand this music, you'll soon come to love it, and you won't want to listen to anything else."

Isabella sank down on the sofa, Thomas went to bed, and Isabella listened and went on listening, then said, "Yes, I think so, too. I think so." And she meant what she said; every single word.

The day after Rosa Angel came to the white villa, Isabella Mermaid makes her way up the hill to the Angels' house.

The day after, Isabella has forgotten to look in her appointment book. The day after that, the summer has come to an end.

"You forgot to look at the appointment book," says Kayus with delight.

He's already stuffing his summer library into a brown suitcase. Isabella Mermaid gives in, shaking out white sheets, which settle over the furniture in the big room.

They hear a honk coming from the forest road.

It is the Angel family majestically sailing through the trees in their white Chevrolet Chevelle, towing a trailer that holds all their stuff.

Still. This summer, 1962, the summer before the summers with Rosa. Thomas walks into a hornet's nest in the forest. He is badly stung and runs out of the forest with hornets all over and after him. He runs along the path to the beach, across the smooth rocks and out into the water. Kayus follows him, still wearing all his clothes, wades out into the water and tries to chase away the hornets that keep circling above the surface of the water. An audience gathers on the beach. At least May Johansson, Erkki Johansson, and Renée stand there staring. Afterward, in bed with a high fever and behind drawn curtains, Thomas has time to think about all of it. That they stood there staring. Did they laugh? Did they smile, even slightly? In that case—although his temperature keeps going up, he is alert enough to put the thought into words quite clearly: *In that case it would serve them right if he fell ill and died.* Thomas's body swells up, and his temperature keeps rising. In the middle of the night Isabella gets dressed and goes up to the house on the hill. She says that of course it's a lot to ask, but could Gabby possibly drive her and her son Thomas to the hospital right now? It is an emergency, after all, and this summer Gabby's white angel is the only car in the summer paradise.

Thomas is wrapped in blankets and placed on the backseat of the white angel. Afterward all he remembers is lying there staring up at the dark sky as it slowly grows lighter, his temples throbbing, the engine growling, and the radio glowing dully between the two front seats. The usual radio stations have stopped broadcasting long ago but Gabby says, *It's no problem whatever finding a little light music on FM.* He fiddles with various knobs, but the radio merely hisses and crackles. In the end Isabella leans forward, laughs a mermaid laugh, and twists another knob, so that silence falls in the car.

Gabby laughs, drums his fingers on the wheel, and hums *Two of a kind, two of a kind.*

When Thomas comes back from the hospital, he boasts to Renée that he almost died. They play the Peter Pan board game, and Renée fixes it so that Thomas is taken prisoner and held in Captain Hook's cave and has to miss three turns. Then she leaves in the middle of the game. Thomas is left behind in his room, convalescing and confined to the house for three days, shut up in Captain Hook's cave. Renée saunters off. Through the window Thomas sees her orange back disappearing across the yard.

II

summers with rosa 1963-1965

If we're to have any hope of understanding one another, we have to speak in metaphors, in images. We always do so in the simplest contexts of everyday life, and we must do so as well when we are trying together to learn something about reality. Real scientists never say: This is it! They say: This is an image of the way we think it is.

instructions for use, skeleton, thomas's birthday present in 1963.

Only a few days into the Angel family's second year in the summer paradise, in 1963, Rosa stands in the kitchen doorway again. Isabella and Thomas are having breakfast. They're eating homemade yogurt, lifting their spoons high above their bowls and letting the yogurt run back down into the bowls in long viscous threads. Again and again, in precisely the way that drives Kayus crazy. But Kayus is not here. He has gone to work in the family's new Austin Mini. And his vacation is still a long way away.

Rosa leans against the doorpost, smiling, arms folded across her stomach, then she smiles some more. She wears sandals on her feet, leather sandals with white straps around her heels. Thomas gazes at them intently, for suddenly he feels shy—so shy he dares not even raise his head.

It is her self-confident way of standing in the doorway, as if she had stood there heaven knows how many times. Not just on that single occasion last summer, when she came with the Mickey Mouse cup, which she left behind on the table. Isabella took it back to the city, placed it under the triple mirror on her dressing table, and filled it with her curlers.

She is wearing a bathing suit and a robe, something she calls the picnic basket is hanging over her shoulder; it is a cool bag, dangling from a strap, and it is "excellent for holding reading matter and soft drinks and suntan lotion and all the things you might need in the sun on the beach on a hot day," as she explains later, down at the beach. "Though this isn't really a beach, too many rocks and too little . . . too little sand for that." She will toss her head back so that her dark hair flies about, laugh a little, and tap a cigarette out of the pack, light it and inhale, blowing smoke out through her nostrils in a straight, significant jet.

"Though I must say I'm not all that crazy about sand. It's so san . . . dy. I prefer smooth rocks. Hot summer rocks."

She lies on her back on the rock, gazing straight up into the sky where a plane is flying past. "Ah, Bella," she says then.

“Airplanes. I love airplanes.

“You’ll let me call you Bella, won’t you? Isabella is so long.”

Still. At this moment. She is standing in the doorway, on one of the first days of the first summer with Rosa. And she says the words that etch their way into Thomas, words he will remember for a long time, for all of his life.

“Let’s go now, Isabella. To the beach. It looks like it’s going to be a lovely day.”

the beach women in a picture

Thomas snaps the picture of the women on the beach one day in July 1963. He uses Rosa’s camera, a wholly automatic Instamatic, which adjusts distance and light by itself, so that the person taking the picture only has to push a red button above the viewfinder.

Bella and Rosa are lying on the beach blanket on the smooth rock just above the point where Thomas is standing. Bella and Rosa are propped up on their elbows, shoulders just touching. Bella and Rosa are wearing, respectively a yellow and a white bathing suit, but the colors will not show on the photograph because the film is black and white. Both of them have put on their sunglasses.

Behind Bella and Rosa, in the gap between their slanting bodies, the bay is a glittering blue in the sunlight. Tupsu Lindbergh is water skiing in the wake of the Lindbergh’s shiny mahogany speedboat.

Tupsu Lindbergh is wearing a white bikini and has fair hair, at the moment protected by a red, blue, and white scarf.

She looks beautiful.

What could be better on a photograph of the women at the

beach than Tupsu Lindbergh on water skis in the background? At least Thomas can't think of anything. He tries to get Tupsu Lindbergh into focus.

Then Renée arrives. She sits down on the rock behind Bella and Rosa, her back to him, so that her orange T-shirt fills the entire space between Bella's and Rosa's backs. Renée pulls up her legs, flings her arms around them, and rests her chin on her knees. She is pretending to be absorbed in the view. Thomas fiddles with the camera to gain time. But he knows it is pointless; she is not going to budge. By now Thomas and Renée can read each other's minds, but in this situation that talent does not come to Thomas's aid. Ordinarily she detests being photographed.

"Push the red button, Thomas!" calls Rosa.

A strand of hair blows across Bella's face, and she brushes it away impatiently. "Hurry up, slow poke! If you don't take it soon, the wind will turn and I'll be stuck with this expression on my face for the rest of my life."

Thomas knows he can't drag the moment out any longer. Bella and Rosa have to get up, put on their robes, roll up the blankets and tuck them under their arms, pick up the beach bag and the cool bag and make their way up into the shade and permanent coolness of the birch-lined avenue.

He has to take the photograph so it can be turned into a memory.

Thomas pushes the red button.

At that very moment, a breeze blows in from another direction, and the wind turns.

On the smooth rock behind the women, with her back to him, sits Renée, not speaking.

■ ■ ■

If you walk from the white villa along the birch-lined avenue, down to the beach, the other houses are on the left: Rosa's and Gabby's timber house farthest up the hill, the Johanssons' house below, and slightly to one side, the red-painted cottage where Johan and Helena Wikblad are living this year with their blue baby, who is sick and who will die in the autumn.

To the right are the Rotwoods. In the Rotwoods spindly trees grow close together straight up from the ground, some so delicate they can be uprooted by hand. In the Rotwoods cabins are built and pulled down, the ground is flattened for paths. In the Rotwoods they simulate a motocross race on their bikes—that is, Renée and Thomas and Erkki Johansson, Nina and Maggi occasionally, but not often. Nina and Maggi Johansson mostly keep to themselves in the changing room of the Johanssons' sauna. There they keep their boyfriends. No one else knows they are boyfriends, except Renée and Thomas, who, after a while, know everything worth knowing in the summer paradise. The boyfriends are cardboard that was once wrapped around cable drums delivered to the summer paradise in the spring, when, at Gabby's initiative, all the houses except the red cottage are electrified. Maggi's and Nina's boyfriends are called Klas Lindbergh and Peter Lindbergh, and by chance Thomas happens to find out that there's a third one as well, a considerably grubbier piece of cardboard given the name Lars-Magnus, who was Renée's boyfriend, since Renée is the youngest of the girls and, however stupid Lars-Magnus is, the Lindberghs only have three sons. When Thomas finds out, he uses the knowledge to improve his relationship with Renée, and eventually Thomas and Renée secretly take all three boyfriends out into the main forest and tear them to shreds over a mossy puddle.

Rosa and Isabella are lying in the sun on the rocks down at the beach. Isabella sleeps under a gray blanket when her body has had enough sun. She has rubbed herself all over with suntan oil; it has a distinct pungent smell and stays on her skin through all the days of summer. The bottle's label shows a dark-brown boy wearing white bathing trunks. A similarly tanned woman in a yellow bathing suit is kneeling in the yellow sand beside him, in the background are blue sky and blue sea and beach umbrellas. The boy is holding a bottle of suntan oil in his hand, squirting it on the woman's back, the stream of oil white and cone-shaped. If you look at the label long enough, you can see that there is no end to the picture. The bottle the boy is holding has exactly the same label. On that label is another woman in a yellow bathing suit, a boy with a bottle of suntan oil with the same label. Thus the picture goes on into infinity.

The woman on the label looks like Isabella.

Thomas, on the other hand, has a pale skin that has been diagnosed as very sensitive. Too much sun gives him a rash. And his trunks are blue with red stripes.

Isabella's and Rosa's sunglasses slant upward at the sides. When both are wearing theirs at the same time, they look like each other, almost like twins. The same dark hair, the same brown faces. But Isabella is the one with a yellow hair ribbon and Rosa the one in the pink robe, white bathing suit, white sandals, and white nail polish on her toenails.

When the time comes to go swimming, Isabella, still asleep, shifts uneasily under the blankets.

Rosa says she loves the sea, goes into the water, and swims a long way out. When she comes back, she sits on the rock and lets the sun dry her body as she gazes out over the bay. On days when there is no sea mist, you can see Tupsu and Robin Lindbergh's summer home on the other side, far beyond the smaller islands. When the light falls a certain way, the villa looms like a shadow over the bay. Tupsu and Rosa are friends. They were neighbors in America.

"Green lawn next to green lawn in Washington, D.C., Bella. That brings you *close*."

Isabella moves in her sleep. Thomas is snorkeling and finds a fishing lure of the kind called a trolling spoon in the sludge. Renée is lying in the shade of the alder on the shore, waiting for an alderbug to fall on her stomach. She wants to see what happens when it wriggles its way into her skin. A test.

But sometimes it is too hot even down at the beach. Bella and Rosa get to their feet, roll up their beach blankets, wrap themselves in their robes, gather up all their things, and go up to Rosa's and Gabby's house.

They draw the living-room curtains. Rosa switches on the air-conditioning and pours soft drinks from the gleaming refrigerator-bar. Bella sits in a black butterfly chair on one side of the table, Rosa in a tan one on the other side. Bella and Rosa light cigarettes, smoke, and watch the gray smoke hover in a soft haze over the room.

Then Rosa starts talking. At first it is mostly Rosa who does the talking.

"We're crazy about airplanes," says Rosa. "It was our fascination with planes that brought us together. We met at an airport. I was an attendant there.

"A *ground* attendant, Bella, not *flight*. But it's almost the same thing.

"You're not in the air so much, that's all.

"Gabriel came every Sunday. He and his buddies, they were always with him. Stood for hours staring out over the runways.

"One day I went over and introduced myself and said I bet that we were all fascinated by the same things.

"Then, Bella, we got married, we eloped to America."

"Eloped?" asks Bella.

"Oh, Bella, that's just our way of talking. We love each other almost too much. *On the wings of passion you elope to freedom*.

"I wanted to be free, Bella.

"Do you see what I mean?"

Bella nods.

"Mmm," she says.

"You want to watch a movie, Bella?"

Bella nods. They watch a movie. It's always the same movie. There is only one. *Family Memories IV* the box reads in black magic marker.

"We forgot to bring the others, Bella. We've lots and lots in the same series. But this is the only one we took with us for the summer."

The projector is called *Private Eye Family Viewing*, and it is a box model. The movie is threaded onto spools under the screen, and then you watch it just like television.

The movie flickers and jumps a little, but that doesn't matter, the movement actually seems part of it. It starts out on a green lawn. Children in sun hats are playing in a round, inflatable pool. The pool is blue, the children are small, and they splash in the water. Two rabbits lollop around the lawn. They are mottled and eat grass. They keep on eating, and if they are not shut up in their cage periodically, they will eat themselves to death, Renée explains to Thomas in another context.

Gabby comes into the picture, pushing a lawn mower.

"Like a thresher, Bella," Rosa says, laughing. "Lucky this film has no *sound.*" Water spurts from a sprinkler. Gabby leaves the lawn mower and unhooks the hose from the sprinkler. A white car fills the screen. Gabby turns the hose on the car and sprays it. Rosa comes tripping across the lawn, heading straight for the camera, balancing a tray of soft drinks. The camera suddenly wobbles unsteadily, more than usual, as if at any moment Rosa might lose her balance and fall down, tray and all. But that doesn't happen. She stays on her feet—it's only Gabby doing *tricky* things with the camera. "Gabby's always teasing," says Rosa every time they come to this part of the movie.

Her mouth is almost square as she smiles. She comes closer and closer. Her face becomes larger and larger. Since the camera does not back away, in the end her face is so close to the lens that its outline dissolves into a blur.

The movie ends at the sea. Rosa in the sand on an almost empty beach. The waves are high, and a wind is blowing. In the foreground children in sun hats are plowing paths in the sand. Rosa has turned her back and is gazing out at the sea, holding a shell to her ear.

She is listening to the roar of the ocean inside the shell.

"Pretty crazy, really, Bella, listening to a shell when you've got the whole ocean in front of you.

"We're restless people, Bella.

"Sometimes you have to get away. Follow your nose. *Take your home too, and go.*

"But, Bella, America's big.

"And when you've got small children.

"In Arizona, for instance. In some places the temperature can be over a hundred.

"Fahrenheit, Bella. Not Celsius."

"*Ich bin ein Berliner,*" cries Kayus on his veranda one evening at the end of June. "Great things are happening in the history of the world, Thomas."

Thomas does not reply. World history is of no interest to him. He is thinking about his birthday. All he wants is a model skeleton and a certain brand of trolling spoon he's seen in one of Huotari's fishing magazines. Kayus switches off the radio.

"Want to go and have some fun, Thomas? Want to go down to the beach and make something for Isabella Mermaid? A diving board?"

"Mmm." Thomas mumbles something in reply. Then Isabella herself appears on the veranda. She is wearing white slacks and a yellow sweater and has not heard anything about a diving board.

"Come on all of you," she says. "We're going to Rosa's and Gabby's. They're having Shangri-las in Rosa's garden."

"Welcome to our little electric summer cottage. Open, Sesame!"

Gabby pulls aside the kitchen curtain and they are faced with a huge stove. It has four burners and a hinged panel that holds the dials to adjust the heat of the burners and of the oven. Gabby tips the panel up and down. He says it is just like the navigation panel on a spaceship. He turns to Thomas. "Isn't it?" he asks.

"The rockets, Thomas. Gemini. The Apollo series.

"We'll soon be on the moon, Thomas.

"We live at the heart of incredible times."

To the adults he says that you need a son to be able to discuss these things properly. He pats Thomas's shoulder, then discovers the stove all over again, as if for the first time, pats it and says: "*Flameless cooking*."

"You can try out your recipes here." Gabby smiles at Bella and Rosa, curling one corner of his mouth up in the manner of Gene Pitney. "We menfolk never say no to a good cake." Gabby's hand lands on Thomas's shoulder.

Isabella laughs her mermaid laugh. "Thanks, but I don't bake—"

"We're not exactly an ordinary family," Kayus fills in. "We've got music in our blood. We listen to a lot of music. To jazz."

Gabby brightens. "*Music*. I like *music*, too."

"Miles Davis, Charlie Parker, Bill Evans . . ." Kayus begins his list.

"I will *go in to music," says Gabby*. "Tape recorders, Kayus. Cassette technology will knock out traditional recording technology in this decade. Want to bet?"

"Thanks, but . . ."

"Great things are happening in music history. I'm going to be part of it. Throw your record player in the garbage, Mr. Jazz."

"Thanks, but . . ." Kayus begins again, and now it is his turn to put his hands on Thomas's and Bella's shoulders. "Vinyl will be fine for us."

Bella frees herself from Kayus's grip. She is still where she had been when she was interrupted. "I don't bake in the traditional way," she says. "I use a mix."

Rosa comes into the kitchen with a tray of Shangri-las. She recognizes the remark. "In that case, Bella," she says with a laugh. "We're two of a kind."

Gabby starts. He looks at Bella and Rosa, from one to the other. Then he smiles the smile Rosa calls his *irresistible wolf grin*.

"And as far as music is concerned," says Gabby, "I would describe myself as an *omnivore*.

Thomas turns red. He can feel Renée's eyes on him. He looks around. She is no longer standing behind him and the wall of adults. He goes out. She is at the foot of the hill on her way to the forest. He runs down the hill and follows her.

Rosa tells about their return journey from America: "There was so much we wanted to take with us. We couldn't possibly take it all on the plane. So we split up. Gabby took a ship with Renée, Nina and I flew, so that we'd be at the pier to meet them. But in the middle of the Atlantic Ocean there was a storm. Hurricanelike conditions."

Thomas can see it in his mind's eye. Renée and Gabby on a ship in mid-Atlantic. Huddled far belowdecks, in the hold, along with all their things. Right at the center of car, stove, air-conditioning unit, lawn mower, and gleaming refrigerator-bar, its handsome teak door swinging in the swell. Fierce rolling, water everywhere.

Then he thought about himself. He had been in a square courtyard below a balcony in a third-floor apartment. He had been one of a number of children who had called out; "Mom, come to the window." It had been a kind of competition. You wanted to impress each other with your mothers. Again and again Thomas had felt the same warm pride welling up in him when Isabella came to the balcony, leaned against the railing, all eyes on her. For there can be no doubt that Isabella is the most beautiful mother in the courtyard, with or without curlers. "What is it, Thomas?" she called rather impatiently, apparently unmoved by all the attention paid her. Thomas had been unable to reply; he had not really wanted anything. She had shrugged and gone back into the apartment. He had gone on calling. He had called and called until she showed herself again. Again and again, several days running. She had been annoyed, but it hardly mattered because it had become a kind of game. Thomas had begun to enjoy the ritual. He calls and she comes. Maybe not right away. But sooner or later she appears.

One day she whistles him up to the apartment, threads a key on a ribbon, and hangs it around his neck. She says that from then on he will have to come up to the apartment on his own, unless it's a matter of life and death. "I'm not at your beck and call, Thomas," she says. "No one is. That's something you have to learn."

Thomas nods eagerly. He has no objection to having his own key. So he becomes the first child his age in the courtyard to have his own key. He goes out again and starts chewing on the ribbon so that everyone can see. A bitter taste. The ribbon tears. When it is replaced, he chews that one to pieces as well, and several more, so that two years later he has used up four ribbons and one key.

During those same two years among other things Renée did the following: traveled across the continent of America in a white angel, been to the Pacific coast, seen with her own eyes the air turning into jelly in the heat above the highways of Arizona, splashed in a blue plastic pool on a green lawn in Washington, D.C., and as she says, owned and killed two rabbits. And last but not least, she has crossed the Atlantic in a ship that nearly sinks in a terrible storm. And not even been seasick.

"Incredible kid," Rosa has said. "She must have nerves of steel. *Or perhaps she's just a kid born to the sea.*

Thomas thinks that he's not impressed. But of course he is.

Thomas and Renée walk in the forest, this summer and all the other summer. It is Thomas's triumph that he knows the forest better than anyone else. Better than Renée, too. They squabble about it, of course. Though not that much. Thomas believes that he doesn't have to prove anything. It's enough to feel privately triumphant when it turns out that he's already familiar with all the places she takes him to and claims to have discovered.

Sometimes they take Erkki Johansson with them to the forest. Sometimes they leave him there, in some particularly horrible place, beside various kinds of mosses above which gnat-like insects fly in buzzing clusters, they leave him in scrubby, impenetrable places, where musty shade prevails at all times of the day. Then the two of them go away, though not as far away as Erkki thinks. In actuality they hide quite close by and spy on him. Erkki Johansson stands still. He looks around uncertainly. He waves his hands to shoo away the insects all around him. He listens. He peers around, alert to the slightest sound, the slightest movement. For a moment. There is silence. Nothing happens. Erkki's face crumples. He folds his arms, clenches his fists, and presses them against his body. His face creases even more. The tears come, as if squeezing their way out of Erkki Johansson, although he tries to hold them back; at first quietly and uncertainly, but after a while and when still nothing has happened, the crying increases in volume and intensity. It feels strange being in a hiding place, watching Erkki Johansson—exciting and upsetting at the same time. Confusing. Sometimes Thomas and Renée emerge from their hiding place and make themselves known in order to get rid of that feeling, claiming that they've been nearby all the time. Doing something. Why are you blubbering, Erkki? Did someone do something to you? Did you get bitten? Serves you right. Why did you stay in one place? Of course the gnats find you if you're too stupid to move.

"Anyhow, Experimental Subject," they say in the end. "The experiment has been a success.

After a while Erkki Johansson stops bursting into tears when he is left behind. He stands still, looking around watchfully, attentively, and he squats, pressing his fists against his body, his face crumpling. But not a sound comes out. He looks around, twisting his head from side to side. He seems to know Renée and Thomas are nearby, and he is just waiting for them to appear to tell him he has been a subject in an important scientific experiment. Then they'll produce a scientific explanation to clarify further what it's really all about, what the experiment has achieved.

Thomas and Renée go away without making themselves known. They walk back to the summer paradise, or they take an entirely different direction in the forest. Erkki is left behind and has to make his way home all by himself. He does actually manage it, at long last. It may take time, particularly at first. But sooner or later they hear May Johansson's voice from the yard at Johanssons'. "What've *they* done again now?"

May Johansson's voice makes Erkki Johansson start crying again. But he does not tell on them, or at least he tells as little as possible. He does his best to be a perfect experimental subject. In all kinds of weather. A person who keeps a straight face, who does not leak scientific secrets to outsiders.

Do Thomas and Renée have guilty consciences? Not really. They do not think in such terms. Thomas believes that it is thanks to him and Renée that Erkki gets out into the forest at all to learn how to find his way on his own.

Maggi and Nina live in the triangle formed by the Johanssons' sauna, the Johanssons' house, and Gabby's and Rosa's house on the hill. May Johansson goes off into the forest only in the bilberry season; then she certainly hurries off *at full tilt* along with Pusu Johansson, cousins, and picking machines, because the Johanssons are a poor family with a lot of mouths to feed, and it is a matter of gathering the bounty of the forest before anyone else gets there. Kayus is on his veranda with his detective stories and his music. Gabby does not like going anywhere that you can't drive to. Johan and Helena Wikblad—they are the ones with the sick baby. And Bella and Rosa—after all, they are *beach women*. Occasionally they take a walk along the path. To the mail box. And back.

So it is only thanks to Thomas and Renée that Erkki Johansson's horizons are expanded to extend beyond even the homes in the summer paradise. No one else moves as freely in the forest as Thomas and Renée do, no one else can teach Erkki Johansson about the forest as well as Thomas and Renée can.

■ ■ ■

In the evenings, when the weather is right, Thomas and Huotari go out in Huotari's boat to fish in the open sea. They put out nets and rods with spinning reels. Then they go back home and light the sauna. They bathe, and when they are done, they cool off on the steps, sitting with towels around their middles and eating sausages they have grilled in tin foil on the hot stones of the sauna. They talk about boxing. Or rather, they do not talk much, but when they do talk, they talk about boxing.

From the steps of Huotari's cottage there's a fine view of all the inlets of the summer paradise straight ahead of them, fifty yards across the water. In the evenings they lie in shadow. They are empty and look abandoned.

But there is movement on the path. Two figures come into view on the beach. One is yellow, the other pink. The yellow one is carrying a pan—the white villa's dishpan, which can be seen a long way away because of its flame-red color. The pink figure is carrying two bowls and wears towels around her neck, a little like a boxer.

Bella sets the bowls down at the place where they do laundry. Rosa scoops hot water out of the dishpan into the two bowls. Steam rises. For a moment the air turns to jelly around Bella and Rosa, sort of like the air you see hovering over the concrete highways in Arizona when it's really hot, over a hundred degrees Fahrenheit. The women disappear almost completely. Then the air clears. Rosa has added cold water from the bay.

They bend over their bowls and wash their hair. They cry out that the water is cold and that shampoo has run into their eyes. Even Huotari looks up. As always, Thomas is proud that it is his mother who is the most beautiful, his mother handling her incredibly long hair, her mermaid hair. But he doesn't say anything. Just keeps quiet, enjoying the moment.

When Bella and Rosa have washed their hair, they wind the towels into turbans around their heads, put on their robes, turn the bowls upside down at the laundry site, pick up the dishpan and go back up the avenue. Quiet descends.

Thomas takes a bite of sausage. Huotari reads from his magazine: "*I'm the best, the most beautiful, the strongest, the quickest, the most phenomenal, the most admirable, and the most incredible.*"

Thomas starts. Now he can see something else. Something orange on the very edge of Gabby's and Johanssons' joint breakwater. Holding its head up in a peculiar position, sniffing the air rather like an animal. Its mouth opens and emits a strange sound.

Thomas looks away. Huotari is deep in his magazine. Thomas slowly turns his eyes back toward the jetty. Renée has gone.

"What did you say?"

"I'm the best, the most phenomenal," says Huotari.

"Yes, I heard that. But who's saying it?"

"Clay, of course. This is how it goes on. *Cooper is lazy, just a punching bag, a jerk* . What d'you think, Thomas? Which one will win?"

"As if there could be any doubt."

"Which round, Thomas?"

"First," says Thomas.

He turns out to be right. Clay knocks out Cooper in the first round.

■ ■ ■

But then, a dull rumble. At first nothing can be seen. Next, a white angel comes rolling along at a leisurely speed. It appears at the Johanssons' house, glides past the corner of it, continues on across May Johansson's little rock on the beach and May Johansson's patch of grass. Straight on. For a moment it looks as if it is going to continue on into the water.

An illusion, of course. The car stops abruptly at the Johansson's sauna. The door opens. Gabby emerges and slams the door so that it echoes all over the summer paradise. Gabby unwinds the hose they share, turns on the water, and starts to wash the car.

Rosa and Bella go up to the house on the hill and draw the curtains. They sit in the butterfly chairs, sipping soft drinks and smoking cigarettes.

"Want to watch a movie, Bella?" says Rosa.

"Yes."

"Which one?" says Rosa.

"Guess," says Bella with a cautious laugh; they have seen the same movie a number of times, and there is only the one.

Rosa laughs, too. She puts the projector on the table and turns it on.

The lawn, the pool, and the children. The tray of drinks, Rosa's wobbling body dissolving into a blur when she comes too close and Gabby does not move. Gabby is always teasing.

But she does not say so. This time Rosa says nothing. Then the sea, the final clip. Rosa sitting on the beach with her back turned, a shell held against her ear. The roar of the sea, as she usually jokes. Now she says nothing. She gets up from the tan butterfly chair. The air-conditioning whirs, the movie projector buzzes. She goes to stand by the window. She draws the curtains back with a whoosh. The picture in the projector is wiped out, the screen turns white. She crouches by the air-conditioner, watching the white propeller flapping around behind the white grid. Then she grasps the cable and jerks the plug out of the wall. The propeller flaps hesitantly a few times more before it stops.

"This," says Rosa, pointing at the propeller, "is probably the nearest Gabby will ever get to an airplane."

She fixes her eyes on Bella. "I talk nonsense, Bella. Nothing but nonsense.

"Listen to me now.

"I don't know anything about airplanes.

"I'd met him at college. I recognized him. I went over to him and asked if he remembered me.

"It was there, all right, at the airport.

"I was an attendant, Bella. *Ground*, not *flight*. There's a big difference.

"Including that you're on the ground all the time.

"He didn't make pilot's training. He couldn't pass the simulator test. He was too nervous.

"And that," says Rosa, snapping her fingers, "is that story."

She falls silent again. Bella also says nothing.

It is really quiet, even the projector has stopped buzzing.

"Shall I tell you something?" Bella asks abruptly.

"Kayus and I didn't meet at the Charlie Parker concert at Topsy's. I've never even been to Stockholm, Rosa. I've never been anywhere.

"We met at the amusement park.

"I was a mermaid.

"Someone who sat on a shelf waiting for someone else to

come and throw balls and make a direct hit on a board below my shelf. And when someone did, my shelf tipped over and I screamed and fell into the pool below. Kayus came and Kayus threw. And Kayus hit. Bull's eye.

"So, Rosa, it went *splash* and I landed in the pool below."

"What are you thinking, Bella. Right now?"

"Nothing. That I still feel sticky. That awful oil everywhere."

gabby's white angel, 1963

Thomas's birthday is on the fourth of July. In the morning the sun shines and there is a party at the white villa. Thomas, Renée, Erkki Johansson, Maggi Johansson, and Nina are all standing in a circle in the garden. They are playing a game Nina is directing so that it will be fair and no one will have too many turns being "it," especially not Erkki Johansson, because he is the youngest and most stupid, and he is always "it" when he plays games with Thomas and Renée.

In the middle of the game Renée leaves the circle and sits down in the shade by the kitchen steps. She pulls a piece of grass out of the ground and sticks it in her mouth, chewing on the stem and looking around, her face expressionless. It is impossible to persuade her or bully her into coming back to the game, now being played half-heartedly. Thomas thinks that they look funny, and he goes over to sit down beside Renée on the kitchen steps. He also pulls up a grass stem and chews on it, making an effort at a deadpan look. Nina is angry and runs into the white villa, where Bella and Rosa are, to tell Rosa all about it. Rosa comes outside, and when she sees Thomas and Renée on the steps, she says with delight that they look fabulous, like little gangsters. "Stay where you are, kids!" she cries. "Freeze in your positions!"

She runs back into the house for the camera. But when she is about to take the photograph, it turns out that all the other children have gathered on the steps, grass stems in their mouths, blank expressions on their faces. Then Thomas realizes that the game is no longer any good and he goes indoors to open his gifts. From May Johansson he receives the darkblue sou'wester handed down from the cousins, who have outgrown it, which is still too big for Erkki Johansson: since blue is a color for boys, the sou'wester looks better on Thomas than on Maggi Johansson, who might otherwise have worn it until Erkki has gown into it. *Many happy returns*. That's May Johansson's reasoning.

Gabby's and Rosa's and Nina's and Renée's present is the Swedish version of the game called TRIUMPH. Triumph—what an appropriate word for the birthday atmosphere that marks the day. Warm joy washes over Thomas. Erkki Johansson also feels something of the kind, for suddenly there is a sly look in his eyes and he runs off, calling out that he has to go home to get something. A few minutes later he is back, his hands full. At first no one can see what he is holding because he has cupped his hands secretively until he holds them out toward Thomas with a triumphant gesture, opens them cautiously and says, "Here you are." And there are all the miniature rubber animals from Erkki Johansson's collection of rubber animals, including the yellow giraffe with an elastic neck that can be knotted, Erkki Johansson's special personal favorite. But the next moment Erkki starts to cry. *You're giving away what you'll never get back*—May Johansson has rushed up in time to stop any further handing-over ceremonies. Later there may be smiles at May Johansson's definition of what a present means, since, strictly speaking, this definition does not seem to apply to the Johansson family's official birthday present. But there is no occasion for laughter now. Erkki Johansson has understood only one part of May Johansson's explanations: He will obviously be stopped from offering his contribution to the birthday. His hands fall to his sides, the animals scatter all over the floor—the sun goes behind a cloud. Well, not really at just that moment. But Erkki's tears are somehow a bad omen.

The afternoon begins. The guests go home. Clouds roll in.

"It comes over you sometimes," says Rosa to Bella. "You have to get away. Don't you ever feel like that? She asks but doesn't stay for an answer. She gathers up her things and hurries away across the yard, home to change into boating clothes. She's going to take the motorboat and go to visit Tupsu Lindbergh, to see if any Fourth of July festivities are in progress at the Lindbergh's house, on the other side of the bay.

Bella starts clearing away the birthday leavings. She carries cups and plates out into the kitchen, lines up eight candles on the brick woodstove. Puts the dishpan on the gas and fills it with water. Stops halfway. Wraps herself in her yellow robe and starts walking.

Bella walks through all the rooms on the ground floor. From the kitchen to the attic entry to the big room to Thomas's room. Barefoot in her yellow robe, her footsteps provocative, as if she wanted to think up something different and amusing now that the weather has turned bad. And involve Thomas in the new amusement. But for once Thomas is not interested. He is sitting on his bed, occupied with fastening his new trolling spoon to the end of his fishing line. He thinks that when he has accomplished that, he will slip down to the beach. On his own. You can't go fishing with Bella. She doesn't sit still for a minute, and she talks all the time.

Clonk. Clonk. There go Bella's sandals, hitting the wall. Bella stands barefoot in the middle of Thomas's room, signaling her presence. But Thomas won't look up. The line is slippery, and he needs to concentrate if he is going to tie all the complicated knots needed to attach the trolling spoon.

Then she is in the big room, where horseflies come in through the open windows. She is talking about thunder. Listing all the different signs of thunder in the air. Says, "Isn't it, Thomas?" after each one. "Mmm," Thomas replies without listening. Then he is on his way. And the last he sees of Bella is her standing before the mirror, holding up her arm.

"Look, Thomas!" All the sun-bleached hairs on her arm are standing straight up.

She clenches her fist. For a brief moment it looks as if she were going to drive her fist into one of the panes of the mirror. Then she lowers her arm, wrinkles her thick, dark eyebrows, and lights a cigarette. Smokes, blowing smoke rings at herself in the mirror. Though Thomas is no longer there but is down in the avenue. On the beach Renée appears from the Rotwoods and takes his rod away from him. "May I try?" she says, but by then she is already out on the jetty and casting for the first time.

Now Renée is on the white villa's jetty with Thomas's rod. She casts and reels in. She reels swiftly, far too quickly, not at all with the caution and calm you should use to reel in a spinning rod, which no doubt she could exercise if she wanted to. She does not want to. Thomas knows; he is half-sitting behind her on a post of the jetty, staring at her orange back. "A bite," says Renée, reeling even faster. A bite. She says the same thing several times, each time reeling in with nothing on the hook, each time casting again. And reeling in. Quite unflustered by Thomas.

"It's my turn," says Thomas, though he knows that talking only makes things worse.

"A bite," says Renée, going on reeling.

The trolling spoon hangs carelessly above the water, dripping and clean, swinging back and forth with her careless handling.

Thomas considers calling for help. Whom should he call? There is no one nearby. He and Renée are alone on the jetty and on the beach. The Johanssons' house is empty, not a sound comes even from the sauna, where Maggi and Nina can usually be found. Huotari's island is deserted. It is midweek, and Huotari's vacation has not started yet. Deep in the inlet to the left a chimney is fiercely sending out smoke, the only sign of life in the whole bay, and that house is a few miles distant, although it looks so close by.

Renée has the upper hand. Thomas cannot persuade her now. They both know it. She keeps on reeling in.

"Give it to me!" Thomas reaches for his rod anyway. Swiftly Renée jerks her hand aside. The line is not properly reeled in, and it snaps back, the hook brushing Thomas's cheek. He backs away.

"Idiot, watch out for my eyes."

The wind drops, and the rain starts. Suddenly there is a downpour.

Renée takes no notice. She reels in and casts again. With a plop the spoon sinks a little farther out. This time she pauses once she has the line out, so that they both have plenty of time to imagine the spoon falling through the water to the bottom, burying itself in the sea grass, and becoming stuck. She starts reeling in again. The end of the rod bends in a deep curve. She jerks the rod. The end springs loose with a whistling noise that sounds terrible to Thomas's ear. She goes on reeling in.

Thomas is the first to see that the line is broken. A transparent end floats on the water. Curled and slack. Renée goes on reeling in for ages, carelessly and jerkily, as if she had not noticed or realized what has happened. Thomas is furious. His anger grows as he watches her. The smell of smoke penetrates his nostrils, and his temples throb. Then he hurls himself at her from behind, snatches the rod out of her hand, so that it falls among the stones supporting the jetty on the beach side.

But as soon as Thomas holds the rod again, it is no longer important, and he does not care what happens to it. He knocks Renée down onto the jetty. They wrestle, but he is angrier and stronger now, and soon he has her flat on her back beneath him. He half-sits on her, his knees on her arms to keep her still, and hammers her stomach and face with his fists, pulls her hair, trying to get a hold so that he can bang her head against the boards of the jetty. She wriggles under him more and more vehemently, and somewhere at the back of his mind Thomas senses that he is going to lose his advantage. He dives down toward her T-shirt, his teeth clamping on skin, a real bite. His mouth is filled with fluff and a disgusting taste. Is it blood? He pushes her away, and she falls onto the stones in a horrible way, head first. Her T-shirt has hitched up, revealing a patch of white back, which he sees before him all the way as he runs up the avenue. She rolls on, her feet, shod in blue and white sneakers, dipping into the water. Thomas's mouth is full of hair and fluff, but he is running now. Along the avenue, toward the white villa. As he runs he shouts for Bella. Renée will remind him of this later, when they are alone.

"BELLAAA! BELLAAA!"

But it was his birthday and his new trolling spoon. It had lain shiny, in the box he had withdrawn from the yellow wrapping paper that morning. Bella and Kayus had come into his room, singing, carrying his birthday tray, and he had put his hands over his ears and slithered down under the sheets so that his head was almost at the foot of the bed. But that was just a game, something that was part of Bella's being given the chance to snatch off the covers and hop into bed with him for birthday hugs. Kayus stood beside his bed, as he did on every birthday, ready to hold out the tray of cocoa and sandwiches and everything Thomas had ever wished for in the whole world. A skeleton model. And that trolling spoon.

Thomas is up at the white villa. The disgusting taste of T-shirt and blood is still in his mouth. He has stopped shouting and has slowed down. In fact, it is as if his speed slowed more and more over the last piece up the hill to the white villa's yard, and as he goes up the kitchen steps, his feet are already heavy, dragging. He spits to rid himself of something horrible in his mouth. Fluff. And he notices that he is holding his rod. The spinning rod; for a moment it seems completely foreign. He flings it away roughly and it lands in the middle of the sere lilac bushes below his window.

On the porch he says Isabella's name again. The door swings shut behind him. But it is not quite dark. Daylight trickles through an opening above the kitchen door. He stands in the dim light for quite a while, listening to his own voice. It sounds different now, hesitant, as if searching.

"B-e-l-l-a," he says, spelling his way through the name like an alphabet.

Then he turns the stiff key, opens the door, and slips into the kitchen. His steps quiet and hesitant, he stops at the center of the blue kitchen floor. He turns rigid, listening. His own breathing. Irregular panting, still out of breath after running along the avenue. A horsefly bumps into the window, slamming against the pane again and again. Rain is pouring down on the metal roof. In the attic it sounds like machine-gun fire, down here it is a distant patter. On the old brick woodstove in front of him are the remains of the party. Bits of cake on the platter, birthday candles with dried whipped cream on the ends. Napkins. Like some kind of proof that there was life before all this happened. A birthday.

It is as if what happened down on the beach is blown away. With everything else. *Everything is suddenly elsewhere*. An unpleasant, mysterious feeling.

Then he starts, abruptly aware of being observed. Slowly he turns his head to the left, toward his room. The box for the model stands upright on his table. The skeleton depicted on the lid is grinning at him, hollowly. The grin brings Thomas back to reality.

Time returns, the spell broken.

He runs again, through the ground-floor rooms and up to the studio.

He finds the yellow robe on the floor of the studio. A bathing suit hangs over the banister. Her sandals are in his room, one under the bed, the other by the tiled stove, wherever they landed when she kicked them off earlier in the day. The top drawer of the bureau in the bedroom is open. That is her drawer. Bits of stockings, sleeves of blouses spill out in an unmistakable Bella mess. And everywhere, all over the white villa, a faint whiff of her perfume, "Blue Grass."

Thomas is out of the house, setting off along the forest road, running straight ahead in the pouring rain without really knowing where he is running to. But past the big birch, the Johanssons' woodpile and out into the open, where the meadow begins. And you can see a long, long way.

Perhaps fifty yards farther on, where the meadow ends and there are only one or two bends in the road, where the mailbox is and the buses run, she is walking along, a red umbrella over her head. In one hand she holds her white case, her traveling suitcase, which she and Thomas have packed several times in fun, as a game. Her coat is beige, her walking shoes have heels, though not too high, just right to walk in comfortably. And the yellow dress, shimmering through the heavy rain. Now she turns around and catches sight of him. Stops, puts down the umbrella.

And so they stand on the road looking at each other through the rain, which is pelting down on both of them.

Thomas is on his way. Lands somewhere in her clothes.

"Thomas. What is it? What's happened?"

Or else he is still in the dim light of the porch, pronouncing her name like an alphabet. She hears the noises from outside, opens the kitchen door. Stands in front of him, barefoot, in her yellow robe, warm, wet, pink gloves that she wears to wash dishes on her hands.

He cannot get a word out. His mouth is full of fluff again. Orange T-shirt fluff, it's enough to make you want to throw up.

Of course he starts crying, too. He cries until she takes him by the shoulders and shakes him. Then the story pours out of him. Everything that he's almost forgotten already. A story called "Little Boy Goes Fishing." And the outcome, catastrophic. But he does not mention Renée. He doesn't know why. She simply does not fit into the picture.

But Bella knows the score. She holds his head between her hands so that he must look her straight in the eye.

"Not the expensive one Kayus gave you?"

Thomas nods slowly.

"Come on, Thomas," she says then, her voice almost happy. "We must go to Johanssons' at once and phone Kayus to tell him the whole sad story."

And while they change and run across the yard to the Johanssons,' the rain stops, the sky clears, and the sun comes out.

Kayus's red Austin Mini drives into the yard at six o'clock. The white angel is right behind it, brakes, the window winds down, and Gabby sticks out his head.

"Ha, ha!" he calls. "Nearly caught you!" and then he revs the car and continues up to the Angels' house. Sometimes Kayus says that Gabby drives like a madman on the main road. He himself is definitely not going to get involved in that kind of game. *The road is totally unsuitable for racing*.

But today Kayus does not pay any attention to Gabby. He opens the car door, gets out, and without a word starts tearing off his clothes. Tie, shirt and finally his shoes, so that they fly across the yard. Is down the avenue, running to the beach and out to the jetty, from where he leaps feet first, still wearing his trousers. Swims underwater for several yards, and not until his head appears and, snorting, he shakes it, does he start talking. He calls out that he has been longing for this all day. There was no refreshing thunderstorm in town as there was here. It was so hot there that the sidewalk bubbled under his shoes. He swims far out, doing the crawl, and Thomas goes after him, also leaping into the water with all his clothes on. Kayus waits for Thomas, and when Thomas has caught up, they turn and swim back to ashore, side by side.

Bella has waded out into the inlet. She stands unsteadily in the water, now up to the edge of her shorts, her hands up in front of her, and she looks rather doubtful. Kayus and Thomas call to her to stop fussing and to come on in. Bella stops and shakes her head, smiling. The water is too cold. Thomas and Kayus swim closer to shore and start splashing her. Bella squeals and runs back to the beach. Thomas and Kayus follow. So Bella is chased all the way up the avenue and into the white villa and through the downstairs rooms. Not until much later do they calm down, wrap themselves in robes, set the table, and hang up their wet clothes on the line in the yard. At dinner there is a brand-new trolling spoon by Thomas's plate. Exactly the same kind.

Renée comes in while Thomas and Bella and Kayus are having dinner. She nods, goes through the kitchen to Thomas's room, where she sits down at his table, takes paper and crayons, and starts drawing. Thomas peers at her over his plate of split-pea soup. She is concentrating on the drawing without looking up. She is wearing a different T-shirt, a dark red one. But there is no other trace of earlier events.

■ ■ ■

When Thomas has finished, he goes into his room, sits down opposite Renée, and starts drawing drops of blood. She draws drops of blood, too, for the chamber of horrors they are going to set up in the attic space next to Bella's studio. They plan to cut out and tape together strings of blood drops to hang in front of the doorway. Then they will take Erkki Johansson there and frighten the life out of him. Not that they have anything against Erkki Johansson; they choose him merely because Erkki Johansson is the smallest, and the only one who might be frightened senseless by a chamber of horrors.

Renée takes a clean piece of paper and starts drawing mugs with ears and noses and mouths, which communicate with each other by way of speech bubbles. She hesitates over what to write in the bubbles; Thomas knows that this is because she cannot yet write very well. Thomas picks up another piece of paper as well, and starts drawing figures who speak to each other with various kinds of short, sharp cries, which he writes out in big cloud-shaped surfaces over their heads.

They stop drawing and turn Thomas's room into a rocket. Renée sits on Thomas's table in the position an astronaut assumes when he is ready for liftoff. Thomas crawls under the table and tries to get the starter thing going. He fails time and time again, until Renée grows impatient and says that Thomas will have to go in a separate rocket. Thomas climbs up on the low bureau under the window and curls up into the liftoff position, drawing his legs up against his chest, wrapping his arms around his legs, and pressing his chin between his knees, because a space capsule is very small, no bigger than the driver's seat of a small car, and a small car is the same size as Kayus's Austin Mini.

Then Rosa suddenly appears with her camera. "Stay where you are, kids! Freeze!"

Thomas and Renée turn their heads at the same time. They are surprised by the flash. Rosa is surprised, too: she had not realized that there was so little light in the room that the automatic flash would go off. When the picture is developed, it turns out that both Renée and Thomas have their eyes fixed on the camera. Fabulous, Rosa will say, just like Little Valentina and Comrade Cosmonaut Bykovsky in June, circling the world in their spaceships, keeping radio contact. Rosa cuts out a funny newspaper caption, which she will stick under the photograph in the album she will put together the following winter.

"Bella! Kayus!" Rosa puts the camera back in its case and calls in the direction of the big room. "Where are you? Gabby and I were expecting you for cocktails."

"Tonight too?" Bella appears from the direction of the veranda. Yellow and happy but slightly confused, because it had been cocktails with Gabby and Rosa the previous evening as well. Kayus is behind Bella, he's holding a mystery novel, on the jacket a buxom blonde's red-painted mouth screaming at some unknown terror. Though the blonde is quite irrelevant to the content—as Kayus explained when Thomas wanted to know more about which character in the book the blonde was, and what exactly she was afraid of—anyone can see that Kayus is not as happily surprised as Bella is.

"Why not?" says Rosa. "There's always a good reason to celebrate a little. And Gabby and I happen to be people who like to have people around.

"So we thought," Rosa goes on, laughing, "that if Mohammed won't come to the mountain, the mountain will have to go to Mohammed. Gabby's right behind me in the car."

A moment later the white angel drives into the yard. The gleaming refrigerator-bar is lifted out of the trunk and wheeled onto the veranda, where the evening sun is shining—they are having a heat wave, and there isn't anywhere in the white villa where drinks can cool. When the narrow teak doors of the bar are opened, they reveal interior walls inlaid with mosaic mirrors. Then sounds of ice and glasses, chatter and laughter, sounds that merge into a restful buzz, which carries from the veranda all over the white villa, even to Thomas and Renée in Thomas's room, where Renée is still having trouble with her rocket, the engine keeps stopping. Thomas does not interfere with her mechanics. He presses his chin harder into his knees and lifts off.

Rosa and Bella are in the kitchen. They are talking to each other, but quietly, and since they are also banging pots and pans, you can only make out odd words and parts of sentences. When Bella and Rosa talk to each other alone in that intense way, you know they're not talking about houses, husbands, and children. The others say that they're discussing Elizabeth Taylor's love life. The way they say it makes it clear that Elizabeth Taylor's love life is nothing but unimportant rubbish. But Thomas knows, though he can't explain how he knows, that they're wrong. Bella and Rosa aren't discussing Elizabeth Taylor's love life. Not because it's unimportant rubbish. It isn't. It's merely that there isn't anything interesting about it right now. Everybody knows Elizabeth Taylor is going to marry Richard Burton, no matter how much both deny it in public.

No, Bella and Rosa are talking about something else and in a different way.

" . . . and at Tupsu's, Bella," Rosa is saying in the kitchen.

"Today. It was so dull. *Boring*. Incredibly boring. I longed to be back here every minute. As soon as I set out, I was sorry. Halfway across the bay I thought, What am I doing here? I'll turn around and go back home. I don't know how to explain it. Do you know what I mean?"

Her voice is soft, calm, so that it is suddenly difficult to understand that it belongs to the same person who dashes around with the camera, chasing after immortal moments to immortalize in the family album.

"Mmm," says Bella. Thomas recognizes Bella's *mmm*. Bella always says *mmm* in the same way when she isn't sure that she understands but is determined to hide her feelings in case she's wrong.

But she laughs, and her voice sounds really happy. *Cool*, thinks Thomas. They're both *cool*. Bella is *cool* like the jazz she listens to in the city. A way of listening that spreads all over the room, inseparable from cigarettes, magazines, curlers, UltraNet hairspray, and chatter tossed back and forth, chatter about *all kinds of stuff*, including Elizabeth Taylor's love life. But Rosa is also cool, like when you put your hand inside that gleaming refrigerator-bar and sketch lines in the icy mist on the walls with your fingers. Not like the cool bag; that's just a useful kind of cool. Or that camera.

Bella and Rosa: they suit each other, they are alike.

"Shall we join the others, Rosa?" says Bella.

"Yes," says Rosa. "If you like."

With a winning smile and nerves of steel, one Sunday, brunette Valentina Tereshkova soared out into the hitherto exclusively male world of space.

"This is no good." Renée kicks the table leg and goes out.

Thomas follows. They stand on the kitchen steps, thinking. They start walking, she first, Thomas behind, his eyes on her red back. The very next day she is wearing her old orange T-shirt again, mended by herself with thick yarn into a white, now gradually graying lump on the shoulder. And she tells anyone who asks that she tripped and fell into the forest.

But Thomas hides his new trolling spoon. And from then on Renée and Thomas do not go fishing together. Thomas rows over to Huotari's island when Huotari's vacation begins. Renée puts out nets.

She takes Pusu Johansson's nets off the hooks on the porch of the Johanssons' sauna, late in the evening, when everyone else has gone indoors. She rows out into the bay and flings out the nets. In the morning she gets up early to empty them. But in July the water temperature rises to over twenty-five degrees on this side of the sound and the sea grass grows well above the seabed, so that the Lindberghs' shiny mahogany speedboat roars with sea grass caught in its propeller. And sea grass is all she will catch as well. Since the nets are empty, she doesn't bother to clean and scrape them as you should. She leaves them on May Johansson's rock in the inlet. They stay there in gray piles, drying out and smelling, ruined by the hot sun that burns for a few hours every morning on the Johanssons' side. She herself has long since gone somewhere else, occupied with other matters.

Renée repeats the same procedure three days in a row, until she has used up all of Pusu Johansson's nets. It's no use locking the sauna door and trying to hide the key in different places. She always knows where it is. For that matter, Thomas also always knows where the key is. There are no secrets in the summer paradise that are a secret to Thomas and Renée.

Pusu Johansson goes to Gabby to clear the matter up.

"Let's not go on about it," says Gabby, taking out his wallet. "I'll pay."

All the same, he's a little embarrassed. "Why can't she take an interest in ordinary things?" he cries after Pusu Johansson has gone. "Girl's things. Dolls or . . . or parachute jumping?" Nevertheless, he cannot hide the fact that his voice is almost faint with pride.

"She's very special," says Rosa. "If only she'd get a haircut."

"It's great," says Bella. "Wild, somehow."

"It's all right for you. You don't have to comb the snarls out after washing it." And Bella laughs. No, she doesn't. Thomas has a crew cut for the summer, like a hedgehog. Almost flat on top.

"Revolting," says Nina about Renée. She has just discovered the word, and according to her, it fits someone like Renée exactly.

"She's so little, she doesn't understand." Someone else says that—Thomas. She is suddenly among them, making ugly faces. She hates being called little. Covertly he sticks his tongue out. Discreetly she moves closer so she can pinch him. But Thomas leaves, takes his rod, and rows over to Huotari's island.

But later, sitting on Huotari's cottage steps, he stares at Renée on the other side. Huotari does not notice. He is busy with his magazine.

"He's coming here in the autumn, Thomas."

"Who?"

"Listen. The guy knocked out Floyd Patterson. He's coming to the amusement park. Want to go and watch him? With me?"

But then, one day in the middle of summer, just when you've grown used to her appearing every morning, one day she doesn't. Rosa doesn't come. As usual, Thomas and Bella are sitting together at breakfast, both facing the door. It is the end of July, vacation time. Thomas and Bella dip their spoons deep into their bowls of yogurt. They raise their spoons high in the air and let the liquid run down to their plates in viscous threads. They are waiting. They do not tell each other that they are waiting. Anyhow, they have lots of fun together on their own, playing with their food in a way that sometimes gets on Kayus's nerves. But Kayus is still asleep, and a watch is ticking somewhere, on the chair by Thomas's bed, where he left it one evening at the beginning of summer and forgot it the following day and the next day and all the days after that. Suddenly a watch wasn't necessary. Suddenly that kind of time did not exist. Not no time but a different time, a different measure of time. But now he would like to get his watch and look at it. Suddenly he can feel the ticking in his body. Gradually the cinnamon dissolves completely before his eyes. For a few moments the acidulated milk turns into a sloppy and incredible mess. Not until that moment does Thomas slide off his chair. He says that he must go find Renée. They have agreed to do something together.

"A secret," he says, loudly and clearly. Ordinarily he never tells Kayus and Bella or anyone else what it is he is going to do with Renée. And they do not arrange it. They just appear. Or simply come from anywhere. At any time. In the middle of meals, if necessary. May Johansson says that is a sign of having no manners. On the other hand, May Johansson is a person who knows nothing about anything that you'd want to know about.

"Yes. Yes, Thomas. Off you go."

Bella starts clearing the breakfast table. Putting one cup

inside another. Stopping, as if suddenly remembering Kayus, who is still asleep. Puts things back. Taps a cigarette out of the pack and lights it. Smokes it. Looks out at the fine day beginning outside.

Thomas runs up the hill to Rosa's and Gabby's house. He pulls at the door. Locked. He walks around the house and tries to see through the windows. Curtains drawn everywhere. Then he starts looking around seriously. Finds that Gabby's car is gone. Then he knows what has happened: The Angels have grown restless and have gone to sightsee out in the world.

Thomas runs back down the hill to the white villa and gets his bike out of the woodshed. He rides to the mailbox as fast as he can. Suddenly he is certain that there must be a message from the Angels somewhere. They cannot have left just like that. And what more natural place to leave that kind of message than the mailbox on the main road?

A two-day-old newspaper is in the box. A strange name on it, not someone from this summer paradise. Anyhow, it is Sunday and there is no mail delivery.

Thomas rides back. Bella is sitting where he had left her.

"They've gone." Thomas's agitation and breathlessness fill the kitchen.

"Who?" Bella looks at him without understanding.

"The Angels," says Thomas impatiently. "Gone away to go and take a look at the world."

"Oh," is all Bella says. As if she were not interested at all. For a moment Thomas is really annoyed.

"I KNOW," he says angrily, emphatically.

"What is it the two of you know?" Kayus comes into the kitchen in shorts and a summer shirt. Rouses himself with a roar and bellows out before anyone has time to answer, "I feel like a lion, Thomas! Ready for great deeds. Want to go down to the beach today and build something?"

He winks at Thomas as if they shared a secret. Thomas tries to look away. "The Angels have gone," he says gravely.

"How nice," Kayus sits down at the breakfast table, takes a bowl of yogurt and starts slurping it down by determined spoonfuls. "So we'll have a bit of peace and quiet for a while."

"Stop being like that, Thomas," he adds. "If you stay indoors and sulk on such a fine day, the sun will go down before you get out." For a moment he looks serious. But then he laughs; what he said sounded so funny. Thomas thinks the same and cannot help laughing also.

"Come on now, Thomas," says Kayus. "Let's go and build something."

Bella stretches as energetically as Kayus has just done and starts listing all the things she has to do. Weeding the strawberry patch. Darning socks. Washing the floor in the big room. And more.

She drops her hands on the table. Gazes meaningfully from Thomas to Kayus. They all know what that means. Loafing. Bella has decided to do nothing at all and just loaf.

"I just have to change first." She goes up to her studio. Three hours later she comes back. By then it is time for lunch, and Kayus and Thomas, who have been making things down on the beach, are as hungry as lions. Bella starts cooking oatmeal and explains that she felt tired.

"I fell asleep. It's lovely to sleep."

But she is awake now. She has sprayed herself with perfume, something she does only when she is in a particularly good mood and prepared for some fun. "Blue Grass." Kayus sniffs the air.

But then May Johansson arrives. In the middle of their meal the door crashes open.

"I'm sorry to disturb you like this, in the middle of . . ." But she has lit the fire under the boiler in the Johansson's sauna. And now she is thinking she and Bella could do a really big laundry together.

"Take care of all our sheets."

Thomas and Kayus eat oatmeal, their spoons scraping their plates. Bella looks around. Nowhere to hide. After the meal Bella rips the sheet off all the beds and follows May Johansson's energetic gabble down to the scalding-hot boiler, the enamel bowls, the soft soap, and the hard scrubbing brushes in the Johanssons' sauna.

Kayus puts on his straw hat and picks a really good book from his summer library. "Come on, Thomas. Never mind building things. Let's go out to sea and enjoy total freedom."

Thomas and Kayus are drifting in the bay in the white villa's rowing boat.

"*Up the lazy river*," says Kayus. "That's a manifestation of the idea of total freedom. Every human being should try something like it sometimes. Are you coming, Thomas?"

Drifting on the tide in a boat is something Kayus has to do at least once a summer if the summer is to be considered a real summer.

"Are you coming, Thomas?"

Of course Thomas is coming. Kayus is so funny when he puts on the straw hat he calls his Huck Finn hat and picks a really good mystery from his summer library. Thomas and Kayus row out, ship the oars in the middle of the bay, and lie down on the boards at the bottom of the boat so that they cannot be seen over the side. Kayus looks up at the sky as the boat drifts to wherever the tide takes it. It reminds him of his childhood summers and his childhood's favorite book, *Huckleberry Finn*.

"Huck Finn was friends with a boy called Tom Sawyer. Tom, that's Thomas in American. Tom Sawyer and Huckleberry Finn had lots of adventures on the Mississippi River.

"Huck Finn lived a life of his own. He didn't care that he had no real home, like Tom Sawyer, or that he was poor. He had a life of his own. He understood how to enjoy life and total freedom."

Thomas peers over the side of the boat. Discreetly. He is a spy now and it is important that everyone who sees the boat floating in the bay should believe it to be empty. Kayus has grown tired of looking up at the sky and enjoying total freedom. He has opened his book and started reading. Thomas has been looking at the jacket. A buxom blonde on some kind of attic stairs, terror in her eyes and her lips painted bright red. A white wrap around her, so thin that the curves of her body are clearly visible. Thomas has been wondering how the wrap is fastened. It seems just to cling to her, since she is holding both hands in front of her to protect herself from some danger. He has not come up with any sensible answer, and fed up with his own thoughts, he has scrambled to his knees and started showing an interest in his surroundings again.

There is life and movement on the beach. Bella and May Johansson are rinsing the laundry on Gabby's and Rosa's and the Johansson's joint breakwater. May Johansson's mouth is moving. You can't hear what she is saying because the wind carries her words in another direction.

But it does not matter which way the wind blows. You do not have to guess. It is just as it seems. May Johansson is talking about the women's traditions inherited by the women in her family. From branch to branch in a wildly branching family tree, in which May Johansson and the cousins' wives are the last shoots for now. Laundry day in the sauna. Embroidering monograms on the sheets.

That evening Bella will say, as usual, that she cannot stand that woman. She will plead a migraine whenever May Johansson comes up with another idea. Thomas and Kayus will smile slightly. Bella will be serious. Seriously, Bella will say that she means it.

From a distance May Johansson and Bella rinsing the laundry look rather cozy. The children rush around. Erkki Johansson runs back and forth between the white villa's jetty and Rosa's and Gabby's and the Johansson's shared breakwater, his hand up in the air. What is Erkki holding? You can't make it out, so his stance looks pretty funny. Perhaps it's nothing. Just one of the products of Erkki Johansson's imagination. A miniature airplane, maybe. Something like that.

Maggi Johansson is keeping an eye on Erkki Johansson. She is standing beside May Johansson's patch of grass, her hands thrust into the pockets of her blue pants. You can tell by looking at her from as far away as you like that she thinks things are dull. Then she starts chasing Erkki Johansson, trying to retrieve whatever it is he's holding. Apparently successfully, for Erkki Johansson grows angry and starts attacking Maggi in typical Erkki Johansson style by butting his head into Maggi Johansson's stomach like a buffalo. Maggi laughs. Maggi's laughter only serves to make Erkki angrier than ever, and he goes on butting Maggi until she loses her temper and they fight in earnest. May Johansson looks up and shouts that Maggi and Erkki must play together nicely.

Near the white villa there is a half-finished diving board. All summer, ever since early June, when Kayus had the idea of surprising Isabella Mermaid with a diving board on their own beach and wanted Thomas to join him in the work as well as the planning. Thomas has known that there is something wrong, fundamentally wrong, with the diving board. Even if he wasn't able to—and still can't—say exactly what and how. And like this, seen from the sea, the planks of the diving board suddenly look quite innocent. Merging into the landscape perfectly well.

Then a familiar engine sound, the Lindberghs' shiny mahogany speedboat appears from between the islands in the bay. Robin at the rudder, Tupsu Lindbergh behind the boat, on water skis. Tupsu Lindbergh *goes water skiing*, Rosa usually says with a laugh when Tupsu Lindbergh parades in front of the jetties, and Rosa tries not to notice all that much, for she has hardly been to Tupsu Lindbergh's at all recently. As if water skiing were not all that interesting. That's stupid, of course, an outright lie.

"Mmm," says Bella, not taking her eyes off Tupsu Lindbergh.

"Though it does look lovely," Rosa is finally forced to admit. She takes out her camera and lies down on the rock beside Bella. "Thomas, take our picture." So, while Tupsu skis in the bay, Thomas snaps a picture of Bella and Rosa, and Rosa laughs and says that now they are wonderful women by the sea.

Bella has stopped rinsing. She is standing on the Johanssons' jetty, quiet for a moment, the laundry basket at her feet.

Tupsu Lindbergh waves, swings around elegantly, and races back across the bay behind the Lindbergh boat. Bella raises her hand, then lowers it. Then she firmly runs it through her hair, picks up the laundry basket, and goes back to where May Johansson is standing by the Johanssons' clothesline. Bella and May Johansson shake out wet, clammy sheets and clip them to the line with clothes pins. Clean white sheets, which will eventually flap in the breeze so that they look like sails.

Time passes. A time when good jazz comes from the radio. Otherwise all is quiet, a calm, restful silence settling over everything.

"It hasn't been this quiet all summer," says Bella one evening over cups of tea. But she does not get up and start breaking the silence as she so often does. Clattering pans, drumming her feet on the floor. Does not laugh. Stays where she is.

"In the middle of summer it suddenly grew quiet," says Kayus. Bella and Kayus take the transistor radio with them into the big room and listen to jazz, staying up far into the night.

At night Thomas lies in bed staring through the door, which is ajar, at the dim light of the big room. Bella is a shadow moving across the floor, which creaks softly under her feet. She stands by her window, her cigarette glowing. The glow from the cigarette is the only point of light in the room apart from the radio's dial, gleaming yellow in the reading corner. Although the white villa is electrified, they have not really become used to thinking in those terms in that house. Thomas's room is the only one with an ordinary overhead bulb.

"It's so long since I've listened to real music," says Bella suddenly. "I've missed it."

"Have you?" says Kayus.

"No other music is so good to dance to."

"I'm glad you think so."

"Oh, Kayus. Let's dance."

Kayus and Bella dance. Thomas lies in bed following the orange dot that is Bella's cigarette swooping in slow, lingering circles out in the big room. Then he turns to the wall and goes to sleep.

"Welcome back," says Kayus.

"What?" says Bella. "I haven't been away."

This is a time when nothing but good jazz comes from the radio. Chet Baker sings "My Funny Valentine." Kayus and Bella discuss Chet Baker's musicianship. They say Chet Baker has wonderful phrasing, really fantastic. Kayus says that is because Chet Baker uses his voice just like a musical instrument, like his trumpet. You can hear that if you listen carefully, paying attention to all the musical nuances. That is his secret, says Kayus, and Bella nods. Bella agrees. Though occasionally Kayus laughs and says that somehow it is also silly, for *you cannot analyze anything by taking it apart into its component parts*. The talk fades away into a great, calm silence. Darkness, glow of cigarette, perhaps music in the background.

Thomas smiles to himself when he hears them. When Bella and he discuss Chet Baker at times when Kayus is not with them, they talk about quite different things. For instance, Bella says that Chet Baker is *sweet*, just as if Chet Baker were Paul Anka or some other charmer without musical merit, not a serious musical artist.

"Just like you, Chet," says Bella to Thomas.

"My name's Thomas," says Thomas. Though that's not too

bad. Sometimes Bella has a way of saying silly things so that they sound okay.

"Of course, young man," says Bella airily.

"My name's Thomas," says Thomas sulkily. Young man: that is much worse. When Bella says *young man*, you know she doesn't mean a word of what she is saying, or she is thinking about something quite different, something she's not going to tell Thomas.

Once Thomas goes up to Bella's studio. He is alone in the white villa, Kayus and Bella are pumping up bicycle tires in the yard. He stands in the middle of all her things, clothes, curlers, makeup, magazines. Breathing in the smell of tobacco, of "Blue Grass." Notes: he hasn't been in the room for a long time. Remembers the rain rattling on the metal roof, the magazines, the talk about all kinds of stuff, the mermaids, the good life. Bella humming, "That's why the lady is a tramp."

"Something will happen soon," Bella said, but it goes on raining, this being the time before the Angel family came.

For they should not be there: They were going to the mermaids, the good life. It was a game they brought with them, right from the beginning, from the apartment in the city out to the summer paradise. The going-away game. Thomas! Are you coming with me? *Shall we go*? One had to ask the question so that the other could answer. The answer was YES. YES. YES. And then you rushed to get ready. Packing bags, changing into traveling clothes, and taking *all kinds of stuff with you*. When you were ready, that was the end of the game. When Thomas was little, he had not really understood. He had started crying when, after they were ready, they never went anywhere but started taking off their traveling clothes, removing makeup, cooking a meal, cleaning up, taking Paul Anka off the turntable and putting on Bill Evans instead, because Kayus would soon be home, and starting the pea soup.

"Oh, Thomas," said Bella. "Don't sulk. When you're older, we'll both go. Together. You just have to grow up some more first."

"Would you like to, too?"

Thomas is up in Bella's studio, trying out his old tone of voice. His voice sounds really harsh.

Then he notes: It's been a long time. He has not been in the room for a long time.

"What are you doing here, young man?"

Bella has come upstairs.

"My name is Thomas. Aren't you going to ride your bikes?"

"Of course, Chet. I just came in to get the insect repellant. Have you seen it?"

"My name is Thomas," says Thomas.

Bella and Kayus ride off along the road. Kayus has fixed his bicycle, and Bella has removed May Johansson's Monarch. They have taken the bilberry cans with them in case they run across a really good patch. When they get back, the two cans are nearly full.

"Ha!" says Kayus. "We got there before May Johansson and the Johansson cousins, with their picking machines." Bella bakes a bilberry pie. Thomas has several helpings. That night he demonstrates that he is allergic to bilberries. But his reaction is fairly mild, a tightening of his throat. Not too bad, and by morning he is fully recovered.

Erkki Johansson and Thomas have a caterpillar project. They catch caterpillars near the Johanssons' sauna, then they put them into jars they have filled with leaves and soil to simulate a natural caterpillar environment. They bore holes in the jar lids and screw them on tightly so the caterpillars won't escape. Gradually they assemble a variety of different caterpillars in different jars. Maggi finds another kind of caterpillar, nothing remarkable in itself, brown and hairy like most caterpillars, and yet not quite like any of Thomas's and Erkki's caterpillars. Maggi puts her caterpillar into her own jar, and she is snooty about one being quite enough. She does not have to collect everything that crawls on the Johanssons' land. She manages without dozens of caterpillars in different jars, a veritable exhibition of caterpillars on the Johanssons' sauna porch. Thomas and Erkki go to see Helena Wikblad in the red cottage, because Helena Wikblad is the only one who owns a real insect book. Keeping a respectful distance from the screaming baby in its carriage out on this summer day, Thomas and Erkki look through Helena's book to identify their caterpillars and find out what butterflies they will become. They turn out to be quite ordinary. Sulphur butterflies and others they cannot be bothered to remember the names of, since they flutter about all the time. And some will not become butterflies at all. Particularly Thomas's fattest and longest caterpillar, the one with a blue-spotted nose and thin orange feelers. Helena Wikblad carefully pronounces the name of a certain beetle, in Latin. She tries to make it sound grand. But everyone knows that only butterflies are lovely. Maggi Johansson unscrews the lid of her jar. Helena Wikblad can tell by just looking that the caterpillar belongs to a rare species. The beginning of a swallowtail, the book says when they look it up. Maggi gives a superior smile to Thomas and Erkki Johansson. Erkki and Thomas go away. Maggi stays For several days Maggi Johansson and Helena Wikblad sit in the grass outside the red cottage, making grown-up conversation. Grown-up conversations are not about beetles and caterpillars but about life, babies, and all that stuff. Maggi sticks the pacifier into the baby's mouth. The baby spits it out. Maggi sticks the pacifier into the baby's mouth. The baby spits it out.

Erkki Johansson and Thomas go into the forest. At first they merely walk aimlessly, but after a while they carry out some scientific experiment or other. After some time has gone by, Erkki Johansson suddenly says that now he wants to begin practicing for when Renée returns.

Renée. That name goes right through Thomas. At first it sounds almost foreign. Thomas realizes that he has not been thinking about her at all. And yet, he understands now, he has really been thinking about her all the time.

It is the middle of this turbulent summer. To his own astonishment, at first it seems to be running its course perfectly well without the Angel family—a summer of caterpillars in jars on the Johanssons' sauna porch; later on, fish fries in leaky buckets, and sea grass to feed them on; Helena Wikblad and Maggi Johansson, their fair hair combed into identical ponytails, by the red cottage with a baby in the carriage beside them; Kayus's diving board still under construction and rising more and more ominously on the white villa's beach; Bella's cigarettes in the evening in the big room; Kayus's and Bella's talk about jazz; Kayus and Bella ringing their bicycle bells, ting-a-ling, "Thomas! We're back!" Erkki Johansson's,

"Thomas, what are we gonna do now?" "Thomas, you're the smartest person I know," "Thomas, you can have my giraffe later, when Mom isn't looking" "Thomas, what experiment shall we do now?" "Tell me now, Thomas."

This. You idiot. Squelch, squelch.

Sound of footsteps and nothing else. Feet on their way to the forest. And the forest: there's no direct connection with Erkki Johansson. Or with scientific experiments in general.

But Erkki Johansson is stubborn, and Thomas has to give in. In the name of science he finally gets Erkki Johansson up on the lowest branch of quite a high tree, a swaying birch that is steady at the bottom but thin and dangerous farther up, because that is what it has to be like for an experiment to feel like a challenge. Erkki Johansson clutches the branch, his arms and legs twisted around it like a monkey. It takes a while before he dares to jump back down to the ground, but when he's done, he says; "When Renée comes back, I'll climb all the way to the top."

"Don't believe you," says Thomas.

"Why don't you wait and see?" says Erkki Johansson.

"Wanna bet?" says Erkki Johansson.

Renée. Eventually everything he sees and does has something to do with her. She is the one to whom he will tell everything. Then he begins to experience and observe his surroundings with that thought in mind and only that. Whenever something happens, it is transformed in his mind into a story, a description, an anecdote that he will tell her. Eventually the telling in his head never stops. He fills himself with stories. Finally he's ready to explode. And yet she does not arrive.

He grows impatient. Where is she? Why doesn't she

come? Then he returns to what had puzzled him at first, what would go on puzzling him the entire time the Angel family is away—where are they, what are they doing? What are they up to this minute, this very second? When are they coming back? What if they never come back?

More and more often he finds himself on the empty patch of gravel below the Angel hill. Peering up at the house, the dark windows, the drawn curtains.

He goes home, sits at his table, and goes on putting the skeleton together. Reads the instructions:

> *If we are to have any hope of understanding one another, we have to speak in metaphors, in images. We always do so in the simplest contexts of everyday life, and we must do so now as well, when we are trying together to learn something about reality. Real scientists never say: This is it! They say: This is an image of the way we think it is.*

She is there again. A glimpse. *Just like her.*

But where is she?

"Where do you think they are now, Thomas?"

Thomas looks around. Bella has come into his room and is looking out the window, speaking in a low voice, gazing out intently, as if the whole world inhabited by the Angels were spread out beyond the villa, just outside the window.

"I don't know," says Thomas. "No idea."

Bella shrugs and leaves the room.

"Let's take a bike ride," suggests Kayus. "Borrow the Monarch?"

"I'm tired," says Bella. "I have to rest."

It can't possibly be true. Lately Bella and Kayus have done nothing but sleep. Sometimes into the afternoons.

"I'm going up to the studio," says Bella when no one believes her. "I want to be left alone to think."

"Think!" Kayus says brightly, as if thinking were a scientific impossibility in conjunction with Bella. He means no harm. Sometimes Kayus and Bella talk like that. As if Bella were that mermaid, and mermaids don't think a lot but react instinctively and emotionally, according to their respective temperaments. And Bella will not say anything. She often joins in, and sometimes she laughs.

But she is not laughing now. She says good night although it is only eight o'clock. They can hear steps on the attic landing, and the studio door closing.

"Was she angry?" says Thomas.

"No," says Kayus gently. "Everyone needs to be left alone to think sometimes. That's how it is, Thomas.

"On second thought, I think I'll withdraw for a while. I'm in the middle of a good book on the veranda. Want to come with me?"

Thomas shakes his head. "I'm busy." He goes into his room and continues putting his skeleton together.

Kayus's diving board is finished. Dark and straight, it juts out above the shimmering blue water. Kayus comes down to the beach in bathing trunks. He has rubbed himself all over with suntan oil. It does not look as well on him as it does on Bella because Kayus's skin is like Thomas's, just as pale. He has brought along the transistor radio. And the camera.

Kayus puts the camera down on the rock and walks out on the diving board. He lies down flat on his back, switches on the radio, and starts sunbathing. After about thirty seconds he sits up and calls to Thomas to come and take a picture.

Bella is asleep face down between her beach blankets, in the shade, her face buried in the yellow robe she has piled under her head. Thomas snaps a picture of Kayus. Kayus turns the radio up so high that Bella can't help waking up. Kayus calls to Bella that she must come out on the diving board. Bella says that she doesn't want to.

"I want to be in the shade," she calls. "I get sunstroke from too much sun."

But because Kayus can be stubborn when he really wants something, Bella finally ends up on the diving board, dazed, her hair untidy, but undeniably beautiful in her yellow bathing suit and dark, soft skin. Kayus goes to stand on the rock with the camera. He zooms in on Bella and calls instructions to her how she is to lie, on her side, propped up on one elbow, her face turned to the camera. Bella says that she is getting splinters in her bottom from the unplaned planks. Even at this late stage, Thomas thinks, Kayus must see how wrong, how really wrong, the diving board is. But Kayus sees nothing. He is suddenly quite blind, absorbed in his photography. He clicks and clicks, then he hands the camera to Thomas and goes out on the diving board himself. He calls to Thomas to take a picture. In the viewfinder Thomas sees that Bella has turned her face toward the Johanssons' sauna and only Kayus is looking straight ahead. Thomas adjusts the light aperture and the distance, and suddenly it does not seem at all a bad thing that Kayus's camera is not a practical Instamatic like Rosa's but has all manner of buttons and adjustments. "Go on!" says Kayus, and Thomas realizes that he has to. But then he feels something strange tickling his knees. He glances down. Of course. Classic. The camera has fallen open, and the strip of film is dangling down in a shiny spiral. Kayus is angry at Thomas. He thinks Thomas did it on purpose.

And that is when they hear a honking above.

A familiar honking—they know what it is at once. There is not another honk like it in the whole summer paradise.

Bella scrambles past Kayus out on his diving board, leisurely at first, retaining some dignity, then with an increasing eagerness that is difficult to control. Away from the diving board, she puts on her robe, and up the avenue she runs, up toward the houses, actually calling some excuse over her shoulders, something improbable like, "Have to pee."

Kayus and Thomas are left on the beach.

"Can I try it?" says Thomas. He means the diving board. Of course he would prefer to go back up like Bella, but he realizes that he cannot simply run away, as Bella has done. That would be rough on Kayus, and on Kayus's diving board, Thomas thinks, although he himself had a part in building it, more than just holding the level.

"If you like." Kayus tries to wind the ruined film back into the camera. He winds and winds. But he is not at all angry anymore. He is completely over his fit of anger.

Thomas tries the diving board. He is right: quite useless. The planks are too thick to bounce on, and if you dive in head first, you have to watch out, because the water is at most a couple of feet deep under the end now that the heat wave has gone on forever and the water level is at a record low.

"You think we should take it apart?" Kayus asks suddenly

while Thomas is trying to bounce up and down on the diving board as well as look interested.

"Yes," Thomas says at once. They start immediately, working quickly and methodically. Soon all that is left of the diving board is an innocuous pile of planks on the rock by the beach.

"How about we make a raft with the planks?" says Thomas.

"Good idea," says Kayus.

He is silent for a moment, but then he starts talking again and actually seems really eager.

"We have to have regular floats. We have to design a test model. We have to calculate how much float material we need for the raft to float properly. You need mathematics for that. Exact calculations."

"Yes." Thomas agrees.

"On our raft no one's going to get wet, are they? Our raft will be the finest raft in the whole bay."

"That's not difficult," says Thomas. "There aren't any other rafts in this bay."

"Hm," says Kayus.

"Hm," says Thomas, imitating him.

"Know what I'm doing now, Thomas?" Kayus grimaces so that the left corner of his mouth moves toward his left ear and trembles slightly. "I'm smiling a crooked smile."

"In the Gene Pitney way," Thomas fills in. And they laugh, for now they are of one mind again.

Several hours later he finds her on the beach, in the exact place of the diving board, now a harmless pile of planks on the beach. Thomas is grateful for that pile. Just how grateful he does not realize until now, now that he sees her again. How difficult it would have been to explain, and he would have had to.

She is just the same, wearing the orange T-shirt whose shoulder is mended with large stitches, pulling a strand of brown hair through her front teeth. Thomas, brimful of stories, observations, secrets he has accumulated while she was away, comes up behind her. Sits down beside her. What about her? What has she been up to? He glances at her as if searching for traces of sun hat, sunglasses, and the road, *take your home and go*. The only new thing about her is a beige cloth dinosaur tucked under her arm. Neck and head showing. Not *Tyrannosaurus rex* but one of the herbivores.

Thomas opens his mouth to start talking. Tupsu Lindbergh is waterskiing out on the bay behind the Lindberghs' shiny mahogany speedboat, sweeping past quite close to the beach. Waving. Calling, "Wheee, there she goes." Thomas automatically raises his hand.

"They'll run out of gas now," says Renée.

"What?"

"They'll run out of gas now."

"Hee-hee," says Thomas. What else can he say?

And yet. At that very moment he sees it beginning to happen. The engine roars. Coughs, stutters. The stutter reproduces itself along the towrope to Tupsu Lindbergh's body. Two strong ones. The engine stops. Tupsu starts sinking. Slowly, then more quickly. Tupsu Lindbergh disappears below the surface of the water. But before she disappears, she looks around, her face twisted into a grimace that is the remains of a smile. She does not understand what is happening.

"Go on, for Christ's sake!" Tupsu cries to Robin Lindbergh in the boat. But Robin Lindbergh can do nothing. He's powerless. He leans against the windscreen, looking at what is happening through his aviator sunglasses.

"Step on it, Robin," calls Tupsu Lindbergh.

But it is no use. They have run out of gas. Tupsu Lindbergh disappears below the water.

Oh, of course that is not what happens.

Robin Lindbergh sweeps on toward the Lindbergh house, Tupsu Lindbergh behind him on skis, her knees rather too bent but not so that you would notice if you did not look too closely. Her bikini bottom sags slightly because Tupsu Lindbergh is so thin, like a skeleton. The red, white, and blue boating scarf she usually ties around her head to protect her fair hair from the blazing sun at sea has slipped and is a little crooked, so that a few fair strands flutter freely and untidily around her head; but all these details take on meaning only a year or two later, when Bella and Rosa go waterskiing and comparative material is available.

So that is that.

But Thomas is angry.

In some way. Just because Renée says, "Now they'll run out of gas," they do. Then he sees it beginning to happen right in front of him. The engine's roar and stutter. Tupsu Lindbergh's grimace. Tupsu Lindbergh sinking under the water.

"Nit." Thomas gets up and walks away. He goes along the avenue up to the white villa, walking with angry steps. In the middle of the avenue he turns right, crosses diagonally through the Johanssons' yard, and turns into the path to the forest. She comes after him. He can hear her footsteps.

But then there is a third sound. A squelching that is not so familiar but is quite distinct. No. He is not imagining it. And in the end he cannot help himself. He has to turn around to check.

"Okay, Experimental Subject," he mumbles. "You're with us."

"Yes," says Erkki Johansson formally, almost before Thomas has even begun to speak.

But still in the middle of the day. Breathless, in soaking wet swimming trunks, diving board splinters in his feet, the inside of his hands smarting from dry, unplaned planks. Thomas stands on the threshold of the big room, his skin hot from the sun, his feet firmly on the warm floor.

Rosa has already arrived, in sunglasses. She is describing life on the road and all the places they have visited. Or is she? Thomas is not listening very carefully. It is not so important.

Rosa and Bella are trying on what they call sunsuits in the big room, now bathed in sunlight. Sunsuits consist of knee-length skirts and separate tops, both made of cotton. The same model for Bella and Rosa, but in different colors. Rosa's is pink, Bella's yellow with white dots. Big white dots.

Rosa bought them in Sweden as a souvenir for both of them.

And she laughs, then she sees Thomas.

A strong, definite joy wells up inside Thomas. He realizes that this is the moment he has been waiting for all the time, despite everything. So has Bella. *When they come back*. No, there is no back to anything else any longer.

"I don't think," says Rosa Angel in her sunsuit in the big room, "I'm ever going to leave here again. At least, not this summer."

"I know what we'll do now," she adds. "We'll send the men on an outing and arrange a party."

And a few days later Bella and Rosa are standing with bare breasts in the skirts of their sunsuits, yellow-and-white and pink, up on Gabby's and Rosa's hill, in the spot where you are visible to the entire summer paradise. They have flung the tops into Rosa's arbor, where all morning they've been having their own party. But now they are hot and are off to the beach to cool off and swim.

They walk past the red cottage where Helena Wikblad is sitting on her steps, an open book in her lap and the blue baby in the carriage beside her. Rosa and Bella wave and cross the Johanssons' yard. Helena Wikblad waves back, but crouching in the potato patch with a hoe, May Johansson pretends not to see them, although she has the best vantage point through the wild jungle of stalks.

Of Bella's and Rosa's breasts the following can be said:

Bella's are round and full, Rosa's somewhat smaller, perhaps sagging just a little—microscopically so but nevertheless. Rosa's nipples are dark and stand straight up. Bella's nipples are adequate.

A few steps behind them comes Renée, pulling her dinosaur. With all her clothes on, long pants, sneakers, orange T-shirt.

But this is something no one else sees. Thomas, for instance, can only imagine it. The day Bella and Rosa fling away their tops for the first and only time, Thomas has gone on an outing with the men in Gabby's white car. He is squashed between Johan Wikblad and Kayus in the back, he strolls on the gravel in the blazing sun among old military planes or, as Gabby calls them, *fine flamingoes*.

"See that, son."

Gabby reaches out his hand toward the flamingo, touching the metal, burning hot under the sun. Gabby pulls his hand back and says, "Oh, son. Why are they sitting there? They should be in the air. What's a plane for if not for flying?

"Yes, son," Gabby goes on. "In America you can say *son* without its having to be your real son you're talking to."

"I know," Thomas says, suddenly remembering. "Paul Anka said it."

Gabby looks at him in astonishment. "Aha, Thomas," he says. "Now I'm really curious. Tell me more."

Without being really aware of it, that is just what Thomas does. He will talk, a story literally oozing out of him, a story which is not a secret but which feels sort of like one all the same. An old story, something private among Bella, Kayus, and himself.

In the car on the way home Gabby winds down the window and rests his elbow on the rim, presses his foot down on the accelerator almost to the floor, and they race away at a seventy-five miles an hour, at least.

Gabby says, in the middle of the joy of speed, "He's a real entertainer, this Thomas of ours."

Of course Thomas had not wanted to go with them. The night before, he'd eaten an orange, secretly popping several segments into his mouth in the kitchen. Not a lot, but enough to bring on a mild allergic reaction. He went back to bed and waited. He fell asleep, but nothing happened. No big reaction set in, and there is no valid reason for him to refuse the place reserved for him in the car's backseat, between Johan Wikblad and Kayus. Since Pusu Johansson is the largest, he sits in front beside the driver.

The driver sets off at sixty miles an hour on the main road. The driver winds down the window and looks at Thomas in the rearview mirror. "Thomas, do you understand now what is meant by the joy of speed?"

Thomas nods, though rather stiffly. At the beginning of the outing he is rather like that, stiff, somewhat distant. He makes an effort to think distancing thoughts. Like this: That one disadvantage of being the smallest of all the men is that you have to answer stupid questions, questions grown-ups would like to ask each other but don't dare just because they're grown-ups.

They stop at a gas station, they eat steaks on plates, drink beer. The men drink, all except Gabby, who is the driver; when it comes time to pay, he holds up his hand to stop them and says this feast is on him. They see airplanes, the goal of the outing. An exhibition of military planes at a military base at Porkala Point. Though the goal is not important in itself. There is an intrinsic value in just rushing along the main road and feeling the joy of speed.

Mixed with that emotion is its opposite. The emotion is not complete if you don't have an idea of the opposite at the back of your mind, as a contrast or as a background against which to feel the emotion. That is where what is called *women and children* comes in. While the men race along the highways, tasting adventures and freedom, the women putter about, doing their thing in the summer paradise. Lazing around and talking about home, husbands, and children and laundry day and about Elizabeth Taylor's love life, which has nothing to do with real life in the way that highways have.

When the men get back from their outings into the world, the women are waiting for them, empty and receptive, ears and eyes open for the sated weariness of men, for men's stories, men's adventures, stories that are allowed to be a little childish, so that the contrast can become palpable again. The contrast between the adventurer and the mature, clever woman who does not need such follies when everything she has ever desired has been given to her—husband and children and a summer paradise in which to laze.

That is how sea chanties come about, myths of the open road, of mobility, of vagabondage. Someone who is not free to go is always needed, someone who does not roam the seas or the roads, as a background against which the sailors, the vagabond, can be delineated.

Naturally Thomas does not think in such terms. He is only eight and not particularly inclined to philosophy. But he feels it. For he knows what the men do not know or want to know: That in the summer paradise, at this very moment, a party is going on and he is not there. *Shangri-la party in Rosa's garden*. And it is very different from what the men imagine it to be.

Even if he can't say precisely how.

Like this, for instance:

"Surprise, surprise. The party's canceled," says Rosa when Bella comes up to the house on the hill after the men have left.

"Mmm," says Bella. But her uncertain smile, the big cheerful dots on her sunsuit cannot hide her disappointment. Can you have a party with only two people? She, at least, has never heard of one. Where are Tupsu and all the other women, the ones who live in the villas on the outer edge of the islands, where Isabella has never even been?

"Oh, Bella. I didn't invite anyone else," says Rosa happily. "Not Tupsu and not my other friends. I've got the house *brilliantly* full of Shangri-las. Won't suffer from the lack of anything. We can be alone together all day long.

A little later Rosa is speaking: "There's another possibility. We could leave. Get out into the blue. Bella, are you listening?"

"Where would we go?"

"Anywhere. Wherever your nose leads you."

Even later Rosa takes off the top of her sunsuit and flings it into the arbor. Bella follows suit; what else can she do? It's only a game, a game with words.

They look at each others' breasts in the shade of the arbor.

Rosa takes Bella's photograph with the Instamatic. Bella is telling her something, perhaps about Kayus and the diving board.

"Do you mean like this?"

Rosa opens the camera with a triumphant gesture of feigned shock. Then she laughs. "I didn't put any film in it. This stays strictly between us."

"What are we going to do, Rosa?" asks Bella, suddenly impatient. "Now?"

Quite right. Rosa can't answer the question.

Since they cannot think of anything else, they pick up their things and go down to the beach, the two of them.

Entertainer: that is someone who makes other people laugh at his incredible stories.

"Fine flamingos. Fantastic birds." Thomas has been piloted around among the airplanes. Gabby's heavy hand has rested on his shoulder. Gabby has been producing facts about the various kinds of planes. Thomas has listened, nodded, and agreed. In all this he has forgotten to distance himself. In all this he has been right in the middle, wanting to tell something himself, a story of his own.

Entertainer: someone who entertains others with his

incredible stories. In the car Gabby's voice is friendly enough, and he does not say anything to the other men about what Thomas has told him. Nevertheless, Thomas wants to sink through the floor of the car, down into the hot roadbed along which they are racing at terrifying speed. Luckily Gabby turns on the radio. Turns the volume up high. They can hear crackling and foreign voices. Foreign voices and more crackling.

"You see," says Gabby, "how good this angel is at finding *a little light music* on FM.

"Want to see how much this angel can stand? It's a lot. Do you believe me or do I have to show you?"

Of course Gabby has to show them.

"What did you think of the planes?" whispers Kayus.

"Really good," Thomas whispers back.

The airplanes, yes. He will remember them like this. The way they were lined up on the barren surface outside the military base, looking like giant grasshoppers from a far-distant, primeval age. He will develop that thought in particular, dressing it up in words, illustrating it with specific details that further emphasize the ghostlike sense of heat and stillness and timelessness and emptiness that hangs over the exhibition space. He will erase Gabby and all the men. He will try to tell the whole adventure to Renée at the house on the hill on the evening of the crayfish party at the white villa, and he will be as truthful as possible. To his surprise she will listen. She will even appear to be interested.

Thomas and Renée row out into the bay. She has brought her dinosaur. In the middle of the bay she puts it in the water, its brown cloth stomach facing up. She orders Thomas to go on rowing. Thomas does not want to. He is angry. There is nothing he owns that he would even consider treating this way, and that includes things he doesn't care for and has not played with for a long time. But it is no good protesting. He rows on.

The following day the dinosaur floats ashore on Huotari's island; Thomas is the one who finds it and takes it to Renée. It is hard for her to conceal her delight, though she pretends to be unmoved. She hangs the dinosaur up to dry on May Johansson's clothesline, where it dances in the wind alongside May Johansson's sheets, and once it has dried, she drags it around for several days, something inseparable. Just, Thomas thinks slightly later, as if the dinosaur had passed a test and been found especially worthy.

The last thing to happen in the summer paradise this year is a crayfish party at the white villa. Bella and Rosa get the crayfish from the river that runs through the forest. They go out in the middle of the night and do not let anyone else go with them, although Thomas keeps whining about it. They gather two full buckets. The crayfish are boiled in the dishpan, and the kitchen table is brought out to the veranda. The summer library and the transistor radio are banished to the bedroom. Rosa covers the table with red paper and brings out crayfish plates, crayfish knives, crayfish napkins, and crayfish lanterns. Gabby has a lot of drinking songs photocopied at his office in town. Thomas and Bella make little red hats on which they print the names of all the people who are going to be at the party. The hats are put on each plate, since everyone has been assigned a place at the table.

Gabby and Rosa arrive at the party in the white angel. They bring along the gleaming refrigerator-bar. It is the dog days of summer now, and there is still no way to keep drinks cool in the white villa.

May Johansson wears a blouse and a summer skirt. She brings a bouquet of flowers as her contribution. She picked the flowers in the meadow below the forest road, enough for a wreath as well, and this she wears in her hair.

"Smell." May Johansson thrusts her head under Kayus's nose. "Fresh scents from a summer meadow."

"Mmm. Good." But Kayus is just being polite, he does not really smell any flowers at all. Nor any other scent, except one, Bella's perfume, "Blue Grass." Bella has come out on the veranda in her yellow dress, her hair up. Her hair looks black in the twilight. She is wearing no jewelry. So, except for her hair and the dress, she is all tanned skin.

Rosa's dress is white, silvery threads running through it in thin, almost invisible patterns, shimmering in the soft lantern light spreading over the veranda as it grows darker outside. Thin silver bracelets around her wrists, tinkling when she moves her hands. Her dark hair is combed into a pageboy, and she really does look a little like Jacqueline Kennedy.

"Standing here in the dark, are you?" Thomas is in the attic entry, spying. Helena Wikblad, wearing long pants and a T-shirt, walks past with a dish of dill. He shakes his head, picks up his things, and sets out for the Angels' house.

All through the crayfish party Thomas and Renée are in the house on the hill. They had originally made big plans to spy on and sabotage both the party and the job of babysitting for which Nina, Maggi, and Erkki Johansson have been engaged at the red cottage. But the plans all come to nothing and they stay where they are, all evening long. They never get started.

For no particular reason, just that time passes.

They talk about all kinds of stuff. About dinosaurs, for instance; Renée has a book with pictures of the different species, and they discuss facts associated with them. Also facts associated with other things—airplanes, rockets. Even rockets, which don't normally interest Thomas.

They play the TRIUMPH game. Or the LIFE game, as it is called in Renée's version. You move across the board in small cars. The cars have little holes for plastic pegs. Girls are pink and boys light blue. Whichever you are, you put it in the hole at the wheel, beside it a space for *spouse*, and behind that, two roles of holes for *children*. If you have more than four children, you have to squeeze together, just *like in real life*. And if you don't manage to land on the really good squares that give you a profession, you become a Ph.D. You can have as many children as you like. Especially if you are Thomas, and a Ph.D. Children mean expenses for schools, activities, and stuff. So far this summer Thomas always lost because his children were so expensive. Renée has been a lawyer and therefore as good as childless, and she has sped on to the Millionaire's Mansion, where the game ends and all the money will be accounted for on the Day of Reckoning. That means she has always won.

Then, suddenly Thomas starts winning. It becomes the most vivid memory he has of that evening: the way he wins; wins and keeps on winning. It itself, there is a natural explanation for it. He studied the rules of the game, and he discovered that there is another way out if you are at a disadvantage in relation to your opponent. You can stake everything you possess on a number on the Wheel of Fortune; if the right number comes up, you can increase your assets according to the number and become a Very Important Person, and the

VIP is usually the one who wins the game, particularly if you've staked everything on a high-enough number.

Thomas picks the number ten. He spins the wheel, ten comes up, and he increases his assets tenfold. Becomes a VIP and wins the game again. Again and again, several times in a row. He himself is surprised at his unbelievable luck.

"One more time." Of course Renée pretends that she cannot believe her eyes. She tries to copy him, staking everything she possesses on the Wheel of Fortune. But it doesn't work for her—her number doesn't come up. She is swept off the board, car, plastic pegs, and all, and ends up destitute in a place called the Poorhouse.

So they drink tea and eat bilberry turnovers. They paint each other's faces with Rosa's makeup, look at Nina's pictures of horses, and take a look at her diary. Renée is impressed when it turns out that Thomas can open the lock without a key perfectly easily. "Dear diary" it reads on almost every page. Thomas is wearing Renée's nightgown, a long sleeveless one, which will keep him shivering that night. Renée is wearing Thomas's helicopter-patterned pajamas, his favorite pair, and of course she refuses to give them back to him after the game. She gets into Nina's bunk bed above her own and pretends to go to sleep. Then she really does fall asleep, abruptly. Slurp; and all the air goes out of her. Thomas gets into Renée's bunk with that silly dinosaur smelling of salt water and sea grass. He lies in the dark for a long time, thinking that he will never fall asleep. The house is very quiet. The moon is shining. A crayfish moon, as Rosa told Bella it is called. In any case he does not remember the party. And you can't really see the moon, it is no more than a dull yellow glow, casting sharp shadows in the forest that starts beyond the window.

■ ■ ■

When he wakes up, he is lying on his stomach, pressing the comforter to his face, rubbing his face against the comforter cover, hard. Must have started rubbing in his sleep, because his skin feels sore and tender. But the itching and prickling go on, apparently coming from beneath, from under his skin. Thomas is not at all surprised. He knows exactly what is happening, an allergic reaction setting in again. Bilberry turnovers and makeup, not a particularly good combination, and he should have expected it. He forces himself to stop scratching, because scratching only makes it worse, and turns over on his back. It is light outside, the trees glisten in the sun outside the window, their leaves wet with dew. But the way the light slants makes him realize that it is early: five past six; there is an alarm clock on the table. And Renée? He lies still for a moment, listening. He cannot hear any sound from the upper bunk. For a moment he thinks that she may have gone off and left him alone in the house. But then he hears. Breathing. Thin. Or light, as they say when you are sleeping heavily. Or do they say that? Thomas closes his eyes and tries to go back to sleep.

But it's no use. He can't feel himself. The allergic reaction is well under way, throbbing and unmistakable. He must do something to stop it.

He gets up and pads out to the living room. The mess from the previous evening strikes him: clothes strewn all over, the horse pictures on the table. Closet doors stand wide open and makeup in Rosa's bedroom is scattered all over Rosa's little pink dressing table. The beds are empty. Gabby and Rosa have not come home yet.

No, he can't be bothered. Suddenly it seems impossible to

start hunting for his own clothes in the mess. But he knows one thing: His skin is throbbing. He must get out.

He takes a bathrobe off a hook, sticks his feet into a pair of big boots, and leaves.

The houses in the summer paradise loom silent in the bright summer morning. The white villa farthest away, so white with black windows. The red cottage. The woodshed and the grove of trees hiding the white villa's yard. The Johanssons' house nearest, below the hill. The Johanssons' yard, open to view. May Johansson's potato patch, May Johansson's pots of nasturtiums, May Johansson's desiccated apple trees. Between the trees he can see the Johanssons' sauna and a shimmering patch of bay. The wind has not yet risen. On the whole everything is desolate, as if you were the only survivor after a natural disaster. In some circumstances that thought could be exciting. But not now.

The party. Thomas has been reminded of it. Acutely. As soon as he is outside the house, the light poured over him, dazzling him. Petrified on the hill. The party. Suddenly he remembered the party. How could he have forgotten?

He stands outside the Angels' house, at the very top of the hill, where you have a view over almost the whole of the summer paradise. But at its very center he feels only pitiful. A little like Erkki Johansson maybe, crouching in the forest. Where is everybody? Why is it so quiet, so empty?

All that lasts for only a moment. Then everything is back to normal. In all this great emptiness someone comes walking from the direction of the white villa, moving with typical hurried little steps over the mound where the Johanssons' land starts, crossing the Johanssons' yard, up the steps and into the house. Closing the door with a bang. Not a particularly loud bang, but in the silence all sounds are magnified, and it echoes through the summer paradise. Thomas knows at once what he has seen. He has seen May Johansson *leaving the party when it is at its most enjoyable*. Somehow the slam of that door has told him something else as well: May Johansson has not been included in what is most enjoyable.

But the party does not stop just because May Johansson has left.

The sound is turned up.

Voices in a foreign language pour out into the silence. Voices in another foreign language, voices in several foreign languages merging together. Fading away. Ssssh. Heard again. Merging into other voices in other foreign languages.

Then Thomas truly sees what he has actually had before his eyes all the time but had not really been able to take in because it has been so misplaced, so wrong.

Farthest away of all, in the meadow below the white villa, is the white angel, its front doors wide open so that they actually do look rather like wings. Inside it someone is taking in *a little light music on the FM band*. One of the dark stones in the meadow starts to move, walking purposefully to the car and getting in. The doors slam and it's quiet again. Of course it is not a stone. Or if it is a stone, then it is a very special kind, called Isabella Mermaid.

Thomas runs down the hill and across the Johanssons' yard down to the beach. On the rock he flings off the bathrobe, boots, and Renée's nightgown and wades out into the water, swims, washes his face. Rubs hard. Rinses several times. Then he gets out, puts on the robe, and walks on up the avenue to the white villa, not looking around at all now, just walking. He goes into the villa, into his room, draws the curtains and closes the door, crawls under the covers, and falls asleep. Not until he is deep into sleep does he remember that he should not be there at all but in the house on the hill with Renée.

It is twenty-five minutes to seven. Gabby's white Chevrolet Chevelle starts rolling down the meadow.

It rolls into the Rotwoods, plowing a great furrow as fragile trees bend and break. It turns into the avenue and drives along for a short while. Then turns left again and continues in the Johanssons' yard, brushes past Johanssons' house, close, so close that the metal panel almost touches the corner. But no one wakes; both May and Pusu Johansson are fast asleep, May Johansson in her bed behind drawn curtains, Pusu on the sofa in the big room of the white villa, the only leftover from the party, so well did May Johansson clean up before leaving. Pusu Johansson's huge body is the only thing she wasn't able to shift. Gabby's car goes on, across May Johansson's patch of grass, down towards the Johanssons' sauna. There it slows for a moment and almost stops. But then the engine revs up again, and the car drives straight into the water. Rolls on the surface of the water for a little, sort of arbitrarily, as if it really could manage such a trick. An illusion, of course. Gabby's white angel is only a car. It sinks. Slowly at first. Then all the way.

The front doors open at almost the same moment. Later there will be many versions of what Gabby really said as soon as he opened the door on his side after the car rolled into the water. This is one, the best: "Look, it's floating!" cries Gabby.

But at that very moment it begins to sink. And in the very next moment nothing remains to be seen above the water but a patch of the car roof. And even that patch rapidly vanishes as the car sinks deeper into the mud under its own weight. Bella wades ashore. She says nothing amusing. Not even that she is going home. But she does.

"We were playing hide-and-seek," Bella tells Thomas afterwards.

"Ha, ha," says Thomas sourly.

"Don't sulk, Thomas."

"Ha, ha," says Thomas sourly.

"Well, sulk then."

Bella shrugs. She goes to Kayus, who is on the veranda. She spends the rest of the summer there.

But a mermaid has stood on the floor of Thomas's room. A mermaid in a wet yellow dress. More mermaid than ever, Muddy—and with some imagination it is possible to imagine fronds of sea grass, green and leafy around her legs, naked and dark, and the arms and the body, and the dress clinging to skin. But no one saw her at such a moment, no one who, at the sight of her, allowed his thoughts to drift and engage in fantasy.

She was alone there in the room, and cold, shivering in her soaking-wet dress. She wriggled out of it, bundled it up, and was just about to fling it in the garbage can when she changed her mind. The garbage can has been emptied, May Johansson having emptied it. May Johansson: and Bella looked around. Not a trace left of the crayfish party. It has been cleaned up. May Johansson's flower vase on the table. "Greetings from May Johansson" on a note under the vase. May Johansson really did tidy away the party, all on her own!

That made her even more dizzy, even more exhausted, confused. The party, where is it? It was here just now. There was to be a party. Her party. Where is everybody? And what is she doing here, soaking wet, standing in Thomas's room?

Suddenly she had no idea.

A pink bathrobe on the floor. Rosa's bathrobe. She picked it up and wrapped it around herself. Suddenly no longer confused, just tired, beat, sleepy, she walked through the big room straight past Pusu Johansson, who lay fast asleep on the sofa, into the bedroom where she threw herself on her bed and fell asleep.

A moment later Kayus came in. Actually it was some kind of game. He and Rosa have been walking along the road, on their way somewhere, sort of like hide-and-seek. After a while they realize no one would come to look for them, least of all Gabby, who is "it," self-appointed. So they turned around and walked home.

Kayus spread a blanket over Bella, undressed, folded his clothes neatly on a chair. Drew the curtains and lay down next to Bella, shaping his body around hers.

Seven o'clock one sunny morning in the summer paradise.

In the afternoon of the day after the crayfish party the Johansson cousins arrive with tractor and towrope. The car is laboriously hauled out of the mud. For the rest of the summer the angel stands on May Johansson's patch of grass near the Johanssons' sauna. In the evenings the hood is raised and the men gather around it. Even Kayus and Johan Wikblad join in occasionally, staring at engine parts, fingering, theorizing, offering opinions, bringing tools in heavy boxes, and Gabby sits on the porch of the Johanssons' sauna reading the manual. These activities are fruitless, all their efforts are in vain. In the end Gabby gives up. He kicks the car and says that the showrooms are full of new cars. He leaves the beach with rapid, angry strides, his white shirt flapping in the breeze. The other men also drift away. Darkness falls, and all is quiet and still.

But what Gabby has said is not true.

Huotari, on his island, tells Thomas once again about regulations for the tax-free import of new cars from abroad. Thomas and Huotari are sitting on the steps outside Huotari's cottage. They have had a sauna and are wearing towels around their middles as they eat sausages they have grilled in aluminum foil on the sauna stones while they watched the men's actions at the car hood on the opposite beach, like a play.

They go into Huotari's cottage and play cards and talk for a while. Huotari once again tells one of these stories Thomas likes to listen to although he knows that they are not true. Huotari tells him about things seen on the outer rim of the ocean, where the archipelago ends, things seen by sailors who have run into trouble during autumn storms and have almost drowned or been shipwrecked. Those who were rescued have had amazing tales to tell about what they experienced at their very last instant, when you are past all such feelings as fear and panic. That was when they came, the mermaids. Appeared abruptly, swam up to the men or in some other way showed themselves and intervened to make the crucial difference.

Glittering fins at the outer horizon of the ocean. Thomas stares into the yellow flame of the oil lamp and draws the smell of wood, soot, fish, and sausages into his nostrils. He knows that Huotari is lying on purpose because Thomas is a child, to whom you can tell such a story. Nevertheless. Mermaid's tails, miracles, the world at the bottom of the sea. For a moment all those glimpses. So he leaves. He must go home and to bed.

He pushes the rowboat out through Huotari's reedy inlet. It is not yet fully dark, but the stars are out. The only sound is the creak of oars in the oarlocks and the blades of the oars breaking the surface of the water. He stops rowing and listens. Splashing. Nearby. The next moment the boat rocks, two hands appear, they grasp the stern, and someone rises.

A face comes into view above the edge.

"Chet."

It is Bella, her dark hair piled high on her head, some strands loosened and sticking to her neck in dark, wet lines. But Thomas says nothing. He just stares.

What is Bella doing in the middle of the bay in the middle of the night? Bella, who cannot swim. How is it possible?

"You mustn't believe all you see, Thomas," says Isabella Mermaid. "Shall I tow you?"

"Ha, ha," says Thomas.

But the next moment she has taken the stern towrope and started swimming ashore, Thomas and the boat gliding slowly behind her.

"Ha, ha," says Thomas again, though this time rather more hesitantly.

Thomas spends most of the rest of the summer with Erkki Johansson or with Huotari or in his room in the white villa. He lies in bed reading old Donald Duck comic books or drawing submarines with crayons on white paper; he keeps busy with his model. He finishes the birthday skeleton, sees Johan Wikblad going past on the track from his window, and names the skeleton Johan. He puts it on his table, from where it gives off a hollow grin at night. It is a good effect. He runs across the yard with Kayus's camera and shoots a whole roll of film of

Helena Wikblad and the blue baby. Helena Wikblad poses with some surprise, and the baby poses alone while Thomas clicks, and both Helena and Thomas are slightly embarrassed, but when Thomas is back at the white villa, he feels something like triumph because he has overcome his discomfort about the baby, and he opens the camera to look at the film inside. Of course it's the same exposed roll that has been in the camera since that business with the diving board that made Kayus lose interest in photography.

Some time later, when it is almost autumn, Thomas goes to the amusement park with Kayus and Huotari. Sonny Liston, the King of the Beasts, works out with a punching bag to music, "Night Train." Night train; there are crowds there, men in hats and boys of his own age. Men in hats like gangsters and gangster kids. Thomas gets an autograph.

"Probably the only thing he can write," says Kayus dryly as they drive home. "His name." As if he were not in the slightest impressed.

"Night Train" and the sound of a nard fist hitting a punching bag stay in Thomas's and Huotari's minds for a long time and make for a tough, dogged mood between them in the car on the way home. Only Kayus has the energy to talk.

The last day of August comes. They pack and leave. Dust sheets are spread over the basket chairs and the sofa in the big room. The summer library is packed into a brown suitcase arranged as closely as possible in alphabetical order. Skeleton, trolling spoon box, the TRIUMPH game, and the yellow rubber giraffe with the knotted neck will go too, as will sunsuits and robes, stuffed into bags to be washed in the laundry room back in the city and then stored for the winter in yellow cardboard boxes with "Summer Things" written on them, placed in the closet in the city apartment. Rat poison is sprinkled on saucers that are set out in the pantry.

They leave. Up on the main road, where the buses run, they see Johan and Helena Wikblad with their baby in a carry-cot, wearing backpacks. Kayus honks twice before he turns and sets off along the main road. That's the last they see of both the baby and Helena Wikblad. The following summer there is another woman in the red cottage. Her name is Ann-Christine and she is large and boisterous, a Ph.D. with many interests, including Nordic mythology, country-style furniture, and the French language.

About a half a mile along the main road a truck drives up behind Kayus's red Austin Mini. Then roars past. Renée is sitting in the open back clutching a blue duffelbag. Thomas hails her with a raised hand. Renée nods. Thomas nods back.

A winter of nothing special follows. Renée turns seven, and her birthday party takes place one evening in November. Thomas is not invited, since no connection exists between their city lives and their summer lives and Gabby and Rosa and Bella and Kayus live at opposite ends of the city. But Tupsu and Robin Lindbergh are present, and most especially their youngest son, Lars-Magnus, the one Renée secretly calls *the runt*, and who, for a while in the summer had been a cardboard boyfriend forced on Renée. This last is a sore point with Renée, and Thomas has succeeded more than once in shutting her up by just mentioning it. Lars-Magnus Lindbergh has the honor of handing Renée the official Lindbergh birthday present. It is a record the Lindbergh family bought on vacation in America, and it's called "It's my Party and I'll cry if I want to." Although President Kennedy is not yet dead, and the name is still only the meaningless title of a meaningless popular song, it is nevertheless some kind of ill omen.

"There isn't going to be a party," says Renée as soon as all the guests have arrived. She goes into the bathroom and locks herself in and only one of the little girls, Charlotta Pfalenqvist, is allowed in with her. When Renée and Charlotta come out hours later, the following has happened: The birthday cake has been eaten, President Kennedy was shot in Dallas, Texas, and died shortly afterwards, sulky little girls in pink dresses and with bows in their hair have struggled into prickly leggings on the floor of the hall under the supervision of shocked mothers and fathers. President Kennedy is dead. They stare out into the November darkness. What is going to happen now, to everything, to the future?

And no one really knows what Renée and Charlotta were up to in the bathroom while Kennedy was being shot and died. They have used up all the cleanser that Nina Angel put on the bathroom shelf in a glass jar. "Don't forget to clean the sink after use. Renée too," a label Nina pasted on the jar read. And the sink is clean. Renée and Charlotta scrubbed it. With a toothbrush.

Thomas has no idea what he is doing when President Kennedy is assassinated. He will be one of those who do not remember. At the end of 1963, what was going on? November, November . . . no. His head is empty. Yes, one thing: That was the autumn they got television. He did not hear or see anything about the murder on television. They did not watch television much at the time, especially the news. Bella was too restless to sit still before a television screen. But they did see Jayne Mansfield, the whole family. Jayne Mansfield was on a public-relations tour and appeared with swelling breasts in a low-cut gown, and she was unforgettable because of the size of her breasts and her platinum hair. But Jayne Mansfield was eager to prove that she was a serious artist, not the dumb blonde she looked to be, and that her blondness and her bust were not responsible for her success in a profession in which only real talent counted. As a lead-in to this demonstration, Jayne Mansfield had brought a violin. She placed the instrument quite grandly beneath her chin, near the neckline of her dress, so that you could concentrate on the deep, dark cleavage when you couldn't be bothered to listen to the music, which was something by Johann Sebastian Bach and which Jayne Mansfield had learned to play at the conservatory, where she really had studied.

They had also brought in a musical expert to give his opinion of Jayne Mansfield's playing. He established objectively that the platinum blonde played the violin *not at all badly*. It was a flat-out lie, and everyone heard it—the expert as well, of course—but Kayus explained that it was all part of the script for him to say what he did. Mansfield played horribly, that was indisputable to Kayus and Bella and Thomas as they sat on the sofa in front of the television being entertained, the whole family all together.

And it was Tragic To Watch.

"She has no integrity," said Kayus.

"She's prepared to do anything to stay in the spotlight," said Kayus.

"Selling herself." Kayus sounded as if selling yourself was the worst thing anyone could do. Bella nodded in agreement.

On the screen they asked Jayne Mansfield about her most deeply felt wish.

"TO BE HAPPY" replied Jayne Mansfield, her bust bobbing

up and down. Happy: she said that was what she was at the moment. And she would go on being happy for the next hundred years. And smiled. It was tragic again; although Kayus did not say anything, he implied it, the whole performance—the low-cut gown, the violin, and the musical expert with his opinions. They could all see that hers was not the smile of a happy and balanced woman. The false eyelashes alone were too long and too dark for that.

"A lie as good as any other," said Kayus, turning off the television set, because in this family they did not like dumb blondes, and Kayus put on a good jazz record instead. Bella smiled again and agreed that Kayus was right.

He was found to be even more right. Jayne Mansfield was actually not to be anything at all in a hundred years. She was to die just like President Kennedy, not murdered but from driving straight into a mountainside in a car at too many miles an hour only a few years later, when the era of the busty queens had definitely passed and no one would still be interested in Marilyn Monroe clones. She was to go on a spree through Europe on yet another tour only a month or two before her death, wild and uninhibited. Like living proof that every syllable of Kayus's words held true. A lie as good as any other; before *crash-crunch*, or whatever it sounds like when a car hits a mountainside, and exit Jayne Mansfield out of this story, out of history in general.

In the fall of 1963 Thomas is overcome by a sense of rebellion. He has listened to Jayne Mansfield playing the violin and looked at her, both the violin and the cleavage, and he has thought about it, then decided that he really does believe the following, which he states in a quiet voice: *"There's nothing wrong with blondes either."*

Kayus and Bella look at Thomas with astonishment. Then they laugh and Kayus says, "Now you're the one, Thomas, who stole the show."

"Sometimes, Thomas," says Bella, looking searchingly at Thomas, "you say incredible things."

But by winter nothing much is left of the summer. City life and summer life are two separate things. Thomas gives Bella a scarf for Christmas. It is red, white, and blue. Not until Bella ties it under her chin does Thomas realize that what he has bought is a Tupsu Lindbergh scarf, though considerably plainer. Everyone notices, but no one says anything. Bella crawls into the gift tent still wearing the scarf.

Exactly: a tent. That is the main Christmas present from the family to the family, and it has been set up on the living-room floor next to the Christmas tree. It is orange, a domed model, big enough for a family. *Take your home and go*. For a moment it races through them, perhaps . . . something from the summer. A feeling, an aura, then it is gone. Thomas and Bella crawl into the tent and play at storms until the downstairs neighbors below ring the doorbell and complain about the loud thumps. Bella and Thomas lie absolutely still in the tent while Kayus talks with the neighbors. When Kayus comes back, he looks terribly serious. Just when his seriousness is about to infect Thomas and Bella, his face cracks into a huge smile. Kayus crawls into the tent with them, and all three fall asleep and do not wake up for hours.

all the days of summer, 1964

In May 1964 Johan Wikblad and Ann-Christine are looking for bargains at auctions. They redecorate the red cottage, put in a long table and benches and copper tubs for heather and twigs, and they install country-style cupboards and hang woven pictures on the walls.

No great changes take place in the white villa, nor in Gabby's and Rosa's house on the hill, except that Gabby has a sturdy garage built below the hill and takes a television set up the hill in a wheelbarrow, which tips over halfway up, and the television falls out and breaks.

The Lindberghs have a new mahogany speedboat, even more shiny, with a small cabin under the foredeck and greater horsepower. For two weeks in August Klas—or is it Peter—Lindbergh roars around the bay with a girl who suns herself on the foredeck. The girl has long, straight hair, and when the boat swings really close to the white villa's rowboat, Huotari's outboard, or the shores of the summer paradise, you can get a really good look at her. "Not bad," says Gabby in passing, before he even has a chance to meet her. But the sound heard everywhere whenever the engine is turned off and Lindbergh's shiny mahogany speedboat drifts lazily in the sun is the music from the transistor radio on deck. One song in particular rings out over the bay.

My boy lollypop
You make my heart so skiddiup
You make my life so dandy
You're my sugar candy . . .

That's roughly how it goes, but the song's outstanding characteristic is that, whether you know the words or not, once you've heard it, you can't get it out of your head. May Johansson stands on the outer edge of Gabby's and Rosa's joint breakwater and says, "How weird. You can't get any peace and quiet even on your summer vacation."

May Johansson's words don't make the music stop. Huotari says, "That one's a knockout." Thomas says nothing. The previous winter Cassius Clay trounced Sonny Liston in a boxing match that would become legendary. The following day Cassius Clay adopted a new name, Muhammed Ali. "A megalomaniac personality, that Clay," says Huotari. Thomas and Huotari both backed Liston because they'd seen him at the amusement park. Thomas says nothing. He does not deign to ask what *megalomaniac* means.

In mid-July, Huotari and Thomas catch an eel on a long line in the bay. That's an unheard of event. "No one ever caught an eel in this mud puddle before," says Huotari, his voice triumphant. For the rest of the summer and the whole of the following summer, which will be Thomas's last year in the summer paradise, Huotari talks about little else. What it felt like to hold the eel (revolting), to kill it (revolting, it would not die but went on wriggling, no matter how long you hit it on the head), to eat (revolting, revolting, revolting), and most of all what you have to do to catch another eel. The thought of eels gradually so obsesses Huotari that he loses interest in boxing. Thomas, for his part, is squeamish when it comes to fish.

Renée has a Beatles sweatshirt Gabby bought when he was doing some business with the English. It is orange and has the Beatles' heads in black on the chest. She wears it for a few days. Then she changes back into her usual old rag.

Thomas and Kayus drift in the bay, in a rowboat, Kayus reading a detective story, Thomas staring up into the blue sky or at the terrified blonde on the book jacket, poking at Johan the Skeleton, who has been allowed out to sea to have some ideas of what total freedom is.

Just down the river.

Thomas leans over the side and drops Johan the Skeleton into the water. Johan the Skeleton does not float. As Johan the Skeleton rapidly sinks to the bottom, Thomas tries to remain unmoved. But he regrets his act, no question. On the other hand, there are new feelings.

When he turns nine on the fourth of July, he receives a kite as a birthday present from Gabby and Rosa and Nina and Renée. A kite like Renée's. Gabby has been to China and stood on the Great Wall during the winter. "A historic moment. All Chinese look alike," Gabby said. "But it's a big market." And in your mind's eye you saw billions of Chinese with billions of yellow tape recorders. Ribbons ending in bows hang from the kites, and they twirl when the kites rise above the treetops, but by the end of the summer both kites are broken. Thomas's gets caught in a tree, and Renée's lands in the water, and though it dries, it never flies as well afterwards. Renée grows tired of it and gives it to Erkki Johansson, which is the same as sending it to its death. And that's what happens. After only an hour or two of Erkki's brisk treatment, the kite stops being a kite.

SWISH—the Lindberghs' shiny mahogany speedboat comes racing up towards Johansson's and Gabby's and Rosa's joint breakwater, Klas or Robin Lindbergh at the helm, Tupsu Lindbergh on the red leather seat in the stern. Rosa leaps on board to accompany Tupsu on a visit to their friends in the villas on the outer edge of the archipelago. Rosa calls to Renée,

"Renée! Come on!"

The runt is also on the boat—Lars Magnus Lindbergh. Renée is supposed to play with him *as well* that summer. But of course Renée does not come when called if the runt is in the boat. Thomas can see her from the water. She is a dot among the reeds.

"Renée! We're not going to wait for you."

Rosa goes on board. The Lindberghs' shiny mahogany speedboat races off across the bay and into the sound and out to the open sea.

"Let's go ashore," Thomas says to Kayus.

"Why?"

"It's dull here. Nothing happens."

Thomas rows ashore. Kayus goes up to the house. Thomas walks to the other beach. She is coming. They go to the forest.

New year, new songs. The Girl from Ipanema. Bella stands by the window in the dim light of the big room. She walks across the floor.

She looks straight ahead
But not at me . . .

Kayus grabs her, and they dance.

Bella and Kayus dance with each other. When they are not dancing, they sit in the basket chairs and smoke, not saying much. Just smoking. In that way it is a quiet summer, despite the nonstop racket of music from the bay. Sometimes Thomas doesn't hear them stop and go to bed. He merely sits bolt upright, abruptly, as if woken by some external sound. He peers out into the darkness in the big room and sees that Kayus and Bella are no longer there. A calm silence at first. Then gradually, toward the end of the summer, a kind of nervous quiet full of little, meaningless sounds, the kind that occur when you can't sit still.

Then more silence again. In another way. Merely silence.

Sometimes, toward the end of the summer, when Kayus and Bella are in the big room, Bella turns on the overhead light and sits in the reading corner, saying that she has to do something that requires light.

"What?" says Kayus with a smile. "Darning stockings?"

"Darning stockings," agrees Bella. But she simply sits in the reading corner in the bright light. Sometimes she gets to the light switch in the middle of "The Girl From Ipanema." Turns it on. Turns it off. Turns it on. Laughs. Turns it off. Toys with the switch until Kayus comes and grabs her, almost roughly, and whirls her off into a dance. Thomas has turned his face to the wall. He is asleep.

In the middle of summer Kayus abandons the veranda to build a tiny sailing dinghy with Gabby. Kayus and Gabby go into town in Gabby's new car, which is in no way special except for the name—PLYMOUTH is hard to pronounce—and when they come back, they bring back white plastic letters, and they think it would give Thomas and Renée enormous pleasure to screw them on the stern of the boat, which looks more like a matchbox than like something that floats on the water. It's been decided that the boat will be called GOOFY. Thomas uses a screwdriver to affix the letters, while Renée is assigned the task of finding something they can use for the Y because they didn't have one at the store. She comes back with a piece of Y-shaped plastic, and that is stuck on the boat with epoxy glue borrowed from Johan Wikblad; according to the writing on the package, it's so strong that you could stick a donkey's tail back on the donkey permanently—if, that is, the tail fell off in the first place.

Plop into the waves.

Thomas and Renée are in Thomas's room, at Thomas's table, drawing mugs with ears and eyes and mouths—mugs that communicate through speech bubbles—when Gabby and Kayus come walking across the yard with life jackets, ropes, and other gear. Thomas and Renée learn that the stuff is called gear in the language of sailors that Gabby and Kayus use, without any evidence that they are entitled to use a single one of these words. No one knows as little about boats and sailing as Kayus and Gabby together. Of course Thomas has no proof of this fact. Not yet, not this summer; but he has an inkling.

"Out into the fresh air, kids. We're going sailing."

Sailing: That means Thomas has to wear an orange life jacket, and Gabby pushes the boat out into the sea from the trailer and guides it along the side of the jetty while Kayus brings the mast, the sail rolled around it, and sticks its base through a hole in the foreseat and unfurls the sail and boom and fixes the rudder in the bow and helps Thomas down into the boat, which is unsteady. (Thomas's first impression is confirmed: absolutely unseaworthy), presses the centerboard down into the center slot, says, "Sheet in, and steer," and shoves Thomas away, who is holding the sheet and the rudder without the sheeting and without steering. Nevertheless, the next moment he finds himself in the middle of the bay, a hundred yards from the jetty, where Kayus and Gabby are both shouting. When things begin to happen on the water, Kayus and Gabby run back and forth between Gabby's and Rosa's and the Johanssons' joint breakwater and the white villa's jetty, still shouting. The boom swings over sharply, the boat heels, Thomas holds on to the sheet, the boom swings over again and again, until Thomas's head gets in the way and the boom whips right past his ears. Gabby shouts that Thomas is to run before the wind. Kayus shouts that Thomas is to lift up the centerboard and go down from the wind's eye, as he has learned to say from a book called *Windward Sailing, Free Wind and Running Before the Wind* that he keeps in his summer library on the glassed-in veranda, and tack. To Thomas it does not matter what they shout, and he no longer even tries to listen. He has noticed the blood on his life jacket, on the sail, in his mouth, and on his face. And he realizes one thing: He will not be able to deal with this situation by himself, on his own. *He has to be rescued.* But who will rescue him? Kayus and Gabby are both busy shouting. Thomas looks around. A moment of icy panic. There is no one.

But suddenly he is lifted up into the air. The next thing he knows, he is lying on a deck with his head close to a transistor radio, which is blaring into his ear. What deck, which transistor, and which boat is immediately clear.

"Watch the paint!" Klas or Peter Lindbergh is looking down at Thomas from above the windscreen. Thomas sees himself bloody and mercilessly doubled, for Klas or Peter Lindbergh is wearing those aviator sunglasses that have mirrored lenses. But Klas or Peter Lindbergh did not rescue Thomas, that is clear at once. It is the girl with the long brown hair, the one who looks like an Indian. She jumped into the dinghy and in no time had the boat under control. She hauls in the sheet and sails the dinghy ashore.

Thomas is taken to the jetty in the Lindberghs' shiny speedboat. Both Kayus and Gabby are still shouting. Without a word Thomas wrenches off his bloodstained life jacket and walks away without looking back. Shortly afterward the girl in her dinghy climbs on the jetty, and Gabby helps her up. He thanks her exhaustively and is given an opportunity to introduce himself: "Gabriel Angel. I'm in music."

She, the Indian girl, says that her name is Viviann.

"You lost my Y," says Renée that afternoon.

It is her turn in the afternoons. She sails to windward, before the wind, adjusts the centerboard, hauling in and letting out the sheet and tacking as if she had done these things all her life, as if she were born to sail, as if her stubborn body had merely been waiting for this moment when it is allowed to step down into a sailing dinghy called GOOF. She sails back and forth before the jetties of the summer paradise, but not content with that, she sails farther out, farther and farther, until she disappears behind the small islands in the middle of the bay. Gabby says it is instinct.

Thomas goes to the Johanssons' sauna and puts on a show with Nina and Maggi, whom no one has even considered putting into a dinghy; he is the master of ceremonies, and he lip-syncs to a song they play on Nina's tape recorder.

Wonderful evening for a show
Wonderful just to be
Cold outside is autumn
Warm and light are we
Music and a lovely girl

A man who is a swinger
Wonderful evening for a show
And an old, old lovely song

Just as well that the summer is at an end.

Bella covers the furniture in the white villa with dust sheets. Kayus arranges his books in bags as alphabetically as possible. Thomas puts the trolling-spoon box and his books into the red duffel bag Kayus and Bella gave him for his birthday. Rosa and Gabby have rented a truck for all their possessions. The truck drives by on the forest road. Renée sits in the open back, her arms around her pale blue duffel bag, looking around with a forbidding expression. Thomas nods. She nods back.

But Bella and Rosa, the beach women, what are they up to, where are they? Yes, of course they are there. On the beach, sometimes in Rosa's living room in the afternoons, but mostly on the veranda of the white villa, or in the big room, for a few hours at some time during the day. Rosa drinks coffee and talks. She is explaining about an idea she and Tupsu Lindbergh are working on, they will be the first to launch it in this country: the dream Tupperware for the perfect modern household. "For the perfect modern household," says Rosa Angel with a laugh, but not the kind of laugh that seems to contain its opposite, the laugh of the moment just before you toss the top of your sunsuit into the arbor but not to show your breasts to anyone, the laugh before you yank the plug of the air-conditioner out of the socket and say that you're talking nonsense and start on another topic, something quite different from Elizabeth Taylor's love life, which is what everyone is so sure you are discussing.

But an ordinary laugh. A light laugh. A laugh that makes you believe, can't help but believe, that Rosa Angel means exactly what she says.

She glances at the gleaming refrigerator-bar left behind in the white villa after the previous year's crayfish party, just about the only real reminder of the previous summer. "There it stands, our bar," says Rosa, showing no inclination whatever of wanting to do anything about it, such as asking Gabby to get it in the car. "I'm white this year," says Rosa, wearing pink as if that were some kind of reasonable explanation. And the bar stays in the white villa, for good.

Anyhow, it is now obsolete. Great strides have been made: they buy a regular refrigerator for the summer place the year after the crayfish party. A television, a stereo. On the whole, the only thing that doesn't change in the house on the hill over the next few years is the stove, so large and heavy it can't be moved. The air-conditioning unit has been set on the floor by the open fireplace. Just for one evening, they put it back on the table and turn it on. That is in September 1964, when all the summer people have left and a car suddenly comes rushing along the forest road in the darkness of the summer paradise, where as yet there are no other people beside the summer visitors. Two people get out of the car and go up the hill and into the house. A girl pushes a button and walks onto the floor of Rosa's living room and dances to the monotonous whir of the air-conditioner. The girl has long brown hair and looks like an Indian. Gabby follows her movements intently from the butterfly chair.

"So, Viviann," he says in English. "What can I do for you?"

"I want to be a flight attendant," she replies in Swedish.

Gabby says that shouldn't be too difficult to arrange.

■ ■ ■

"I'm white this year," says Rosa Angel that summer of 1964, dressed in pink, laughing and talking to Bella. But sooner or later she always gets up and says she has to go, because Tupsu Lindbergh is coming to pick her up at the jetty in the Lindberghs' shiny mahogany speedboat.

"We're going for a spin on the ocean. The breeze is great out there."

"Maybe you could come with us sometime," she occasionally adds, but you can tell that she's just being polite. Bella nods and knows that there won't be a sometime. Rosa leaves the white villa and crosses the yard. Bella stays behind in the big room, over and over again that summer, the multifaceted mirror reflecting her face shattered exactly the same way.

But Rosa, what is she thinking about as she walks rapidly across the yard and to the house on the hill to change into sailing clothes, paint her lips a shade of pink, and tie a white ribbon around her hair so that it will not blow in her face out on the open sea? Are things as they look? Is she thinking about the Tupperware she and Tupsu will be the first to launch in this country, for the perfect modern household, as she has just explained to Bella in the white villa? Is she thinking about the perfect modern household? About Tupsu Lindbergh's deep friendship, which means so much to her, which she has also just explained? About all the other stuff you might think she might be thinking about? Gabby's flight attendants, for instance, who have begun to come into the picture these last few years, serving chiefly as a reminder to Rosa that she was a ground attendant, not a flight one, and that *actually there is a great difference*? About what her attitude should be? Which of the few acceptable attitudes, none of which appeals to her, should she choose? Martyred courage or hurt pride? No, no, no. Rosa Angel is certainly not interested in any of those. She is not thinking at all.

This is Rosa's secret. This summer. The sun is shining, the sea is refreshing. That's all. Her mind is blank, is Rosa Angel's.

But one thing she has decided: not to think.

She has no camera this year. The photographs from last summer—Thomas was absolutely right—were not pasted into an album during the autumn. That camera—it was really just camouflage.

Though she did not know that herself, either, not until the autumn when, having spread the photographs out on the table, she suddenly did not know what to do with them.

All those photographs. All *memories*, suddenly a totally incomprehensible pattern.

And she went on staring at a single photograph, the one of the women on the beach, of course.

That somehow made it impossible to go on pasting them into the album and adding amusing captions.

Her mind a blank, but consciously so.

Tupperware for the perfect modern household, that is an idea she certainly does not believe in, and she and Tupsu Lindbergh are certainly not going to be the first to launch the concept in this country—not on your life! She would rather die. But she needs the ideas as a front for something in herself, a facade for stuff she does not—well, ye gods, how can you describe it?

The fact is, behind this facade there is someone or something inside Rosa that goes around humming "Bella-Rosa, Bella-Rosa," with a foolish smile.

But one thing, it isn't a game.

She realized that as early as the first days of that summer.

Last summer it was easy to sit in the arbor with bare breasts and Shangri-las, talking about another life and pretending.

When it had been a game.

On the wings of passion you fly to freedom.

But what does that mean? In this context? Really?

No idea. Something that isn't. Something for which there is no single image. Like falling in space.

And yet you can't get the song out of your mind. Bella-Rosa.

But Bella-Rosa: in reality it is like falling into space.

So, this is the passion seething in Rosa Angel.

Rosa walks down the forest path toward the beach in clean sailing clothes, freshly made up for an ocean voyage, in her absent-mindedness running straight into May Johansson's washed sheets decorated with elaborate family monograms.

Smack. Rosa Angel kisses them.

Lipstick stains on the sheets. Rose-colored, clammy.

Rosa looks at them and laughs.

Lipstick stains on sheets, the beach, Tupsu Lindbergh in the boat, and the wind that will soon be blowing in her face again. All that is here. And now.

After the crayfish party the previous year, they had talked about how Gabby scuttled the white angel. And Bella had been there with him. What a tremendous thing it had been.

But Rosa remembered something else. The car had not

ended up in the meadow by itself. Earlier, it had started off from the white villa's yard. Then it had taken off. Bumping through the yard down toward the meadow, where it finally stopped near the potato patch. And two other people were inside.

"This isn't anywhere near where we were supposed to go," was Rosa's comment after the car stopped. Bella had looked at her, had been angry. Rosa had never seen her so angry before.

"Rosa," cried Bella at the wheel. "You aren't listening. You've forgotten. I can't drive. I don't have a license."

Did it really happen? Nothing was said, no one mentions it ever again. Not even soon after the event. Sometimes Rosa herself has her doubts.

But whether or not it happened, Rosa had wanted it to happen. And to have a different ending. But what ending? To think like that was like falling into space.

And Bella? She remains in the big room in the white villa, near the mirror, with her magazines, her cigarettes, her variously colored lipsticks. She is sitting in the reading corner close to the oil lamp, lighting it, putting it out, lighting it again with her cigarette lighter. What is on her mind? Nothing. She is not particularly inclined to philosophizing.

That something *has* to happen.

In the winter she takes a job in a drugstore in a shopping mall. She gives it up. Cannot get there on time. Tries to listen to music. The music no longer says anything to her.

Winter 1964-1965, the winter Bella stops listening to music. In December, Thomas and Bella are on the balcony of their apartment.

"Want to see if this record has wings, Thomas?"

"Yes," says Thomas, in as neutral a voice as possible. Of course the record does not have wings, they both know that. But they *both want* to see the record skimming the air over the courtyard and land in the snowdrifts by the rug-beating stand. Bella takes the record out of its sleeve almost formally and weighs it in her hand for a second or two. Then she throws it like a boomerang, and the record zooms away. They can't see it too well as it flies, because it's dark. But its whistling echoes beneath the walls in the square courtyard. The disk plops into the snow.

Chet Baker Sings. Pacific Records 1956.

They can no longer see the record, and gradually they grow cold standing out on the balcony without coats. Thomas and Bella go back inside. But when Chet Baker begins to resound from some other apartment a little later, Kayus looks at Bella with a questioning, perhaps a rather sad expression. Just as if he knew what had occurred. Even though he hadn't been home at the time.

"We have to go on growing," says Bella. "I need new challenges."

She has not sprayed on perfume. Kayus says nothing, and Bella says nothing, so that is what it is like. No new challenges appear. Bella gives up music, although only Thomas really notices, for when Kayus comes home, he puts his music on as usual, and Bella goes on sitting in the same room, with the stockings she is mending or the cigarettes she is smoking. But she is not listening. In the daytime, when Kayus is not at home, she does not even turn on the radio. Only Thomas knows this, because he is home in the daytime, after school, before Kayus comes home from work.

"Thomas. Let's sit and just listen to the silence," says Bella.

"It's boring, I know," she says after a while. "Deadly dull." When she can't think of anything to do, she picks up a magazine and reads a story aloud. "Listen to this, Thomas."

"Huh," says Thomas. He goes into his room and starts up his steam engine. He is nine years old, and those magazines no longer interest him. They are full of all kinds of stuff that has nothing to do with his life. His life is steam engines, model sets, other hobbies. Bella stays in the other room with her tales, her stories. A moment later she goes into the kitchen to start supper.

"We never have any fun," she calls out to Thomas.

Thomas shakes his head. He stares at his steam engine.

all the days of the summer, 1965

The summer of 1965. This summer waterskiing is the thing—skiing behind the Lindberghs' shiny speedboat and after Midsummer, behind Gabby's outboard, an Evinrude handed down from Robin Lindbergh. Now Bella and Rosa are skiing. If you look closely, it's clear that Tupsu Lindbergh's face has become freckled all over, and that's not particularly becoming; her fair hair is peroxided, and she's thin as a rail. Everyone knows that it's because she is so thin and plain, and not because she has a cold, as she claims, that she can't take part in any water sports. There's something nervous about Tupsu Lindbergh. At Bella's party at the beginning of the summer Tupsu Lindbergh sits quietly on the veranda of the white villa or in the yard of the white villa in a camp chair or on the beach of the white villa while Bella and Rosa water-ski and Tupsu talks about Tupperware. Not only about Tupperware, but Tupperware is the overall subject.

Rosa explains to Bella it's as if Tupsu Lindbergh were made for Tupperware. The dream of a perfect housewife.

"The dream of the perfect housewife," says Rosa. That's one of her first comments this summer. "Tupperware, Bella. There's a big market. But who cares, Bella? When it's so dull. Boring. Boring. Boring." And she turns over on her stomach and dozes off in the sun. When she wakes a few minutes later and sees Bella again as if for the first time, she smiles in recognition and says loudly and clearly, "I want something else, Bella," as the trees rustle. "I want another life."

So Rosa's back. But she doesn't come and lure you out into the fine day, as she did two years earlier. She doesn't stand in the doorway smiling and expectant while you eat your endless breakfast. No, you have to spoon up your yogurt yourself and then make your way down to the beach on your own, to find her already there. She's lying on the smooth rock in a white robe, pink bikini, and sunglasses. The part of her body that's visible is tense, her skin softly tanned, especially early in the summer; the tan is largely a leftover from the previous year. This year both their tans will fade because it starts raining. And it goes on raining. It keeps on raining for most of June, July, and August. And their tans, Rosa's and Bella's, slowly fade instead of deepening.

So Rosa is asleep in the sun when you get to the beach, and what catches your eye is the way she's sleeping—on her side, directly on the rock, without a towel or blanket under her. She has wrapped her robe loosely around her, drawn her knees up to her stomach, sort of like the astronaut position, as you called it two years ago, when you were still little and played rocket launching. But the rocket capsized, as if it had been tipped over. Very early in June the astronaut Edward White walked in space. *What was Ed White thinking about as he floated in space, before his enthusiasm grew so intense that he didn't think about anything at all?* If Rosa were an astronaut in space, and not a beach woman glued to a rock, Thomas would be able to answer, on her behalf, that she is thinking, "Where is the spaceship? Has it left without me?"

Although Rosa is wearing a bathing suit and a robe, she looks naked somehow.

But whenever you go to the beach, Rosa wakes up after a while and sits up looking dazed. Looks around, her hair mussed, catches sight of Thomas, and starts speaking in English.

"Rosa's back again," she says, laughing. She lies down, stretches out on the rock, and falls asleep.

With Thomas's help Bella tucks a corner bit of her blanket under Rosa. Rosa moves in her sleep, and her head is suddenly on Bella's arms. Bella has also found a place on the rock with all her beach stuff. They remain in that position, the beach women, Bella and Rosa, until a few minutes later, when the strange thing happens. Lindberghs' shiny mahogany speedboat comes whooshing across the bay. But it is not heading for the Johanssons' and Gabby's and Rosa's joint breakwater, nor does it turn midway, swing into the sound, and disappear in that direction. No, it continues straight on, toward Bella on the rock in the white villa's inlet, toward the white villa's short jetty, where it never stopped before. Bella is the only one to see it. She is a little nervous; what will she say, what should she do? She tries to wake Rosa. But Rosa is sleeping soundly and does not respond. So Bella has to run down to the jetty by herself and make smalltalk with Robin and Tupsu all by herself, to prevent them from seeing Mrs. Gabriel Angel lying drunk on the rock. But when the Lindberghs have gone, Bella wakes Rosa by slapping her cheek and telling her that there is going to be a party at the white villa on Saturday and that the

 Lindberghs are also invited, since they happened to come by while Rosa was asleep.

"I want to have fun," says Bella. "I want something to happen now."

Strictly speaking, that is the first remark Bella has made to Rosa this summer.

But Rosa looks at Bella with wide-open eyes. Suddenly it is as if she had remembered something, a thing which had felt so unreal last summer, which in some ways she feared, feared so much that every day she had to dress in blue-and-white sailing clothes and leave the summer paradise to go out on the refreshing water with Tupsu Lindbergh.

Yes. She is in space now.

But being in space. In some places that is also a wonderful, weightless feeling.

She runs into the water, swims far out, dunks her head under the water several times.

"I want to clear my head," she calls to Bella, who is still on the beach. "Be more awake than ever before in my whole life. Is there any coffee in your thermos?"

But the sun goes in and it starts raining, so Rosa and Bella have to take their coffee indoors, up into Bella's studio. They collect their stuff in baskets and bags and run up the avenue to the white villa, up the attic stairs, and they close the door behind them. They end up in Bella's studio, Bella and Rosa. And there they stay for days, weeks, hours, and minutes. Behind a closed door, and though no one is forbidden from opening it, somehow it represents an insuperable barrier, a boundary.

Thomas does not know whether he thinks that's a good or a bad thing. He stays in the attic space beyond the wall. Some days, not always. Sometimes when he is in the space, he looks up and finds that someone has come in without his hearing. Sometimes it is Erkki Johansson, other times someone else. Someone who does not exist but is given a name: Viviann. Sometimes Renée. But mostly not.

Up there in Bella's studio the song that is everywhere that summer arises. A tune almost without words, to be hummed. It spreads and swells out all over the summer paradise.

"Bella-Rosa, Bella-Rosa," it goes.

"*I'm James Bond, James Bond*," Gabby cries out to everyone within earshot that year. All the women who come his way are his Bond girls. "*Who's that pretty girl?*" cries Gabby from the highest point on the hill when he sees May Johansson coming out of the Johanssons' sauna and going out on to the jetty in her blue-checked monokini, which comes all the way up to her navel.

Monokini: one-piece bikinis, bottoms only, no big deal these days. Everyone goes swimming in a monokini. The newspaper even claimed that based on his own investigations on an experimental bathing beach in Baden-Baden, a German scientist maintains that for medical reasons women should *sunbathe in the nude*.

Bella and Rosa no longer take their clothes off. Now that everyone undresses, they wear both bottoms *and* tops. Or one-piece bathing suits.

"Bella-Rosa, Bella-Rosa," Gabby drums on the arm of his chair up on his hill, on the highest point with a view over the whole summer paradise. He has carried his personal canvas armchair up there, the chair he calls his James Bond chair because Gabby is James Bond this year.

"Bella-Rosa, Bella-Rosa," hums Gabby. "The one is good red wine to a steak, Thomas. Steak. *And* red wine.

"The other flutters like a butterfly.

"I've lots of weaknesses, Thomas.

"One of my weaknesses is good food.

"A rare steak and a full-bodied wine. It doesn't have to be vintage.

"Though I like butterflies, too, Thomas. Butterflies in my stomach, Thomas. Like on a roller coaster. The amusement park, Thomas. I assume you like riding on a roller coaster?"

Thomas nods. He has to admit that, like any other child, he has no objection to riding roller coasters.

Renée is competing for the sailing club. At first she's called a fair-weather sailor, because she's a girl who came out of nowhere and starts winning, or pushing her way in among the best in her dinghy class, and they're inclined to think that her successes are pure chance, explained by certain qualities of the boat's hull and the wind that is so slight at the beginning of summer. But then the weather turns almost stormy, and a great many boats give up, capsize or sink, and she goes on to win just as easily. With a lightness and nonchalance that infuriates her rivals.

More and more GOOF becomes Renée's boat. Thomas doesn't mind, though Kayus points out repeatedly that Thomas ought to step up and assert his rights.

Well, rights—Thomas's relationship to sailing is quite different. Thus it's pointless even to try to explain it to Kayus or Gabby, or even Bella. They wouldn't understand. Bella has never even been out to sea. Gabby and Kayus just talk or read books, and then they go around handing out vaguely phrased good advice.

Thomas knows now, this summer, he knows for the first time, unquestionably, that it's possible to behave differently. During the autumn and winter Thomas became an active member of the Balco Baloo Cub Scout den, though he would have preferred to belong to another den called Shere Khan, because the name is better. He went on the autumn club outing. The first night he stood the middle watch with Assistant Scoutmaster Buster Kronlund, and he was allowed to steer for almost half an hour; Buster Kronlund was pleased, he said, "Perfect course." The following night Thomas had been below deck with five Cubs when Dennis Kronlund, Buster's brother and patrol leader in Shere Khan, took middle watch and navigated incorrectly and steered the boat right up to a light house, and it had taken several minutes of heaving and levering in the raw cold autumn air before Thomas realized it was not his fault.

Thomas does not go to the sailing club to cheer Renée on from the beach or from a following boat. He pretends to be, and in some ways he is, totally uninterested in Renée's success in the races. He puts on his underwater goggles and flippers, sticks the snorkel into his mouth, goes out into the water, and disappears into that silent world. Occasionally that summer they form a diving club, the bay's Society for Underwater Research: Erkki Johansson, Thomas, and Renée. All three adopt other identities. Erkki is Jacques Cousteau, the man who wrote a book Thomas has read; Renée is called Tailliez, but since that name is so difficult to pronounce, they just call her Renée; and Thomas is Frederic Dumas, Didi—who best and most completely embodies the society's motto, to live entirely for research into the life of the silent world. That means not having any earthly ties stronger than the ties to the silent world. In contrast, for instance, to Jacques Cousteau, who sometimes had to take his entire family with him under the water ("The author with his wife and child on their usual Sunday trip under water at their home in Sanary-sur-Mer": the photograph, taken with an underwater camera, shows three pale, jellylike phantoms—two big ones, a smaller one in the middle—and *they are holding hands* as they descend into the green depths).

> "Dumas catches a stingray at a depth of thirty-six yards off the island of Porquerolles."
>
> "Tailliez tries to catch a sea bream with a knife. It raises its spinal fins in defense."
>
> "Here Frederic Dumas discovers that a sea bream can open its jaws so wide that its mouth is as large as the circumference of its body."
>
> "An embarrassed octopus, which does not wish to dance with Dumas, moves away, releasing a cloud of ink."
>
> "Dumas tickles the stomach of a pei-qua, the goby of the Mediterranean."
>
> "On a distant shore in French West Africa, Dumas and Tailliez find a colony of monk seals. This species was thought to have become extinct in the 1690s. Here Dumas and Tailliez are crawling up the beach to make the seals' acquaintance."

Thomas tries to become obsessed by life in the silent world. He dives underwater. Without goggles he sees mud; with his goggles his view is slightly clearer and he makes out mud formations and sea grass on the ocean floor. The sight is both beautiful and fascinating. But it is no use, he is the first to grow cold. Erkki Johansson can stay underwater for the longest time. Any length of time, to be more precise.

The summer of 1965. What else?

Thomas finds a knife in the Rotwoods. Suddenly it lies gleaming before him, under some ferns. A long blade, not at all rusty. Who could have dropped it? Who goes around with a knife in the Rotwoods? Later it turns out that there is a perfectly natural explanation. Johan Wikblad went out to collect fresh twigs to put in a metal dish, a bargain Ann-Christine found at an auction. Thomas conceals the knife under his T-shirt, takes it up to the attic space, and hides it under a floorboard. Later he says nothing when Johan Wikblad asks if anyone has seen his expensive new knife. Thomas doesn't know why. The knife remains in the attic space until some time later, when it disappears. Who took it? It's not hard to guess.

The Johanssons go off on a long trip.

"Now it's the Johansson family," says May Johansson, "who is going out to see the world."

"I'm not going anywhere with my crazy Mom and Dad," says Maggi to Nina in Johanssons' sauna. Maggi and Nina speak Finnish to each other this summer.

Kayus's radio breaks down. Simply falls silent. Right in the middle of the weather forecast.

But Isabella in the sun just before it disappears behind the clouds. One morning there is a party at the white villa. She has come out on the veranda steps in her yellow dress, laughing in her pink lipstick, smelling of suntan oil and perfume, "Blue Grass," for although she changed brands long ago, "Blue Grass" remains for Kayus the collective term for every perfume Bella sprays on herself, "Just like her, Thomas, sort of topsy-turvy, because grass is green, not blue, but if Bella says grass is blue then it's blue," and you look at her, of course. The point is that you're meant to look at her, everyone in the yard is supposed to look up when she stands there with a tray of rainbow drinks and slowly, as if in a sort of fake unsteadiness, she starts down the steps so that the tray wobbles, and if you had a movie camera to film the movie star, her laughing face would come closer and closer and finally so close that it would lose its contours and dissolve in the lens. But you have no camera, this isn't a movie, it's real life. The last summer in the white villa in 1965, the third summer with Rosa, and she is Isabella Mermaid for real, Thomas's mother, Rosa's friend, a good steak with red wine, steak, Renée *and* red wine, Jazz Kayus's dream, and for the rest of time, which begins after this summer, it will be found locked in a closet in an ordinary city apartment in a suburb east of town, and a lot more, all kinds of things, Thomas. And she is down in the yard now, walking among her guests, laughing, quite real, you can touch her, holding out the tray and saying ALMOST HEAVEN and offering drinks.

out into the world, 1965

Why are waterskiing beach women beautiful? Irresistible? Inescapable? In their yellow and white bathing suits, though one of them wears an orange life jacket as well?

Philosophical questions. Thomas is nine, nearly ten. He has no leanings to philosophy. Not even later on, for that matter. He is just like his mother, a person who will never have *a philosophical disposition*. His mind is concrete. To him, everything is concrete.

He is in his summer paradise, trying to do all kinds of stuff. Spying and sabotaging and roaming through the forest, developing new interests and meeting new people. But it is pointless. He always ends up in the same place. On the beach, that is. Where the beach women are in the bay. Waterskiing behind the Lindberghs' shiny mahogany speedboat. First one, then the other, taking turns.

Actually he isn't the only one. All the others, at least most of them, gradually go down to the beach. Drawn there. Even entire parties. Move on to the beach even before all the rainbow drinks Bella has invented (that is not remarkable in itself, she uses almost the same ingredients as for Shangri-las, except that the drinks settle into variously colored layers in each glass because of the gelatine she puts in, nevertheless Thomas is as impressed and proud as Bella is while they prepare for the party in the morning) have been consumed at the camp table that Tupsu Lindbergh only has to glance at for it to be called the ramshackle barbecue table in the white villa garden, as the yard is called after that kind of party. The beach women threw off their party dresses long ago and wriggled into bathing suits. Got up on Lindberghs' water skis and gone into the water. The towrope grows taut. The engine roars. Off they go—*Wheee*—and they're gone. The joy of speed. And everyone claps. No, not everyone. Tupsu and Kayus are sitting on the hill pretending to be talking about this and that. Thomas is lying face down on the Johanssons' breakwater, staring between the boards into the water, busy visualizing a skeleton in front of him on the seabed, thus what it is legitimate for people of his age to do, *childishly pretending*.

For your head is not filled with waterskiing if you are a boy that age, building models and activating steam engines for your own pleasure in your free time.

But everyone else is down on the beach. Finally ends up there.

So: early one afternoon, some Saturday or other, at the beginning of the summer, Thomas is roaming his summer paradise. He walks along the path that starts behind the white villa's woodshed and the outdoor privy. He comes out into the yard of the red cottage, where Ann-Christine is scraping old paint off a washbowl she is going to repaint, she says, so she can plant herbs in it. She lists the many different kinds. Thomas listens, but not one is familiar to him.

"I'm sure I'm allergic to all of them," says Thomas. Ann-Christine ruffles his hair and says, "*charmeur.*" Thomas blushes, but not too deeply. Ann-Christine has a way of saying things in such a way that they sound okay. Thomas has charm. Ann-Christine has said so right from the beginning of the summer. *As a child, Thomas is quite simply charming*. Johan Wikblad was there, and he added, "Charmer." That sounded seriously stupid. Thomas told both Ann-Christine and Johan Wikblad to stop it.

Ann-Christine is one of those people who is always busy with different projects. On one of the first days of summer, when Thomas and Ann-Christine were getting to know each other, Ann-Christine was peeling oranges to make orange wine for Midsummer. Thomas helped for a while, because it was a time when Rosa was not around and Renée was trimming GOOF's mast down on the beach, so insistently that Thomas had plenty of time to do new things and get to know new people. The container for the orange wine was put under the house. Nina and Maggi tasted it, pouring off an empty Cinzano bottleful for themselves, with Midsummer in mind. Thomas knows, although he hasn't mentioned it to anyone. So does Renée. It is still true that there are no secrets in the summer paradise that are secret from Thomas and Renée. At least, that is their intention.

Thomas ate some of the oranges, only a few sections. That night he was ill, developed a rash, and ran a temperature. A high temperature. Bella and Kayus were sorry for him, united in their pity as they stood by Thomas's bed in Thomas's room behind drawn curtains. "It's a curse to be so sensitive," said Kayus as Bella shook down the thermometer, which had risen to great heights. But a curse. This wasn't a question of curse. Thomas took a considerably more sober approach. He saw the phenomenon from a scientific perspective. Oranges, that was merely another discovery, another item to add to the seemingly endless list of the Allergies of the Allergic Subject. There were no limits to that Allergic Subject, a truly interesting phenomenon. Thanks to his scientific point of view, Thomas was able to detach himself from the Allergic Subject and make observations in a way that was the ideal in the hard sciences: *with great astonishment and a child's curiosity*. He lay in bed analyzing his symptoms. Continued analyzing until the list became too long and he lost control of the situation and started bawling like any little kid. When he was better, he was unable to think back on his sobs as anything other than a defeat. And he did get better. He himself and all the others had also known that all the time. In no way was he going to die. And yet he lay in his bed and cried. Thomas goes and sits on the steps of the red cottage beside Johan Wikblad. Johan

Wikblad is designing a house; he's holding a slide rule, pulling it in and out and taking his readings, writing down figures in the margin of the graph paper on which he is drawing the plan. Johan Wikblad has planned the house himself. It has four rooms, a kitchen, and a sunporch. The plan actually has a caption that reads "Sunporch." Thomas and Ann-Christine have some fun with that, since Ann-Christine can't help pointing out that the only chance of fitting a building as fancy as the one developing on Johan Wikblad's graph paper on the site of the red cottage is to build so that what is to be the sunporch faces directly on the first thick spruces in the big forest. Johan Wikblad is not at all amused. He looks worried and insists that there must be another solution.

Thomas studies some of the earlier plans. He asks questions. The same questions he asked many times during these early summer weeks. "Where are you going to build it?" asks Thomas.

"Here," says Johan Wikblad, loudly and clearly, so that Ann-Christine will hear him. "On the precise spot where we're standing."

"Are you going to demolish the red cottage?" Thomas asks.

"The red cottage will be demolished," Johan Wikblad replies, just as loudly and clearly.

"Over my dead body," Ann-Christine calls from the yard, flakes of paint whirling around her in the wind. Thomas laughs. That is why he asks. He wants to hear the sound of Ann-Christine's voice saying *over my dead body*. Funny somehow. And also. To imagine, elaborating on the idea and pretending. Ann-Christine's body. It is quite big.

"I'll buy it first," says Johan Wikblad firmly. "Then pull it down."

"Over my dead body," Ann-Christine calls into the wind. She laughs, and Johan Wikblad laughs with her.

Thomas crosses the Johanssons' yard and walks past the Johanssons' house. The Johanssons are not home. May and Pusu and Erkki have gone to stay with their cousins to look at the sloop the cousins have bought. Maybe the Johanssons will borrow it later on in the summer, when the weather's warmer, then set sail out to see the world. Thomas walks over May Johansson's little rock on the beach, slants across May Johanssons' patch of grass where GOOF usually lies upside down on wood trestles unless there is a race at this or another sailing club. Thomas goes into the Johanssons' sauna.

Two beds line the walls in the changing room. Nina is lying on one, Maggi on the other. The floor between the beds is strewn with all kinds of stuff: mostly magazines and a radio, turned up full blast although it's only the news. Maggi is lying on her back, fiddling with a necklace she has threaded on her fingers. She is making figures. The Eiffel Tower. The Spider's Web, which is the most difficult. She tugs at the necklace quite hard; it is long and consists of tiny little pearls. In the middle of the performance Thomas thinks that it would be great if Maggi pulled a little too hard, so the necklace broke. The pearls would scatter all over the floor with a noisy clatter. It would be a good effect.

Maggi pulls at the necklace. It does not break.

"Look, Thomas. What's up, Thomas?"

Thomas has been standing by the door for a while before Nina looks up from her magazine and sees him. It is always like this when you go to the Johanssons' sauna this summer. You have to wait until the *young ladies will grant you an audience*, as Rosa once put it with a smile. Thomas nods, though he does not know what *granting an audience* means.

Thomas shrugs.

"Renée's gone to a race."

"Yes," says Thomas. "I know."

"I'm sick of listening to the news," says Maggi, sitting up on the bed. She kicks at the radio on the floor. But although she is angry, her rough kick misses its mark. The necklace is still threaded on her fingers, but nothing happens to it. On the other hand, the radio tips over.

"Hey, careful, Maggi." Nina also sits up. She glances out the window. Sort of listlessly, in passing.

"Hey, look. Bella's skiing on one ski. Or was."

Thomas sees too; he certainly does. Bella, on water skis in the bay, skids backward, drops the towrope, and the next moment is flat in the water in the middle of the bay in her orange life jacket.

"Your mom's swimming out there in the bay. Still chattering away. Doesn't she ever shut up, Thomas?"

Thomas shrugs. There seems no point in answering Nina's question.

"Hey, Maggi," Nina says next. "Let's go and have a smoke. I feel like one. You coming, Thomas?"

"Coming, Thomas? You can have the butt of mine, if you want."

Maggi winds the necklace around her neck several times. Nina and Maggi leave.

Thomas doesn't reply. He is already out on the Johanssons' and Rosa's and Gabby's breakwater. On the beach again, with the beach women. Bella is an orange dot in the water. Perhaps fifteen yards farther to one side.

"No. She's not swimming. She can't swim." He merely thought it, did not say anything.

Though that is not true, either. Well—true. You don't really know what the situation is. A few years ago he was still busy pondering things like that. Now he no longer thinks about them so much. A few years ago he was still a child people told stories to, the way people do tell stories to children. So it wouldn't be very dramatic if it should turn out that she was, in fact, objectively and indisputably, able to swim, or that he was not the only one to know she put a dark dye in her fair hair. It wouldn't matter so much. He would not feel disappointed or horribly deceived. He had accepted that previously he was a child to whom people told stories—the kind of stories that do not always stick to the truth. But to realize that, to stop believing, was not so dramatic, either. Roughly like ceasing to believe in Santa Claus—*a necessary stage one has to go through in one's development*.

In addition, there are other reasons not to stick to the truth, apart from wanting to lie, or to deceive someone, or cheat. Once, early in the summer, Thomas tells Rosa about Bella's swimming in the bay that evening in late August a year or two earlier. He has no idea why he is telling Rosa. Certainly not because he thinks about the incident all the time. It is the first time Rosa has come to the white villa to take them down to the beach this summer, which started rather awkwardly, not only because of Thomas's allergic reaction and Renée's mast trimming, but also owing to a certain *Rosa Angel dot dot dot* on the rock on the beach, as May Johansson put it, while she was on the beach hanging her everlasting sheets on the line, keeping on hanging them as she peeked. But now Rosa is back to normal and they are walking along the avenue. Thomas stays a few steps behind because he likes having Bella's and Rosa's backs before his eyes. Suddenly Rosa slows down, dropping back, too, idling until she is almost level with Thomas. Only Bella walks on without noticing, yellow and happy on this lovely summer's day. Barefoot, on hard soles. So hard they can walk over any terrain.

Thomas suddenly feels like telling Rosa something. About Bella, a private story of his own. And so he does.

". . . kind of funny, really, 'cause she always says she can't swim."

Rosa listens but does not seem surprised. Just says, as if that were the most natural thing in the world, "People have to have their secrets, Thomas. If they want to. It doesn't matter if they're true or not.

"Do you understand?"

"No," says Thomas. But of course he understands. And Rosa's way of putting it is a good way of putting it.

Lindberghs' shiny mahogany speedboat chugs past Bella as she lies in the water. Rosa flings out the other ski she has picked up somewhere in the bay. Bella will start straight out of the water. Rosa is trying to throw out the towrope with the handle on the end. Rosa is kneeling on the afterdeck in a pink sunsuit and white cardigan, twirling the towrope around her head like a lasso. Throws it out. Misses. Throws again. Misses, over and over again. The fact that she misses every time is because she does not concentrate properly. She is so busy laughing and making a fool of herself. Bella, too.

They call and squeal and laugh so much that if you merely try to keep up with them and get into the spirit of what they are up to, you never notice that the sun disappeared a long time ago and the rain will start coming down any minute now.

"I'm drowning!" Bella cries from the water.

"You'll be the death of me," laughs Rosa, throwing the rope and missing.

Robin Lindbergh is at the wheel of the boat. He leans against the windscreen in that indolent way familiar from advertisements. Nevertheless there's one thing he cannot hide: Robin Lindbergh is bored stiff. Thomas also sees that Robin Lindbergh may well leave Bella in the water. With or without a life jacket. Able to swim or not. Robin Lindbergh really couldn't care less. He has no interest whatever in knowing what kind of mermaid is splashing around in the water before his very eyes.

Robin Lindbergh is thinking about other things.

Only a short while later, when Bella has got herself back on the skis and has whooshed around the bay a few times, then let go of the towrope and curved in to shore as the first drops of rain fall mercilessly on her, Robin will streak across the bay toward the sound. He will turn and disappear. And Rosa will be with him.

"I tried to tell him to turn back," says Rosa to Bella afterward. "But he didn't hear. Just went on."

Out to sea Robin Lindbergh was angry with Rosa and said that *What is more, she goes around offering herself. She and that demimonde*. You know what that means, Robin Lindbergh said, you, who read French. And Rosa and Robin Lindbergh quarreled and started fighting in the Lindberghs' boat out on the open sea.

In the middle, however, they stopped to consider that they are family acquaintances. They tried to clear up the painful situation by going to the clubhouse to see how things are going for Renée at the races and for Gabby in his capacity as sailing parent having to relinquish the party in the summer paradise, at least the first part of it. Well, it turns out. Renée came in second in the first race, then gave up in the second without a good reason.

"What did Tupsu say?"

"She has a migraine." Bella and Rosa will laugh at Tupsu Lindbergh in the studio. Sometimes you would not believe, as Kayus says, that *they are two grown women with husbands and children* when they're in the studio. In certain situations there is no great difference between Bella and Rosa and the *young ladies* in the Johanssons' sauna.

The beach women are waterskiing. On the white villa's beach Tupsu Lindbergh is wearing a navy-blue boating jacket. Kayus is pouring coffee into mugs. Tupsu and Kayus drink coffee, their mugs steaming. They chat, pretending to be deeply involved in their conversation.

Thomas lies face down on the jetty staring into the water through the cracks between the boards.

"Catch anything?" They start calling to him from the other beach. It's Tupsu Lindbergh's voice. Thomas does not reply. Anyone can see he isn't fishing.

"Come over and talk to us for a while," Kayus adds.

"Come and tell us, Thomas." Tupsu Lindbergh again. "What do you usually do on gray days like this? Don't you have anyone to play with?"

Thomas cannot believe his ears.

He is very busy imagining. This is what he imagines: If a dead person were lying underneath him, he and the skeleton could lie like this, each in his place, and grin at each other.

Thomas opens his eyes and mouth wide, imagining dark eye sockets and clattering jaws from the silent world. Though he knows such a thing is a scientific absurdity. The human skeleton decomposes underwater in record time. That's because of the consistency of bone. That was another thing that often astonished Didi and Tailliez and Cousteau when they were investigating wrecked ships on the ocean floor. *That they were so empty*. Whole ships could be intact. Interior and all: things, furniture, cabins with all their fittings. There was a bathtub. Didi was a person who liked practical jokes, and he got into the bathtub, grabbed the bath brush and pretended to scrub himself as he sang behind his diving helmet the way some people do, so that bubbles bubbled all around him fifty yards below the surface. Cousteau, who took the photograph with his underwater camera, laughed so much that he almost strangled in the tubes of his aqualung.

"Thomas! When someone asks you something, you're supposed to answer." Kayus is angry. Thomas registers his mood objectively.

"Mmm," he says. That was probably not heard over on the other beach. Bella has risen on the skis now, right in front of everyone. She calls out and laughs even more, and the Lindberghs' engine roars. When Thomas does not answer, Kayus and Tupsu go on talking about him in the third person.

"Lars-Magnus is quite lonely, too," says Tupsu Lindbergh. "Perhaps Thomas would like to come over some day to play with Lars-Magnus. There's such a difference in ages between Lars-Magnus and his brothers.

"And there isn't time to take him to visit his friends farther out in the islands every day.

"Especially now, before his sailboat has been delivered."

"No problem," says Kayus firmly. "We'll just put him in the rowboat one day. Then he can row over."

Row on your own. Thomas stares down into the water. His fantasy has blown away. *Damn Kayus*.

The next day Thomas will go to Kayus and tell him about the runt. How dumb he is. That anyone knows what will happen when the sailing dinghy specially made for the runt comes from the factory and can at last join in the clubhouse races. The runt will be the dumbbell of all time. The runt will capsize, will be wrecked, and will be in such distress at sea that it will not make the slightest difference that the dinghy has a fiberglass hull. Can't Kayus see that? Thomas can't possibly prove his statements, since none of this has happened yet (but it will happen, with astonishing precision, though not until the following summer and by then Thomas himself is no longer there to witness fulfillment of his predictions, one after another). Kayus bears it in mind.

"Did Renée tell you?"

Thomas is taken by surprise. "What?" is all he can find to say. He does not understand. What has it got to do with Renée?

"I was just thinking it would be good for you to be with boys of your own age," says Kayus in a more friendly, sort of matter-of-fact tone of voice.

Thomas says nothing and walks away, to his tent in the yard.

"But if you don't want to, then don't," Kayus's voice pursues him through the villa. Full of all kinds of things, leaving no doubt that Kayus considers Thomas a spoiled lazy boy, taking it for granted he can always do just as he pleases, and Kayus certainly rowed much farther than however far it is across the bay and back when he was a boy.

Thomas crawls into his tent. He gazes at nature appearing in shadowy orange-colored patches on the canvas. A moment later Kayus appears. He sticks his head in through the tent opening and says winningly, calmly, "So this is where you're living now, is it?" Thomas nods. It is.

"*Thomasss!!*" But all that comes later: the yard, the tent, the quarrel with Kayus, that is not now. NOW Bella is skiing in the bay. Describing great arcs, surfing back and forth over the waves made by the Lindberghs' boat. Her body tilting backward perfectly. Legs absolutely straight. Dark hair flying.

"Thomas!" calls Bella. "Wheee!"

She races past Rosa's and Gabby's and the Johanssons' breakwater. Close to the end of the jetty she almost overshoots the mark. Drops the towrope a few yards farther on, glides into the beach right under the noses of Kayus and Tupsu Lindbergh. Is going at such speed, that she hits the beach with her skis still on. Jumps off them and flings off her life jacket. Shakes her head, laughing, scooping her wet hair into her hands and wringing it out. Says she has never had such fun in her whole life. Hops on one foot to get the water out of her ear. Dries her hair, rubbing energetically with her towel, winds the towel into a turban around her head, and pulls on her robe. Digs in her pocket for a cigarette, sticks it in her mouth, lights it. Looks around. Notices for the first time what everyone else has noticed long before she has.

The Lindberghs' boat is no longer in the bay. It has raced off into the sound and disappeared. They can hear the noise of the engine dying away, then silence, total quiet. The last they see of Rosa is her sitting on the afterdeck. Glowing white against the blue and violet sky.

"Where are Robin and Rosa?"

It starts raining.

For a moment Bella is disconcerted. Her features smooth out, all expression obliterated. Her eyes dart around. Fasten on Tupsu and Kayus.

"Where did they go?" she asks. Almost angrily, as if Tupsu and Kayus were to blame.

Tupsu Lindbergh gets up and wraps her arms around her body. Shivers, saying that she's cold. Kayus packs the thermos and the coffee mugs in the beach basket.

Bella catches sight of Thomas, still on the Johanssons' and Gabby's and Rosa's breakwater. Then she brightens up again.

"Come on, all of you," she cries, as if speaking to an entire schoolclass on the beach. "Let's go up and get a bite to eat. The water makes you hungry."

"Thomas, too." She waves to Thomas. Now the rain is really coming down. Thomas cannot help raising his hand slightly in return.

He walks toward the white villa in the rain, through the Rotwoods. Finds that knife there—Johan Wikblad's knife, as it turns out later. Takes it, hides it under a floorboard in the attic space. It stays there.

Thomas is in the attic space, the rain splattering against the metal roof. The splatter of rain mixes with Bella's voice coming from the ground floor. The only voice on the ground floor that goes on and on, unceasing, despite the awful weather. A party is in full swing, and more rainbow drinks. "Doesn't she ever shut up, Thomas?" He suddenly remembers Nina's words. No. He smiles to himself. Shut up? Why should she?

In the background Tupsu Lindbergh says that she wants

something for her headache. Kayus turns on the radio. The weather report comes on. Gusty north winds are forecast, measuring five on the Beaufort scale. The radio falls silent. It is broken. Kayus pushes various buttons. No point to it. The radio does not come on again.

The rain comes down harder.

Thomas looks out the window. Kayus is in the yard now, folding up the camp table and the four camp chairs they used for the morning garden party. The chairs are constructed so that they can be folded up and put inside the table, which in its turn can be folded into a bag with a handle. This set was also a Christmas present. From the family to the family. But as Thomas is the child and the one who enjoys presents the most, like the tent, his name was on the package.

Kayus goes across to the slope, opens the door. Suddenly it starts pouring. Kayus, the slope, the yard of the white villa, all disappear for a few seconds behind a dense, pale gray curtain of rain.

When the sky clears, the scene has changed. Two bright figures come running along the avenue, their hands over their heads as if to protect themselves against the rain, though they are already soaked. A moment later the white villa is filled with new voices. Rosa's, and a few words from Robin.

But two dark phantoms are approaching from the other direction. Splashing across the Johanssons' yard in high black boots. One larger, the other smaller, but both in identical black oilskins. Trousers, coats. The hoods of the coats are up, hands are pulled inside sleeves, arms are held slightly crooked against their sides, so that the rain runs down the sleeves and hits the ground.

■ ■ ■

Soon the whole of the white villa is shaking with a single voice.

"She sailed ashore right in the middle of the race: I thought she'd damaged it but not at all. It was NOTHING. She was second after the first race. SECOND! What you do with a kid like that?"

It is Gabby who is shouting, of course. But though he is pretending to be upset, it is quite evident that his voice is almost thick with pride.

"WuaWuaWua," he goes on the next moment. "Where's the party? If there's one thing I've been wanting all day, it's a good party."

"What was that, Gabby?"

"What?"

"That wail?"

"It's a new dance I've just learned. The song goes on, and in the middle of it you lie down on the floor and wail like a Red Indian. Want to try it?

Of course they do.

The party warms up again.

"I just felt like it. Don't you ever?"

She's standing at the opening of the attic space. Dripping, in her dark oilskins.

"Don't you want to sail?"

"Hi, idiot. This isn't about sailing. Come on."

"Where?"

"Come on, now."

"It's raining."

She is already on her way down the attic stairs. Thomas pulls on his waterproof jacket and follows her out by way of the veranda.

■ ■ ■

Thomas puts up a tent in the yard. He sleeps in the tent for almost ten days, right up to Midsummer. He pretends to be a Red Indian, a settler, a wanderer in the wilderness, a tent tester. Or merely a lone overnight hiker, lying on a foam mattress studying the movement of shadows on the canvas—shadows cast by trees, butterflies and flying birds, by insects creeping and by *all kinds of stuff* on the canvas. Sometimes the night is pitch dark.

"Ugh." May Johansson's voice from outside. "Me Paleface. What a handsome wigwam."

"It isn't a wigwam."

Thomas comes out. "It's a domed model for four people. Family size."

"Yes, yes," agrees May Johansson, as usual not listening very carefully to what others are saying, especially when, in May Johansson's words, it *comes from the mouths of babes and sucklings*. "Here's Erkki. Now play together nicely."

Erkki Johansson is in his medicine-man's feathered headdress. He is holding a toy tomahawk.

"I'm a cowboy," Thomas says in greeting.

"I'm a cowboy, too." Erkki does not hesitate, although everything about him reeks of Redskin.

"You're Red Indian all over," says Thomas. Erkki pretends not to hear.

Renée comes into view. She's strolling along the road, apparently aimlessly. But definitely in their direction. Her lips are moving, as if she were singing some kind of song. This is what she usually does, so that she seems to be talking aloud to herself. She has no singing voice. Or else, Thomas thinks, her head is full of monotonous tunes no one else knows. When she is in a good mood.

And her hair in a great shaggy mop on her head.

Thomas has an idea. "Should we scalp her?"

"Idiot," says Erkki Johansson. "Palefaces don't scalp. Redskins do."

"Huh," says Thomas. Actually he can't believe what he's hearing. It is so completely unlike Erkki Johansson to express an opinion diametrically opposite to Thomas's. The thing about Erkki Johansson is that he agrees.

Though this self-assertion is fleeting. The very next moment Erkki Johansson is Erkki Johansson again. "Though we could anyway," he says calmly.

"I'm a cowboy," Thomas assures him once Renée is within earshot.

"I'm a cowboy," Renée replies.

There is no further discussion. All three are cowboys and swagger into the saloon in May Johansson's kitchen, draw their guns, and fire in every direction. When they can't think of anything else, they arrange a rodeo. Thomas is the wild bronco. Everyone is surprised. Being the wild bronco tied to the big birch in the white villa's yard would seem to be a role tailor-made for Erkki Johansson, giving Thomas and Renée time to slip off into the forest or somewhere else while the wild bronco is tied up. Even Erkki Johansson himself looks a little bewildered. Erkki and Renée depart along the road, but they return quickly. They have no idea what to do on their own. Thomas is sitting on the grass under the tree. He had wanted to find out what it would feel like. As he had thought, it's nothing special.

"So this is where you're living now, is it?" Kayus comes to Thomas's tent. "May I come in?"

Thomas shifts on the foam mattress. Kayus crawls into the tent and fastens the mosquito net.

"I'm playing," says Thomas.

"What?"

"All kinds of stuff."

Redskin. Settler. Wanderer in the wilderness.

Tent tester. Someone designated to find out empirically how a domed model for four works. Capacity, durability, and comfort.

Kayus pinches the canvas. "Fine tent, this. It shouldn't be moldering away in the yard. It should be out camping."

"I don't know," says Thomas matter-of-factly. "It's kind of small. Considering it's supposed to hold a whole family.

Kayus laughs.

"You're pretty funny, Thomas."

Pretty funny. It sounds a little like when Ann-Christine says he has charm. Thomas is embarrassed, but it isn't too bad. Right now Kayus has a way of saying things so that they sound all right. A minute ago he and Bella had been squabbling in the white villa. Thomas is grateful that Kayus didn't bring the squabble with him into the tent.

They sit in silence. They stare at the canvas, they listen to the summer sounds outside.

"You know what I think?" says Kayus after a while.

"No."

"Maybe we could go away. When my vacation starts. Sometimes it's good to get away for a while."

"Where?"

"Anywhere. To Sweden, if you want. Would you like that?"

"Yes," says Thomas, in a low, unemotional voice.

But YES. His hand squeezes the sleeping-bag pillow. What

 a question. Of course he would like that.

"What do you say, Thomas? Want to surprise Isabella Mermaid with a little trip out into the great big world?"

"Bella," says Thomas, correcting him just as unemotionally. Kayus is the only one who still uses the old name. There's nothing wrong with it in itself, but it belongs to another time, when you were smaller and played different games. When they told you stories. Stories you believed, like Santa Claus and all that stuff.

But yes. Yes. Yes.

"Bella," says Kayus with a little laugh, as if the name made no difference. "But the tent. We'll leave that at home. For one thing, it's far too small."

"The tent's good," says Thomas coolly. "But here, in this place."

"We'll stay at a hotel," says Kayus.

"Isn't that expensive?"

"Sure it's expensive, Thomas. But if worst comes to worst, we can always rob a bank.

"Are you coming in to bed now?" says Kayus as he leaves.

"No."

"Come in later if it gets too cold. Or if you get tired of playing."

"I'm not playing."

"Ha, Thomas. You've fallen into your own trap. You just said you were playing."

Kayus ruffles Thomas's hair. Thomas laughs.

He creeps into his sleeping bag and falls asleep. Of course he isn't going in. June nights do not get cold.

Redskin, tent tester, settler, wanderer in the wilderness.

Of course: Kayus and Thomas both know other things as

well. They know the great silence in the white villa. In the evenings, at night. It cannot be ignored, and it is made more palpable by the fact that the radio broke. A silence they brought with them from the city apartment to the summer paradise. Perhaps you were also surprised when that happened. Only Thomas's falling ill with a high fever as a result of eating oranges united Kayus and Bella at the side of his bed as they shared their pity for him. But the silence continued afterward, when he recovered. Then Rosa came, and the days filled with sounds again. But in the evenings, at night, silence fell as before.

When did the silence begin? Thomas can't say. Perhaps as early as last summer, the last weeks in August, when Bella kept turning the light on and off instead of sitting quietly and calmly in the dark, listening to jazz or dancing. Perhaps later. In the winter, when the silence had quite definitely set in.

In the evenings, very early, Bella goes up to her studio. She says she's tired. She wants to sleep, *tomorrow is another day*. She isn't angry, just firm and pleasant. It's possible that she really is tired and needs to sleep. In the daytime there is a lot of activity, of Bella-Rosa, Rosa-Bella, life on the beach on changeable, cloudy days, before the rains begin, conversations in Bella's studio with endless pots of coffee. Once or twice Kayus says, "We never have any time to ourselves." But by the time he speaks, she is no longer in the room. Footsteps can be heard on the stairs, and the door to Bella's studio closes. Most of the time Kayus says nothing. Reads detective stories on his veranda and stays up late.

But in the daytime life goes on as usual. At those times the silence seems unreal. Like something you pretend, with the lively imagination they say you have in such lavish measure.

■ ■ ■

Sometimes Thomas spends time in the attic space. He listens to Bella and Rosa talking together on the other side of the wall. Or keeps on listening, catching only occasional snatches.

Rosa does most of the talking, as usual, Bella interjecting "Mmm," "Yes," "Mmm," laughing, agreeing. But sometimes Bella does some of the talking.

Once Bella starts to tell a story.

"Want me to tell you a story?" asks Bella. "Once, in the middle of the summer, I was going to leave. A few years ago. Everything seemed to be sticking in my throat. I was bored stiff. Or, no, I don't know if that was it. I just suddenly felt that I didn't know what I was doing here. That I ought to be somewhere else. Do you know what I did? I packed my suitcase and left. I walked up the forest road, straight up to the main road, where the buses run. It was pouring rain, I remember that. But suddenly, in the midst of it, I realized what I was doing. Had I gone mad? Where was I going? I had no idea. So I turned around and came back here. Did you ever do anything like that?"

"No," says Rosa thoughtfully after a while. "I haven't. I wouldn't want to leave everything. I want to *take everything with me*."

Rosa laughed, and then Bella and Rosa began talking about something else.

Thomas felt peculiar, without really knowing why. Yes, two things. She had not even mentioned him. Hadn't told that he had found her on the road and run after her. And what was most important: it was a game. The game they had played long ago. The going-away game. To the mermaids, the good life, all of that.

But he cannot bring himself to think about it anymore. Goes out into the summer again. Crawls into his tent. Imagines all kinds of stuff.

And there is another reason, in all seriousness. Redskin, tent tester, settler, wanderer in the wilderness, lone overnighter, experimental person. A reason as good as any other. Worth neither more nor less. He likes sleeping alone in a tent in the yard.

When Gabby comes back from town on Midsummer Eve, a pair of water skis is tied to the car's roof rack. "WuaWua WuaWuaWua," Gabby cries from his James Bond chair in the summer paradise. His vacation has started. But there won't be time for waterskiing until Midsummer Day.

On Midsummer Eve, Gabby and Rosa go to a party on the outer islands. A boat comes to get them. Not the Lindberghs' boat but another one, a boat no one has ever seen before. Two levels high, so that it can only just get into the bay under the bridge across the sound, where the headroom is less than ten feet.

Rosa tells Bella that she'd prefer to stay with Bella in the summer paradise. But Gunilla Pfalenqvist has phoned. Gunilla's husband, Ralf "Raffen" Pfalenqvist, and Gabby do business together. *So it's sort of business*, says Rosa Angel, and she runs down to the boat waiting at Gabby's and Rosa's and the Johanssons' joint breakwater.

The Johanssons are throwing a bring-your-own party. Bella is standing at the mirror in the white villa, putting on lipstick.

"It's weird how the children can't manage to play nicely together in this summer paradise." May Johansson comes in, dragging with her a weeping and extremely recalcitrant Erkki Johansson.

"What do you want me to do about it?" Bella turns around, her lips bright red and her voice harsh.

Bella and May Johansson would have ended up seriously quarreling if Kayus had not come in just then and introduced a lighter note. Meanwhile Thomas and Renée slip discreetly out of the attic space, by way of the veranda, to the road down to the meadow, to pick seven kinds of flowers, to put them under their pillows and dream about their future.

The fact that Bella and May Johansson are almost at each others' throats is not a particularly good start to the Midsummer celebrations. The mood at the Johanssons' is subdued, and the party never really takes off. Bella and Kayus leave early. As they walk home across the white villa's yard, they look into the tent. Thomas and Renée are asleep inside. They look nice and innocent. Almost like little angels.

Thomas and Renée snuggled on foam mattresses inside their sleeping bags, are dreaming about their future. They have put seven kinds of flowers under their pillows. When Thomas first wakes up, it is very early. Perhaps about six. It is a cloudy morning. Renée is already awake. She is dressed and is rolling up her sleeping bag.

"Snow," she says, pulling the strap tightly around the sleeping-bag sausage. "Like on the TV." Thomas laughs Laughing, he forgets his own dream.

"I'm going now. Bye." Renée leaves. Thomas falls back asleep, and when he wakes up again, it is much later, full morning, and a shadow darkens the orange canvas. Erkki Johansson's shrill voice is calling from outside.

THOMAS, I WANT TO BE WITH YOU."

It is a request that cannot be ignored. Thomas sticks out his head and peers into the bright sunlight.

"Go get your equipment, Jack. Conditions are perfect. Today we'll dive for wrecks on the seabed."

"Yes," Erkki Johansson agrees devoutly. He nips off home; if he had been a dog he would have wagged his tail.

This is what happened: On Midsummer Eve, Erkki Johansson was standing in a ditch in the meadow, his feet in the mud, high over his ankles, where his sneakers stop and his pants start. On his way down. Deeper and deeper. At least, that's how it seems. And alone.

May Johansson came through the tall meadow grasses. She was picking flowers to put in vases in the Johansson house, for the Midsummer Eve party. She thought she heard strange noises. No, she was not wrong. She looked over the edge of the ditch, and there, my goodness, there was Erkki, in the ditch, sobbing his heart out.

For this was the situation: Regardless of how useful Erkki Johansson knew himself to be in the service of science, he was suddenly not at all sure that he might not go on sinking and gradually be swallowed up by the earth. He had second thoughts—and for once Erkki Johansson had plenty of time to think as he stood stuck in the mud. Erkki Johansson had more thoughts than all the previous times together when he eagerly volunteered to be the subject for various experiments in the name of science. It is precisely what this experiment is about. *To investigate whether, in a certain kind of clay in this hemisphere, it's possible to sink to any depth, just as one sinks into quicksand in other parts of the world.* And of course, it seems that you can. Erkki Johansson should have had a number of interesting observations to share with those who were running the experiment. But they are elsewhere. They have left. As usual. And Erkki Johansson, as so often before, has had to realize that he must get out of this predicament on his own. He has started struggling to get free. An act that maybe shouldn't have been so difficult. But the fact is, the ditch is wide, and he can't find anywhere to take hold. Then it was difficult to move at all, next to impossible, and in addition, Erkki Johansson had to admit that his legs are too short. *He's so damned small.* That was what he was swearing about to himself, just before his sense of hopelessness took over and the tears came. Those damned tears, he still can't keep them at bay, though he's already of an age when he shouldn't be crying. And on top of that, the tears turned out to be utterly unnecessary. When they began, he already knew he'd sink through the earth and turn into dust and ashes. May Johansson's face appeared over the edge of the ditch, her expression making the situation even worse.

"We're not playing," Erkki Johansson tried to explain, but his voice broke. "We're making scientific observations."

The next minute the whole story comes pouring out. The ultimate secret: that he's the Experimental Subject. *The Experimental Subject, that's him.*

Of course May Johansson is angry. Furious as all hell, as she explains later over and over. What makes her particularly furious as hell is this: Perhaps only five minutes before she found Erkki Johansson in the ditch, she met Renée and Thomas on the road. They cheerfully said hello to her—something May Johansson later realizes ought to have aroused her suspicions, since Thomas, otherwise such a nice boy, is sullen and morose when he is with that peculiar girl. The girl always looks sullen and angry. But children are children, and Midsummer is Midsummer, and May Johansson was in a good mood because she still hadn't the slightest idea what was waiting for her in the ditch below the meadow. Encouraged by her good mood, May Johansson began to tell Thomas and Renée what children used to do at Midsummer when she was a child. They went out on to the meadow and picked seven sorts of flowers and put them under their pillows, and then they went to bed and dreamed about their future.

"Boys can probably do that, too." May Johansson winked at Thomas and went on to the meadow.

But the following day, Midsummer Day, they are all at the beach again, Kayus and Bella, Gabby and Rosa, Ann-Christine and Johan Wikblad, May and Pusu Johansson. A day roughly like most other days early this summer. Sunny at first, then clouds rolling in, and rain in the afternoon.

Rosa is wearing her white bathing suit. She has stepped into her water skis and waded out into the water. She is lying down so that the tips of the skis stick up into the air, because she does not dare to start directly from the jetty, afraid of falling and hitting the wooden boards if the boat starts off too quickly. Gabby's speedboat is chugging in the water ahead of her—the Lindberghs' old Evinrude, at full throttle. Gabby flings out the towrope. Bella catches it in midair and hands the end to Rosa. Bella goes into the water behind Rosa and supports her from the back. The rope grows taut. Gabby sets off at top speed. Rosa comes up out of the water, her knees bent, her body leaning far forward.

"Straighten up!" shouts Bella. But too late. Rosa falls headlong into the water between the skis. Rosa and Bella laugh. Try again.

The second effort is more successful. Rosa stays on the skis for the first difficult part, manages to straighten up, to stretch her legs, to lean back in perfect balance. She swooshes over the bay behind Gabby's boat. Gabby veers sharply in one direction, then another. But Rosa has no problem keeping up. She surfs over the waves in splendid swoops.

May Johansson is having a rainbow drink from Bella's beach bag.

"Chin-chin," she says. "Aren't you guys going to keep me company?" She looks tired. The fact is that, regardless of what you think of her, seen objectively, May Johansson has spent a dreadful Midsummer. It is more than Erkki and the party that bombed. The discussion that morning had centered on Nina's and Maggi's drinking of orange wine in the woods on Midsummer Eve. Afterward they went down the main road to look for other young people in a forest clearing above the fire station, roughly where the cousins live. May Johansson knew nothing of this beforehand, of course, but towards morning she was so worried because Maggi Johansson had not come home that she got out her Monarch, bicycled away, and found Maggi and Nina by the roadside.

Maggi and Nina spend Midsummer Day under house arrest. When Ann-Christine arrives at the beach party, she says, "No wonder they're feeling ill. That batch turned out badly. I emptied the container this morning."

May Johansson cannot face getting into another dispute, getting into anything. She had thought it was her turn to have fun. And she made an effort to think only about waterskiing and beach balls, an effort to be nice. Ann-Christine brought her knitting, a fisherman's sweater for Johan Wikblad. To be friendly and show an interest, May Johansson asked to see the pattern. Numbers of rows and stitches jumped about before her eyes, since she hadn't had much sleep the night before. Then it crossed her mind almost rebelliously that she doesn't care about the pattern or anything else, and she reached for Bella's beach bag and helped herself to a large mug of rainbow drink without gelatine.

"*Chin-chin*." Ann-Christine has moved into the shade. "That means *cheers* in Italian."

"*Chin-chin*." May Johansson repeats. "Aren't you guys going to keep me company?"

Somehow she always ends up with the same question and gets no further. The beach women are waterskiing. Pusu Johansson is nipping at his vodka flask on the sly, though everyone can see. Johan Wikblad pulls out a pack of cards, and Pusu and Johan start playing gin rummy. Ann-Christine moves into the shade. May Johansson is left on the rock with her rainbow drink.

Nevertheless, in the end someone sees and responds.

"Chin-chin." Kayus keeps May Johansson company. At least for a minute. Until he catches sight of Bella again, gets up, and goes down to where she is standing in the bay, her back to him.

Rosa has skied away. Bella is left alone in the water. She looks across the bay. Rosa and Gabby are far away, two dots between the center islands. The sun has gone in; it's afternoon. Bella's long hair is loosely gathered on her back with a black velvet ribbon. Her hair curls down her spine in a clammy braid.

Not far to one side of her, Renée and Erkki Johansson are diving with snorkels and goggles. Bella asks them what game they are playing. Erkki mumbles something inaudible. He cannot speak. The diving club is a secret. Has to be, otherwise there would be no point to it.

Thomas is sitting on the rock on the other side of the inlet, shivering under his towel. His teeth are chattering. He started getting cold a long time ago, and as usual he had to be the first to come out of the water.

Bella turns toward the adults on the shore. May Johansson raises her mug but does not have time to say "*Chin-chin*" before Bella looks away again, splashing water at random, twirling her hands under the water like a propeller, and she is about to turn to Thomas and call to him when Kayus leaves his place beside May Johansson on the rock, throws off his robe, and wades out into the water toward Bella. He's wearing red trunks, the color glowing against his white skin. Kayus reaches Bella and puts his arm around her shoulders, grabs her dark hair, and pulls it. Not hard, but he does pull it. Bella laughs. Kayus puts his hand on the nape of her neck and moves farther out with her. She laughs.

Thomas looks away. Suddenly he understands something: She is not really laughing, it just looks as if she were. *What's happening is something else*.

But now Gabby's boat comes racing toward the shore at top speed. When he quite close, he makes an abrupt turn and goes out again. Rosa lets go of the towrope and glides toward shore. She is not going fast enough to remain upright on the skis all the way. Just as she reaches Bella and Kayus, she stops completely and falls in the water.

"I'm siiiiinking!"

"Wait!" Bella tears herself out of Kayus's grip and wades out toward Rosa. "I'll save you!"

It's really silly. The water is probably no more than a couple of feet deep where Rosa is on skis.

Thomas looks around. Suddenly he meets May Johansson's eyes, which are focused on him from the rock on the other side of the little bay.

May Johansson raises her mug and says, "*Chin-chin*."

Thomas is the only one to see or hear her. Pusu Johansson and Johan Wikblad are playing cards. Ann-Christine is knitting and has moved away from the others.

"Into the shade," Ann-Christine has said. But that was when the sun was still shining. Now shade is everywhere. Only a matter of time before the rain starts.

Thomas smiles kindly at May Johansson.

Suddenly he is feeling sorry for her. She looks lonely. Bella and Rosa are shouting and laughing in the inlet. *And nobody asked May Johansson if she'd like to go waterskiing.*

At this moment, with Bella's and Rosa's voices in the background, the waves from the boat washing against the shore, Thomas has some understanding for May Johansson. He can imagine even listening to her, taking her seriously, all her versions of the story. Only then. Not later.

Unfortunately it is later when May Johansson's mouth gets going. In August, when the Johanssons return from their trip and what May Johansson calls *The Disaster* has become fact. May Johansson will stand in the yard of the white villa and explain. Thomas will close his ears as best he can. He would leave if he were not so busy lashing stuff to the roof of the car, his hands busy with the rope, Kayus on the other side of the car.

"I didn't mean her any harm." May Johansson will stress the *I*. Then she will make a speech Thomas will forget the moment he hears it.

Here is what May Johansson has to say:

May Johansson says that she was always prepared to take Isabella's side. For instance, as against the cousins who did not see Isabella as a normal person in the same way May Johansson did. The cousins called Isabella "the movie star." May Johansson says she repeatedly pleaded the cause of Kayus and Bella and Thomas when negotiating with the cousins. For instance, over the question of the lease. The lease for the white villa was signed annually. Once a year, at the end of the summer, when it was time to renew the agreement for the following season, the cousins came to the white villa, to be charmed by Isabella. When Isabella finished charming the cousins, a lease for another year was signed. Always just for one year at a time. The cousins wanted it like that. For them it was like a fixed point in their schedule to come to the white villa once a year to be charmed by the movie star, sort of like dancing the polka at the firemen's ball on the same Saturday in August every year. And at heart, the cousins were not stingy. This meant that the white villa was naturally also included when Gabby's plans to electrify the summer paradise were realized in the spring of 1963. The red cottage, for instance, which the cousins also owned was left out.

"The movie star must have light to . . .," the cousins had said. Then they had to ponder the situation a little, since they couldn't immediately come up with what a movie star might need light for. After a while they agreed on the following: ". . . to read *Elle* and look at herself in the mirror." Of course those reasons were not very far from the truth. Since Isabella undeniably liked looking at herself in the mirror and she also read a lot of magazines—if not necessarily *Elle*. All this, May Johansson says, made her feel strongly on Isabella's side. And on Isabella's behalf she always spoke out in favor of a five-year lease instead of an annual agreement. May Johansson tried to explain to the cousins that basically Isabella was a nice, ordinary woman, primarily the mother of a nice boy of about Erkki's age and the wife of an ordinary man, an engineer by profession. But she definitely had nothing to do with the movies. The cousins preferred to turn a deaf ear. They preferred their own delusions to May Johansson's version of the truth.

In May Johansson's version, what she calls The Disaster, which occurs later in the summer, will be due to Bella, who otherwise is basically a nice, ordinary woman but who, by virtue of having no people—no family and no traditions—and all the things some others have, was perhaps more susceptible to various influences, her head more in the air than her feet were rooted in the ground, like May Johansson and the women in her family, down the generations back to the beginning of time. One had to have some understanding of these circumstances. May Johansson tried to be understanding, to make herself accessible, and she wanted to share whatever she could and thought about things.

May Johansson's forehead creases as she recollects the time, long ago, before they knew *those people* who came to the summer paradise and built a timber house up on the hill and thought well of themselves. May Johansson and Bella had been on the beach washing sheets, which was a summer tradition in May Johansson's family. While they were doing this laundry, she—that person—had come tripping down from the hill, cigarette in hand. She had gone past the laundry place and happened to see the monograms embroidered on May Johansson's sheets. She had said how beautiful they were but then added, "Good heavens, embroidering them!" and volunteered that she was lazy and loathed doing embroidery. She used cheap sheets at their summer place, since that was the most practical alternative. "You just throw them away when you've used them. No one wants to waste a lovely summer day washing sheets."

Thomas remembers that time, too, but he remembers it somewhat differently. The monograms and sheets made no impression on him. But this:

The way Rosa held out the pack of cigarettes to Bella. The way Bella took a cigarette and lit it with Rosa's lighter. A gold-colored Dunhill she held herself so the cigarette would light in the spanking fresh wind. The lighter remained in Bella's hand. The Lindberghs' boat arrived, and Rosa hurried out to the jetty. That was the first thing Rosa gave Bella, even before the Mickey Mouse measuring cup. A cigarette lighter, Dunhill. Bella saved it. Put it in the drawer of the dressing table, along with all her other stuff.

But pffft. Kayus and Thomas are supposed to have gotten into the car before May Johansson fell silent. Pffft—or whatever it sounds like when a car, an Austin Mini, leaves a summer paradise for all time. And silence in May Johansson's silence for all time.

May Johansson has emptied her mug and is lying back on the rock, dozing. It's Bella's turn to ski. She starts from the jetty and makes such a fuss that you'd think she was performing a feat of great derring-do. She puts on the orange life jacket, sits on the edge of the jetty, thrusts her feet into the skis. Gabby chugs alongside with the outboard, hands Bella the rope. Bella gives the all-clear signal, Gabby sets off. Straight across the bay without unnecessary swings. Bella is up on the skis as easily as anything. The last they see of Bella before she disappears among the islands in the bay is her dark hair in a long thick braid, sharply outlined against the orange life jacket. The sound of the engine dies away. Quiet descends. A thin rain falls.

Renée comes out of the water. She hands the goggles to Erkki Johansson.

"I have made an interesting find!" cries Erkki Johansson. He puts on the goggles, sticks the snorkel into his mouth, and dives. Renée fishes up her towel from the rock near Thomas, wraps it around her, and sits on a boulder in the high grass just above. Thomas knows no one except Renée who can sit in prickly, itchy grass when it's wet.

May Johansson is asleep on the rock. Rosa and Kayus are sharing the last drops of rainbow drink from Bella's thermos. Rosa is lying flat on her back, her head on Kayus's stomach. Kayus is half sitting, leaning back on his elbows. Pusu Johansson takes a drink from his flask—quite openly, since May Johansson is asleep. He is holding Rosa's foot. Kayus, Rosa, Pusu: together they make a pretty funny combination.

Ann-Christine puts her knitting and yarn and pattern back in her knitting basket and says, "It's a pretty nice *still life*."

Johan Wikblad smiles. Ann-Christine has a knack of making anything she says sound amusing. The gin game is over. The back of the sweater is finished. Ann-Christine and Johan Wikblad will get up and do other things in the red cottage for the rest of the day. Thomas does not know what *still life* means. He isn't really interested, either. He is lying face down on the rock, thinking about other stuff.

He is listening to the patter of the rain that is just beginning to fall harder. He thinks it strange that he goes on lying there although the rain has started. He smells the rain. A special smell when it hits warm rock. Charred, spongy.

The rain starts coming down harder.

When it rains harder, you can't lie there pretending that it's not raining. You have to get up, pick up your stuff, and go back to the house. There had been talk of a joint lunch—marinated herring and potatoes. Everyone seems to have forgotten who was supposed to share and why. Thomas gets his comics and lies down under a blanket on the sofa in the big room. Kayus goes into the kitchen and puts on the potatoes. Then he sits down in the reading corner and starts playing solitaire. The only sound is the patter of rain. Thomas wraps himself more tightly in the blanket.

"Are you cold?" asks Kayus.

"A little. I feel hot."

He closes his eyes.

The beach again. It's no good. You have to go back there. Stay there a little longer. Though you don't want to, though you want to get away as quickly as possible. Away from the beach. But you can't get it out of your mind.

In those moments just before the rain really starts coming down.

Thomas is lying on the rock smelling the rain. Something lands on his head. A towel. It is Renée's. Thomas sits up. He isn't surprised. He's been waiting for her to announce her presence in the grass up above him. He is about to call out when he realizes that she is no longer there. And May Johansson is sitting up on the rock on the other side of the sandy bay.

"Erkki," she says. "Where's Erkki Johansson?"

Looks around with wide open eyes. Dazed. As if she had had a nightmare and had woken with a start to find that she has landed in another nightmare.

Renée is already in the water. The moment after, Kayus and Pusu Johansson, both still wearing their trousers. No, it is impossible to describe afterward. It is so ordinary. Exactly as you would imagine it. Thomas and Rosa are standing together in the sandy inlet, just staring. Kayus is carrying Erkki Johansson out of the water. Erkki Johansson's body, slack, lifeless, in his arms. Exactly as you imagine it will be when something really awful happens, when someone drowns. They put Erkki Johansson down on the rock. His goggles have slipped off. Pusu Johansson and Kayus bend over him, trying to bring him back to life, giving artificial respiration, all that stuff. Rosa puts her arm around Thomas. She tries to say something, but nothing comes out except a few short squeaks. Those squeaks, that's all you can hear, though Pusu's and Kayus's voices are loud and agitated.

The next minute everything is back to normal. Erkki Johansson revives. He had only passed out. Swallowed some water. He coughs, spits, brings up a little liquid. But he's alive. There is nothing wrong with him.

May Johansson comes running over with towels. She's angry. Her terror has left her, but she is still in shock. May Johansson is angry in a way no one has ever seen her be angry before. She dries off Erkki Johansson, rubbing him roughly, almost shaking him. How could he do something so stupid? What could he have been thinking of? No, she does not scream. She wants to get it all out, but she can't. May Johansson is silent, just like Rosa a little while back, unable to get a word out, only squeaks, and Erkki Johansson starts crying.

Renée wades up out of the water. She is holding Erkki Johansson's snorkel. May Johansson catches sight of her. Then the strange thing happens. May Johansson lets go of Erkki Johansson and reaches out to Renée. Maybe, you think, she is going to pat Renée on the shoulder or something, thank her for her part in saving the boy's life. May Johansson grabs Renée. Shakes her hard. Hard. As hard as she shook Erkki just now. Perhaps harder. Yes, of course. And she shouts all kinds of stuff. Suddenly words pour out of her. Incredible words. Is Renée sick? Is she crazy? Some kind of animal?

Not until then does Thomas understand that May Johansson holds Renée responsible for all that happened. He cannot understand it, because the true situation was exactly the reverse. Renée was the first to notice what had happened and ran out into the water to save Erkki Johansson. Thomas goes over to them to correct the error. No, he does not. Instead, he is paralyzed, like the others. Says nothing. Like the others. It is only a matter of seconds, but these seconds last an eternity.

Until Renée wrenches herself out of May Johansson's grip, runs away across the rocks and into the Rotwoods in nothing but her bathing suit. Rosa looks at May Johansson. Takes a few steps forward, as if thinking of attacking her. But then she turns abruptly, picks up her robe and Renée's towel, and runs into the woods after Renée.

"Lucky nothing worse happened." Kayus is shuffling the deck of cards in the reading corner. "Things could have gone really badly."

Then, at last, the dam in Thomas bursts, and he manages to get the words out. "It wasn't her fault!" he cries. Almost sobbing under his blanket among his Donald Duck comics.

Kayus does not speak at once. "I know," he says finally, quietly and seriously. "Thomas. Everyone knows." Then he falls silent again.

Lights the oil lamp. Shuffles the cards. Lays them out. The rain comes down harder. The rain comes in stages. Grows heavier, stops, starts again, grows heavier. Thomas tries to lose himself in his comics, letting himself be carried away. No use. One thing.

It throbs in him.

If everyone knows. Why don't they do something? If everyone knew. Why didn't they do something?

Kayus goes to the kitchen to check the potatoes. He comes back to the reading corner. Thomas must have dozed off after all, for the next time he opens his eyes, a mermaid is standing in the middle of the big room.

Wearing a wet, grimy bathing suit, a robe. Barefoot, hair down her back, streaky, tangled. Her face patchy with mascara. Mermaid—that was long ago; and yet she is more mermaid than ever. You can almost see the twisted strands of seaweed curling around her wet arms and legs.

"Where did everybody go?" Isabella's voice is thick and muffled.

"The engine failed. We could have used some help."

She is almost crying.

Kayus gets to his feet. "I'm sorry, Isabella. The potatoes are boiling." He walks in her direction but passes her. Goes through Thomas's room into the kitchen.

"Where is everybody?"

Isabella stays put. Thomas won't risk looking up.

"Where is everybody?"

Thomas stares at his Donald Duck comics.

Nevertheless. *He wants to go to her*.

"Where is everybody?" she asks. Now more angry than forlorn. And turns to follow Kayus into the kitchen.

"We were all going to eat together!" she cries. "We were going to have a party. It's Midsummer!"

You hear clatter, Isabella's cries. Kayus's shouts. More clatter, shouts. The door slams in the attic entry. Quick footsteps on the attic stairs. A door slams again. Hard. Then silence. Dead silence.

Kayus and Thomas eat marinated herring and potatoes.

Kayus plays solitaire. Thomas reads comics.

"Thomas," Kayus tries at one point.

But Thomas does not respond. His face is turned into the sofa.

Kayus gets one of his detective stories and starts to read. After he has read for a while, Thomas gets up and slips out into the attic entry. The door to the attic stairs is closed. He goes to the door, pulls at it. It is locked. He presses his ear against the wood. Silence. Nothing. Thomas sees himself thumping on the door. Thomas the Door Thumper. Hammering on the door to the attic stairs with clenched fists.

He just stands there, very still.

"Thomas!" Kayus comes out of the big room into the attic entry.

"Want to have some fun, you and me? Want to go to Sweden?"

He is just talking. Pretending that Thomas isn't standing by the door they both know is locked.

"Later," says Kayus. "When the weather clears."

"I want to go to Sweden, too!" For a moment Thomas is

almost convinced that she is with them. That by some magic she has opened the locked door and has put on her yellow summer clothes and washed off her runny makeup and pulled her comb through her hair. *Now we're the ones who will travel!* But no, it never happened. The door remains closed. Kayus goes back to the big room and closes that door behind him.

"Come on, Thomas."

Thomas takes his weatherproof jacket from the hook in the attic entry and goes out by way of the veranda. He walks along the avenue down to the beach. At Gabby's and Rosa's and the Johanssons' shared breakwater Gabby's boat is moored in the usual way to its own pole on the left of the jetty. The water skis are on the bench in the prow. They have SUN RACING printed on them. The towrope is in an untidy heap on the bottom. And something black—Isabella's hair ribbon. Soaking wet. Thomas picks it up, wrings it out, and puts it in his pocket.

He gets Pusu Johansson's swivel rod from the terrace of the Johanssons' sauna. His own rod is in the white villa. He goes to the other beach and out on to the white villa's jetty. He casts and reels in several times in swift succession. Doesn't hook so much as seaweed, reeling in far too quickly. Stops at regular intervals. Looks around. Emptiness everywhere. There's a light in the Johanssons' window.

He places the swivel rods under the spruce near the white villa's beach.

"Follow me." He is speaking loudly and clearly. He walks toward the forest. Walks. After a while he turns around. Silly, of course. No one is there. And he knew that all the time.

Where is she?

For the first time, Thomas has to admit that he doesn't know.

That he has no idea.

He goes home. Across the yard where the tend stands in front of the woodshed, dripping and dark from the rain. That game is over. Thomas moves back into the house.

The following day: Bella comes down from the studio. Dressed in yellow: shorts and summer shirt. She takes a bowl of sour milk off a rack and sits next to Thomas at the breakfast table.

"How about we pop some corn?" is the first thing she says. "How about a popcorn party?"

Kayus's Austin Mini has driven off along the road. Kayus's vacation has not yet begun, and today is a weekday after the big holiday.

"I mean," says Bella, lifting the milk high up in the air with her spoon. "Your birthday is coming up soon."

The sour milk runs off the spoon onto the plate in a long, expressive stream. Thomas sticks his spoon into his bowl and imitates her. Bella laughs, ruffles his hair, and gives him a punch of the kind they tend to give each other at the breakfast table on those mornings when they pretend to be members of a band of thieves. Not until then does Thomas dare to look at her properly. Just the same as always. Not a trace of the day before.

Then the dam bursts again, and he can't hold it in any longer. "We're going to go to Sweden," he exclaims, bursting with the surprise.

Then Rosa appears. Opening the door, standing in the middle of the kitchen. Wearing navy-blue trousers and a blue-and-white striped T-shirt, painted lips, sunglasses, a white ribbon in her hair. Says that it's chilly out. Clutches her shoulders to illustrate.

Is otherwise just the same as always.

"Gabby's gone," she says, as if in passing. Takes off her sunglasses. Sits down at the table opposite Thomas and Bella. Fixes her eyes on Bella, smiles. Perhaps the smile is a little uncertain, but the uncertainty is mostly because she cannot immediately figure out Bella's mood of the day.

"Where to?" asks Bella in a perfectly ordinary voice, pushing her bowl away.

"Oh, God, Bella." Rosa laughs. "He doesn't know what he's letting himself in for. He's taken the young ladies with him. Nina. And Maggi Johansson.

"He had to go immediately. Immediately. Not one of us wanted to go. He can be so stubborn, Bella. When he gets restless, he has to go. He went on and on about it. But I refused.

"I've never refused before, Bella.

"In the middle of the night I had to go down to the Johanssons' myself to ask if Maggi could go too. That was Nina's condition. She was the only one he could persuade."

"Renée wouldn't budge.

"Me, either."

"We thought about having a popcorn party," says Bella, smiling. "Soon it will be Thomas's birthday."

"We're going to the floating shop with Renée," says Rosa, meeting Bella's smile with an even broader smile. "That was really why I came. I was supposed to ask you if you wanted to come with us. Do you want to come?"

Of course they do. Bella just has to change into some warmer clothes first. Thomas runs ahead down to the beach.

Renée is in the little outboard. He sees her from a long way off. An orange dot in the gray landscape, yellow reeds in the background. She is taking the motor apart. Has raised the hood, unscrewed some parts. She has arranged these on the bench in front of her in a neat row. Presumably she has been at it for some time, since a sizable number of engine parts are lined up.

"The spark plug," she says before he even has time to ask.

"The spark plug doesn't go there," Thomas explains decisively. To be honest, he has no idea where the spark plug goes on outboard motors.

Nor has she. That's what he knows.

"What wrong is UNDERNEATH ON THE BOTTOM." She peers at him from under her bangs. "Idiot."

Glares; just as she has a hundred times before.

"We're going to Sweden," says Thomas then, happily, loudly and clearly.

"To what?"

She is pretending not to hear. But that is perfectly normal behavior in someone like her. And it turns out that they have to row to the floating shop. She can't get the motor reassembled correctly.

There is a padlock on the big outboard. Gabby is the only person who has a key.

"Where did they go?" Bella asks in passing, in the rowboat.

"I've no idea, Bella," says Rosa. "But if I know Nina and Maggi, not all that far. To be honest, Bella, I don't care. It's something I just can't be bothered with."

"Maybe you think I don't understand, but I do understand, Bella. I've been through this before."

"Through what?"

"Gabby."

"We just had an engine failure."

"I've told you, Bella. I want to be here. With you. In the summer paradise. That's all that matters.

"And for once, Bella, I thought I'd say what I mean."

That evening Thomas walks along the road. Turns off into the forest at one of the places where there are no paths at all and continues at a rapid pace over rough ground. When he is deep into the woods, he slows down. Sounds in the background.

"I'm going to the forest." Erkki Johansson catches up with him. "I'm going to carry out a scientific experiment."

"It's a secret," he adds.

"Liar," says Thomas.

They walk on in silence.

"I drowned, Thomas," Erkki finally says. "Do you want to know what it feels like?

"Want me to tell you?"

"Go home." The words are on Thomas's tongue, but Erkki Johansson changes the subject.

"We went into town, Thomas. I bought a birthday present for you. With my own money. Guess what I bought?

"Want me to tell you what I bought?"

"No," says Thomas. But there's no stopping Erkki Johansson.

"Want to guess? Want me to give you a hint?

"Want to bet, Thomas?

"Want to bet that you get the most presents from me?

"Even more than from your mom and dad?

"Guess how many presents I'm gonna give you?

"Guess HOW MANY, Thomas?"

Erkki Johansson can't hold back any longer. *"Forty-eight counting the big ones."*

Nothing has changed. Except that Kayus is unrelenting.

"When are we going?" In the evening Thomas goes to the veranda.

"Where?" Kayus looks up from his detective story, abruptly, confused.

"To Sweden."

"Later."

Kayus closes his book and puts it down on the table. He says nothing more, just goes on looking at Thomas with a worried expression.

"I want to go to Sweden, too." Bella is suddenly standing behind Thomas. And she is really here, it is not merely his imagination. "Were you planning to leave me behind?" But although she has addressed them both, she is really only speaking to one of them. To Kayus. Just as if she knew the answer beforehand. She laughs with a touch of defiance, a kind of confirming laugh.

A deathly silence spreads on the veranda.

Thomas has left. He is charging along the forest road at great speed.

He has suddenly understood something: That the correct answer to Bella's question was yes, that was exactly what they had planned. Leaving her there. That was the point of the question Kayus had asked in the attic entry the previous day. That *she* was no longer included, that she would not be allowed to come.

All that was earlier; the conversations and plans in the tent, the ideas, they were just dreams.

Regardless of what they were: After yesterday they could not, in any case be realized. Because of the grimy mermaid in the middle of the big room. Or just the memory of her.

No, of course not. That's not a total impossibility, an impossibility from now to eternity. The point is that all of them should be at peace in their separate corners. *Think the situation through*. Bella in particular should think and arrive at the awareness that the grimy mermaid in the middle of the big room was an absurdity. She should accept the consequences and become herself again.

Meanwhile Thomas and Kayus should go out into the world and have new experiences together, father and son.

Damn Kayus. Thomas really does feel that he's been deceived.

"But you promised." Even later, when it is almost night, Thomas approached Kayus again. But it was useless.

"We had an agreement," Kayus said suddenly. Just as if it were Thomas who had broken it.

In the photograph, taken on board the *Forsholm III*, the woman wearing a tailored suit has her arm around the boy's shoulders. The woman is crouching, so that she is almost level with the boy. The woman and the boy are on deck. It is the classic photograph: Family on Deck, mother and son with wind in their hair, sun in their eyes, lips open and laughing. The woman is wearing dark shoes with suitably moderate heels and carrying a dark shoulder bag. The tailored suit is light-colored and the jacket has dark buttons. It looks expensive. It is new, bought in a small shop that very day. The woman's hair is cut in a long page-boy, backcombed and bouffant, a few strands blowing in her face. She is holding them back with her free hand, the one not on the boy's shoulder. Thomas, who is the boy in the photograph, is peering at the camera. The woman—she is Isabella, Bella-Isabella, and when Thomas finds the photograph, he hides it carefully.

But Renée in her orange T-shirt. Shoulder-length tangled light-brown hair. And no comb will go through it, a matter of honor. Hasn't even tried since May. Renée chewing on a strand of hair. Toot! Off goes the car along the forest road. Gabby and Bella in front because Bella wants to have a full view of the road and Rosa does not mind either way. Rosa and Thomas in the back. Thomas with his game of Battleship and a book about a sailor making his way along across the Atlantic in terrible weather. Renée chewing on a strand of hair. When Thomas comes back from Sweden, her hair is going to be cut short and trimmed and backcombed in a peculiarly uneven way in the Johanssons' sauna.

This is how things are for Thomas and Bella: they have an idea, a dream, a plan to go away. It was a game. The Going-away game they played in the city apartment when Thomas was younger. And they took the game along to the summer paradise, a little, and played it there, too, a little, during a rainy period before the family called Angel came. Packing your suitcase, putting on your traveling clothes, and going.

Going where? To the mermaids, to the good life. What is that? The mermaids, who were at the amusement park with Bella, who later scattered to the winds and waves, who went out into the world.

But mermaids is also a collective term. They are people with restless souls, searching for something, not necessarily a place in the sun, least of all a place in the sun. For life is many places, life is several lives, encapsulated like Chinese boxes, multiplied lives, and you had to travel around from life to life.

On Thomas's birthday there's a popcorn party in the house on the hill. Thomas opens his presents. Kayus and Bella give him a model he can build, a miniature of the *Santa Maria* in which Christopher Columbus sailed across the seas to discover America. From Gabby and Rosa and Nina and Renée Thomas receives a book about a sailor who sailed alone in a vessel until it was mysteriously lost in a distant sea. Slocum, Joshua. Erkki Johansson has contributed his tiddledywinks. The game is very simple, considerably less sophisticated than TRIUMPH, which Thomas and Renée no longer play because it becomes pretty monotonous, with the Very Important Person and all the millionaires in the Millionaire's Mansion. And considerably more domestic. After they have spread all over the floor in a hideous muddle, all the green, yellow, red, and black tiddledywink families are flipped toward the empty pot on the floor with a special tiddledywink larger than the others. The pot is the home, and all the participants have a family of their own color, and the player whose entire family is the first to land in the pot wins the game.

Immediately after handing over his present, Erkki Johansson wants to demonstrate all the intricacies of the game, with the result that he drops the jar and all the tiddledywinks spill, rolling all over the floor and under the dining-room table, where the popcorn is served. Since everybody is busy with popcorn and birthday excitement, the tiddledywinks remain scattered as long as the party lasts.

Kayus joins them for a while. Then he goes to the beach to go fishing with Huotari. They have bought little Baltic herrings, which they're going to fix on the hooks of the long line as bait for the eel they are determined to catch one of these days.

To Sweden. Thomas and Kayus have stopped talking about Sweden. Together. But Thomas alone has talked. Talked and talked, so that no one in the summer paradise can avoid knowing what he WANTS, what his plans are: to go to Sweden. He has turned whiny and angry, like any kid who's ignored.

"Thomas has turned so restless," says Rosa, laughing.

Thomas looks sullen.

"Thomas is sulking," says Bella with an amused expression.

"Oh," Rosa said. "I know just how you feel, Thomas. Things are like that sometimes. You have to get away."

Well, that's partly it. But only partly. The main reason why Thomas is obsessed, as Kayus calls it, is Kayus himself, sitting on his veranda and continuing to be unrelenting. From the day after Midsummer up to the day they actually leave. When he does not go with them.

"I've work to do. Gabby has business in the north. You're going to Umeå."

"You promised."

"I'm sorry, Thomas."

"It was going to be a surprise for Isabella Mermaid."

Kayus says nothing, he simply looks even more knowing. As if the mere sight of his expression would remind Thomas of the grimy mermaid who has been forgotten by everyone except by this one man, who is unrelenting in not forgetting . . . .

But Sweden. It was their idea, Kayus's and his, and it had nothing to do with whatever happened. That is what it was. And it is to maintain the right to his version of the story that Thomas continues to harp on Sweden until the decision to go is made.

Though suddenly it does not feel as he had thought it would. Kayus isn't coming. Nor is Renée. She can't be persuaded, is adamant, so that Thomas finally gets angry and goes home, up to the attic, takes the knife from its hiding place under the floorboard, and conceals it behind the wallpaper instead. At least she is not going to get that while he's away.

But in the middle of the birthday celebrations someone else returns. Someone who can turn dreams into reality.

"It's weird," cries Gabby as soon as he is through the door, clearly upset. "You give them what they ask for, and then they change their mind." His trip with Nina and Maggi Johansson out into the world has been a flop. Gabby wanted to do all kinds of stuff: go to the trotting races and bet a reasonable amount or even a little more, go to the parachuting club and watch the parachutists. He was even prepared to treat Maggi Johansson to a jump, although Maggi Johansson isn't even a member of the family.

Or just drive along the road, straight ahead at seventy miles or more an hour.

Whatever the young ladies want. But the *young ladies* did not want anything. And whatever Gabby wanted you could be sure that the *young ladies*—who are at the age when the last thing you're interested in is being a Bond girl to anybody, least of all to a man of their dads' age, and least of all their own dads—did not want the same thing, and most of the time, generally speaking, they did not want anything at all except for the time when they stayed in Nina's room in the city apartment—for that is where they end up—giggling and whispering and enjoying themselves and, every time Gabby comes in, falling silent and making faces, generally behaving in such a way that it is impossible to get a sensible word out of them. The record department of the big store is the only place they agree to visit.

Then Gabby catches sight of the birthday boy, who also grew restless, it is explained, during Gabby's absence.

Gabby brightens.

"Good thing I got home this particular day. Just in time to put some life into the party."

So the party ends with Gabby sitting in his James Bond chair on the hill and Thomas approaching him, standing beside him, considerately and discreetly. Gabby turns his head, catches sight of him again, and right there, on the highest point of the hill, he says, "Now, son, it's our turn to go. Out to take a look at the world."

The cabin is green and it has a round window called a porthole, Thomas explains to Bella, who has it wrong. There are two bunks, one above the other, and a little table and a narrow closet. Bella takes a dress from her white leather suitcase and hangs it in the wardrobe as if this journey was going to last for months. It is the yellow dress. The one that shimmers, Thomas's favorite. *Let's go now, Thomas!* Thomas clambers up onto the top bunk, lies face down, and looks out. White geese on the sea. Green and gray water merging with the sky.

Thomas holds his ticket in his hand. The ship is called the *Forsholm III*. When he first caught sight of the *Forsholm III* in the harbor, Thomas was a little disappointed. The ship is so small. Low and long, with the captain's bridge in varnished wood. But it takes no longer than a few hours across to Umeå. The gulf is at its narrowest at this point. Gabby parked the car in the harbor garage, and they took their bags and went on board.

Gabby and Rosa knock on the cabin door. Gabby has a bottle, and the idea is that they should all squash into Thomas's and Bella's cabin for cocktails. Gabby, Bella, and Rosa sit on the lower bunk because there is nothing else to sit on; they have to lean forward because you cannot sit up straight, and Thomas in the upper bunk looks down on to three heads with three parts in dark hair. Gabby is in great form, pretending to be James Bond. Bella and Rosa are his Bond girls, and Gabby is being witty and Bella and Rosa are laughing. The mood becomes almost unbearable at times, especially when Gabby suddenly decides he must establish a rapport between male travelers, with Thomas. He starts talking about the lone sailor in the book Thomas got for his birthday. Thomas says, "Hmhm," the *Forsholm III* leaves the dock, and Thomas presses his face against the glass of the porthole. The ship slowly makes its way out into the wind and the waves. For there is a high wind. On the radio they said that it reaches six on the Beaufort scale.

"It's a fantastic enterprise, all right," says Gabby about the sailor's sole voyage.

"Navigare necesse est, vivere non necesse," says Gabby. The very words printed on the matchbox they found on the table when they came into the cabin.

"You mispronounced it," giggles Rosa. "It's Latin, and you

should say it this way." Rosa says it her way, and Bella giggles, Gabby raises his glass and says, "Bond—James Bond," and Thomas almost glues his face to the pane. They are all the way out in the water now. He climbs down from the bunk and asks if he can go outside.

Thomas goes up to the top deck. On the way he bumps into teenagers drinking beer out of bottles. One boy, perhaps fifteen or sixteen, holds up his bottle and says, "Hi," as if they knew each other. They do not, but Thomas nods. They have a radio and it is playing the Rolling Stones. Bjöna's older brother has the record in his rec room in town. A rec room is made by emptying a room of all nonessentials, laying down mattresses, turning a wooden box upside down to serve as a table, then sticking candles into empty green bottles and scattering cushions over the mattresses and the floor. Then you put the Rolling Stones on the turntable and listen. Bjöna and Thomas are called in and have to sit on a mattress and keep quiet while Bjöna's older brother solemnly lowers the needle on the record. So Thomas and Bjöna keep quiet while the single plays once from beginning to end; after that Bjöna's older brother turns off the record player and tells Thomas and Bjöna to split. But all that—that belongs to another time. Another life. Thomas's city time and Thomas's city life. Not now. Now it is summertime and roaring sea.

Thomas is alone on the top deck. The *Forsholm III* passes the outermost islands in the gulf. The water here is low, and sometimes when the sun comes out, you can clearly see patches of underwater rocks. There are such patches everywhere, on both sides of the channel.

This is where the open sea starts. When Thomas looks straight ahead, all he can see is green and white. The waves are coming straight at the ship, waves that are sheer and high. The *Forsholm III* is small, he was right about what he thought in the harbor, it was far too small to cope safely with rough seas. After they have been on the open sea for a few hundred yards, the waves have grown so high that the ship hurtles down into the troughs, her prow dipping. White foam spurts in all directions. Thomas holds on to the railing.

He is thinking about her now, perhaps. Viviann, or the woman Renée says is called Viviann. Viviann: the woman who looks like an Indian, who sailed GOOF ashore last summer and came to his rescue. Thinks about her now as he has thought about her occasionally. Viviann: as he thinks about her now, the name suddenly seems foreign. Viviann, that is not who she really is, and now he imagines her as the possessor of the name, more anonymous in a way; she just becomes the girl with long brown hair and a white blouse with many buttons, the Indian-looking girl who came to his rescue and to whom now, a little later, he, in turn, would be able to tell all kinds of stuff about the ocean. She might be here now in all this gray, this white, in all this roar of the sea, holding on to the railing beside him and listening to him, the seafarer, holding course perfectly in the middle of the night through the great swells of calm after autumn storms, on dog-watch with Buster Kronlund—not merely an ordinary sailor, master of a small dinghy. He would tell her his story of the sea—not so that it sounded foolish but so that it was true.

For that was what you went to Umeå for: for the sea, the roar of the waves; not for the ponies in the stable, where Thomas is going to go for a ride the following day, or to be able to buy Gold Blend at Tempo—and Gold Blend is good coffee—or to eat strawberry cake with a FORK at a guest house called The Arrow.

Exactly. But Viviann isn't here. He has merely been making believe again. Viviann is a creature of his imagination and therefore of no interest, and now, here on the slippery deck with water sloshing on the boards and with the wind ballooning his jacket, Thomas grows up for a few seconds and truly understands that he is inventing everything to do with himself and Viviann; he knows nothing about her, he is a dreamer, trying to shape reality to fit his own desires.

Gabby comes walking along the deck below. Against the gray and green and in the sun which is now shining between the clouds, he appears in sharp outline. Like a figure in a comic book, confined within black lines. Thomas, in his green jacket, merges more easily into the background. Almost disappears into it.

But luckily the background is wide. It is *everything else*: the sea, the sky, the *Forsholm III*.

Thomas turns and goes down a different stairway. He opens the door to a lounge with a bar and a cafeteria. It is also full of teenagers. One wall holds a display showing the ship's route with tiny bulbs, which light up as each sea mile is covered. A girl is sitting beneath the display; her legs are crossed, and her eyes are fixed on her hands, which she is twisting in such a way that she almost seems to be dog-paddling. Thomas stares at her hands. He cannot help it. He has to force himself to look away, concentrating on the display, the yellow blinkers lighting up sluggishly but regularly. The ship keeps lurching, first one way, then rapidly the other way, and back again. Thomas stumbles, almost loses his balance, and grabs at the first available sleeve.

"Hi," says a girl whose jacket he has grabbed. Thomas recognizes her: one of the girls among the teenagers he met on his way up to the top deck.

"Hi," Thomas mumbles.

"Who are you?" the girl asks.

"Thomas."

As soon as he has said his name, he wishes he had said something else. Thomas—it suddenly sounds foolish. Rather childish. He needs another name when talking to this girl, who behaves as if they were contemporaries although there must be at least two or three years between their ages. A name that is somehow more appropriate.

Thomas mentally runs through his names. Not at this very moment, of course. But later. For he will reenact the scene in his head again and again, changing the remarks and the course of events in various ways, so that it becomes a long conversation between him and the girl about the sea, the weather, the ship's course, and the whole journey in general. So that everything does not end with Bella's sudden appearance, taking him by the arm and shaking him, asking loudly and angrily why he ran away from Gabby and the others.

Thomas goes through his names. *Bykovsky*, Comrade Cosmonaut. Didi, Frederic Dumas. *Tom Sawyer*. A Perfectly Incredible Person. The Charm Troll, Entertainer. Slocum, Joshua. Chet. *Mister Chet*.

It's awful.

He becomes aware that he is still holding the girl's sleeve and lets go, but as soon as his hand is free, the ship gives another lurch, and he has to grab again.

"Just hang on," says the girl. "I'm very steady on my feet. Do you want a beer?"

Thomas shakes his head.

"Any brothers and sisters?"

"What do you mean?"

"I just wondered. Are you traveling alone? Did you run away? I ran away once."

"I'm traveling alone," says Thomas, suddenly the Lone Traveler. "I didn't run away."

"They caught me on the other side. There's a stable over there. I was crazy about horses. So I ran away."

Then, suddenly, there is someone else. A boy leaning heavily against the girl's shoulder, over which he looks at Thomas and at the display board. He catches sight of the other girl, the one with her legs crossed, twisting her hands. He asks her why she does that. She looks up.

"Why not?" she says. "It's fun."

But she does not smile or change expression in any way. It is kind of interesting, Thomas thinks. Reminds him of someone. Though her hair is different, short and fair. But Thomas thinks he would be able to talk to her, too, just as he is talking to this girl who was crazy about horses and ran away to a stable on the other side of the gulf. But it turns out to be impossible, for the next moment Bella is there, and she is both angry and loud. She is wearing her yellow dress. She has put on high heels, and the whole lounge smells of her perfume, "Apple Blossom," sweet and sickly. An old-woman smell. Thomas is ashamed. No one else in this lounge is wearing a sleeveless party dress. Or any kind of dress.

"Come away at once." Bella takes hold of his shoulders harshly. "Why did you run away from Gabby? Come on. I've told you, we're going to eat now."

Thomas is dragged away so quickly that he has no time to explain.

■ ■ ■

The restaurant is behind a glass wall next to the saloon. Luckily they have a window table, and Thomas can make himself invisible to the teenagers who thought he was lying to them, turning his back and looking out. He eats sausages and French fries and drinks Coca-Cola. The water splashes on the glass pane, so that it runs down the inside. Gabby explains that this is the effect of the pressure, but what he means is unclear, since the very next moment he is already ordering schnapps to go with his veal cutlet. And wine. *Sangre di Toro* says Gabby in a language he does not *parlez*. BULL'S BLOOD he translates when the bottle comes, because there is a bull's head on the label, and the color of the wine is as dark as Thomas's Coca-Cola. Cheers, Thomas! Bella raises her glass. She has forgotten the interlude in the lounge and is in excellent spirits again. Rosa says that she doesn't want any. Rosa is quieter than before. But Gabby is in great form, no storm at sea will stop him ever again.

"Anyone who's been in a storm in the Atlantic is immune for the rest of his life. That was seafaring, that was, Thomas." And the restaurant sways, the ketchup bottles roll across the table, and Thomas nods, nods, and it takes a moment before he realizes that Gabby is talking about the crossing from America he made with his daughter, Renée, who has nerves of steel, and all their belongings. "It's called baptism at sea, Thomas, or Christ knows what it's called, but here's to James." Gabby talks all the time, and when he is not saying something else, he says that that's who he is—James Bond. Bella laughs. Bella laughs with her mouth open, her breasts bobbing under the yellow dress, *the lovely firm breasts that are the principal trait of a Bond girl*. No one is wearing a party dress in the restaurant, either. Rosa and Gabby are in the same clothes they wore in the car, except that Gabby has put on a tie patterned with musical notes.

"I want to ride ponies," Thomas says suddenly.

"Ride ponies," Bella repeats, as if Thomas has said something provocative or tremendously amusing. "Why?"

"There's some stables there. In Umeå."

"Of course we'll go riding." Gabby puts his arm around Thomas on the men's side of the table. "On second thought, a good ride would do us all good. The way we're stuffing ourselves."

Bella meets Gabby's eyes and laughs. Thomas registers coolly that Bella seems to have only one response now—laughing in such a way that her mouth turns into a big black hole. Thomas wriggles out of Gabby's grasp. Gabby raises his glass.

"Here's to James."

"There's no talking to you," says Thomas, suddenly feeling sorry for himself.

"Excuse me." Rosa tries to get up. "But I have to. . . ."

She sinks back again.

"Heavens, I do feel ill."

But there is not much left of this journey. You can already see the coast up ahead, and the sea is not at all rough. Gabby has followed Rosa to their cabin, and Thomas and Bella are alone at the restaurant table amid the veal cutlets, sausages, French fries, Coca-Cola, and Sangre di Toro.

Bella asks Thomas why he acts that way toward Gabby. Thomas does not reply until he realizes that he must say something, since Bella does not stop looking at him with a questioning and rather worried expression. So he asks her what she means by that way.

Bella puts her knife and fork down on the plate with a clatter. She lights a cigarette, puffs on it angrily for a moment, not speaking.

Thomas cannot say anything. He looks at the sausages, split open on the plate, at the mustard in the cracks. Glances over at the window. Can't she see? Can't Isabella see the *roar of the sea?* Traveling by sea? Being on their way? Is she completely blind? He does not say anything. Merely asks himself a few questions. Unobtrusively, in passing, trying to avoid her eyes.

"Thomas," says Bella. She stubs out her cigarette and starts eating again, her voice almost warm. Pleading in some way.

"Thomas," says Bella. "We could try to have a good time, couldn't we?"

Bella's party dress shimmers. Thomas stares at the material. *Handwoven Thai silk*. He knows the words by heart, has known them as long as he can remember. He swallows. And softens. Suddenly he feels sorry for Bella in her shimmering dress among the ketchup bottles rolling across the restaurant table. "Apple Blossom" mixed with the faintly sweet smell of seasickness and vomit all over everything now that the crossing is almost at an end.

In spite of everything. Though she does not see.

Bella is on one side of the table, Thomas on the other. She is there now, and he is here. Bella raises her glass of wine. She smiles, as if they had an agreement, as if they were sharing a secret. They do not.

Somehow so lonely in her yellow dress.

Thomas grasps his Coca-Cola. The whole bottle. They drink to each other.

■ ■ ■

The guest house is called The Arrow and is a blue wooden building. Their rooms are on the first floor, Bella and Thomas in one, Rosa and Gabby in another. Rosa feels better as soon as she has firm ground under her feet.

Gabby takes Thomas to the stables in a taxi. Thomas's pony is dark brown and tall, Thomas is surprised how tall. He has never been riding or even sat in a saddle before. He scrambles up on the pony's back. Two young women who work at the stables lead the pony once around the paddock. No pony is tall enough for Gabby, so he can only wait. Gabby has brought the camera and when the ride ends, he calls to Thomas, "Keep smiling, son!"

He clicks, immediately puts his sunglasses back on, then looks from one young woman to the other. The second one is perched on the fence outside the stable he is leaning against like one of the Cartwrights. Gabby helps Thomas down from the pony. Thomas has a big space between his legs—or rather, that is what it feels like to be a real cowboy. Gabby leaves a generous tip, and when he and Thomas walk down to the road to the waiting taxi that Gabby has ordered, he puts his hand on Thomas's shoulder just as he did two years earlier, at the air show. Thomas has no objection to the taxi. He likes riding in taxis. With Kayus they never take taxis because they are too expensive, and there's really no need to go out to eat at restaurants when the food is so much better and cheaper at home. Thomas has the whole backseat to himself. Gabby sits next to the driver. He chats with the driver about business in general and comments on the *progress of the nebulae in the solar system*, because that is what they are talking about on the car radio. Gabby pronounces words like *solar system* and *nebulae* with emphatic clarity, so that Thomas realizes that Gabby thinks Thomas is really interested. Over and over again in recent years it has surprised Thomas how little interest he has in space, the moon, and who will be the first to set foot on it. Even airplanes are more interesting. But suddenly he also realizes that Gabby has to find something to talk about, that Gabby may not know how to act with Thomas, who has said no more than two complete sentences during the hour they have been on this adventure together.

Renée and Gabby, Thomas thinks. What are they like together?

Renée and Gabby lift the sailing dinghy onto the motorboat so that it rests across the outer edge of the stern. Gabby casts off. Renée starts the motor and backs away. Gabby makes sure the dinghy is in place. Renée accelerates, and they go out into the sound at ten knots at least, though the speed limit is three knots. Not a word is exchanged during these maneuvers.

"Yep," says Thomas to Gabby from the backseat, trying to sound enthusiastic.

"Yep," Thomas says again. "Yep, yep, yep," until Gabby falls silent and looks out of his window, Thomas looks out of his, and the driver, a taciturn man, turns off the radio because it's started playing pop tunes. The silence does not last long. Gabby has to break it. He starts whistling, slapping his hand against his knee in time with the tune coming from the radio before it was turned off but is still going on in his head. I can't get no satisfact . . . donk. And back at The Arrow they have Coca-Cola and strawberry cake eaten with FORKS.

Bella is wearing a new light-blue suit. Rosa's clothes are also new. A sleeveless dress, light-blue. At a distance Bella and Rosa look alike in their light-blue clothes and identical sunglasses. Rosa smiles, takes Bella's arm and says, "Now we're twins," and they all get into a taxi. "Here's to James." Gabby still isn't tired of James Bond, although it is already the next day and time to go home. Gabby does all the talking. He has opened the window all the way, so that there is a fierce draft in the back. This time the driver is an animated man; he has lost a lot of money at the trotting races. Gabby gets this out of him while engaging loudly in a chain of associations; Thomas finds that he cannot, after all, help being a little impressed. Starting with ponies that are too small and a ride consisting of being led once by a stable girl around the paddock, Gabby manages to bring the conversation quite naturally around to jockeys, wagers, and *the atmosphere of gambling that prevails at the races*. Thomas laughs a little to himself. He's in the back again, between Bella and Rosa, the light-blue women with dark hair and sunglasses. Bella gives a slight laugh, perhaps amused by the same thing as Thomas, perhaps not. Perhaps she is just laughing at nothing in particular, as she has been doing lately. Thomas looks at the pebbly material in her suit. *Wool georgette*: that is what the material is called. Rosa's new dress is of thin cotton, and that along with the fact that it is sleeveless, makes you think that now Rosa is the one who is overdressed and Bella the one who is wearing warm, comfortable traveling clothes. It has grown quite cold, although there is practically no wind. But the air is slightly raw, it may even be that a touch of autumn is already in the air.

Later, as they stand on deck giving a final look at Sweden, Rosa has to get a cardigan, and while she is gone, a certain photograph is taken at a railing below the captain's bridge. Then, wearing the cardigan, Rosa will fall asleep on the sundeck, which is empty except for her.

Rosa is also laughing now, in the taxi, like Bella. But Bella laughs more, and gradually Rosa falls silent. Then they are back at the harbor. Walk from the taxi and go on board.

"Well, Thomas," says Bella in the restaurant. "What did you like best?"

Thomas's mouth is full of food, sausage and bread. Isabella is smoking and sipping a glass of wine. Rosa is drinking water. Gabby orders coffee, strong black coffee. He rewinds the film in his camera. There it is now, inside the black box, a certain photograph, the last shot on the roll. Thomas is still a little dazed by the flash, which went off because it suddenly grew so dark, right in the middle of the day.

"Calm." Rosa looks out over the sea, "I think I'll go and sit in the sun."

"It's gone in," says Thomas, but Rosa smiles faintly and says that the sun usually comes out as soon as she goes outside.

"I have that effect on the weather, Thomas." Rosa gets up and leaves. Thomas plays with a matchbox. Safe at sea, it reads on one side, *Navigare necesse est* on the other, but he makes an effort to keep the Safe-at-sea side in sight, so that Gabby will not see the other side and start mispronouncing Latin again. Gabby is drinking coffee out of a large mug.

Bella leans back and blows smoke through her nostrils. She says that she does not ever want to go back home. "I'd like to live out of my suitcase. A vagabond life. From life to life to life." Bella's suitcase falls over. They do not have cabins on their return journey but have assembled their luggage around them at the table. All three of them look at the suitcase. It is so round, not the usual shape of a suitcase, in any case crammed full for a longer trip than a simple ride across to Umeå.

"Damned shame he got there first." Gabby holds the camera

up to his face and looks at Bella through it.

"Who?" asks Bella with a laugh.

"Mister Jazz." Gabby presses the button. Clicks. "Only a joke." He grins his lupine grin and puts the camera down on the table.

"The roll of film is finished," says Thomas, because it is.

They enjoy his remark. At least Bella does. She finds everything amusing. Thomas sees: Bella is no longer on the ferry from Umeå. She's crossing the Atlantic, and Thomas knows it and knows as well that he is not with her. She is going out into the world, and he is on his way home to his models, attaching wings to the bodies of miniature fighter planes with epoxy glue, painting the parts in camouflage colors. Gabby smiles and is pleased that they are all enjoying what he has to offer. He does not mean merely the wine in Bella's glass but the trip, in general, the light-blue suit, two pounds of Gold Blend coffee, and English licorice. He clicks the camera to record the event but only as a joke, because the film has already come to an end.

Thomas is embarrassed. He thinks that Isabella is being silly. He regrets letting himself be photographed just now, and he is sorry that he grinned in that way that will make him blush later, when he sees the snapshot. He gets up and leaves the restaurant. Not many people are on board today. No young people with bottles of beer, no girl twisting her hands in the air as if she were dog-paddling. Nor does he have any sense of the roar of the sea up on the top deck. It is almost dead calm. The sun comes out for a while, then disappears behind the clouds again, and everything is gray.

Below Thomas, in a white chair, is Rosa. She is wearing her sunglasses. Her head has fallen slightly back and to one side.

She has propped her legs on another chair. All the chairs are empty—Rosa is the only person on the sundeck. Thomas waves. Rosa does not see. She sees nothing. She is asleep.

Thomas, in sharp outline. His white T-shirt glows. Sharp, individual, against a backdrop of gray-blue sky. Isolated, all by himself. Thomas the Traveler. Thomas the Lone Traveler.

The last happening on the trip to Sweden is Gabby's turning into a gas station to fill up the car. They are roughly an hour away from the summer paradise, the gas station is perfectly ordinary, and they had no intention of stopping to have the car washed. The car is not particularly dirty, but for the last few hours Bella has laughed at every single thing Gabby has said, and so, for that matter, have Rosa and Thomas, though they have said much less, since both are tired and slept most of the way. Then Bella notices the huge brushes in the automatic car wash and thinks that it looks like a lot of fun. She would really like to try it. So what happens is that Gabby and Bella sit in the car while it goes through the car wash twice, out of curiosity and a desire for adventure. Thomas doesn't care, he is merely dazed, like Rosa, when they are made to get out because Bella and Gabby—who can see himself offering this, too, if that is what she wants—want to drive alone through the rotating brushes and the lather, with water spurting from several directions at once.

At that moment, because he is tired and only interested in getting home as quickly as possible, Thomas realizes why Bella has dyed her hair: not because she wants to be a brunette, but because she wants to hide what she really is—blonde, of the dumb-blonde variety, the kind who make up the majority of blondes. What she does not understand, because she is so dumb, is that her dumb-blondness is such that no hair dye in the world can get rid of it.

Rosa and Thomas are left standing by the gas pumps while Gabby and Bella drive in under the brushes and the glass doors close behind them, the scene as pathetic and unreal as it seems when described afterward. What are Rosa and Thomas supposed to do while they wait?

"Come on, Thomas," says Rosa after they have kicked at the sand near the pumps for a while. "Let's go and wait in the café. No point in standing around here."

Thomas and Rosa go together to the bar next to the gas station, across from the modern automatic car wash. Rosa orders coffee, Thomas Coca-Cola, although he doesn't really want it. They choose a table that faces the road. The automatic record-player is on, playing that song, the same song heard several times at various places during the trip:

Help, I need somebody
Help, not just anybody

"*You can't do that,*" Rosa says abruptly. It takes Thomas a moment to realize that she is talking about the brushes and the carwash. "It can be dangerous."

"How, dangerous?"

But Rosa can't really explain. Thomas would have been relieved if she could have answered, because he becomes aware the next moment that, using his know-it-all voice, he will have to point out that if water gets inside the car, the interior is ruined and the gas-station owner will be liable for damages because he allowed the driver and a passenger to stay in the car during the procedure, which is forbidden.

Furthermore, Gabby gave the gas-station man some money, and that is even worse, it's totally illegal. Or if the gas station refuses to pay up, you might get reimbursed by your car insurance. Thomas knows about car insurance mainly from the LIFE game that is called TRIUMPH in Swedish. *Graduate, income 2,400.* And the next square: *If you take out car insurance, pay 2,000.*

"Yes, yes, Thomas." Rosa's gaze flickers around the café. People look at her, too, because she is beautiful. Thomas thinks that Rosa is almost as beautiful as Bella, in some ways but Rosa is nicer to be with because she is more restrained, doesn't talk so loudly, and most of all, she doesn't have that laugh or say things that make you suddenly see through her so easily to discover the dumb blonde.

Then Rosa says that she doesn't know a thing about cars. "Yes, yes, Thomas. I know nothing about those things. Are you very interested in cars?"

"I know nothing about cars," says Thomas, looking Rosa straight in the eye.

Rosa laughs. Suddenly she seems a little embarrassed. Thomas has taken the straw out of his glass and squeezes it in the middle so that it flattens out and snaps. Cars drive past on the highway. Thomas goes to the counter to get another straw. He pours some more coffee for Rosa from the pot on the hot plate near the cash register.

Rosa goes on talking. "Look at the highway, Thomas. I love highways.

"A moment like this, Thomas. Exactly the kind of moment you want to include in your memoirs."

Thomas shrugs. What does *memoirs* mean?

"What's memoirs?" says Thomas. But Rosa just laughs,

because her comment was intended to be ironic, and she holds out her hands across the table.

Someone puts that record on again.

When I was young and so much younger than today
I never needed anybody's help in any way
Help me if you can I'm feeling down
And I do appreciate your being around
Help me get my feet back on the ground
Won't you please help me . . . .

Rosa's hands are rough and brown. Darker than her arms, or perhaps the pale pink nail polish and the light-blue dress and the white cardigan seem to accentuate the darkness, so that it seems even darker. Her nails are not as long as Bella's, but they are also carefully tended, even at the tips. Rosa's fingers are drumming although the music has stopped. Then Rosa looks straight at Thomas and says something unbelievable. She says, "You're an incredibly nice little boy, Thomas."

Thomas sits for a while in astonishment. He is disconcerted, forgetting his intention not to drink any more Coca-Cola and emptying the glass in one long gulp, then setting it back on the table. He shakes his head slowly, unable to get out a single word.

For no. He is not a nice little boy. He is not "nice." He is . . . . Thomas thinks very hard and, in this situation, he knows now what he is: He is the boy who started winning at TRIUMPH by staking all his possessions—his money, his property, the car with the plastic pegs that were his family—on one number, the highest number, number ten, and spinning the Wheel of Fortune, then ten came up, every time the number ten inexplicably came up again, increasing his assets tenfold. Renée was unable to do better although she was very rich and independent in the Millionaire's Mansion, where, as usual, she had arrived long before he did. But it was the boy who was Thomas who became the VIP and won the game.

With mixed feelings, Thomas was not one hundred percent easy about suddenly being the constant winner. At once he had felt involved. Now it was he who was affecting others. There was a great difference between being the person having an effect and some poor innocent always losing, walking into a hornet's nest, losing the trolling spoon, being treated badly and unfairly, having stupid things done to him, and able only to complain and feel sorry for himself more or less demonstratively.

Thomas reaches hands across the table to lay his hands beside Rosa's. He grasps Rosa's hands and enfolds Rosa's hands in his. He looks up at Rosa, straight into her dark eyes. Of course he blushes, but not until later, the next second, after Rosa has pulled her hands roughly out of his and picked up her handbag from the table, put it on her lap, opened it, and started a frenzied search through it as if rummaging for something she really needs. She finds a towelette. Tears off the wrapping, unfolds the tissue, which is folded into a very small square, and starts wiping her hands. Then she glances over at the car wash and speaks in perfectly ordinary voice. "They must have done it twice." She crumples the tissue into a little ball and puts it into the ashtray. A gray ball. Ash gray.

"I have to go to the ladies' room, Thomas. Do you want some ice cream?"

Much later in Bella's studio, Bella and Rosa will be amused and amazed at Thomas because of this incident. One of the last times they are up there, just the two of them, in the studio. Rosa has told Bella what in her words is to become *the little incident at the gas-station café on the highway*, not in minute detail but enough to give Bella a clear picture of what happened. Not maliciously, either, but more as an example of what a special little person Thomas is, the specialness not immediately obvious to the naked eye. How little we know about each other, about our own children. With hair all around them. For the last thing Bella and Rosa do together in the summer paradise is to cut each other's hair. The bouffant style has gone out of fashion. They noticed it recently, when they were in Sweden.

"He's an incredible little boy, that Thomas," Rosa will say, and Thomas will be eavesdropping behind the wall. "He has a great many sides to him. A small, not terribly, but just a tiny bit, how can I put it, a little *wolf in sheep's clothing*."

Bella, of course, cannot believe her ears. "Did he really?" Though later she will ponder a little and say that after all, it's not totally inconceivable. "It's just that I never thought about him in that way."

Then they will stop talking about Thomas and talk about other things. All plans, which Rosa is full of at the time, plans for another life. Thomas will go out. It's a fine day, so why is he indoors eavesdropping on others?

But perhaps Bella looks at Thomas differently from then on. Perhaps she begins to discover the wolf in him. Just as, a few weeks earlier, at the gas station by the highway, somewhere in the middle of nowhere halfway between Sweden, the sea, and the summer paradise, he suddenly saw what he called the dumb blonde. That notion had sunk in, could not be erased, no hair dye could hide it.

"Your hair's quite fair at the roots," says Rosa, who is cutting Bella's hair in Bella's studio.

"Yes. I color it."

"So you're a blonde, Bella. Really."

Evening, night: A figure is standing in the doorway. Not Viviann, because she does not exist. Thomas has grown. He knows Viviann is only a figment of his imagination, one of many. This is reality. Thomas screws up his eyes.

"Hi, Only Child. Are you asleep?" Bella will say. Thomas does not reply. But his silence will not stop Bella.

"We must have a talk.

"I'm going to tell you everything now. I want you to listen, Thomas.

"Thomas, dear. Wake up. We must have a talk."

Thomas turns over on his stomach and buries his face in the comforter, grunting in a way he believes is usual for him when he is fast asleep.

"All right, don't, Thomas," says Bella and leaves.

As if they have both suddenly come to some realization. Perhaps very soon—tomorrow, maybe, or in a few days—they will enter into . . . what could you call it? You have to put it this way, it's the only way you can say it: the good life, the rest of time. But they won't be doing it together. Of course this is not an insight that is voiced. Of course it comes with hindsight. It is only much later that Thomas realizes that all the time in the summer paradise he knew, and only he knew, that Bella would not come back after she and Rosa caused a scandal by running away together out into the world at the end of the summer of 1965.

And the other story, *The Wolf and the Blonde*, the story that was barely noticed, that story would never be told.

Nothing would come of it. Thomas is screwing up his eyes tightly although she left the room long ago.

"Don't, then," says Bella once more, before she leaves his room. "Don't, then." Slowly, slowly she goes over to the door, as if waiting for him to call her back. To say something.

But he does not speak. And she goes. He hears her leaving the white villa, although it is the middle of the night and dark and Rosa is asleep. He peers through a corner of the curtain. She is smoking down in the yard. She is looking up at his window. Is she? Whatever. She does not see him. He is hiding in the dark behind the drawn curtains.

Bella comes in again and goes to Rosa, who is sleeping in the bedroom. "I must go NOW."

"I'm coming with you," says Rosa, dazed but without any emotion. It is very simple. That, too, is a possible version of what happened.

Thomas has left the café. He sits on the steps and draws the smell of gas into his lungs. The brushes are still rumbling away behind the closed doors of the car wash, hot, damp steam seeping out through the crack under the door. Rosa's probably right. Bella and Gabby are a little mad. How long have they been? Three or four times "Help," and that's not a long song. Ten minutes? Rosa comes out holding an ice-cream cone in each hand. Thomas says he doesn't want any. Rosa sits down beside him on the steps.

"If you don't want it," says Rosa, "I suppose I'll have to eat both. To be on the safe side, I got my favorite flavors. Chocolate and pistachio. Can you hold this one while I eat the other?"

She hands Thomas the chocolate cone. She has put on

her sunglasses. A wave of something washes over Thomas. Alcohol. She has been to the ladies room and freshened up, had a snort, and now she is pretending that she didn't, while earlier on the trip she made a great show every time she took her flask out of her handbag, a snort because we're on our way, a snort for Sweden, *a snort for the ponies, a snort for Gold Blend, such good coffee*. Thomas holds the cone. Fortunately the ice cream is frozen fairly solid, so it doesn't start melting right away. As Thomas holds the ice cream, he looks across at the highway. Not because he cares about cars but because he is suddenly indescribably ashamed of the way he took hold of Rosa's hands just now in the café. Rosa licks her ice cream, pretending that nothing has happened.

At the same time it is an unbelievable scene. Rosa and Thomas on the steps of a gas station somewhere in the middle of nowhere, halfway between Sweden, the sea, and the summer paradise, the otherwise rather cool summer air thick with hot steam from an aromatic car wash, Rosa in a light-blue dress and a white cardigan, a green ice cream cone in her hand. Thomas screwing up his eyes although the sun's gone in, chocolate ice cream slowly melting in his hand. He does not eat it. He does not want it. It is not his, it is Rosa's. A brown trickle runs over his fingers, so that he has to change hands and lick his fingers clean.

"Want a tissue?" says Rosa.

Thomas shakes his head.

The scene ought to be photographed, for despite everything Rosa is beautiful and Thomas looks as if he were her son. Seeing Rosa and Thomas sitting there on the steps of the gas station, if you were a stranger who did not know them, you would think, What are they doing there, what are they waiting for? Why won't that little boy who looks so nice eat his ice cream? It is melting in his hand.

Rosa gets her camera out of her handbag. It actually seems as if Rosa happened to think of it herself. All this. These moments, which ought not to be included in your memoirs. How absurd, but just because of that perhaps, how beautiful they are.

A moment ago she had been in the café with Thomas, sipping at a cup of coffee and saying, This is just the kind of moment you want in your memoirs, at the time meaning it ironically, while at the same time an uncanny feeling has been growing inside. *On second thought*. But she has no plans for afterthoughts. In peace and quiet she will sit there chattering away until the worst has passed, until a new moment appears for her to be in.

But Thomas does not want to chat. She is alone with her chatter. What is she to do with it?

She has been to the ladies room and taken a great gulp from her flask. There, in the ladies' room in front of the mirror, she has not been able to stop her thoughts after all. They have poured out like water from the tap where she has dipped almost her entire face *to cool off*.

Then she saw herself in the mirror, made herself see. Unlike Bella, the sight of herself in a mirror does not calm Rosa down. Not because she is less beautiful, but because she looks at herself in a different way when she looks in the mirror. Not as if to find confirmation of something she already knows but to search for something she has always known is not there. Something that ought to be written on her nose as it is on her daughter Renée. For that reason she loves her daughter Renée in a way that is different from the way she loves Nina

Angel. But she does not find it. Does not find IT. So her face is a place, only one of the places, where her anxiety begins. Rosa has slapped her cheeks three times. Left cheek, right cheek, left cheek. THERE—now she is normal again. Treated her throat with breath spray, gone back to the bar and bought ice cream cones at the counter. Not seen Thomas. Left the bar. Thomas is on the steps. Sat down by Thomas. Eaten the ice cream. Had an idea. Rummaged in her bag for the camera.

A stranger approaches. He has filled up his gas tank and has come to pay. In a jiffy Rosa has handed him the camera and asked him to take a photograph. "Of Thomas and me," she says putting her arm around Thomas. "This is Thomas." The stranger takes the camera, zooms in on Thomas and Rosa, and clicks. Thomas says nothing. In contrast to Rosa, he knows the photograph will never be developed because the film is already full and the last photograph on the film is called Family on Board. It is the same camera. Rosa took it out of the car in case it got damaged by the heat and damp in the car wash.

Gabby and Bella drive out of the carwash. They get out of the car, now spanking clean, and they go over to Thomas and Rosa on the steps of the gas station. They look insane—their faces red and sweaty, their hair damp. Gabby's shirt is sticking to his stomach and chest.

Bella is just as exhilarated as before. She cries out that she is boiling. It was so hot in there, at least over a hundred degrees.

"What did I tell you?" Thomas mumbles. Bella ruffles his hair and takes the ice cream cone melting away in his hand, for Rosa has finished the first one but appears to have quite forgotten the second.

"It's Rosa's."

"You have it." Rosa lights a cigarette and heads for the car.

Gabby and Rosa head for the car. This is what it looks like. Rosa is walking slightly ahead of Gabby. She flings down her cigarette after only a few puffs, then pulls her white cardigan more tightly around her, shuddering. If this had been an ordinary situation, Thomas would also have seen the following: Rosa flinging away her cigarette. It lands in a puddle and starts burning, the whole gas station explodes, and Rosa and Bella and Thomas and Gabby are thrown into the nearest ditch, Gabby with his arm protectively around all three of them, for he is the man among them, and it would not be a movie about what can happen when you are careless with fire but an adventure tale with Catastrophe and Chaos. And so on, in Thomas's imagination. But this is not an ordinary situation, and Thomas is not thinking anything. He is protected by Bella again. Bella is walking beside him. Thomas is protected by Bella's high spirits and Bella's exhilaration, and anyhow he cannot help being drawn into it. Before he knows where he is, he is smiling at Bella's silly descriptions. A little way ahead of them, Gabby catches up with Rosa and puts his arm around her. She shakes herself slightly, but not so hard that Gabby's arm might drop off her shoulders. They are talking to each other, quietly, so that should they be listening, Thomas and Bella won't hear what they're saying. But Gabby and Rosa are not whispering about Bella and Thomas or anything like that. Their quiet talk is simply exactly what it looks like. A sign that there is harmony, a certain fellowship after all, in all climates. Bella does not see it or else she does not take much notice of it.

"We had it done twice." Bella is the only one still in the car wash and, on the whole, still traveling. All the others are tired and have had enough, on their way home. "It really was quite an experience, Thomas. Like being under water or something."

They get back into the car, Rosa and Gabby in front, Bella and Thomas in the back. The doors slam and Bella waves to the gas-station staff Gabby has bribed because you are not allowed to stay in the car while it's being washed.

"There has to be some adventure in every life," Gabby might say if he had not suddenly been overcome by exhaustion himself. Like after a really good dinner. The sweat dries, Gabby scratches, he itches. His shirt is made of polyester, not the best material to absorb sweat. Gabby's exhaustion settles heavily over the car.

Rosa falls asleep. Thomas looks out the window. Bella talks and laughs for a while, until she falls silent in the middle of a sentence because she has also fallen asleep. It is quiet. Only the engine hums.

Later Thomas will, of course, think that he had no part in that scene. No one he knows—mothers, fathers, kids—would ever do anything like staying in the car while it goes through the car wash and afterwards say that it really was quite an experience. So he never tells anyone about it, neither Kayus nor Ann-Christine and Johan Wikblad, who otherwise will share unforgettable episodes from the trip, stories about ponies, cake, a guest house called The Arrow.

Bella and Rosa sleep almost all the way home. Thomas is wide awake. Bella sleeps with her mouth open, snoring slightly. Audibly. Thomas tries to nudge her discreetly to get her to stop. Gabby says nothing. He drums his fingers on the wheel at regular intervals and drives faster and faster. The drumming gets more furious the faster they go. Thomas thinks it is like Renée when she is sailing. And it does not matter if Bella's snores are heard or not, because Gabby is lost in his own world, far away in speed and freedom.

Thomas stops nudging Bella and makes the most of an unguarded moment to take a peek at the model fighter planes from Sweden in the plastic bag at his feet. He covertly studies the lids of the boxes. In Sweden he had promised himself that he would not even look at them because he is not interested. But he does anyway. The planes look interesting. When Gabby suddenly addresses him from the front seat, he starts like a thief caught red-handed, although they are his models, presents from Gabby. He swiftly shuffles the plastic bag back on to the floor of the car.

"If I could do it all over again and pick something to be when I grow up," says Gabby. "Then I'd be, do you know what I'd be, Thomas? I'd be a race-car driver."

"Mmm," says Thomas.

"What are you going to be when you grow up, Thomas? Are you going to be a race-car driver?"

A very audible gurgle comes from Bella's throat. Thomas leans forward so he can secretly nudge Bella with one hand and, although he had not considered answering Gabby's question, he ends up with his head almost between the front seats, so he has to answer.

"I don't think so."

"What are you going to be then?"

"I don't know," says Thomas. "I haven't thought about it."

Thomas leans back again, Gabby seems to press the accelerator almost down to the floor and passes at least three cars one after another in a way Thomas knows is really dangerous and which Kayus usually calls hooliganism: *Somebody should point out to these hooligans that if everyone drove the way they do, traffic would be utter chaos.* Thomas holds on to the door handle. Bella's head falls against his shoulder. Now almost her entire weight is resting against him. Thomas has to hold really hard on to the door handle to prevent their tumbling together. Bella smells of sweat, but also faintly of "Blue Grass." It actually is "Blue Grass." She bought some in Sweden.

"'Blue Grass.' I've been searching everywhere for it, Rosa."

"Blue Grass:" The scent Kayus used to tease her about. That it was just like her. Kind of topsy-turvy, since grass is green, and not blue, as the vial claims. "But to Bella," Kayus said to Thomas. "To Bella grass is blue if she says it's blue." Several times—in the summer paradise, in the city a long time ago. Thomas and Kayus had been standing watching Bella at a distance; they were in the far corner of the courtyard, Kayus in his overcoat, briefcase in hand, for he had come from work and had just got off the bus at the stop where Thomas had been waiting for him, perched on the sanitation department's sand container for icy winter roads. Paul Anka was on the turntable, thundering out "D-i-a-n-a" through the open balcony door of their third-floor apartment, the top floor in this new block by this courtyard. Bella was leaning against the gray balcony railing, humming and smoking, on the whole in everyone's field of vision. Though she suddenly turned her head as if she could feel she was being watched by somebody, and then she saw who was standing in the corner of the courtyard looking at her. She started waving eagerly. More excitedly than was necessary, maybe, perhaps with a little embarrassment in her way of immediately stubbing out her cigarette in the dark soil of the window box. She was always saying she was going to plant flowers in the spring, but nothing ever came of it because the spring went by so quickly, summer came, and the meadows were full of flowers in your own summer paradise.

Goes in. Turns down the music, closing the door behind her. Nevertheless, she gave a slight impression of being caught red-handed. As if surprised at doing something secret and private.

When Thomas and Kayus came up to the apartment only a few minutes later, they encountered a different person, a cool, smiling, dinner-is-ready person coming out of the silence of the apartment. But the air was thick with "Blue Grass." Kayus sniffed again and again said what he'd said to Thomas in the courtyard. That it was like her, kind of topsy-turvy. . . and so on. As if that were enough. As if that were some kind of explanation. Of something incomprehensible, provocative, characteristic of Bella. But not enormously important. At least, not as important as jazz and family life three floors up above a courtyard.

Yet Thomas knew quite early on: It was not enough. "Blue Grass." That was a name for *all kinds of stuff*. And all kinds of things—real, concrete things.

Thomas looks out the car window and is suddenly angry with Kayus because Kayus does not see it. Somehow seems to refuse to see it. Is content to say "Blue Grass." Music, for instance. When there's other kinds of music. *When the world is full of music*. Different kinds of music. Chet Baker. Bill Evans, and Paul Anka. And lots of other kinds. Those popular songs on the car radio all through their trip: that kind of music, too. And lots of other kinds, lots. Not Blue Grass. All kinds of other, real, concrete things.

"All kinds of things," as she herself said. "I like *all kinds*."

"I'm an omnivore," as someone else had said. Fingers drumming on the wheel. Humming a song. "Two of a Kind. Two of a Kind."

Thomas's shoulder grows numb under the weight of Bella's head and body. But he does not mind any longer. He suddenly has a feeling of PANIC. For this: If she straightens up and takes the weight off him, she will be gone forever. For all time, for ever and ever. Who will he be then, Thomas, if the weight of Isabella is taken off him? He has no idea. A lightweight, but so light that he will hover in the air. A year or two ago Gabby and Rosa and Renée and Nina gave him a Chinese kite for his birthday, and he let go of the line by mistake. The kite hovered freely in the air for a while . . . it looked fine, but then it got caught in a tree—you know, same old story, it was so funny. There was no way to climb up to get it back, it was stuck so high up in the branches, and there it stayed until it fell down, broken and ragged, during a rainstorm.

"If I may offer you some good advice," says Gabby at the wheel, and although only a few seconds have gone by since his previous silly remark, it feels almost safe to hear Gabby again, anyhow better than the kind of thoughts that have been going through his mind. "I think you should seriously consider a career as a race-car driver. There's nothing as marvelous as high speed and freedom."

"Yes," says Thomas.

"I suppose your room in town is full of little cars, Thomas?"

"Yes," lies Thomas.

"Which do you like best, Thomas? I mean, which kind of car?"

Rosa wakes up suddenly. She winds the window halfway down in exactly the way Bella is not allowed to do in Kayus's Austin Mini, because Thomas is sensitive and ends up in the draft in the back. Rosa laughs and tells Gabby to stop asking silly questions for which there is no answer. She turns around and smiles at Thomas, and Thomas smiles back. Then she turns back again and looks at the road and all the cars ahead of them. She asks Gabby whether they shouldn't get one like that now, "Why don't we get that red one, d'you think, that Opel?" and that one and that one and that one. Gabby says, "Of course," pressing down even harder on the accelerator, and they rush past one car after another. "Why don't we see how much this one can stand?" Gabby asks in his turn. They pass that one, too, and Rosa is delighted, opens her handbag, takes out her flask and says, A snort for the highway, and Gabby says, "Now, now, now," in a feigned stern voice, and Rosa takes another snort and says, "Oh, what a lovely burning sensation in my throat." Thomas sits in the back with the draft blowing in his face and Bella's hair blowing into his mouth, but he laughs too. He can't help it. They're all in a good mood. Rosa and Gabby are so funny together. He has never seen them like this before. Like two playmates or something, so alike, sort of like brother and sister. Suddenly he has the feeling that he and Bella are Renée and Nina in the back of a white angel driving right across the American continent and seeing marvelous things. As Rosa once said, "America's big, Bella, so big."

Finally the car swooshes into the summer paradise at fifty miles an hour, which is a high speed for the narrow road. Gabby honks the horn and parks on the gravel patch, slightly crookedly, not even driving into the garage. Rosa puts the flask back into her bag and swings the rearview mirror in her direction, straightens her hair, and wipes the remains of ice cream from the corners of her mouth.

Bella wakes up and looks around in a daze.

"Are we home already?" she says, though it's not a question, for you can hear she knows the answer. Thomas nods. Then there is no more. They collect their suitcases and shopping bags containing Gold Blend coffee, the model fighter planes, "Blue Grass," the postcards they have never sent, all kinds of stuff. They get out of the car.

"Corgi," Thomas says to Gabby before they separate. He's remembered the advertisements in his Donald Duck comics.

"The cars," he lies. "At home in my room in town."

"I'm so tired, Thomas, I could hibernate."

Bella's standing in the big room, her suitcase and all the plastic bags in her hands, sunglasses on, and wearing her new clothes. She looks somehow alien among all the familiar furniture and things. As if she did not belong. Or perhaps it is just because usually she almost always wears yellow?

"It's the middle of the summer," says Thomas. "You hibernate in the winter."

"But I could hibernate NOW."

Bella drops her suitcase and the plastic bags on to the floor all at once. She goes over to the sideboard, takes off her sunglasses, and makes a face at the mirror. Then she vanishes into the bedroom and comes back in her familiar robe, just as if she were on her way to the beach. But she isn't. She goes out into the attic entry, and Thomas hears footsteps on the stairs and the sound of the door slamming. Then footsteps and voices and a door slamming again. The same door, the studio door, since there is no other door up in the attic. Footsteps again, then shortly after that, Thomas sees Kayus for the first time after the trip to Sweden. He is standing in the doorway to Thomas's room, holding a detective story.

"How was it? Had a good time?"

Thomas is taking two fighter-plane models out of a plastic bag.

"I had a ride on a pony that stopped and crapped."

"You had a ride? But you can't ride."

Thomas opens one of the model sets and studies the parts and the instructions. It does not take long to see that at least one of them is far too easy for someone with his experience and for his age group.

"Bella and Rosa and Gabby, then? What did they do? Did they go riding as well?"

"There was a storm when we crossed. I stood on the top deck. Rosa was seasick. I wasn't seasick at all."

"Bella and Gabby, then? Were they seasick?"

"Not at all. They've got nerves of steel."

"Listen, Thomas. I suppose you can manage with Bella for a week or two?"

"Listen Thomas." Thomas is on his way out. Kayus's voice catches up with him at the kitchen door. Nails him to the kitchen floor, his hand on the door handle.

"The two of you."

"What do you mean?"

"I'm going fishing in Lapland."

"Who with?"

"A friend at work. He phoned yesterday."

"We haven't got a phone."

"Thomas . . . I was in town. I told you I had to work. Don't you remember?"

"I'm coming with you." Thomas doesn't know why he says that. It comes automatically.

"There are mosquitoes," says Kayus. "Mosquitoes are quite different in Lapland. Worse than here."

"Mosquitoes don't like my skin. I don't even have to use mosquito repellent."

"There's not much to do there. You'd probably have much more fun here. With Renée and all the children."

Renée and all the children. Thomas is outside.

Sitting in the privy, on the lid, and eventually Kayus drives out of the yard. Not until the car has vanished along the track does Thomas get up and leave the sanctuary.

"But if you really want to," Kayus said, walking through the kitchen, "then of course you can come too. But I think you'd prefer to stay here." The paralysis disappeared. Thomas ran out before Kayus had time to give him a hug.

Thomas goes across the Johanssons' yard. It is quite empty, but the outside door is open, so the Johanssons must be home. For a moment Thomas considers going inside, but then he changes his mind. He would not be able to cope with Erkki Johansson. Erkki Johansson is pretty much okay, but not just now, Thomas thinks, feeling noble at expressing his sympathy for Erkki Johansson in this way. He slants across May Johansson's bit of beach, where their biggest rug is drying on the rock, big stones holding down each of the four corners, so the wind won't catch it. Thomas kicks a stone on one of the top corners of the rug, and the stone rolls away toward the stone in the other top corner, knocking it away like in billiards and in what follows, Thomas thinks he will give one of the model sets to Erkki Johansson, for it's an appropriate degree of difficulty for an eight-year-old. He sees in front of him Erkki Johansson's expression as a gift is handed over, the way Erkki Johansson goes haywire over Thomas's kindness, then he goes into the Johanssons' sauna.

"Look, Thomas. What's new, Thomas?"

Nina and Maggi are lying on the beds in the changing room, looking through magazines, and a transistor radio is playing, though not loudly because it's a talk program. Nina spots Thomas and says something else, but Thomas isn't listening because what he is staring at is a stranger, a girl with fairly short brown hair weirdly fluffed up on her head. She is lying on the magazines on the floor, and it takes at least a minute before Thomas realizes that the girl is Renée.

"Got a smoke?" she says to Nina and Maggi, but she's looking at Thomas. "I'm dying for one."

"Shut up, kid," says Nina. "Don't act tough."

"Piss off." Renée tugs at her hair, but it is so short that she cannot make the strand she is pulling reach her mouth, however much she tries. She starts fooling around with the radio instead and turns the volume up until it makes a horrible racket.

"Ha, ha," says Thomas, but his voice is drowned by the noise from the radio. He leaves.

A strange boat is moored at the Johanssons' and Gabby's and Rosa's joint breakwater. An ordinary fishing boat with a tarpaulin covering the prow. A chug-chug engine that has to be started with a handle. Pusu Johansson is in the boat trying to get the engine going. He sees Thomas.

"Well, Thomas. What do you think of this angel?"

"She's called Selma." Thomas reads the wooden plaque nailed between the portholes. "Did you buy it?"

"I've borrowed it from the cousins. As soon as the summer warms up a little, we'll be off on a long trip."

Johan Wikblad has glued his house onto a panel of yellow plywood. He has made a miniature model—that is, cut the parts out of balsa wood and stuck them together with epoxy, after his own plans; it's light brown and looks rather fragile, but when you touch it—picking it up, for instance, by the perfectly symmetrical square roof—you can feel how solid it really is. Johan Wikblad pokes at the little doors, which actually move. "You go in here," he says, demonstrating, "and out here. Here's the kitchen, with the possibility of adding a sauna when I'm rich."

"It's going to be a yellow house," says Johan Wikblad. "A yellow house with white corners and a green roof. And I'm going to build a garage next to it. A garage will be a good thing to have when I get a car." Johan Wikblad points at an empty space on the panel.

"When are you going to build it?" says Thomas.

"As soon as possible. I'll go to a builder to get estimates. Then I'll buy the red cottage. Pull it down. And build."

Thomas glances at Ann-Christine. She is looking at the model house with large, calm eyes. She does not say what she always said earlier in the summer. She doesn't say anything else, either.

Evening comes. Johan Wikblad makes an omelette. Thomas, Ann-Christine, and Johan eat. Afterward Johan Wikblad gets out the pack of cards, and they play Racing Demon. Ann-Christine loses and Thomas wins several times running. Then Johan Wikblad teaches Thomas the basic principles of the slide rule, and Ann-Christine sews together the parts of the fisherman's sweater she has now finished, then she makes Johan Wikblad try it on. It fits. It is seven-thirty, eight. Thomas looks at Johan Wikblad's atlas, then all three of them go for an evening walk. Ann-Christine and Johan Wikblad hand in hand along the forest road, Thomas strolling just behind, slowly falling farther and farther behind until, unnoticed, turns off toward the Rotwoods. It's silent and empty there.

May Johansson comes along the road with the basket in which she gathers wild mushrooms. She does not see Thomas, either. But that may be because Thomas is pressing himself down into the earth, anxious not to be seen as May Johansson passes.

After the trip to Sweden, Gabby and Rosa are invisible for several days. Renée, too, has vanished. They say that she is at a race organized by another sailing club and *is billeted there*. But no one knows for sure. GOOF lies upside down on the boat trailer on May Johansson's patch of grass all the time, bits of leaves and other stuff blowing down on it from the trees. Green boomerang-shaped seed cases from May Johansson's maple. May Johansson tells Erkki and Thomas that when she was a child, they wet the boomerang ends with spit, stuck them on their noses, and then played a game called Long Green Nose. Erkki's nose falls off almost immediately, and Thomas's stays on for at the most a minute or two. He feels like an idiot. For a moment, like a sweep of radar, he feels eyes on his skin, on him. He turns around like lightning and looks over at the reeds. No one there. His nose falls off and the feeling goes away.

On the other hand, Nina is there as usual. She and Maggi have more or less taken up residence in the Johanssons' sauna. A third person is with therm, too, not Renée but a boy. One of the boys they met in the clearing above the fire brigade headquarters at Midsummer. His name is Jake, and just whose boyfriend he is, Nina's or Maggi's, has not been decided yet. He has not made up his mind, and Nina and Maggi do their best to hasten his decision. Jake is the kind of kid adults have trouble fathoming out. Not exactly a man, not a James Bond, and not a Don Juan, the name May Johansson used when Gabby was sitting in his James Bond chair with the binoculars or just a drink in his hand on Angel Hill, gazing around and shouting into the summer paradise. "What kind of *Don Juan* does he think he is?" May Johansson said, but she received no answer, because neither Erkki nor Thomas knew what a Don Juan was.

Jake twists his hands around each other so that it looks as if he were dog-paddling. His hair is fairly long. Although his family are almost neighbors to the Johansson cousins, he pretends he doesn't know May Johansson; he never says hello to her, for instance, if they happen to meet on the road. So even if Jake were not what he is—*a boy from the district and not an outsider with fancy city ways*—May Johansson would dislike him intensely and take measures to put an end to all that brooding in the Johanssons' sauna. But as it is, she contents herself with dashing to and fro between the house and the sauna, saying that the radio will have to be turned down.

To his own surprise, it puts Thomas in a really good mood to see May Johansson dash back and forth between house and sauna saying that they must turn down the music. This action is familiar, somehow known. Bilberry time. Thomas takes the bilberry can and goes out into the forest to pick almost a canful, which he takes to May Johansson because the Johanssons are a poor family with a lot of mouths to feed and he himself has been diagnosed as allergic to bilberries.

"These are for you."

"Oh, Thomas."

May Johansson flushes up to her ears, not knowing what to say. She just stands there by the sink in the Johanssons' kitchen holding the can and saying, Oh Thomas. It's all really rather pathetic, because Thomas is suddenly just as embarrassed as she is, and he has to run off to the Rotwoods to collect his wits and be alone for a while to think. But when the Johanssons are having their evening meal and Thomas is waiting for Erkki Johansson out in the yard, the door opens at dessert time and Thomas is called in and given a stool at the end of the Johansson table, and May Johansson produces a plate, cuts a slice of bilberry pie, and dishes it up with a silver cake server.

"Thank you very much, but I'm allergic to bilberries." Thomas hadn't intended keeping that information to himself, but there's been no opportunity to give it before. Both Thomas and May Johansson are so embarrassed again that Thomas can't stay and has to go out.

"A charmer in the making," Ann-Christine from the red cottage teases. "*Charmeur.*"

"Stop it." Thomas glances at Johan Wikblad. Johan Wikblad pays no attention. He gets out the cards, shuffles them, and deals for Racing Demon. He asks Thomas where his dad is. In Lapland, says Thomas.

Bella sleeps for almost two days. When she finally comes fully awake, it is the afternoon and she quickly changes into yellow clothes and walks around the ground floor as usual, while Thomas works on his models in his room. She smokes and fiddles with this and that, does some of the dishes, straightens the shelves a little, gets out her sewing basket to mend socks, turns the light on and off in the big room as if she cannot decide whether the light is needed or not. Even in the middle of the day it is fairly dark and overcast outside. But she never finishes anything, and everything ends with her sitting in the reading corner with her magazines. She leafs through them, humming. What she is humming is not jazz, Thomas notices, certainly not, but one of those popular songs that billowed out of the car radio during their trip to Sweden. She turns the page quickly, almost frantically, in a way Thomas knows means that she's only occupying herself temporarily, while expecting something else to happen. As she reads, she keeps glancing out the window. Furtively, then gradually less and less furtively.

Bella in the reading corner with her magazines, Thomas busy in his room. Time passes, a day, two days, almost three. They are not bored, not at first; they talk all the time. They talk about all kinds of things. About the weather and the winds out in the summer paradise. How it is suddenly almost autumn and the very thought of going swimming makes you feel cold. They don't talk much about the trip to Sweden and what happened during the journey. There is no need. They know; both of them were there.

Thomas tells her about the summer and everything happening outside. Not about the boomerang noses, the bilberries, or May Johansson and stuff like that, but that Huotari's vacation is over and that he has moved back to town, and that Thomas and Erkki helped carry his things up to the road where the buses run. There was a postcard from Lapland in the mailbox, addressed to Thomas personally. He does not mention it to Bella, but he leaves the postcard on the kitchen table in full view. He put it there intending to read it when he has time. He tells her about Maggi's and Nina's boyfriend and about Ann-Christine's fisherman's sweater being the right size for Johan Wikblad.

Bella says "Yes" and glances out the window. Gradually not at all discreetly, and gradually not even glancing, but with her gaze fixed unswervingly on the window. On the third day she stops staying in the same place. She puts the magazine down and starts walking. She walks and walks, stomping through the house from the big room to Thomas's room, through the attic entry to the kitchen or out into the big room. She is longer humming nor fiddling with things, and well, there is no point in disguising it any longer. Where are they? Why don't they show up? Have they gone away somewhere?

But no, you know they haven't. They're almost certainly in their house on the hill. In the evening all their windows are lighted, but they have drawn the curtains.

One afternoon Bella suddenly stops in the middle of Thomas's room and asks straight out what neither of them has dared to say before: "Why don't they come? They're here, aren't they? What are they doing?"

Her tone of voice is fairly mean, almost resigned. A tone of voice Thomas has not heard before. But he is not surprised. It is not that. He feels that he has to answer, that Bella is expecting an answer, especially from him, and for once he will have to say it as it is, make a real effort to word it exactly.

"I don't know," says Thomas. "I've no idea."

Bella says nothing for a while. Then, as if establishing the weather or the temperature outside, she says, "We had fun in Sweden."

But Thomas hears the question mark at the end.

He feels he has to answer that, too. "Yes." They had fun in Sweden. Suddenly he knows he means it.

Bella sits down opposite Thomas at the table.

"Has Kayus gone?"

"Mmmm," says Thomas.

"Where? To Lapland?" But it's obvious she knows.

"Mmmm," says Thomas.

"Oh." She gets up again, takes off her robe, and flings it away so that it lands on Thomas's bed.

"I'm going up to the studio to rest. We can talk later."

She walks through the big room out into the attic entry in her panties and bra. Closes the door behind her.

Thomas stays at his table. He's working on his model.

But more and more frequently he makes his way to the Angels' house. Stands at the foot of the hill, on the gravel patch, the parking space, at dusk. Near Gabby's car. It's parked slightly crookedly. Just as Gabby parked it the day they came back from Sweden and were so tired and exhausted, all of them, that they could not even drive into the garage.

Lights on in the windows. Curtains drawn. Otherwise, it's silent and empty. What are they doing?

Word gets around. Someone has seen someone in the James Bond chair at night, or at some incredible time when only May Johansson is present. Someone has also seen Rosa. Rosa Angel dot dot dot swaying like a pine tree in the otherwise unbroken forest behind her house, the next moment tumbling down the hill. In the middle of the day, in full view.

Though not everyone saw. Only someone who happened to be there.

Rosa Angel, a fallen Angel. Snigger, snigger, as if literally.

"Everything people say they've seen, Bella," Rosa herself will say to Bella in the white villa the very next day. "All the rumors. Well, what can I say? They're true. I've no intention of denying a single one. It's all true, and more. God, Bella, you should know how much of it's true. I did actually fall. It was sort of slippery. I slipped. I thought I was going to die. But I didn't, of course. The proof is that I'm here.

"And one advantage of falling and getting black and blue all over is that you're lucky, you're a little stunned. Then you can think clearly."

To say she is black and blue all over is, of course, an exaggeration. She has a few scrapes on her face. You can only see them if you look very closely.

"I've thought very clearly now, Bella. I'm staying here.

"And for once, I'm going to mean what I say.

"I've come to stay. If you'd like me to, that is."

But all that is not until tomorrow and you do not know it yet.

Thomas is standing below the Angels' house, in the dark. Lights in the windows, nothing stirring in the curtains. Not so much as a flutter. And he thinks the following about angels:

Angels are on the move, restlessly roving around. Some probably live somewhere, even have proper homes and summer places where they hang up billowing curtains at their windows. And draw them.

They say a lot about angels. Angels bring good tidings, promises, and presentiments, touched by something else. They appear. When you least expect them. Then you are pleased, because when you see them, you really do realize that you missed them and needed them all the time.

Angels live in real houses with chimneys where the smoke comes out, with patterned curtains in the windows. In the evenings there are lights behind the curtains so you will know that they are at home.

But they do not come down. Unless they themselves have some reason to.

Other times they leave you in peace.

In peace.

Idiot idiot echoes in the forest. Where you do not go. You do not feel like going.

You fetch your goggles and put on your bathing trunks, stick the snorkel into your mouth, and wade out into the water. It is cold, sixty-five degrees tops. You dive down and disappear into the silent world. There you become Didi. D-di. You idiot. You come up to the surface. You are cold.

"Hi, Didi!" Erkki Johansson gallops across the rock in his cowboy costume. He pulls the gun out of the holster, shoots into the air. *Click, click* it goes.

"Dundedundedundedunde da da," cries Erkki Johansson.

"It's *Bonanza*, Thomas. I am Little Joe."

"Erkki! How many times do I have to tell you not to go swimming without a grown-up with you?" May Johansson is soon on the Johanssons' little rock with her reminders. Despite the fact that Erkki is fully clothed.

"Cowboys don't swim," says Erkki Johansson sullenly, so quietly that only Thomas can hear him. "I am little Joe."

"Come back at once, Erkki Johansson! It's dinner time."

Thomas is left alone on the beach, shivering in his towel.

What has happened to your scientific urge to discover? What has happened to your observations of life on the seabed? When you dive into the silent world you see mud and sea grass. Where is your childish curiosity, which is a condition of progress in all the most objective sciences? What makes you suddenly able to see connections where they do not appear to the naked eye? The leaps of imagination? The moment when reality opens up? Glimmers, like fins on the outer edge of the archipelago? The sudden knowledge that reality is greater than reality. When you *know* that is how the greatest discoveries are made.

He does try. Really makes an effort. But it is not enough. Something more is required.

The urge is required.

URGE. *Someone pulling wet hair between her teeth.*

Yes. She's back. He can't get away from her.

Thomas stands by the Angel house. Kicking gravel, which scatters in the dark. Dull *clonks* when the gravel hits the metal of Gabby's red Plymouth. They must hear it. But no one comes out to find out what the sound is.

Though everything has its natural explanation. Thomas does not really know what is going on behind the drawn curtains. But he will soon learn—in fact, the very next day. Rosa is getting ready to go away. She is going to leave all the old things behind her and start a new life. The game is over.

Gabby has intestinal flu. But he's getting better. The next day he is quite well.

"Must have eaten something that disagreed with me," Gabby said the day they came back from Sweden. He began to feel ill almost right away.

"Which?" Rosa asked with a smile. "Of all the things you stuffed yourself with?"

She drank whisky to ward off the intestinal flu. It helped for three days. She really hasn't caught it.

But Gabby's flu, the whiskey, her own smile. All of a sudden they put a stop to the calm companionship she and Gabby had shared on the trip, and occasionally after other excursions. Everything Thomas saw in the car, the last bit, when Rosa woke up and participated in driving on the highway—that was true. It was mutual understanding.

But all the stuff involving Bella was also true.

Suddenly Gabby's weariness, his having had enough, his feeling ill disgusted Rosa. She had to choose.

How many times does she have to repeat to herself that she must stop playing games? Several times these days. In the James Bond chair, Gabby's chair, on the highest point of the hill at impossible times of the day. And finally she slipped and fell, and that has made her think clearly and decide.

In the morning of the fifth day she gets up and draws back the curtains. She patches herself up, rubs her body all over with suntan oil, picks up the cool bag, sweeps the quilt off the bed, and leaves.

The very next morning Renée is down on the beach carrying sailing things to Gabby's motorboat. GOOF has been lifted right over the railing, ready for departure. Thomas goes closer.

"Do you need any help?"

"It's all done." She gives him a quick look from below her

 new bangs. Her hair is hideous. Everything about her looks different. More childlike, somehow.

"What have you done to your hair?"

"I fell downstairs. It fell out."

"It was better before."

"So what? Now it's like this. Help me with this."

Together they carry duckboards, centerboard, and rudder on board Gabby's boat. Gabby appears near the Johanssons' house. He comes walking across May Johansson's a little bit of beach in his boating clothes. He strides past Thomas on the jetty and ruffles his hair. They are off to the clubhouse. Does Thomas want to come? Thomas shakes his head. Gabby unlocks the engine and starts it. Gas has to be pumped because the engine has been unused for such a long time. Otherwise everything is just as usual. Renée casts off and jumps in. The boat gathers speed, and off they go. Just before they reach the sound, they slow down and put on their black oilskins. The wind is high, and the sea is sure to be running high once they are well offshore.

Thomas and Bella are having breakfast, their eternal breakfast, just as usual. Sitting side by side as they do every morning, facing the door. Bella mixes instant oatmeal with her sour milk. She says she has to lose some weight. She is getting fat. Thomas shakes his head. He hardly knows what the word means. In his eyes Bella's body is as nice as ever.

"It doesn't show yet," says Bella. "But it will later. You get bigger and bigger. In the end, you explode. Whoooosh, Thomas." Bella imitates an explosion.

Thomas is eating crispbread. These are the dog days, and the milk won't set. There's only a slightly thicker layer on the top, while the actual bowlful is runny and inedible. He studies Kayus's postcard on the table. "Mosquitoes and midnight sun! A fantastic experience. We must do this together some time." The picture on the front is of a Lapp in a Lappish tent. Tundra in the background. The snow thick on the tundra. The photograph must have been taken in winter.

Sunlight pours over the kitchen table, the first time for several days.

Footsteps outside, the kitchen door opens. She is standing in the doorway again, Rosa in a sunsuit and sandals. Rosa, with a cool bag hanging from her shoulder, her skin glistening with suntan oil.

And she is lugging a quilt. An enormous quilt.

"You can find quilts like this only in America," she says, stepping onto the dark-blue floor. "It's my American quilt. I usually bring it with me from town every summer. I feel the cold, sort of."

She drops the quilt, leaving it in a heap at her feet.

"And now I'm staying.

"I've come to stay.

"That is, Bella, if you'll have me. Of course."

Thomas and Bella just stare.

Rosa comes closer. She has a Band-Aid on her forehead, a dark bruise on one arm. She is not drunk or anything, she is her usual self.

"It's temporary, of course. Eventually I'm going away. The question is, Bella: Are you coming with me?

"And Thomas. Are you coming, too, Thomas?"

Thomas looks down. He is suddenly shy.

The squares in the crispbread zigzag in Thomas's eyes. A postcard from Lapland crinkles softly in his hand. Meaning yes.

He wants to. He will go. Where to? What to? He still has no idea. But that isn't important. The actual setting, the atmosphere is there. That is what counts to start with.

YES.

Days without Angels, days of wondering, Lapland days, all blown away.

And Bella? Thomas glances at Bella.

She is looking confused.

But then she smiles, a smile that seems like an expulsion of all the walking around that took place in the white villa, all the looking at windows, and all the sleeping.

"Heavens, Rosa," says Bella with a relieved laugh. "We've only just been to Umeå.

"Sweden!" Rosa laughs too. "What's Sweden compared to what I'm thinking of?"

"Sit down, Rosa," Bella says. "And tell me what you're thinking of."

Rosa moves into the white villa. She sleeps in the bedroom. Bella lives in her studio, just as she has been doing all summer. They take meals together in the white villa kitchen. Rosa, Bella, Thomas, and Nina; Renée too, if she turns up. They are down on the beach or out in the yard when the sun is out. Thomas works on his models in his room. Thomas moves around the summer paradise, doing different stuff, playing, observing.

There is nothing more peculiar than that. What at first is new and amazing levels out and becomes ordinary. Gradually Thomas has a feeling that it's always been like this. That Rosa has always lived with them in the white villa, taken meals with them. When Kayus lived there, too. And to Thomas there is no conflict in this, as there might be the moment you take a step away from your own land in the summer paradise.

He likes it all. Afterward, should be think about this time—which he will not—he would say quite calmly that the time with Rosa in the white villa was a good time.

But as soon as you head for the Johanssons, May Johansson is there with her truths. DOT DOT DOT. When you listen to May Johansson, you can imagine yourself living through something earthshaking. Something never seen *in living memory*, which for May Johansson is a collective term for the history of the summer paradise. Something that will be talked about for years afterward.

In any case, it is not true. Everyone will quickly forget what it was like when Bella and Rosa lived together in the white villa, planning a life together. They will have forgotten by the following year. And in a few years, they will think that it never really happened, that they only imagined it.

May Johansson looks at Thomas and asks if he is hungry. Thomas cannot believe his ears. Would Thomas like to share the hot meal at the Johanssons' dinner table?

Thomas really does shake his head.

Gabby does, too. When May Johansson *compassionately* invited him as well. He says that he gets meals as good as anywhere at the cafés and gas stations in the area. French fries, hamburgers, beefburgers. And other unhealthy food, says Gabby, licking his lips. *One ought to get a franchise*, he says, and he starts to explain about fast-food chains to May Johansson on May Johansson's patch of grass while indoors her meal is getting cold. There is a big market for fast food. It would sure to be good business.

As soon as Gabby hears herself talking about business, his mood brightens considerably. You expect him to cry, "James Bond" and look around for his Bond girls, all of whom have now disappeared.

Gabby looks around. Frowns. Shrugs. Gets into his car and goes for a drive.

"What a cross to bear," says May Johansson. "But she has to, too."

Gabby is not quite focused, he is irresolute. He does not really know how he should react. For the first few days he goes around shouting and swearing. He stands at the highest point of his hill and says more or less what May Johansson says, that it is certainly peculiar that grown people . . . . Then he stops. He simply does not know what attitude he should take.

Once, when the women are on the white villa's beach, Gabby comes down. He starts nailing boards together on May Johansson's patch of grass. Hammering away with heartrending intensity. The women on the beach take no notice. Renée helps him. Nothing happens. The sun goes in. The women leave the beach. Gabby stops hammering. The thing he is building looks like it might be going to be a creel to keep fish alive in the water. But only half a creel.

Finally he just drives around in his car. Rushes along the forest road and the main road at sixty miles an hour.

In Australia, Miss Eleonora Plum has been chosen Queen of the Air. She is an SAS attendant and has been presented with a fine silver cup, a fine wardrobe, fine makeup equipment, and a fine three-week round trip as her prize. Thomas takes the newspaper to Gabby to cheer him up. And the girl in the photograph is a lot like that other girl, Viviann.

He thinks that this event might put Gabby in a better

mood. No, of course he doesn't really go to Gabby. But he thinks about Gabby when he sees the photograph, and he also thinks that it's a story Gabby would appreciate.

More photographs: On the table in the reading corner there were once photographs. Photographs from different periods in the summer paradise. Scrambled randomly, as if waiting to be arranged into a new order. Photographs taken by Rosa with her Instamatic at the time when she was someone who collects memories. But more recent photographs, too, photographs from the trip to Sweden, for example.

The entire boxful, photographs from the summer paradise—all the same, Rosa never pasted them in an album. Funny little captions, newspaper cuttings and so on, she was going to copy them out or let them inspire her when composing her own captions.

The cosmonauts Bykovsky and Valentina Tereshkova, *Voskov 5* and *Voskov 6*, twin flights in orbit after orbit around the earth.

The two cosmonauts chatting happily to each other and to good friends during the Monday flight. Valya's photograph frequently appeared on Russian television screens, and she seemed to be in a good mood, though it was possible to begin to make out dark circles round her eyes. The duo from space often sounded quite clear over the telephone lines, and Valya even took an unintentional nap, causing some consternation on the ground, where they thought communication had been broken off.

On the photograph to which that caption is attached, both have their eyes closed, he and Renée. The flash took them by surprise. Thomas remembers and smiles.

New photographs, including Family on Board. Quite openly, for everyone to see.

Bella and Rosa looked at them, then they got tired of the pasttime. Left the pictures on the table, abandoned. As if they had lost interest and not known what to do with them.

"I can't be bothered with photographs, Bella," says Rosa. "I want to develop my own life."

Thomas takes Family on Board. He wants it. Somehow it seems private. He no longer thinks about who took it. He thinks that the photo shows Bella and him, on their way. Like a memory. When they were on their way.

Rosa and Bella are planning another life. Rosa talks, Rosa does most of the talking, and Thomas listens. He really does listen, and what she says sounds reasonable. It is quite conceivable to go and live in a house with a garden, Rosa and Bella and Nina and Renée and Thomas.

Bella also listens at first, not saying much but looking interested. Rather like Ann-Christine, the way she looked at Johan Wikblad's balsa-wood house after it had been glued to the plywood panel.

Rosa will go back to school, and Bella will get a job.

"We have to create our own lives, Bella. Start from scratch, pure and simple."

"Mmmm," says Bella.

Thomas nods. He understands Bella perfectly.

And when Rosa sees Gabby racing off along the road in his car, she says, "Sometimes, Bella, I think the only chance for family life the way things are now is life with that Chitty-Chitty-Bang-Bang car, the one with wings and the whole family in it, on their way up among the clouds on new adventures. But there are at least two flaws in that story, Bella. One is that it isn't true. Cars don't fly. And secondly, it's a fairy tale, in which you yourself have been made a character."

"Oh, yes." Bella looks out the window. Sometimes, in time, Thomas has a feeling she watches the car for a long time. Even after it has disappeared up on to the main road.

"And Gabby's flight attendants, too. My role becomes that of the stoical ground attendant. *She who sees but does not see*. You know that story. It's too pathetic. And I don't want to. I don't want to.

"I don't want to live like that.

"I'll fall apart if I have to live like that.

"You have to have vision, Bella. For your life."

"We must try to earn our own living and take responsibility for our own lives."

Gradually, after Bella has listened for a while, she starts leafing through the magazines again. Smoking cigarettes, saying "Mmm" to everything Rosa says in that way that makes Thomas realize that she is not really listening carefully. Thomas suddenly wants to reveal to Rosa some of the things Bella told her that do not make sense, that are pure lies or exaggerations. For instance, telling Rosa that Bella did give up her job at the drugstore because she had her hand in the cash register and was on her own for a few days, but it was because she never really knew what time it was, and that was bad for the business.

But he does not.

He thinks exactly like Rosa all the time.

"You have to have vision, Bella, utopias."

Of course it sounds silly, naive, incomprehensible. But you

try putting into words for the first time something outside the framework, something you have never thought before.

"What does *utopia* mean?" Thomas would like to ask that, too. Not in the same tone of voice Bella uses, but gently and with some interest.

"I don't feel well," says Bella. "I have a headache."

And she goes up to the studio.

And once when Gabby's car goes past, Bella stands for a long time at the window, watching it go. Rosa notices, says something, something *straight to the point*.

"It's not that," says Bella, suddenly almost angry, at least annoyed. "You don't listen, Rosa."

"What do you really want, Bella?" Rosa asks another time. Rather wearily, but probably also with genuine concern.

"To get away," replies Bella. Though not until a few days later. Late in the evening. After she's decided to go away.

She goes to Rosa in the middle of the night.

"I have to leave now."

And Rosa replies, she has to reply like this: "I'm coming with you."

▪ ▪ ▪

But otherwise all the talk about a new life ebbs away after a while, at least the concrete planning of it. The talk is all about ordinary things again. Suntan cream, hair styles, and the floating shop. And when Rosa and Bella go out into the summer paradise, they are the women on the beach again, in sunglasses, alike as two pins, almost twins.

Though eventually Bella is standing in his room, in the evening, when Rosa is somewhere else.

"I'm so tired, Thomas. Tired out. Only Child, *we must talk*."

"I'm busy," says Thomas if he is at his table with his models.

She goes away but comes back. Again and again she comes back. "Perhaps I'll go away, Thomas. But I'll come back."

At night: She is a dark figure in the doorway. Thomas is asleep. She goes away. But the following moment he sits up in bed. He's wide awake.

"Thomas."

"I'm busy." In the evenings: Thomas repeats the phrase, seated at his models.

"You don't want to hear," says Bella, sitting down opposite him, almost wearily, as if all her strength has suddenly run out of her. And there is something desolate and hurt in her voice, which he is not prepared for. After all, he is only a child, with model planes at the yellow table in his boy's room, which was called the nursery not so long ago, and she is the mother who should talk mother talk and ask him this, that, and the other about all his doings, not the other way around, not her babbling about other things, peculiar things.

But he stops, has to stop what he is doing. Puts the airplane wing he is holding back on the newspaper on the table. Looks up, looks at her, making himself look. This is the evening, the last evening, her hair is short, very short, stopping just below her ears. He has never seen it so short before. It looks fine. But different.

He stares.

She does not evade his look. He has to think up something quickly. Otherwise she will start talking.

All the airplane parts are spread over the yellow surface of the table. He knows how they should be put together. He no longer needs the instructions.

He begins to tell her, in a way that almost surprises even him. Suddenly, he can only hear his own voice.

"Like all good stories," Thomas the Storyteller begins, "this story begins in a bar."

So the last thing Thomas does with Bella in the summer paradise is not to ask the questions that have to do with what she wants but to babble, producing a story of his own.

"In the bar the American fighter pilot, Jimmie Angel, met a mysterious man, an Adventurer."

He goes on with his story, on and on, losing himself in the story: The mysterious Adventurer promised Jimmie Angel, himself a real daredevil, a great deal of money to carry out a secret assignment in the South American jungles. Off they went, without maps, the Adventurer insisting that Jimmie Angel should fly only according to his directions. They landed in the jungle and the Adventurer disappeared, but Jimmie Angel was not allowed to go with him and had to stay with the plane. When the Adventurer came back, he had with him a case full of gold and diamonds. Jimmie Angel just stared and secretly swore that when this assignment was over, he would return, on his own, and find out where the gold and diamonds were. And that is what he did, years later, when the Adventurer himself was dead.

But he happened to land high up on a mountain and flew straight into a muddy pool. The plane became mired in the mud and could not be budged. So instead of searching for gold and diamonds, Jimmie Angel had to make his way down the mountain on foot, through terrain that was almost impenetrable, along the Indians' secret paths. The journey was not in vain, however. That was how Jimmie Angel discovered the highest waterfall in the world, which was named after him. The plane stayed in the mud. Forever.

"It was a flamingo," Thomas the Storyteller concludes his story, "a fine flamingo."

"Thomas." Bella's face cracks into a smile, and she stares intently into Thomas's eyes. "That's an absolutely marvelous story. Did you make it all up yourself?"

"No, it's on this."

Thomas shows her the model box, the inside of the lid.

"On the lid. In the space for *interesting background facts.*"

Or had he imagined it? Had he ever told a story at all? Had she ever sat down opposite him? Had she ever listened? Hadn't she said for the umpteenth time: Only Child, we must talk....

Perhaps he had already gone out through the veranda. Surely he is already standing on the edge of the Johanssons' and Rosa's and Gabby's joint breakwater? In his pajamas, his robe, his boots? Looking across the dark water, the dark islands of which Huotari's is the nearest, scratching his arm in the moonlight? For the moon is almost full, on the wane, and the last week of summer is about to begin. And after summer comes autumn, winter, spring, and more summers. The promise of other summers.

No. He is in his room. She is standing on the kitchen steps, smoking. Quick, nervous puffs. She does not see him. He has turned off the light. Now she turns around, opens the door, and pads through the kitchen to the bedroom where Rosa sleeps.

Because it does not help to tell stories, produce stories. Pictures, pictures of the good life. This is what Thomas—suddenly only Thomas and no one else—knows.

Of the good life, a picture from city life, long ago: Kayus is ill. Thomas is given Kayus's ticket. Thomas and Isabella go to the theater together. The performance? Afterward Thomas and Isabella cannot remember the performance. But when the curtain came down, balloons rained down from the ceiling; little bottles of bubble-bath essence dangled from their strings. Thomas and Isabella caught more balloons than anyone else in the audience. They remember that. They went home and split their booty. Thomas was given the balloons, because he is the child and likes balloons. Isabella appropriated the bottles of bubble bath, because she is the woman who loves bubble baths, and the kind of bubble-bath essence in the small bottles on the balloon strings is her favorite brand. Isabella and Kayus get into the bathtub. Isabella empties a whole little bottle of bubble bath into the water. Kayus takes the record player into the bathroom, and Thomas goes to bed. He ties the balloons to the bedpost, turns out the light, and lies in bed staring up at the dark silhouettes of the balloons on the ceiling until he falls asleep and he is an airship that is flying, floating through time and space. But when he wakes up before dawn, all the balloons have drifted down to the floor, crumpled, and they have SKIN like on hot cocoa or on Kayus's and Isabella's bodies because they fell asleep in the tub. They look dead. Thomas went to the bathroom to pee. The record player is still on. The record is whirling round and round on the turntable, although it ended long ago. Thomas turns off the record player, and the turntable stops. He stands next to the tub for a moment and looks at Isabella and Kayus sleeping in the water, which is cold. He dips his finger in the water to feel before he has an impulse to grab Kayus by the arm, shake it, and whine as only a boy who has woken in the middle of the night and is frightened can: "Wake up. Get up now."

He does not do it. He really knows. They are not dead. Isabella's head has slipped to one side, so that her cheek is resting on the edge of the bath. Kayus is sitting almost upright, his eyes closed, his mouth half-open. The funny thing, which makes Thomas want to laugh although he is frightened and it is the middle of the night and the whole place is quiet, is the sight of their legs, so spookily milky white in the green bath water. The white flesh is horrible, soft, shapeless somehow, especially in contrast to the dark hair on their legs. Both Kayus and Isabella have hairy legs. Isabella usually shaves hers for the summer when she is going to wear a bathing suit. But it is not the hair that makes Thomas laugh. It is the way Isabella and Kayus are lying. The tub is not very long, and they cannot stretch their legs out. But the way they are lying, their feet seem to be pressing against the other's body. Kayus has buried one foot in Isabella's dark armpit, which is also hairy in the winter. Isabella is lying slanting to one side, her feet are on Kayus's stomach. Or rather, *in* Kayus's stomach.

All the bubble bath has dissolved. Isabella wakes and sees Thomas. She is almost alarmed. She asks where she is. And she looks at Thomas as if she had come to the wrong place.

Rosa carries the beach basket with peanut-butter cookies and another kind. She has black coffee in one thermos, orange juice in the other. Bella carries towels, the beach blanket, and the suntan oil. Rosa has tied back her dark hair off her forehead with a pink ribbon, Bella wears a scarf around her head. Rosa is propped up on one elbow on the rug and is saying something to Bella which is inaudible. Rosa hands Bella a mug of coffee, and Bella takes it and sits down on the rug beside Rosa. She stretches out, her body glistening from suntan oil and the water she has just splashed on to herself in the inlet. Her body is very beautiful, although her skin is not nearly as tanned as it is most summers.

This is what Bella and Rosa are like on their last afternoon on the beach in the summer paradise. In scarcely half an hour they will go back up to the villa, cut their hair, never to return.

Rosa taps a cigarette out of her pack, puts it between her lips, and holds the pack out to Bella before lighting hers. Bella shakes her head. She scrambles up into a sitting position and looks across the bay. Haze and poor visibility. Even Huotari's island, which is so near, is barely recognizable. Rosa sits up, too. Rosa says something and laughs. Bella laughs.

May Johansson comes along in her robe. The belt is hanging loose, so that her huge monokini is very visible at a distance. Rosa and Bella do not notice May Johansson, so it is not May Johansson they are laughing at.

Thomas dives under the water. He sits on the bottom, where the sand turns into mud. He looks through his goggles. Rays of sunlight trickle into the water, the particles of mud floating up around him whenever he moves his foot are grayish-brown, spiky like snowflakes when they're big and falling slowly and thickly and the thought that there is nothing wrong with winter either, takes you by surprise.

He has to surface to breathe. On the surface, Erkki

Johansson is playing with a dark-blue beach ball stenciled with NIVEA in big white letters. He has busied himself with it for some time and has not come up with anything more interesting than throwing the ball a little ahead of him in the water and running after it shouting, as if there were a great hurry. There is certainly no hurry. The wind has dropped, although it is noon. Quite abruptly the bay has smoothed out, although it is noon, when there should be a fresh afternoon breeze. But the main reason why Erkki is so demonstratively and noisily playing with the ball is that he wants to get Thomas'ss attention. Thomas knows that. But does not feel like responding. He is cold. But he will overcome his susceptibility to cold, wean himself. That is why he stays in the water although he is cold, and why he tries to stay below the surface. It is warmer below than in the air if you stay down long enough.

"Throw the ball, Erkki!" May Johansson is on her way out into the water. She has tossed her robe below the alder, where Renée usually sits when she is not somewhere else in the Rotwoods, in the root cellar, behind the Johanssons' sauna, or in one of her other places all over the summer paradise. Thomas can no longer tell her exact whereabouts. Only roughly. *One of several alternatives.* If he thinks about it. He does not. At the moment he is in the water, his head full of other stuff.

May Johansson has run into the water, holding out her hands toward Erkki Johansson and the ball, which is actually hers, Pusu's *and* May Johansson's beach ball, originally reserved for *adult water games* exactly as recommended in the advertisement. But the ball itself was bought before the summer. In May, when they had gone through the stores pushing a shopping cart, getting ready for the summer season and believing that they could buy the roar of the sea and the happy laughter on the beach, glowing skin, cool evenings, and hot days when the sun has gone behind the trees, shimmering mosquitoes in the last rays of the sun trickling through the trees over the bay.

Erkki throws the ball to May Johansson. May Johansson catches it. She stands in the water, which comes to the top of her monokini, not very far from where her sagging breasts begin. She glances at Bella and Rosa sitting on the beach by themselves, talking so quietly that she cannot hear what they are saying. She wonders whether she should wave to them. Before she can decide, Rosa and Bella have lain back down on the rug, Rosa with her head on Bella's stomach, Bella with one hand in Rosa's hair, stroking it absentmindedly, while Rosa gazes up into the sky and talks, talks.

Bella and Rosa will leave in a minute. Get up, stretch their arms and legs, brush off their bathing suits, roll up the beach blanket, put the coffee and juice mugs and packages of cookies back in the basket, shake out their towels, and hang them around their necks like boxers. Rosa will shove her feet into her sandals, the same white sandals with gold buttons and leather straps across the instep. Bella just walks barefoot. So they will disappear up the avenue. Not quite yet. But in roughly five minutes.

Thomas is now trying to beat his own record of holding his breath under water. He counts the seconds to himself, although he knows he cannot rely on his own counting. The fact is, you do not count the same way each time, so that counting is not an objective measurement. He thinks that he should have a stopwatch. He goes on thinking that he will ask for a stopwatch for Christmas, a waterproof one, one like Renée's that hangs in a red plastic case around her neck like a key on a string, when she takes part in races, a watch that has also been used to keep time during the foot races at May Johansson's Olympic Games in the Johanssons' yard, recently arranged because athletics is a way of promoting friendship between all nationalities of the world; and May Johansson in particular has had a guilty conscience over a certain incident on the beach one hopeless day long ago, when the Society for Underwater Research still existed. She has arranged for prizes and all kinds of stuff. And when Thomas begged to be America and Renée begged to be America, and naturally Erkki Johansson also begged to be America, May Johansson said that there are sure to be a great many athletic talents in America, and so all three have been America, and eventually Erkki Johansson was the only athlete on the track, because two of the athletes sustained devastating and incomprehensible injuries, first Renée, then Thomas. Under the water Thomas thinks that once he has a real stopwatch, he will have an objective measurement of how long he can stay under water, and starting out from this objective measure, he will then be able to set up a purposeful training schedule to become even better, to be able to stay under for even longer.

But Christmas presents, Christmases. Doesn't he wonder what is going to happen about Christmases, for instance, and celebrating Christmas in his new life?

Perhaps, a little.

He comes up to the surface. He has to breathe.

Then he is angry with himself. Christmases, Christmas presents; is that the kind of thing you should think about on the brink of a new life? And yet, at the same time, again that voice in his room, Bella's voice, the voice he cannot get rid of.

"Only Child, we must talk."

■ ■ ■

No. Thomas shakes his head, snorts, looks at the beach women on the rock, Bella and Rosa, in his mind holding on to them forever.

Rosa and Bella are still lying on the rock. Rosa has taken off her sunglasses and is buttoning her blouse, a white sleeveless summer blouse with lots of tiny little buttons down the front. Bella's fingers are in Rosa's hair. Pulling at a few strands, measuring them with her eyes. Long, aren't they?

But May Johansson, standing in the water by the shore, ball in hand, her monokini slowly and unpleasantly getting wet with cold water, is suddenly, briefly, seized with irresolution. She is holding the ball. The ball is blue, the white letters on it are big, challenging. The sun is shining, and it is time for happy water games. But: *what should she do with the ball?* Suddenly she has no idea.

She feels completely out of place. *Really pathetic,* to use May Johansson's language. She is a grown woman, after all. Why is she standing there in the water, her breasts bare, making a fool of herself?

May Johansson's feeling of being out of place lasts only a few seconds, then Thomas's head appears above the water. May Johansson sees him and thinks that if Thomas stays above the surface where he is now, and Erkki Johansson stands slightly diagonally to one side, as he already is, then they form a kind of circle, the three of them, Thomas, Erkki, and May Johansson. So all they have to do is throw the ball from one to the other and then to the third. Somewhere behind them, Pusu Johansson comes out of the Johanssons' house and May Johansson calls out to Pusu to go get the camera and take a picture.

"Pusu! Go and get our Instamatic. Come and take a picture."

The women on the beach get up. Now they are on their way.

Thomas is shivering, his teeth are chattering. Erkki is not at all cold. He laughs at Thomas, his mouth wide open, and he would certainly wag his tail if he were a dog, and just as Thomas is thinking of getting out and not catching the ball flying in his direction but letting it go on out across the water—and on and on with the wind, because the wind is rising up again, blowing offshore, too—then he thinks, no, Erkki Johansson is not a dog, he is May and Pusu's boy and two years younger than Thomas, but Erkki is quite okay after all. It is not Erkki's fault that he has the silliest mother with the droopiest breasts in the summer paradise. Thomas suddenly feels sorry for Erkki because of that. *A wave of tenderness* washes over Thomas for Erkki Johansson, and he decides to stay where he is and play ball, although Pusu Johansson has arrived with the camera held high, and never, according to Renée, could he imagine himself voluntarily being in a photograph of that kind, *with Erkki Johansson and May Johansson in a monokini.*

And although in some dim corner of his mind he is aware that Rosa and Bella have packed their things and are now leaving, slightly subdued, without the fuss they usually make.

They are going up to the studio to cut their hair. Their hairstyles are out of fashion. As they walk about the avenue, Rosa slips her arm into Bella's. Bella lengthens her stride, slipping out of Rosa's grasp.

■ ■ ■

Pusu Johansson is taking pictures. Erkki and May Johansson and Thomas laugh and splash each other. Thomas, too. But his teeth keep chattering and his lips will be blue if the film in the Johanssons' camera is in color. It isn't. And it isn't an Instamatic either. A perfectly ordinary box model; it's just called Instamatic. Then, suddenly, May and Pusu and Erkki Johansson are gone, walking to the Johanssons' house at the bustling pace that expresses May Johansson's eagerness, when, as she puts it, *she feels like a child again.* They are cold now, the Johansson family. May Johansson is pulling at Erkki, who is resisting. They have to go to the house for dry towels, have to dry themselves off, eat a little because they are hungry, change their clothes because the cousins are coming for a good-bye visit, because the time has come for the long voyage, tomorrow or the next day or the day after that, depending on the weather.

Erkki tries to turn around to say something to Thomas, but all he can manage is a wave, which remains incomplete because he drops the ball and has to run after it. And once Erkki has the ball again, they are in even more of a hurry, the Johansson family. They have to get up to the house and busy themselves with whatever it is that is next on the family-summer schedule.

Thomas waves back, but Erkki does not see him. He rubs himself hard with the towel until he is dry and warm again, puts on his clothes—long trousers and a heavy wool sweater. The sun has indeed been out all day, but there is certainly no heat wave; the wind is quite cold, and there is still a rawness in the air that makes you think of autumn.

Renée comes out of the Rotwoods. She crosses the rock, passing Thomas, and goes on down to the jetty and the white villa's rowboat, casts off, and rows away.

"Wait!" Thomas calls. But she does not wait.

Thomas is sailing GOOF toward Wind Island. He can see her from far away, a bright dot in the reeds. He is running before the wind, which is steadily increasing, and it is going well. He feels it again, the joy of speed. Wheeee! Once it even bubbles up inside him, that song, the Viviann song but now somehow detached from Viviann. My Boy LolliPop. Only a tune. A popular song like any other but with an undeniably catchy chorus.

GOOF races toward Wind Island at such speed that even Renée leaps out onto a stone in the reeds and stands fully visible, waving her hands and shouting at him to watch the hull. She does not like him to use GOOF when she is not with him. He knows that, although she never says anything. But she can't reasonably stop him, because the boat belongs to them both. Not until the following spring will Gabby telephone Kayus at the city apartment to ask whether he may *buy out* Kayus. Thomas takes no notice of Renée. He pretends not to hear or see. Not until he is right up by the edge of the reeds does he haul in and heave to, drop the sail, raise the centerboard, and jump out of the dinghy into the water, barefoot, his trousers already rolled up. Then, with Renée's help, he cautiously hauls the boat a little way up on land and lashes the sail to the mast with the painter.

"This island's private," says Renée as soon as GOOF is in place.

"Oh, shit. Who cares. Grump."

Thomas goes straight over to the other side. Following the shoreline, stumping along, things crackling underfoot. There are special Wind Island insects, which do not bite but are otherwise disgusting, just crawling all over your body under your clothes. The rancid Wind Island smell of reeds, eggshells, rotten fish, and fish bones crawls into his nose. He comes to the other side and looks out at the Lindberghs' beach. The shiny mahogany speedboat is moored at the jetty, covered with a green tarpaulin. Klas or Peter Lindbergh and an unknown girl are on the jetty. A girlfriend, that's clear, but not a Viviann. This one has thin, fair hair and a dark-blue peaked cap on her head. They go on board. The girl starts undoing the tarpaulin with practiced hands. Casts off, Klas or Peter starts up, and they set off. It is quiet again. The runt? No runt in sight anywhere.

A crash behind him, and the next moment he is on the ground, face down, with reeds and rotten island smell deep inside his nose. She is on him, and it is not a game, as it sometimes is when, giggling, she has jumped him from behind unexpectedly, saying that he is an alder bug—"It eats its way in just here. It has to be twisted counterclockwise to get it out. I've tested it. Now I'm twisting"—as if she wanted to establish an alibi for squeezing the back of his neck. Today she is serious. She is angry for some reason, he can feel her anger in all her movements. He shouts in real pain. She has dug her teeth into his arm. Bitten him right through his heavy sweater.

There will be a bruise later. Scars remain for a long time. Though fairly soon all you can see is only an ordinary red patch that looks like any old rash.

Thomas wriggles underneath her, thrashing to free himself. He flings her off, but he hurls himself back at her and they wrestle, fight, he pulls her hair, the little that is left of it, kicks, he's out of his mind—until he stops and lets go. Stops fighting.

Gets up and stands still. Brushes himself off. The pain in his arm wanes.

For there is no point.

She is also taken aback, surprised by his violent and total retreat. Stands a little way off, looking at him, breathing. Loud, agitated breathing, slowly calming, silent, ordinary.

He feels his arm. It is tender.

"Let me see." She comes closer. Her voice is ordinary again. Even slightly curious. As if wishing to show an impersonal interest in the name of science.

"You're sick in the head," he mumbles.

"Serves you right," she says then. "Idiot."

And leaves. Back into the bushes from where she rushed out and attacked him from behind. Straight through them she goes, making way for nothing. Twigs breaking and snapping.

Thomas goes back to the boats on the shoreline. He puts on the life jacket and prepares GOOF. Lashes everything that is loose in the boat; the wind is still high, and tacking will be hard. The bay lies spread out, gray and shimmering white foam ahead of him, somehow wild in the sunlight sweeping over it for a few seconds when there is a break in the solid whitish-gray cloud cover.

Her orange T-shirt, the lump of stitches on the shoulder, white once, now no longer. He has it in his eyes now, in the corner of his eye. She is there again, leaning, half-sitting against the prow of the row boat not far from GOOF, small pebbles in her hand, throwing them into the water in front of her in the reeds.

Plop, plop: very small pebbles. The sleeves of her T-shirt

 are rolled up; the skin on her arms is not quite sunburned, but anyhow patinated, rough, summer dry, so that when scratched, white powdery streaks are drawn in it. Just like his.

"Let's take GOOF in tow," she suggests. "Otherwise you'll have to tack."

Kayus is back from Lapland. Everybody knows except Thomas. When Thomas got the postcard with the Lapp and the tundra on it, Kayus was already back home, in the city. Thomas has spoken to Kayus on the Johanssons' phone, and somehow or other he thought he was talking to Lapland, although there was no mention of any place during the call. Kayus said they ought to go to Lapland together some time; Thomas nodded, but you couldn't hear his nod over the phone.

Thomas takes the large bilberry can and goes out into the forest. He is there for several hours, because he runs into Johan Wikblad and Ann-Christine, who are looking for cloudberries. Thomas shows them a place only he knows about, a deep hollow a fairly long way off. The red and yellow glows intensely in his eyes, and the smell is heavy and prickly in his nostrils.

"You only see something like this every ten years if you're lucky," says Johan Wikblad as he starts picking. And they go on picking. They pick and pick, clearing the whole hollow.

When Thomas gets back to the white villa with his can full to the brim with soft yellow cloudberries and pale yellow and red hard unripe ones, the house is empty. Pink foot-shaped notes are lying on the kitchen table and in the big room. Thomas recognizes them. They are torn off Rosa's *Happy Feet Memo* block. The first pink foot reads:

"Thomas! We've gone to Copenhagen to see the world.

We'll be all right. There are some sandwiches in the cupboard and soured milk on the stand. Kayus is coming this evening. Hugs. B." It is in Bella's handwriting. "From me, too," it says underneath in sprawling Rosa letters. The sentence is circled like a sun, with ray-like arrows pointing to the word hugs.

On the note in the big room Bella has written: "Thomas! Look in the blue jar on the bottom shelf of the sideboard. You'll find some surprises."

Thomas finds the blue jar, which in the white villa was always kept for cookies and candy but is usually empty because Bella and Thomas have eaten their cookies and other goodies straight out of the packages and finished them before they could be put in the jar. He lifts the lid and inside finds two of his favorite kind of chocolate bars and a bag of English licorice allsorts, also his favorites, probably bought in Sweden because the bag is Extra King Size and that size is not available in ordinary stores. Special goodies. Things you usually wrap in fancy paper and give away as Christmas and birthday presents.

Thomas tucks the footprints away in his pocket, picks up the cloudberry can, and goes out. Johan Wikblad and Ann-Christine are having an omelette in the red cottage. The cottage smells of frying and somehow also of a hot-dog stand, like in the amusement park, but that is only a quick association in Thomas's mind; he thinks about the yogurt in the stand, which will not set because it is the dog days, and then he feels sorry for himself, so much so that his lips and face muscles start to tremble. But only for a moment, then everything is back to normal. Ann-Christine and Johan Wikblad's cloudberry bucket is just inside the door, where he stood for a moment in the dim light. Forest, cloudberries, and the smell of cloudberry moss take over, and Thomas puts his can on the table and sits down on the long bench, Ann-Christine gets a plate and serves him; the omelette has sausages in it. Afterwards Ann-Christine and Thomas and Johan Wikblad clean cloudberries until Gabby comes back with the news that Rosa and Bella have gone to Copenhagen to see the world, leaving the children exposed to the elements, as May Johansson's version has it, as it gradually spreads, and finally reaches as far as the red cottage.

Kayus comes back that night. He carries Thomas from the red cottage to the white villa. Early in the morning Thomas wakes up in his own bed. He gets up and slips into the attic space. The knife he had hidden in the wall is gone. He is not surprised. He had almost always known it would disappear.

He puts on his clothes and goes back to the red cottage. He crawls under the blanket on the country-style sofa where he had fallen asleep the evening before. He kicks off his sneakers and undresses under the blanket. Wriggles out of garment after garment until he is quite naked and the blanket prickles unpleasantly against his skin. For some reason he will remember that detail in particular. The way he undressed, although it was quite unnecessary and he could easily have worn underclothes as pajamas.

■ ■ ■

Thomas is living the red-cottage life. Long days, semi-cloudy or overcast. Thomas and Johan Wikblad sit at the country-style table in the evenings and paint Johan Wikblad's balsa-wood house with Hobby paints while Ann-Christine does other things. The house becomes very nice—yellow walls, white trim, green roof. The work requires great concentration so the paints are even and don't run. Ann-Christine reads aloud out of the *Edda,* which she says is as good a book as any adventure story. Ann-Christine whistles. Ann-Christine bakes bread, cans the cloudberries, speaks French to herself to keep up her skills, and Thomas and Johan Wikblad do not understand a word she says. Thomas laughs at Ann-Christine just as he has done all summer. Everything Ann-Christine says is so funny, something about her, and when she says *Over my dead body*, he can still see Ann-Christine's dead body in front of him, huge, insuperable. To him it is only funny and not as morbid as it sounds, but he knows better to keep it to himself. Kayus turns up now and again. Nor does Thomas react when there is a telephone call for him from Copenhagen and May Johansson comes panting across the red cottage yard in the clothes she will wear on her long trip. NOW the Johanssons are on their way, since this morning the sun is out slightly longer, so that you would almost think the summer has come back. Out to sea, says May Johansson, looking like adventure and the wide world, though she does not say so aloud owing to the present circumstances. Maggi Johansson is taken on board by force. She is not interested in leaving the summer paradise where she and Nina have taken up residence in the Johanssons' sauna and are waging a long struggle over who, in the end, will have *him.* On the first night of the Johanssons' long trip, when they lie at anchor off Porkala Point and all the others are asleep, Maggi Johansson goes ashore and walks and hitchhikes back to the summer paradise. The next night she is outside Gabby's and Rosa's house, throwing stones at Nina's window. When Nina and Gabby hear the noise, they think it is Renée.

Thomas does not go to the telephone.

"Aren't you leaving soon?" he says to May Johansson. "If you don't leave soon, the sun will have gone in," he mumbles in a slightly lower voice, though no doubt audibly, and if May Johansson had not known that it was tough on Thomas, that Thomas was now a poor little child, as it says in the hymns in May Johansson's head, if she thinks about Bella and Rosa and all the others, and not about the long voyage, sun hat and out in the world, she would have taken it as insolence.

Thomas goes with Ann-Christine and Kayus and the other children in the summer paradise—Nina and Maggi—to the amusement park. Kayus thinks that they have to get away and have other things to think about, "The show must go on, sort of," says Kayus. Thomas looks at him without understanding. *What is Kayus babbling about?* Thomas is already thinking about other things. Thomas is thinking about Johan Wikblad's balsa-wood house, about certain scenes from the *Edda*, about what Renée is up to in the forest, and about what May Johansson will say when she sees for herself how high the waves can be in Porkala Bay. Not to be compared with this puddle exactly. So Kayus is wrong, but that doesn't matter, either. It's okay. The amusement park is a stupid idea but okay. Thomas is standing beside a round counter; miniature planes circling above it drop pointed bombs on a piece of paper in the table when you press a button. The bomb lands on a number, and what you have to do is push the button at the right moment. The person whose bomb sticks into the highest number gets another turn and wins the prize of a forty-five EP record. Thomas's bomb lands on ten. He wins his turn and gets that record of "Help" by the Beatles. Thank goodness the record player is still at home in town. For a moment, *a fleeting moment,* Thomas has a vision of hands, hands held out across a table in a café at a gas station. His hands and Rosa's hands and how he blushes, still, although that happened weeks ago and the present situation is quite different. In Kayus's car on the way back, Thomas gives the record to Nina Angel. It is a stupid song. Everyone in the car begins to think that he is in love with Nina. Maggi, Nina herself, Kayus, and Ann-Christine in front, all laugh equally in agreement. Nina puts her arm around Thomas. Thomas shakes her off and looks out the window.

"Dum-de-dum-de-dum," yodels Maggi meaningfully. Thomas thinks she is jealous of Nina because he gave the record to Nina. Now Nina has both the record and Jake. Though actually no one knows that yet, and nor does it belong in this story, though it might be some consolation for Maggi to know that though Nina has Jake now, Maggi will get him later on. *To put up with for the rest of time,* an eternity, as May Johansson used to say sometimes to Bella long ago, when she was in a joking mood, just what she had to with Pusu Johansson. That was the time when she and Bella were washing sheets down on the beach like real womenfolk, and Rosa Angel was just an Angel in white with fancy city ways, who came tripping down to the beach, past Bella and May Johansson, out onto the jetty, and just before the Lindberghs' boat came to take her to the villas on the other side of the sound on the outer edge of the archipelago, and said heavens above, how industrious you are, she could never cope with scrubbing sheets like that in the middle of a beautiful summer.

Thomas thinks he should explain to them all that he gave the record to Nina and not to anyone else in the car by sheer chance. Nina happened to be nearest to hand. He does not do it. He says nothing and looks out the window.

Kayus's fingertips drum cautiously on the wheel.

Ann-Christine says something amusing.

Kayus laughs and honks the horn, and so they drive in on the forest road. Dusk is falling. Darkness comes early in August.

"How was it in Lapland?" Thomas says that same morning he returned to the red cottage by himself and Kayus appears a few hours later, then hangs about in the doorway looking miserable, not knowing what to say. Thomas, naked but with the blanket wrapped around him, is sitting on the long bench at the country-style table waiting for breakfast. Kayus says the mosquitoes were a nuisance. Ann-Christine comes out of the kitchen alcove with a tray of cocoa, bread, and jam. She asks Kayus to sit down at the table and join them. So all three of them have breakfast. Kayus, Thomas, and Ann-Christine.

The following summer there will be a new girl in the red cottage. Her name is Annette and she is prettier than Ann-Christine, prettier even than Helena Wikblad. Annette wants a big family, and she will give birth to three children in three years, and Johan and Annette and the children become a large family, too large for the red cottage, so they ask the Johansson cousins about the possibility of renting the white villa, which has stood empty every summer since Thomas and Kayus left the summer paradise in 1965. The cousins agree: Johan and Annette can have the villa on an annual basis. Though Annette is not the same kind of person as the movie star. It is not the same pleasure to be charmed by Annette as it was to be charmed by Bella-Isabella, who made a real effort to be charming and movie-star-like when the cousins came to visit once a year to discuss renewal of the lease, which was always settled on an annual basis.

At the beginning of the 1970s the white villa is put up for sale. The cost of maintenance swallows a considerable share of the cousins' budget, and they never have enough cash. Of course Annette and Johan Wikblad cannot afford to buy the white villa, so in the end it is May and Pusu Johansson who clinch the deal.

"Let's not bicker," says Pusu Johansson, putting a handsome sum on the table. So May and Pusu Johansson buy out the cousins' share in the white villa, for their own use, and renovate it almost beyond recognizability, painting it red with white gables and outside trim, lowering the roof because of the cost of heating, ripping out the old tiled stoves that do not draw, and walling up the open fireplace in the big room.

The cousins sell a small plot of land to Johan Wikblad and Annette in what was once the Rotwoods. There they build a timbered cottage of their own with a place for a boat and swimming rights, not to the white villa's, or as they say now, "the villa's beach," but to the breakwater on the shore alongside, which is still half-owned by a family once called Angel but who almost never come to the summer paradise because they have acquired "a little place" in the real archipelago, and eventually they rent out the house on the hill permanently.

And, of course, yes: The cousins have a considerable part of the big forest cleared; they obtain a very advantageous loan for the purpose.

And so on and so forth, the story of the summer paradise goes on into eternity. But that is no longer important. There are no points of intersection left in this story.

When they get back from the amusement park, it is pitch dark. Kayus looks appealingly at Thomas. But Thomas goes with Ann-Christine and Johan Wikblad who meet them on the path to the red cottage. Gabby comes toward them holding a flashlight. His lit-up face seems white. He's going out into the forest. "Anyone coming with me?"

Renée has taken her sleeping bag and gone into the big forest. She moves her camping site every day but does not sleep in the tent, at least not on the nights when Gabby, alone or with the others in the "patrol," creep up and surround the tent at dawn to surprise her. Each time they are forced to realize the same thing: She is somewhere else.

It is Thomas's tent, the tent that was a Christmas present two years earlier; he does not really mind, because he left it set up in the yard of the white villa's yard for over a month this summer, and by now it has lost all significance. The material has faded, the mosquito netting is ripped, and Thomas thinks about it so rarely that even he cannot say at exactly what point it disappeared from the yard.

So they are looking for Renée. The children in the daytime, the adults in the evenings, when the men come home from work, Gabby alone or sometimes with someone else at night. A *search party*, but Thomas is the only one who knows that, because he is the only one in the summer paradise whose hobby is scouting. This is what happens: They call, make noise, and hope the person who is somewhere in the forest will hear where they are and come out. Or they do as Gabby does, creeping up, planning, devising strategies. But it does not matter what they do. The result is always the same. She does not come out. She is not found. Thomas himself has long been convinced that he knows more or less exactly where she is in the forest at any time of the day or night. When he is leading the daytime search party, in his capacity as the one most knowledgeable, followed

by Maggi and Nina, he often feels that he is leading them astray.
It is not that he wants to lead them astray. Not at all. On the contrary. He would very much like to find Renée. But he knows the discovery has to happen in another way. Not with a search party through the forest, nor slinking around, planning, devising strategies and ambushing a tent. Gradually Renée abandons the tent as well. Of course. They always find it in the same place. Open. The outer zipper broken. But always empty.

This is not a question of weeks. More of days. Long gray days.

"They're frightening the life out of her," says Ann-Christine. "They should leave her alone."

"She's little," says John Wikblad. "Only a child."

"She can look after herself. Everyone knows that. That's what frightens them. That's what they're really worried about. That she has integrity. *That child* has greater integrity than many adults."

Thomas laughs at *child.* He protests. Renée is no child. Then he laughs again. It sounds so funny when Ann-Christine says *that child.*

Johan Wikblad looks at Thomas in surprise and purses his lips slightly, as if to show that Thomas's laughter, which is not at all appropriate in this situation, upsets him a little. Thomas falls silent. He cannot be bothered to explain.

"She's no less a child," says Johan Wikblad. "With immeasurable pressure on her."

"They should leave her alone," says Ann-Christine. "She'll come eventually."

"Will she starve to death?" says Thomas suddenly.

"No," says Ann-Christine. "She'll manage."

"She's got a knife," says Thomas. "My knife."

Then he remembers that originally it was Johan Wikblad's knife. But Johan Wikblad turns a deaf ear. Or he thinks that in this situation it doesn't matter whose knife it is, Thomas guesses, and in that he is right. *This situation.* That is how Johan Wikblad tells him that Renée took the tent and knife and went out into the forest. As time passes and Gabby gets more and more upset, he also says that *someone has to keep a cool head in this situation.*

"Yes," says Johan Wikblad laconically. "She's prepared to use it, too. She almost stabbed Gabby."

"How do you know?" asks Ann-Christine.

"Gabby's T-shirt is ripped."

"Gabby," says Ann-Christine, "exaggerates."

Johan Wikblad shrugs his shoulders. He has his own opinions. Thomas smiles, for suddenly there is something terribly familiar. Thomas recognizes in Johan Wikblad a striving for scientific objectivity. Again Johan Wikblad surprises him with a foolish smile in the absolutely wrong situation. He purses his mouth. Thomas is sort of sad. He would like to explain.

Kayus is ruled out. He is not with them in the forest. He has gone to his veranda with his books and a new transistor radio. He is already thinking about Isabella Mermaid, long, painful thoughts, though he does not say anything, though it does not show. But Thomas knows, and it is unbearable. For Kayus, everything that begins the day Bella disappeared from the summer paradise and did not come back has already started. He has never spoken aloud this thing that is big and lofty and has a name: The Great Afterward. The Rest of Time.

Early one morning Thomas goes into the forest alone. He takes along sandwiches wrapped in paper with him, Extra

King Size chocolate bars, and a thermos, in a basket. He is equipped as if he were going on an excursion. He and Ann-Christine filled the basket in secret, when no one else was around. He climbs up the highest hill, where there had once presumably been a lookout tower, since there has been a pile of graying, semi-rotted boards on the ground as long as Thomas can remember. Thomas scrambles to the top of the boards and looks around. It is a windy day. The wind is all that he can hear. Thomas stands still. When he stops thinking about the wind, it is very quiet. Really quiet. The kind of quiet when everything vanishes—time, too. The sky is still overcast, and the light is such that it could be any time of day. Any day, any year. Thomas suddenly has a feeling that he is falling out of time. Becomes outside time, alongside time. Time is going on somewhere. Tick-tock-tick-tock-tick-tock a distant clock goes, but in another place. The feeling is not pleasant.

To disperse it, he cups his hands around his mouth and shouts. The wind rustles through the trees. He shouts again. No reply. Nothing. He goes down the hill and walks on. He can go where he likes in the big forest, because he knows it better than anyone else. That is what he concentrates on. Even better than Renée. That is the way it has always been. From the start. He was here before her, so he had a head-start. He comes to the place where he and Ann-Christine and Johan Wikblad picked cloudberries. Suddenly he feels it strongly: She is there. He seems to sense her panting, her heavy breathing, her warm breath very near him. He turns around and goes up on the ridge above the hollow where recently there were so many cloudberries. The smell, the heavy prickly smell, is still there, although the berries have gone. No. Nothing.

"Renée! I know where you are. Come on out!"

And after a while: "Don't then, stupid idiot." He puts down the basket and leaves.

The following day, when he returns, he finds the basket in the cloudberry scrub. The sandwich papers are scattered over the moss, glistening with butter and the night's rain, torn to pieces, in places shredded almost like confetti. But in general it looks as if someone had emptied a basket of rubbish in the lovely scenery Thomas knows like the back of his hand. Thomas sits down on the ridge. Now he *knows* she is there.

"Renée!" he calls. "You have to come out."

Then he stops calling, sits down, and starts unpacking that day's basket. He unwraps the fresh sandwiches and puts them in a neat row beside him. He folds up the paper and puts it back in the basket, which he is going to take back home. Puts out paper napkins, too. He is very calm as he works, and in some way his own activities amuse him. But at the same time he makes an effort to be methodical and take his time, as if he did not know or care whether he was being watched by two gleaming eyes.

Not until he has finished putting the food out as neatly as possible does he get up and go. Though not far away, maybe fifty feet, until he finds a suitable hollow, where he lies down to spy. He lies face down, pressing himself into the ground, and watches.

She appears almost at once. She crouches down by the sandwiches and starts eating. She eats roughly and greedily, crouching all the time, like a baboon or something. Otherwise she is just the same as ever. Nothing special about her. Tangled hair, but when was her hair not tangled? Dirty, her clothes grimy, but you get like that in the forest. She is quite herself. That surprises Thomas somehow, and the fact that it surprises him also makes him feel uneasy.

The jerky movements, the monkey ways—somehow all that is a relief by comparison. *Some kind of reasonable explanation.*

"Renée!"

Thomas gets up and shows himself. She looks up. Seems astonished, though she has known all the time that he was nearby.

"Stop it now!" he calls. "What are you playing at?"

She gets up, too, and straightens. Throws the remains of her sandwich away, sticks her hand under her T-shirt, and pulls out the knife, letting the edge glitter at Thomas, long and fatal. There are perhaps ten yards between them. Thomas is not afraid, it is not that, but the situation is unpleasant, in the way that some things he doesn't want to know about are unpleasant. Thomas has an impulse to stick his fingers in his ears, close his eyes tight, and rattle off some monotonous rigmarole to shut out all other sounds and voices around him. But otherwise he is calm. Really calm. And then he does what he has never done properly before. He turns around and walks away.

For a moment he thinks that she is following him. He can almost hear her panting close by. And he remembers all kinds of stuff: that sudden attack and the bite on Wind Island, and Johan Wikblad's knife, which she stole and used to scratch Gabby's arm. No, Ann-Christine is probably wrong. She could easily consider using it. And yet he does not stop, does not hesitate, does not turn around. He walks. Does not run, does not hurry. Just walks.

As he is walking, a thought occurs to him. Unarticulated at first, more of a hunch. But present and inescapable: this is the moment for which he has been in training all the time, all the days of summer. The moment in the forest.

Not until he is really lost does he look around to find that she has vanished. He is standing at the edge of a field. A wide field. It is quite unfamiliar. He can only establish that he has never been here before. Then it begins to rain. Typical—that it should start raining at this very moment, the first and only time you are really and truly lost in the forest.

By the time Thomas gets home, many hours have passed. It is evening. Kayus has come back from work, and everyone is assembled at the red cottage. Kayus, Johan Wikblad, and Ann-Christine.

Thomas is soaking wet. He is a little cold, but not too bad. Inside he still feels warm because he has run a long way. After roaming around for a long time, he finally came to a place that was familiar, and by then he was a long way away from here.

He is out of breath, standing in the dim light of the porch, breathing in absolute silence as they look at him with troubled expressions. Come toward him, ready to hold him, hug him.

"Where have you been? We've been worried." Thomas starts back. Even if it does not make him happy, it is somehow comforting to hear Gabby's familiar voice from the yard, and the situation feels more normal.

"I'll go after her when it gets light!"

"Are you going to take the shotgun?" Ann-Christine says, not without irony in her voice, through the door Thomas has left slightly open.

"It's not inconceivable that he might," says Kayus dryly. He looks appealingly at Thomas. As if wanting to add: Come on. But Thomas has lain down on the country-style sofa and pulled the blanket over himself. He undresses under the blanket, wriggling out of one garment after another and dropping them in a heap on the floor.

Johan Wikblad goes to the house on the hill with Gabby.

"You never know what he'll get up to." Johan Wikblad speaks soberly, winking at Kayus and Ann-Christine and Thomas over his shoulder, as if they had a special understanding in which Gabby is not included.

Kayus picks Thomas's clothes up off the floor. He shakes them out and hangs them on the line in the little kitchen alcove. Thomas turns to the wall, closes his eyes, and dozes off.

Ann-Christine goes out and stays away a long time. When she come back, she says that the sauna is ready. Not without a note of triumph. "I got inside by myself."

Ann-Christine has broken into the Johanssons' sauna. The outer door had been left open, but the door into the washroom and the sauna department was locked, and she had to break the window in the washroom door and get in that way.

"The height of gall, of course," she says. "But necessity is the mother of invention." She looks at Thomas on the country-style sofa as if he were necessity personified. The pneumonia or something equivalent you get from long cold hours languishing in the forest. The Allergic Subject in pouring rain without sufficient clothing.

"And this is an emergency," adds Ann-Christine.

Thomas thinks that he could have told Ann-Christine that the key to the washroom is hidden in an obvious place: under the hose rolled up on a hook by the sauna wall. But he says nothing. Ann-Christine is so proud of her own daring that he does not want to spoil her delight.

"Go on, now, Thomas."

Ann-Christine pulls the blanket off Thomas. Thomas curls up, his hands in front of him. But Ann-Christine is not looking at Thomas's nakedness. She is taking his robe off the hook and throwing it at him so that it lands on his body.

"Go with Kayus and bathe." She gives Kayus the flashlight. "Take this. It's slippery on the rock."

Down in the Johanssons' sauna Thomas has an opportunity to study the hole in the washroom door more closely. It is not big. Ann-Christine has already pasted a piece of plastic over it. Thomas tries to imagine what it had looked like when Ann-Christine's body made its way through the hole. That is, of course, an erroneous idea, because Ann-Christine said herself that she had only made the hole big enough for her hand to get through to open the door from the inside. But Kayus guesses what Thomas is thinking, pats him on the shoulder, and chuckles in the way he used to.

"Emergency," he says. "This is an emergency all right. Will you scrub my back?"

Thomas dips the brush into the bowl and soaps it, then he scrubs Kayus's back. Hard, because Kayus likes that. Red streaks rise on Kayus's pale skin. The hot-water pan steams when Thomas cautiously pokes under the lid, dips the Johanssons' metal scoop in, and pours some more hot water into the bowl. An electric light above the porch door spreads a faint yellow light over the washroom. The August darkness thickens outside. The windows are dark, the concrete floor is very cold if you don't keep your feet on the wooden boards.

Thomas and Kayus throw water on the hot stones and

sweat it out in the hot room, then they go out and cool off on the Johanssons' sauna porch. Naked, not even a towel around them. It is so dark and late in August that there is no need to worry whether anyone will see them. The cottages on the islands in the bay are empty, lights twinkle only at the farther shore. Thomas and Kayus walk across the wet grass, out on to the jetty, and climb down into the water by the swimming ladder, May Johansson's swimming ladder, from a time when it was important that just May Johansson and no one else thought it up that Pusu Johansson should make it and fix it farthest out on Johanssons' and Rosa's and Gabby's joint breakwater. They climb silently up the ladder and run along the wet boards of the jetty, across May Johansson's patch of grass, back to the sauna. Thomas slips on the slippery cold grass.

Up on the top bench again, side by side. Throwing water on the hot stones.

Yet another thing, there in the water: The compact silence and darkness is suddenly shattered by the sound of an engine. The next moment the boat appears out of the sound. All its lights are on, shining brightly. Glittering on the water. Silver-shimmering. They cannot see who is in the boat. The tarpaulin is drawn over the whole body. It chugs fairly slowly along the sound. Then swings out, speeds up, and races off to the other side of the bay. A glittering island of light. Then the dark and the silence return.

Thomas moves a step down to the lower bench, so that he is by the window. The pane is steamed over. He starts drawing lines in the mist with his forefinger and tries to look out through the lines.

“What are you drawing?” says Kayus.

“Nothing,” says Thomas.

“Don’t be so impossible, Thomas,” says Kayus, suddenly harsh, as if he thought Thomas is teasing him. Thomas says nothing. He is not teasing. It is true what he says: He is drawing nothing. As soon as a pattern or a figure or something that might be something or look like or resemble something particular takes shape, he wipes it away with new lines. He is making a real effort to achieve something that is not anything, cannot possibly be defined, be given a name. He would like to tell Kayus that it is not at all easy, but he does not. On the contrary: almost impossible. At least he does not manage to. And gradually the game ends. He has traced lines all over the window. The pane is clear and dark again.

She is lying face down on the ground. It has stopped raining, but the ground is wet. Soaking. She has waited out the rain in one of her hiding places. Now the rain has stopped, and she has come out again. And is on her way. She presses her body into the ground. The wetness is sucked up into her clothes. They are already damp, so she does not really feel the difference.

She is spying, all her senses alert. It is getting lighter now. It is a matter of paying attention. The wind rustles in the trees. All she can hear now is her own breathing, the throbbing in her body. She can smell only her own smell. Wet clothes, wet earth. Almost light. They will soon be coming. Will be here at any moment. She knows that. She has been waiting for them to come, to be here. She has wrenched off her orange T-shirt. It glows like a traffic light in the monotonous gray landscape. The short-sleeved blouse she wears underneath is blue.

And then there are sounds. She cautiously levers herself up onto her knees, peers between the branches of a bush. They are by the tent. They always start from there. They have surrounded the tent. As usual, shaking it and looking inside. Finding it empty. Finding the same thing for perhaps the tenth time. Idiots. On second thought, stupid idiots. Of course the tent is empty. She has used it for ages. The tent is nothing and is unimportant. Or just camouflage. She scrambles up, crouches down and gets ready.

Fear, what about fear? Am I afraid?

Oh, yes. The fear comes now. It always comes at the same place. Always starts here. *Don't move.* Now they have found out that the tent is empty. They kick the tent, crane their necks, and sniff the air. *No panic now.* You know you are safe as long as you do not move. *Go away!* They come closer. Twigs snap, the ground vibrates with the tramping of boots. Bite hard into the birch branch. Your mouth full of sap. Sweet. Hand fumbles under the blouse. The knife is there, as it should be. Calm now. Let it begin. The time has come, take your places, get set. Up on your feet. Run. On your way.

And they spot her. Call out. To each other, to her. And go after her.

She runs in a zigzag course and in circles. In larger and smaller circles and in other formations. They keep up quite well, but she is swifter. And one thing, she knows the forest and knows how to move in it better than the others. She tires them out. They get lost and lose track. Wearied, they cannot go on. The more tired they get, the less they can cope, the more frequently they get lost, lose track. Sometimes she goes out of sight for long spells. Disappearing completely. But appears again as if it were a game. Showing herself in places where they least expect her to be. They start off. Trying to catch up.

But once she makes a wrong judgment. When she appears, she is far too close. Brushing by, only a few feet away. And then they almost have her, so they can catch her. At that moment she is disconcerted. Turns and runs straight ahead, without a plan. Panic. To panic is highly dangerous. She is also pretty tired, and when you're tired, to be in a panic is an obvious disadvantage. Seriously dangerous. And she knows it.

She runs and runs straight ahead as fast as she can. Aimlessly. Without a thought in her head. Fleeing, in other words; and when you flee, speed and strength are what matter. But she has no intention of giving up, never. Her body is pounding with exhaustion, excitement. They are getting nearer. Nearer and nearer, and in a moment or two, they will be so close that she knows there's no hope. Then, suddenly, she loses her footing and rolls down into a crevice. A perfect crevice, a place of safety, just right for her. She can rest for a few moments, collect her wits, gather courage, prepare herself. Before the voices and footsteps return.

Her hand fumbles under her blouse. The knife is gone. She has dropped it. Where? When? Just now, while she was running aimlessly and without a plan? No time to think? Keep a cool head. Must run. Run.

The forest thins out. She finds herself facing a field. Looks around. Bewildered at first; she does not know where she is. She has never seen this place before. Funny. This field, it is quite unfamiliar. Her eyes calculate the distance. Impossible. A wide field, nowhere to hide and rest. Then she notices how thirsty she is. Tumbles down into the ditch between field and forest. Thirsty. To water now. The ditch is deeper than she had thought, widening in both directions. She chooses one. Onward. Gradually she comes to a place she recognizes, where there is water under the soil: a tributary of the river that runs through the forest and emerges into the sea further away. She drinks. And hears them. But no longer cares.

They can catch her, they can have her now.

Though the moment she thinks that, her strength returns, she knows, just like that. *Just you come.* It will not work. It will never succeed.

The sound of footsteps and voices dying away. Strange. lost again. They have lost track.

And morning comes, afternoon, evening, and dusk.

At dusk she, Renée, crawls through the long grass in the meadow below the white villa. Opens the heavy door of the root cellar and slips inside. Lies down under the table and falls asleep under a blanket. A beach blanket. Thomas put it there, though she does not know that, nor does anyone else, not even Ann-Christine. Thomas thought that it might come in useful. You never know. *And you never can know.*

Rosa goes to get her in the root cellar the next day. Rosa goes straight there as soon as she's back in the summer paradise. A return that occurs discreetly and in a very ordinary way. Rosa walks down the hill and toward the white villa, then continues on down to the meadow. She has no problem finding her. She seems to know exactly what to do to find Renée.

Somehow it seems to be a different Rosa. Thomas notices a new Rosa, an extremely rose-colored Rosa. She is wearing the same light-blue dress and white cardigan that she wore an eternity ago, but the similarity ends there. This Rosa, pulling open the door of the root cellar and fumbling her way into the dim light, is a Rosa whose hands you would never even dream of holding, almost squeezing (and blushing afterward).

The new Rosa stands at the entrance of the root cellar and calls to Renée. Renée shows herself in the cellar darkness. She comes out. Capitulates, unresisting.

Of course, she is ill. She has a temperature, a cough, and a cold, and she has to stay in bed in her room with the curtains drawn. She is cossetted, surrounded by soft drinks, Donald Duck comics, and a Peter Pan game Thomas brings her for two reasons.

First of all because the game is hers and was left behind at the white villa a year or two ago and he wants to return it to its rightful owner, for he and Kayus are clearing up and packing to leave, stowing things in the car and lashing things on to the roof.

Secondly because he wants to check up on something.

"Why did you do it?" he asks. But Renée cannot answer.

"I just felt like it," is all she says. "Don't you ever feel like doing stuff?"

Thomas shrugs his shoulders and leaves. Now he has checked out what he wanted to check out. It makes sense. He cannot get away from the fact that her power to bewitch has fled.

Rosa stands up on the hill and is doing laundry. For a moment Thomas thinks something else. It suddenly occurs to him that at first, long ago, when she went around with her camera taking photographs, photographs she said she was going to paste in an album, which she never did, nothing came of it, she wearied of it, it was no longer of interest, "I'm tired of taking photographs, Bella, I want to develop my own life," she said to Bella one of these summers, summers with Rosa, *Rosa and all those photographs*—those are what are flying around her now, photographs whirling all over the summer paradise, whole photographs and others torn into bits.

"Look, Thomas, look how they fly!"

But it is only laundry. In a bowl, panties and other things you wash by hand even when you have a washing machine. Rinsing out, as they say, every evening, for the Western woman values cleanliness. And when Rosa suddenly looks up from the bowl and addresses Thomas, it is in a low, scarcely audible voice. Not quite a chirp, a little higher perhaps, but almost.

"Thomas," says Rosa.

"Thomas. I meant it. Everything. I can't say more. I can't explain. Just that I . . . yes."

"Yes," says Thomas, though he shakes his head and has already begun to run down the hill. Perhaps Rosa has taken his running away as still another of the innumerable expressions of silence surrounding her from nearly every direction when she returns to the summer paradise. A silence that is eager to tell her one thing over and over: that it was her fault, *that everything was Rosa's fault,* and now we are not talking about only Rosa and Bella and that story but about *everything* from an all-embracing point of view—including the fact that those last few months of summer were no summer at all, as May Johansson says to the left and the right, just as if she were talking about the weather now that she is back from the long trip in time to get a word in edgewise, words in edgewise, with her busy tongue, before Thomas and Kayus leave. She stands by the car where they are lashing their things to the roof before their departure, talking.

But it is not like that, Rosa.

Thomas is mute for the opposite reason. He is mute because he understands perfectly. *About Bella.* But how can you say it? Express it? When you yourself do not know what it really is you understand. Except that you do. Exactly. Definitely.

Say? That is just words, talk.

"Yes." Thomas has run down the hill to the white villa's yard and the car that is almost ready to leave.

So it becomes what it becomes between Thomas and Rosa in the summer paradise.

"Thomas. I'd like to tell you about . . ."

He knows that, too. About the hotel room in Copenhagen, what it was like to wake up one morning and realize she was not there. To wait half the day, knowing perfectly well she was not coming back.

For that was where the story of the Women on the Beach ends. In a hotel room in Copenhagen. There is a perfectly natural explanation, but in this context it is of no interest. For some alleged reason, Bella was to go on to Poland. But nothing came of Poland, for reasons which no doubt exist but which do not belong in this story. And the baby was born months later, in the spring of 1966. But that in itself was unimportant, that baby and who the father was and things like that, which were to make May Johansson shake her gray head meaningfully more than once. Another baby, that really made no difference. Another baby could not stop Rosa. She was off and away and would take everything with her.

Copenhagen—just a little trip in expectation of something more. One morning she woke in their hotel room, and Bella was not there. While she was waiting for Bella to come back, slowly she began to realize that it was going to be like this, she had been deceived. Or she had deceived herself. You don't listen, Bella had said to her at times. But why didn't she say anything herself, Bella?

By then it was already a quarter to three in the afternoon and Bella had been gone for hours. She had taken her things and left while Rosa was asleep.

She had written a note, which she had tucked into her handbag, and when she opened the handbag the next time, she was at a petrol gas station and half a day had passed. She threw the note away and went on. Or she never wrote a note at all.

Thomas is back in the white villa.

"Aren't we going back soon?' is the first thing he asks when he gets there. Kayus is already packing his summer library.

"Give me a hand with this," he says, assembling his clothes and lots of other stuff into suitcases and cardboard boxes, which they then carry out to the yard to stow in the car. The broken transistor radio is thrown away, and Thomas puts his birthday presents, games, model sets, and so on into his duffel bag. Meanwhile the Johanssons are back from their long voyage. When Erkki Johansson comes running across the yard, Kayus and Thomas have just lashed the last of the boxes on the car roof.

"Are you leaving now?" Erkki Johansson stops abruptly, right in the middle of a movement. The movement is as follows: he has held out his hand toward Thomas, then opened it.

In it is a shell. He has picked it himself, right out on the edge of the archipelago. It is a dull yellow color, smaller by half than a pinkie, and filled with brown mud. But it is for Thomas. Erkki Johansson saved the shell the entire long voyage, thinking only of Thomas. He does not exactly say it like that. But it is written all over his face. Erkki Johansson cannot lie. His face is an open book.

"Yes," Thomas takes the shell from Erkki Johansson and sticks it in his trouser pocket. He picks up his duffel bag and gets in the car, in the front, beside Kayus. He waves. Erkki Johansson stays where he is in the yard. He also waves. So does May Johansson, who has been interrupted in the middle of one of her long sentences. That is the last Thomas ever sees of Erkki Johansson in the summer paradise and probably forever.

But he saves the shell. He puts it in the top drawer of his desk in his room in the city apartment. Drops it in among all his other things, but quite near the front of the drawer, so that he sees the shell every time he opens the drawer. Gradually the shell begins to smell faintly of salt and sort of sour. Not a pleasant smell, and although it is not strong, it spreads through the drawer, so that everything in it acquires the same smell. It is fairly nasty, and yet Thomas cannot bring himself to throw the shell away because he thinks about Erkki Johansson on his long trip finding a shell he thought was the handsomest of all shells and deciding that that is the shell for Thomas.

In time Thomas thinks less and less about Erkki Johansson. One day in December 1965 he opens the drawer, finds the shell, and examines it as if for the first time. Full of dirt. What is it doing in his drawer? At that moment he cannot think of a single reasonable answer. He crushes the shell in his hand, grinding it to pieces over the wastepaper basket.

And they never return to the summer paradise.

Thomas becomes a boy without a summer paradise. A city boy who occasionally defects to the country. The next summer and the summers to follow are different kinds of summers, city summers in the main, with occasional breaks for scout camp, scouting excursions, trips to Lapland, and small cottages on inland lakes rented by the week. The following Midsummer will already be one of those new summers. Thomas will stand on a jetty by a lake with a fishing rod, beside another boy of about the same age, who also has a fishing rod. Both of them will be in track suits and exchange swearwords, because they do not know each other very well, while they catch fish. Fish after fish after fish. When they have taken them off the hook, they put them into a white bucket of water between them on the jetty, for the boy is the son of one of Kayus's colleagues at work with whom they rent the cottage to share expenses. Others in the cottage are the children and the boy's mother and Ann-Christine. The boy and Thomas will play football or darts or practice with peashooters, catapults, or whatever they will be doing in a few weeks' time. Whatever boys do when they are together: Thomas lists all the players in the soccer team for which he roots, as the other boy is a fan of a different team. All the players backwards in order of their numbers. And every time he gets in a particularly good shot in goal behind the other boy's back, he says the name of one of the players in the team who shoots just the kind of beautiful goal Thomas would like to shoot if he were interested in soccer. He is not. He is a scout. His hobby is scouting.

Thomas becomes a boy without a summer paradise. That is not as awful as it sounds. Summers. There is life elsewhere.

Thomas becomes someone who really likes the autumn and winter and spring and city life with school and everything. Sometimes in the summer he goes down to the basement and waits for school to begin. He does not know why. He likes the autumn. But he also likes the basement, the basement smell, sweet, tickling his nose a little. Though it gradually begins to smell of cigarette smoke. More and more of smoke. Secret smoke. Bjöna is an orange spot in the dim light, on the seat of an anonymous bicycle placed farther back. Sometimes he smokes several cigarettes one after one another so as not to have to keep going down there. And he talks, out into the dim light.

He talks about music; names the names of different pop and rock groups Thomas doesn't know or has just caught in passing, gabbling words like *tune in, turn on, drop out,* talking about what happens out in the world. Thomas listens carefully, slightly interested, too, but nonetheless always aware that he is somewhere else, not where Bjöna is. The world where Bjöna, Nina Angel, and all those others live is not his world.

But it is not really dramatic. There are no dividing lines that would constitute insuperable barriers or anything like that. Bjöna and he are simply not such good friends any longer. They have different interests. Thomas's best friend is called Dennis Kronlund.

Occasionally he also enjoys Bjöna's stories. Just because they are different. And the way Bjöna also makes an effort to make them different, Thomas appreciates that as well. That summer, those weeks, when suddenly everyone is on the moon, Bjöna kicks the bicycle stand so hard that the basement seems filled with thunder, and he talks about the *disintegration of the myth.* The moon and all that; that's a culmination *in absurdum,* Bjöna says, of a dream that falls apart before your very eyes while it is being enacted before your very eyes. Roughly at the same time as the astronauts land on the moon, the last Kennedy drives out into the water in a car, and he has a blonde with him. *No. She won't be saved.* A slightly blurry photograph in the newspapers, a school photograph of a college girl. Mary Jo: yet another pathetic blonde irrelevant to the context.

Thomas becomes a boy without a summer paradise. But it is not too bad. Instead, his city block, with its three floors, courtyard, shopping center, the whole of this suburb and all the other suburbs around which you move between in blue and red buses, are etched into him. That becomes his mental map, a map that constantly conceals new secrets and reveals new meanings.

A person without a summer paradise. It is not bad. For the world starts outside the summer paradise. Everything else is there, *all kinds of stuff.* Gently, in some way, the world receives him, like the spruce branches he sleeps on when he is hiking in the forest. For he is a scout. Thomas is primarily a scout right up until he stops being one at the end of the 1960s and has his first girlfriend, Camilla, *the psychologist of the class.*

Bella. Yes. He can fall asleep at night and yearn. Probably a longing for someone, something, so in that way he can give it some outline. But another kind. A longing for someone who exists and at the same time does not exist. And you are aware of the discrepancy. It is called the Viviann longing. Though, Viviann: that is just an image of an atmosphere that can be acquired by thinking about a girl with a white blouse, jeans, and long, straight, light-brown hair.

Bella. Yes. But in another way. Not so dramatically. And the official version, the Mermaid Chapter as cultivated in the third-floor apartment in a suburb east of the city with Kayus in the television chair on the other side of the wall—to all that, he is totally alien. It makes him almost angry to think more closely on the matter, staying in the apartment instead of going out, out into your suburb and the other suburbs, to Dennis Kronlund, to Bjöna in the basement, to school, to the scouts, and all kinds of things, *all kinds of things*.

Actually, it is no more dramatic than that.

When Ann-Christine finally leaves Kayus after *four fruitless years,* Thomas is sad, of course, but it is not a great inflated sadness metaphysically full of significance. It's just that he liked Ann-Christine. "Four fruitless years," says Ann-Christine. It is the autumn of 1969, in the hall closet. She goes out into the hall, puts on her outdoor clothes, and leaves the apartment, slamming the door behind her. She cannot cope any longer. So she says. That she does not want to do it. But she does it.

At the time Thomas is in his dark room with a flashlight. They had all been inside the closet, he as well. At first only Kayus and Ann-Christine. They had gone there to work out how they were going to find room for Ann-Christine's things when, after a great deal of discussion, she has at last agreed to move into the apartment. Ann-Christine has pointed at all the yellow cardboard boxes on which Kayus has written Isabella's name with a thick red marker. Then she suggested that they could be taken down to the basement or up into the attic, or they could even sort out the contents first if there wasn't enough space in the attic or the basement, then anything unnecessary could be thrown away. Kayus was uncooperative, as always when it comes to the yellow cardboard boxes, which actually do take up almost a whole wall of shelves. Thomas heard everything and felt he must go to Ann-Christine and Kayus to lighten the mood. As far as he's concerned, the yellow cardboard boxes can go anywhere, *that's not what's important about Bella,* and he has no objection to Ann-Christine's presence in the apartment. On the contrary. So he picked up his scout's flashlight, went into the closet, turned out the light, then switched on his flashlight and put it under his chin so the beam of light falls on his face, then made monster faces to lighten the mood, although he's fourteen and too old for that kind of childish game. Ann-Christine laughed, but only briefly and politely, then had gone out into the hall, picked up her coat, and left the apartment, no less.

Thomas stands by the window in his room and turns on the flashlight. Ann-Christine is standing at the bus stop. Thomas signals with the flashlight—three long, three short. She waves. She really understands. She shrugs and throws out her hands. Then the bus comes, and she's gone. But for Thomas, this is what it's like: He's not sending out an SOS with his flashlight because he's hopelessly lost. He just likes Ann-Christine and doesn't want her to go away on the bus, then go abroad to continue her studies and never come back. And he's ashamed of Kayus. For to Kayus, Ann-Christine's walking out on him is nothing but a symptom of another absence, a considerably greater one, an absence of desert-like dimensions, and that absence is called The Absence of the Mermaid. That's what largely makes impossible all of life's possibilities, at least a life that is other than brooding in the television chair. In Thomas's eyes, that whole story comes under the considerably less flattering heading of the Mermaid *Chapter.*

It's not really like that from the beginning. It takes time before life can find its tracks and acquire a pattern.

Right at the beginning, in the autumn of 1965, when you'd returned from the summer paradise to the apartment and for the first time ever to city life without Isabella Mermaid, there is nothing but silence, muteness. Everything seems incomprehensible. There are no reasons or explanations. Then they come, by themselves. This: In the spring of 1966, at the beginning of March, a baby is born in a maternity hospital somewhere in Sweden. Bella's baby, the baby who will eventually be called Julia Angel.

Thomas is standing in goal during the semifinal match of the school's ice hockey playoffs, and the puck comes flying straight at his face just before the second half and before he has had a chance to adjust the mask. He has to go to the hospital and have stitches in his upper lip and the corner of his mouth, and when he's feeling better, Kayus mentions in passing that Bella has astonished everyone by giving birth to a baby in Sweden. On her own. Without involving anyone else. So there's no name of any father.

"Think we should send her a telegram, Thomas?"

Thomas is ashamed, for Ann-Christine is there, too. And for some reason he is also angry, furious.

He realizes that Kayus still understands nothing about Isabella Mermaid, Isabella Jazz Singer, Isabella Movie Star, Isabella the Most Beautiful Mother in the Courtyard, Isabella Woman on the Beach. To Kayus everything else is just so much Blue Grass, although Isabella stopped using that perfume long ago. Everything Kayus did not understand about Bella he called

Blue Grass, a provocative and heavy perfume, yes, but perfume in general stands for makeup and everything that is unnecessary, of no importance, not real.

Like that summer of 1965: the way Kayus thought it would somehow be enough to go to Lapland or sulk on the veranda and be left in peace. In peace; as if it would be enough for everyone to be left in peace wherever they are, think about what was happening, and calm down, because things would go back to the way they were before, because Kayus said they would, everyone at peace waiting for IT to go away—the implication being that IT was some kind of innate impossibility in Isabella, which would probably go away if she could be left in peace to think, and to think better of it—and then all would be ordinary and happy again, *oneself again,* and they would meet again in the autumn in a city life, then adopt Kayus's version of life again; with all that that entails of listening to jazz and elaborating on the mermaid mythology, plowing deeper and deeper down into its secrets, the two of them, of course, Kayus and Bella, or then, as a family, Kayus and Bella and Thomas—you know, That Story.

"Think we should send a telegram, Thomas?" A reasonable explanation has appeared, Bella made contact by telephone (she called from a public phone booth somewhere, eager to communicate the happy event). There's the possibility of a new story, yet another. Kayus doesn't think his hope shows, but he's an open book. In the new story, beginning in his mind with Bella's coming back (of course) with the baby (why not, on second thought), and since she is temperamental and unpredictable, someone who marches to a different drummer, she has to be indulged, and besides, Kayus's love is great and marvelous—in that story he therefore becomes the substitute father, and the baby girl is incorporated into a new family, which is now a quartet instead of a trio, as before ("Thomas has a sister, a little sister, Thomas, just what you've always wanted?" that jingle). Thomas blushes inwardly and is ashamed, ashamed, even when Ann-Christine isn't there. Well.

Of course she doesn't come back however much she *thinks it over.* Two years later, you hear from her again. She is in Mallorca, works there as a *tourist guide.*

Obviously living the good life, Thomas thinks. And on she goes. From *life to life to life.* All those postcards, those telephone calls, static on the line, rather like it had sounded on the FM in Gabby's angel. Thomas understands completely. It IS the good life.

But he doesn't think so much about it. He is in another life.

"Think we should send a telegram?"

Thomas doesn't answer. He says nothing. He has a doctor's certificate for his silence. Because of the injury to his mouth, he is unable to talk for three days. Mute and clenched, he plays Battleship with Ann-Christine.

The first thing he says when he regains his voice is that he's giving up ice hockey. He's almost eleven, and it's high time for those with no aptitude, or no real interest in taking ice hockey seriously and playing in various divisions, to give it up.

"It will give me more time for scouts," says Thomas, and both Kayus and Ann-Christine look surprised as he explains. There's no need to explain. They accept his decision, after all, as Ann-Christine puts it, in general terms. No need to account for all his doings to them.

Thomas goes to Cub Scouts. He changes patrol. From Baloo Baloo to Shere Khan. It happens like this. Once when

Thomas is on his way to a scout meeting, he sees Cassius Clay, or Muhammed Ali as Clay insists on calling himself. Not really, of course, but on the front of a magazine hanging at a newspaper stand. When Thomas sees Cassius Clay, he remembers all kinds of things connected with boxing. Huotari's and his common interest. Liston, The King of the Beasts, who boxed with a punching bag to background music, "Night Train," an eternity ago, at the amusement park.

Thomas arrives at the meeting not as himself but as another Thomas. In a flash he changes guise and is Thomas the Squabbler and sets about provoking Dennis Kronlund himself, so that a few minutes later the fight is a fact. A patrol leader intervenes, and it's settled. Though afterward Dennis Kronlund tells Thomas that he didn't put his full strength into it. He had allowed himself to be provoked by Thomas, mostly because he was curious about Thomas's sudden change of personality. "Don't lie, you idiot," says Thomas quite firmly. Dennis Kronlund is startled, looks at Thomas with surprise but also quite definitely with approval. Thomas and Dennis shake hands, and Thomas becomes the same old Thomas again. But two things have changed. Thomas and Dennis Kronlund become friends. From now on Thomas and Dennis are inseparable. In their free time and at school. And in his last year as a cub before moving up to scouts, Thomas is Second Patrol Leader in the Shere Khan patrol. He is appointed at Dennis Kronlund's express request.

The following happens to the Angel family:

Gabby's business with cassettes continues well into the 1970s. Anyhow, far too long before he realizes his mistake in time to get out. *He ought to have gone in for chosen*

CDs. Gabby never makes his mark in the history of music. Gabby loses money. Goes bankrupt. Everything down the drain. That's to say, the cassette side down the drain in what at this stage are diversified corporate activities. Gabby has a great many irons in the fire. So it doesn't matter so much. On the contrary, perhaps the bankruptcy has some positive effects on his total long-term economy; Gabby can centralize his activities and channel all his resources into more lucrative projects.

Evidence of Gabby's success is the building of the Dream House in 1970, in the most elegant part of the leafy town where the Angel family has settled. Then he has two summer places, two wonderful, talented daughters, a well-preserved wife, former ground attendants as well as flight attendants to amuse him in his spare time.

There is no shortage of flight attendants. The supply is constantly increasing. If at the end of the 1950s there was a total of about seven thousand flight attendants in the world, ten years later the number is nearer fifty thousand. If the figures are examined more closely, it can be seen that the turnover is also pretty high. Each month about seven hundred and fifty flight attendants leave, but at the same time a thousand more are appointed. And all airlines look for the same sort of young women.

"We're not looking for photographic models or beauty queens," says personnel manager XX of YY, one of the world's leading airlines. "We want the girl at whom the average passenger can look and think 'That was a pretty girl. That really was a nice girl.' "

■ ■ ■

On her own initiative Renée joins a skating class, because for a time after the summer she went out into the forest, she becomes obsessed with the idea of learning to skate, not for ice hockey but figure skating. Like in *Holiday On Ice* or something. Pirouettes and various figures, little leaps in the air. The attempt is a fiasco. She cannot even learn to skate backward properly. Her body grows no less clumsy however much she practices, more than anyone else in the class. Her teacher is surprised, and so is she. Her failure is also something of a humiliation for a successful competitive sailor like herself. She hangs up her skates.

The hook is in the changing room at the ice rink. It is one afternoon in March. Renée leaves in the middle of a lesson. Rosa drives up to the ice rink half an hour later. Rosa waits. No sign of Renée. No one knows where she is. Rosa drives around looking for her. She telephones all Renée's friends from school and her own friends and acquaintances. No one knows anything about Renée.

Rosa takes the skates off the hook in the changing room at the ice rink. She drives home and puts them on the table, then sits staring at them in dread. Naturally they are expensive skates, white with gleaming black heels. Made to be stared at.

But nothing at all has happened. Renée comes home. She says she just felt like it. She has no other answer.

Renée joins the Brownies, but she is a long way behind the girls in her age group. While her contemporaries are Elves or Pixies, the highest possible level in the Brownies, she is struggling with the very first tasks for a Brownie badge. She can do nothing to catch up because the badges have to be earned in order; she tries to compensate by beating all records and collecting as many of the special badges as possible in a month.

 Cleaner Badge, Cookery Badge, Little Home Help Badge, Big Home Help Badge, and more. She breaks the record, but no one seems to care.

Her uniform includes a round cap with a loop on the top and a neckerchief tied in a seaman's knot. At the meetings she sings with the others, "Bring out the best in you, though the road is long, Cross looks are never good, no, laugh and sing, all as one." And while the song is going on, she fixes her eyes on the leader's brown leather belt with its metal clasp on which the letters BE PREPARED dance around. She wants that belt. She goes with them to the indoor camp in Klöverängen, steals the belt, and leaves the Brownies.

She lies in her room in the darkness for a week in April, a behavior that leads to a visit to a child psychologist. What can they say? She is outside any established categories. Once she was a wild creature in the forest. That fact cannot be interpreted; it is untranslatable.

But then summer returns, and sailing. Renée places third in the national championships. They give her a new boat, and she practices diligently. All that costs money, of course, But money these days is not really an object.

Rosa talks on the telephone to Tupsu Lindbergh. Talks and talks, through years and years. Rosa Angel talks about *this and that.* Dreams, dreams, a few thoughts, too. But they are only words.

Some time at the end of the 1960s Rosa ends up on the top of the Auyán-Tepuí mountain because Gabriel is on business in Venezuela.

It is an old dream. To stand on the top of the Auyán-Tepuí mountain where in the 1930s the American fighter pilot

Jimmie Angel landed in his little plane that because inextricably mired in a muddy pool and is still there to this very day—*a fine flamingo*—and discovered the highest waterfall in the world named after him, Angel Falls. To be able to touch the metal of the plane, now a national monument, to be photographed beside it, the gleaming plaque Jimmie Angel's son himself fixed to the plane, In Memory of My Father, and to look down into the chasm and feel dizzy.

One of many dreams. Dreams, dreams, dreams . . .

"Jesus, Tupsu, our dreams go so quickly nowadays. You can't keep up with them coming true. One after another they come true. The second and the third and the fourth. My head whirls sometimes, Tupsu Lindbergh. Sometimes I have a feeling that all those dreams will be the death of me."

"What do you mean?" asks Tupsu Lindbergh.

Rosa cannot come up with an answer that would sound sensible. But really, this is what she means:

Up there on the Auyán-Tepuí mountain, Rosa thinks as she gazes at the Angel Falls and feels dizzy—no, she doesn't think what she ought to think, as Nina Angel points out cynically to her when they are back home again, for this happens after Nina has stopped parachute jumping: "How can anyone discover a waterfall? It must have been there all the time. The Indians are sure to have had their own name for it for ages. Has anyone asked the Indians what the waterfall is called?"—*I'm falling falling falling* . . . until she understands that she is not falling at all. She has both feet firmly planted on the ground. Nor will she fall. The stakes are too high. They have become too high.

That is what she actually says to herself somewhere in those regions inside her where a voice she prefers not to listen to goes on talking; it is not the voice of conscience, either, but a voice full of great plans for a new life, new thoughts, new ideas.

But if you fall from here, you can't just patch yourself up again afterward, leave everything, go away to another life, and say the crash was good for your head because it made you think clearly. The stakes are too high. Tumbling down Auyán-Tepuí. You die, you kill yourself.

"I'm falling falling falling," says Rosa suddenly on the phone to Tupsu Lindbergh.

"Though, Tupsu, that's also an ordinary, banal thought. My mind's full of ordinary, banal thoughts.

"I can't express myself any better.

"And I talk nonsense. Only nonsense.

"I seem to be that sort of person. Babble. Somebody who is exactly what she looks like. What are you having for dinner tonight, Tupsu? I wonder what we'll have."

And blah blah blah. Until they hang up. And call each other again. The next day, and the next. Talking. Months pass, and years.

The women on the beach. Never. A photograph fluttering away on the wind. Flitter-fluttering from the mountain on one of the last days of August 1965.

No. The photograph is probably there. Somewhere. Among all her things.

It is a day at the end of May 1968.

Nina Angel comes sailing through the air. Her parachute has opened above her head. It is lovely in the sunlight. Red, white, blue, and huge. What a day for parachute jumping. No wind, unlimited visibility. Sailing down through the air. Seeing the world from above. That perspective.

Nina Angel, parachute jumper, not a professional but skilled, though not as skilled as her sister Renée is at sailing. Nina Angel has done a great many jumps in a great many different contexts. Even competed some, but only in competitions arranged by the parachuting club to which she belongs.

At the beginning of the jump, this time, Nina concentrates on the usual as she throws herself out of the plane and falls toward the ground while the parachute opens like a flower above her head: the various elements of the jump. Perfecting those elements.

The jump as an athletic achievement. For Nina Angel, that is what it is, that is what it has been. Until now.

For a moment on this fantastic day she forgets herself. Everything she is supposed to think about—the various elements of a jump, together making up an athletic achievement—simply blows away.

For a moment she really does look down on the earth she is hovering above. Is a three hundred feet, a hundred and fifty feet, a hundred feet from the ground, and even closer.

She sees violence, war, injustice. Oppression and provocation. Above France the sky is red from the burning cars in the Parisian street riots.

And Nina Angel asks herself: What am I doing? Here? Hovering up in the air?

And it strikes her, unexpectedly: She does not know. *She has no idea.*

After all, it is quite meaningless.

She looks around in the air. Birds, birds. Doves; even the

doves have a more meaningful task: being the symbols of peace and freedom. At least the white ones.

She doesn't laugh. It is not as amusing as it sounds. Once you have thoughts like that, there is no going back. You cannot come down to earth and pretend not to know what you were thinking up in the air, go on as if those thoughts had never been thought. That would be hypocrisy. Nina Angel knows one thing, although there are those who would say that she does not know very much: She does not want to be a hypocrite. But what is she to do now? The future, all these parachute jumps, all this traveling, and all her brilliant outlook seem preposterous. Nina is seized with anguish. It is a perfectly serious feeling and she has no desire to wallow in it as her mother, Rosa Angel, does.

She must do something.

She sums up the possibilities. It has been said of her that she has a good clear voice, perfect for megaphones.

Her hair is great, too, long, dark and glossy, fairly thick, rather like an Indian's. People have commented on it appreciatively. Everyone certainly knows who her father is: Gabriel Angel. Already before this perfect afternoon in sun and perfect wind conditions, owing to her appearance and background, Nina has been the perfect focus of attention at certain parties she has occasionally attended.

THUD. Nina Angel lands.

She runs. She runs as fast as she can, away from the parachute so as not to end up under its huge panoply, as you're supposed to do, as she has learned by heart, automatic in her already. Then she flings herself to the ground and rolls over. That is out of habit and entirely unnecessary. But she likes rolling on the ground after floating about in the air. Feeling the ground, the earth, not just under her feet but in her whole body. Then she gets up, unfastens the parachute, and goes to her family, telling them that she wants to give up everything that *isn't*.

Her words sound rather clumsy and stiff at first, because her vocabulary is limited. But she learns, studies in order to develop. Very soon she will be fluent in another language, which expresses more exactly whatever it was that caused her anguish and panic in the air.

III

siblings

Our so-called popular music (jazz, swing, bop and back to "progressive" jazz) is the real folk music of our time. It reflects and expresses the uncertainty and nostalgic longing with which most of us look at life today. We're not at all sure, now, that "dreams come true"—at least those dreams we all grew up with—"boy meets girl, boy loses girl, boy gets girl," and "they lived happily ever after." And yet we must keep on hoping that our particular dream will come true. We all want to be happy, but we don't know how to set about reaching this elusive state.

GERALD HEARD ON THE SLEEVE OF *CHET BAKER SINGS*, PACIFIC RECORDS, 1956.

She was only seventeen when I was born, says Thomas years later to his first girlfriend, Camilla, *the little psychologist of the class.* They are in his room in the city apartment, and Kayus is watching television on the other side of the wall. It is the winter after the moon landing, and the television program is repeating the same scenes over and over again.

> *Aldrin with the seismometer. The Eagle has landed in the Sea of Tranquility. Here is an overall view of Tranquility Base with the Eagle in the background. We are now looking forward to a new decade during which the breakthrough that has been made will be used to increase even further the knowledge of this universe, in which our earth is but a grain of dust.*

Thomas is not interested in space and rockets. And yet he cannot help being infected by the general moon euphoria that went on for a few days during the summer. "It's wonderful when someone you like has the opportunity to do exactly what he's always dreamed of doing," Mrs. Aldrin said. Not in those words, of course. But something like it. Anyhow, even if Thomas cannot say what he was doing when President Kennedy was assassinated, he can at least remember where he was when man first set foot on the moon: in a scout tent, in the forest, playing cards with Buster Kronlund, Dennis, and some others. In the middle of the night they walked across a meadow. The moon was out. They stopped, fell silent, and thought about the astronauts up there. But you could not see the astronauts, and Buster Kronlund said something funny about that. They laughed. The sense of a great step forward in the history of mankind was dampened, vanished, and they went back to their dark tent in camp, got into their sleeping bags on the spruce branches they'd spread out on the ground, and Thomas the Storyteller told stories, Buster Kronlund said things you remembered afterward. Among them this: *A woman is at her most beautiful at seventeen.* Buster Kronlund's girlfriend was seventeen. Thomas used to adore them, Buster's girlfriends. In appearance, they reminded him of Camilla in his class at school.

"You look miserable. Tell me. I want to know everything about you," says Camilla from Thomas's class at school, that first evening later in the year, in the autumn.

She comes over to him at the class party. For a long time Thomas sat alone in the corner of a sofa wondering about what it feels like now, after the four beers he has drunk, one after another with the express intention of getting drunk for the first time in his life.

It feels like nothing in particular.

The second evening Camilla says she loves him.

Thomas is speechless. Camilla says that is good. You should not say you love someone until you actually mean it.

The fourth evening, with Kayus safely ensconced in the television chair in the other room, on the other side of the wall, Thomas slips into the closet and lifts down a yellow cardboard box marked "Isabella's things." He carries it into his room, opens the lid, and turns it upside down on his bed so the contents spill out on to the bedspread between him and Camilla. He switches on the bedside lamp so that everything is brightly lit.

"Wow!" says Camilla. "Like the whole of your childhood in a box."

■ ■ ■

Then Thomas says that thing about being seventeen.

He is dissatisfied. Why can't he put things in a better way? That seventeen stuff in his mouth sounds like some dumb popular song.

You can see that now in Camilla's expression. A popular song, that is what's scattered on the bed before her eyes. She picks up something, a photograph torn out of a magazine. The photo is of Anita Ekberg in the most famous fountain in the world. Camilla frowns and asks what it is.

Thomas is speechless. He knows exactly what it is. It is the good life. But he cannot say it. Not for the life of him.

Seventeen: For a moment Thomas wonders why Buster Kronlund can say certain things so that they sound good.

But Camilla loves Thomas. That saves him. Camilla is quick to hear Thomas's silence, his inability to reply. She assumes that she has inadvertently touched on a sore spot.

During those moments when Thomas's speechlessness lies like a desert between Thomas the speechless and Camilla with a scoffing smile on her lips at the question Thomas cannot answer, Camilla tries to put herself into Thomas's situation. As a result she frowns again, the frown lines forming an upside down T, in a way that is unlike, almost essentially different from, Buster Kronlund's girlfriend, his present one, and all the others. But no harm is done. If she looks strange, she won't in the future. Thomas will get used to her. He will learn to love that upside down T, too, like other things about Camilla. Almost everything.

But now it is still Camilla who is doing the thinking.

Camilla sees that Thomas lacks words with which to express himself, and she takes it upon herself to articulate and put things into words, since she is the more verbal one of the two. In one stroke, while Camilla puts herself in Thomas'ss situation, she is transformed into the person she presumes has lain dormant in Thomas and who has now suddenly popped out like the genie from the lamp—or from that yellow cardboard box between them. *The wronged, abandoned child.*

She is still holding the picture of Anita Ekberg in her wet clothes in the Fontana di Trevi.

Then she falls silent.

Her scornful expression dies away. She suddenly understands something she cannot express. *It's wrong. Very wrong.*

She puts the picture back. Among the things on the bed: the photograph signed by Paul Anka; a red, white, and blue scarf Thomas knows is called the Tupsu Lindbergh scarf; an EP record of The Twist; a Dunhill lighter, gold-colored; a bottle of UltraNet hair spray; curlers; the sleeve of a record, *Chet Baker sings*, Pacific Records, 1956; and other stuff, *all kinds of other stuff.*

All kinds of things, Thomas.

Camilla suddenly says, in quite a different tone of voice, "It's nice, Thomas. Really nice."

ALDRIN WITH THE SEISMOMETER AT TRANQUILITY BASE.
THE HIGH POINT OF THE DECADE.
WE ARE NOW LOOKING FORWARD TO A NEW DECADE.

In the other room, on the other side of the wall, Kayus has turned the volume up even higher. He watches a great deal of television these days. Does not listen to records so much any more. The only discussion on jazz between him and Thomas in recent years takes place when Thomas tells Kayus that he read that Chet Baker had had his teeth knocked out by hooligans in San Francisco.

"Good," says Kayus. "That'll shut him up."

Though that is not true, either. Chet Baker still rumbles through the pipes in the building. At first they thought that whoever was playing the records was doing it to annoy them, in revenge for all the music played at odd moments, including in the bathroom, during the time when the mermaid lived there. But gradually they realized that the perpetrator actually loved jazz.

But now Kayus has turned up the sound on the television because he is anxious not to disturb Thomas. He is pleased that his son has a girlfriend, a sensible girl who comes to see him. And this is in the days when prudish people deserve pity. The sexual drive is a natural drive in all mammals, both in younger and older specimens.

"It's nice, Thomas," Camilla has said.

Thomas is speechless.

A moment later he is no longer speechless.

He thinks one thing and says it: "I love you." And turns out the light.

testers, 1973

I think I saw you in an ice-cream parlor
drinking milk shakes cold and long
Smiling and waving and looking so fine
don't think you knew you were in this song

1973, MARCH: Renée Angel, sixteen, in a black wet suit in a fitting room at the department store. The expensive rubber material gleams and clings to her skin. Music is coming from the loudspeaker above her head, near the mirror.

Renée is barefoot, her toenails are long and uncared for. her outdoor clothes, the heavy winter garments, lie in a heap on the green wall-to-wall carpeting. Renée is careless about her clothes, which are of good quality.

All that black on her body in the mirror: her limbs, legs, arms, and knuckles as delicate as chicken wings.

Gooseflesh. Renée unwraps a meat pasty from its greasy paper. She sits down on the stool in the fitting room, leans back against the wall, and eats.

1973, MARCH: Renée goes to Gabby's office. She rides up in the elevator. Sits in a fat brown leather armchair intended for visitors. Sinks deep down in its softness, Donald Duck in an armchair facing a solid desk behind which sits a pig, a red-faced director puffing at cigars and laying down the law. Gabby does not smoke. As happens during confidential interviews in American television series, he tells his secretary to hold all calls during Renée's visit. And it is she who is expounding on her plans.

The delivery of the specially ordered new boat, *Shamrock*, from England in three or four weeks will initiate the coming sailing season. This year she is moving up a class from Flying Junior. But that is not why she is being given a new boat. Every season starts with a new boat. At least one new boat every season. Gabby himself telephones to England. You never know with the English. They are not all equally reliable. As the Germans are, or the punctual Japanese, or even the Finns, those peasant Finns with their peasant brains but their sound peasant common sense. Renée grins. *Arrival on schedule.*

Training camp in France. Two weeks, at the end of April.

Gabby nods in agreement and efficiently takes out, guess what, yes, of course, his wallet. As if somehow he were involved as more than a financier, with a corner in, a participant in, Renée's plans. He is not.

1973, MARCH: Gabby has loads of money. A vagrant drunk-like smell of onions and slushy snow from the pasty seeps out under the green curtains of the fitting room. They move. A female voice. She is dying to draw back the curtain. Makes your fingers itch, Renée hears, but hell, she doesn't dare. They are scared shitless. Renée knows it, and she also knows it, that woman in the suede pumps with fake gold buckles, in which her feet wobble. She doesn't dare. Gabby has loads of money, and no one doesn't know that Gabby has money. That is just as Gabby likes it. Renée is careless with all the good clothes she buys on Gabby's credit card. She does not care about clothes, and yet she buys more and more, spending afternoons, whole days, in the stores, strolling from department to department, shopping absently, with an arrogance that frightens and annoys the life out of the clerks, who do not *have* what Renée *has*, who would like to *have*, but do not *have* because it is Renée who *has*.

The wet suit is the latest model, later than the latest. Renée must have it, of course she must have it, because of the special zipper, because of the brand name, because it costs so much, for the sailing season, but first and foremost, and especially, for no reason at all.

When she has finished the pasty. She finishes it. "I'll take this." She heaves the wet suit on to the counter in front of the lady in the suede pumps, "and this" about a stopwatch lying on the counter, "and this" about a Space Pen which writes under water, from a box by the cash register. And so, of course, she smiles and hands over the credit card Gabby gave her.

Daddy will pay. They clean up after her in the fitting room. They find a sanitary napkin in the waste basket, not very stained, just used, and as if it had been worn for several days.

On this day Renée goes to the record department and asks the clerk for the name of the record coming over the loudspeakers.

She buys it.

It changes her life. Then everything is different.

1973, APRIL: She crops her hair. Puts a henna rinse in it. Buys ivory-colored foundation. Paints her eyelashes black, draws black lines above and below her eyes. Draws, with a trembling hand, a flash of lightning on her forehead. Orange, outlined in black.

1973, JUNE, JULY, AUGUST: The red in her hair fades. Successful sailing season. Everything runs smoothly. Super.

1973, SEPTEMBER: Back to school. New red color. New cropped hair. Cigarettes. Wears a brown leather strap around her neck: symbol. In love.

Time takes a cigarette, puts it in your mouth.

White clothes, glistening satin. Arouses attention, spiky, angry. Walks the dog together with Charlotta Pfalenqvist, a neighbor and in her class at school, along lighted sidewalks. In love with Charlotta's boyfriend Stefan. Stefan and Charlotta have nothing against Renée. She looks so special, and her daddy has money, just as their daddies have money, so it is not the most important thing, but it does stand for the basics; and besides, she is a famous sailor.

1973, SEPTEMBER: They are a gang now. Some from their own class and others from school, some from the district, chosen, regarding themselves as chosen for each other's company because of similar family circumstances. "Snobs, mods, nauseating spoiled brats," says Nina in the bus on her way home from the Solidarity Committee meeting in a timeless green duffle coat that clashes with Renée's Satin Gleaming Coat (two thousand marks). Renée has dusted gold glitter on her cheeks. She goes to the hairdresser's once a week now, to have her appearance Just Right, and in the gang of spoiled nauseating brats, she is the Mascot, the only Space Child, considerably more sophisticated than others seen sporadically in town, with mixed hair colors and faces painted with liquid Mary Quant crayons or quite ordinary Crayola sticks. Renée is the Best Quality Space Child, but she will die soon, so we must not begrudge her this position. But no one knows that she will die, and everything is so different when Nina, with her long, proletarian hair, turns to Renée: "Don't you ever think about other people? About what it's like for others?"

At the Pfalenqvists' there is at least one set of stereo speakers in every room. Renée dances alone. She likes being the Lone Space Child while the others are necking in the darkness of the big basement room with the open fireplace and drink too much. Renée does not drink, she only smokes. "What's that?" says Stefan, tugging at her necklace. She looks dazzlingly into his eyes. "Just one of those things." And moves away. She is so damned shy.

He knows she is in love with him. Everyone is in love with him. On the other hand, Charlotta is the prettiest and has the most luscious lips. The other girls are like copies, yes, all of them except sullen Renée, who is blatantly sexless and can be discounted when it comes to being with someone, copies of Charlotta's blooming blond Val d'Isère and Barbados suntanned face and her bubbling laugh, particularly at dirty stories, of which she herself knows many. She can also be insolent, incredibly and subtly insolent. Sometimes some of the boys bring other girls, girls from town or from the eastern working-class suburbs. They are usually pretty, but their clothes are *too much,* they wear things like *that horrible fake bracelet,* and what they do not do is keep up with the idiom; not so much that they don't have the money to go to Barbados—that isn't what anybody talks about at parties; travel, all the external things, are obvious prerequisites, things you just have, that seem just to exist, in the background, like the unspoken basics—but because they fucking well do not know what they're talking about when Charlotta says to Renée, for instance, that you *blow up,* and then they usually just get drunker than ever out of nervousness, and then it is easy to tell them to piss off for Now Unfortunately All Outsiders Must GO. Unfortunately, unfortunately . . . .

1973, a party at Charlotta Pfalenqvist's, late September: Renée and Charlotta load up on cheap booze and Marc Bolan records. Renée gets drunk for the first time in her life, with the exception of the final festivities at the international sailing races in France, where she ate paté de fois gras and drank champagne in the regatta tent, so much that her legs gave way under her when she tried to get up to dance with the head judge, but that is her sailing life, the super sailing life so alien to this life, with Charlotta and with Stefan, with whom she is in love. She does not know why, that's just how it is. She wanted a friend. Charlotta has become her friend. Charlotta jumps in and out of Renée's basement window during these weeks in autumn, before Renée dies.

Yes, it is true; Renée is living in the basement in the enormous house, the villa Gabby and Rosa had built to their specifications. Living in the basement sounds worse than it is. The ground level of the house contains a sauna, a room, a swimming pool, and what they call the billiard room though it is furnished with only an ordinary ping-pong table before Renée says that she needs it, there is more privacy in the basement. *I have to concentrate.* Renée keeps her sailing cups on shelves along the walls, puts speakers in two corners of the room, sets an enormous beanbag chair on the floor and enjoys plenty of empty space, and that ping-pong table, it is okay, it can stay. Three posters: Angie and David Bowie, the one's head on the other's shoulder. Herself in *Shamrock II*, an enlargement. A dinosaur grazing in a not very lush primeval landscape. She has a bathroom to herself. On the bathroom shelf bottles of perfume are neatly lined up: Chanel No. 5, Chanel No. 19, and Chanel No. 20. Perfume, not toilet water. There's a separate row for TESTERS. She steals other things, too, but they have to be expensive and difficult to steal. It is a test, mostly a test. *You have to concentrate.*

At some time in the middle of Charlotta's party, when Renée is drunk and making the rounds, talking casually to everyone, she undressed and went alone into the sauna. That must be considerably later, for suddenly it is quite silent in Charlotta's house, everyone has gone home, fallen asleep, is necking somewhere, or is in one of the many bedrooms in the house. Charlotta has passed out, that is for sure. Renée has cleaned the vomit off the carpet in Charlotta's room.

Renée is swimming naked in the pool. Stefan comes in. She knows that. She has always known he would come.

New love á a boy and a girl are talking
New words á that only they can share in
New words á a love so strong it tears their heads to sleep
through the fleeting hours of the morning

Stefan jumps into the pool. They swim. Is she dreaming? No, Stefan is there, in the sauna, in the big room, on the sofa; she looks out at the blue water of the pool, a square of which she can see through a window in the room, while—while he comes roughly into her. Stefan's body is dark, his eyes dark, closed, his chest birdlike and fragile, quite hairless, the arrogant crease in the corners of his mouth particularly marked just before he ejaculates all over her stomach. She has been looking at him all the time and out into the blue, all the time holding on hard to his shoulder blades, fragile as wings in the palms of her hands.

Stefan covers her face with his hand as he comes. Not from hatred or disgust, but because he is miles away, somewhere where Renée does not exist. In Lo-ve-land. Stefan.

Stefan falls asleep. Renée wriggles out from under him. She wraps herself in Charlotta's mother's bathrobe, goes into the house, which is empty, into the kitchen, sits on the Pfalenqvists' luxurious washing machine, and smokes a cigarette.

When she goes back down to Stefan, he is sprawled all over

 the sofa. Renée lies down on the shaggy white rug and covers herself with damp towels.

She wakes because someone is pressing against her body. She opens her eyes to make sure that it is Stefan. It is not Stefan, but another space child, a boy with hair cropped as short as hers but not as red and it is a mess, she cannot believe her eyes, though she has seen him before, although she knows who he is, although he is at all the parties, although he has run after her, actually the only one to run after her at parties, although he has imitated her style, someone she loathes, what is he doing here? What happened to Stefan? What happened to the blue? What happened to the silence?

Music is pouring out of all the loudspeakers, and Stefan's hoarse laugh is coming from somewhere. The room is full of new people, new girls, and the person pressing his body against her, thinking that she is asleep, is Lars-Magnus Lindbergh.

She kicks him. In the crotch, in his stomach, hard, as hard as she can. She gets to her feet and goes on kicking Lars-Magnus Lindbergh. The others in the room grin, especially Stefan, who is quite different now, wide-jawed, his arm around two outsider girls, while Charlotta is asleep in her own vomit up in her neat girl's room below her "Ho! We're Going To Barbados!" posters. But there's nothing she can do but let the party go on.

And the party goes on.

1973, a few days later: At the Pfalenqvists, they are taking an inventory of missing and ruined property: broken glasses, stolen cash, refrigerator emptied, and a ruined green carpet (what were those girls from the suburbs called?), house arrest for Charlotta (except for walking the dog in the evenings with

Stefan or Renée, or Stefan and Renée), the blame put on Lars-Magnus Lindbergh, whose parents, Tupsu and Robin, are visited by a parental delegation. Tupsu and Robin Lindbergh promise to keep Lars-Magnus under special observation. He is peculiar, he has started dying his hair and hanging around Renée's house. Renée wants nothing to do with him, nor do Gabby and Rosa. Nevertheless, to annoy Gabby and Rosa, Renée sometimes lets Lars-Magnus Lindbergh into her basement.

Stefan comes too, occasionally, when she is alone, on his way home from walking the dog with Charlotta. He lies with Renée on the beanbag chair or in Renée's bed, and she holds hard on to his prominent shoulder blades. His eyes are closed. He leaves. There's a light in Charlotta's window.

1973, October, two weeks before Renée's death: Lars-Magnus Lindbergh's parents, Tupsu and Robin, send out invitations to a fancy-dress party for young people, closely chaperoned, at their house. In actual fact, they deeply fear falling into disfavor with the Pfalenqvists, well aware that they themselves still live in this leafy little town, where even the dogs are shorter.

Gabby and Rosa take the dog out. Stefan comes and takes Renée on the floor. Nina comes home from the Solidarity Committee, and encouraged by the thought that she does not really belong here, she goes into the house through the basement.

Stefan disappears. Renée bites Nina's wrist and makes it bleed.

"You're crazy. I could get rabies."

Gabby and Rosa come back. Renée has locked herself in the basement. In the bus the next day Nina says, "He's using you. Don't you have any pride, you sick pig?"

Renée knows. She kneels down and spies out through her sailing cups, Champion I, Second Prize, Regatta Queen, spying on Stefan and Charlotta walking the dog together, all three taking short steps on the sidewalk under the glorious autumn colors.

She remembers the blue and feels those shoulder blades, sharp, summoning, in the rough palms of her hands where she bites the skin.

What I have is my love of love and love is not to love/ loving/ love.

It is not the declaration of a program. It is not a formula. It is a jingle, the words of a song.

"Uses her"—of course. The song somehow justifies the feeling. Justifies, does not justify: it doesn't matter.

TESTERS: you have to concentrate.

You may think that harmful, repressed aggressions are accumulating in the big white basement room in which Renée has locked herself to be left in peace to spy on love, which is not to love/loving/love, between all her trophies, which, after all, certify that she is a capable, smart, and really nice girl, one many people envy but what the cups proclaim does not interest her, or at least she can easily disregard these messages in favor of huddling on her table spying on the three swaggering off down Baarman Avenue. You might think that acts of revenge were being forged in that confused mind, which is not used to losing. You might think that perils, perils of puberty, are on the horizon.

Renée stares, establishing the facts. Oh yes, there go Stefan and Charlotta, and perhaps he will come and take her later. Perhaps, perhaps not.

It is the secret of the dog's leash—a kind of masochism, but also revolt. Stefan sees it. Renée knows he sees it.

1973, October, ten days before Renée's death: But there are also other moments. When, for instance, Renée is lying in the beanbag chair reading her international sailing journal to find the right terminology to use in letters to her international sailing friends, who think of her as an equal, who admire her, because she is one of the few girls, perhaps the only girl, with real success in sailing races.

Then Lars-Magnus Lindbergh taps on the window, and the normal changes into the grotesque. He has brought cassettes with him. She lets him in. Lars-Magnus's hair is actually redder than hers now, his face is chubbier, but he is imitating her, that is obvious. At the moment, anyhow, he is not wearing a satin shirt as she is, but a white T-shirt, and his face is painted with Mary Quant crayons, exhibiting that lack of style she detests. Lars-Magnus Lindbergh assaults her on the beanbag chair. She struggles free. He rips off the T-shirt, he turns off the light, and she wriggles away, puts the light back on, receives a blow in the stomach, and they wrestle on the floor. There is a tap on the window. It is Stefan and Charlotta, their sweaters bulging with apples they have just swiped. All four of them eat apples. Things are not good with Lars-Magnus Lindbergh. Renée senses that instinctively. She is the status Space Child, he wants to be in on it at all cost. Things are not good with Lars-Magnus Lindbergh.

All four eat apples. The candles burn.

"Oh, go to hell," says Renée to Lars-Magnus Lindbergh and kicks out at him. Charlotta and Stefan grin, and they go on for a while until Lars-Magnus Lindbergh agrees to be banished. He understands not a thing, the dumb idiot. Then, when they are just three, there is talk about some stupid cassette. Stefan talks, looks at Renée, and urges Charlotta to go and get it, it is on the bed in her room, he left it there. After a great many *ums* and *ifs* and *buts,* Charlotta goes off to get it.

When she has gone, Stefan unzips his trousers. He takes hold of Renée's head, kneels beside her where she is sprawled on the beanbag. And her mouth is full when Charlotta again taps on the window on the other side of the curtains. Stefan opens the door. Renée is in the john, rinsing out her mouth under the faucet. Bits of apple in it. Mmm. *I.like.you.*

1973, a week before Renée's death: Stefan has found, put his finger on, and now goes on pressing Renée's vulnerable point. The secret place, which is the equivalent of chicken wings in Renée's mind, what shows when she is alone in fitting rooms in the middle of the most sophisticated and elegant orgy of consumption, and, long ago, also had its equivalent in a defeat after an attempt to flee into the forest with tent and knife and all. Stefan fiddles with the strap around Renée's neck, presses his hand against Renée's face, and it comes for him, she is open, wet.

It isn't about love/non-love/to love/loving. We've entered a new dimension now. *Testers. You have to concentrate.*

He telephones her from home one Saturday. His parents have gone on a cruise with Charlotta Pfalenqvist's parents.

Renée still has the taste in her mouth. Trala-trala.

He takes her to his room, a boy's room. He locks the door. he takes out a leather strap, thin, a dog's leash. It is pale blue and may have belonged to the little dog he had six months ago, perhaps, perhaps not. Cherry Bomb, the reason why he and

Charlotta got together. Together they cultivated grieving, talked out while they went out with her, Doggie dear, really the whole Pfalenqvist family's but particularly Charlotta's because she is so spoiled. The world is full of dogs.

He fastens the leash to Renée's neck. He ties the end to the bedpost, after jerking on it a few times to see if her head moves. It moves. Renée's expression is not her usual sulky one. It is vacant.

She is sitting on the floor with her back against his bed, allowing herself to be tied up, although she could perfectly well undo the strap and leave. Impossible. Symbol.

Stefan is turned on. Renée has the taste in her mouth.

He draws the curtains, goes out of the room, and leaves her in the dark. That is also calculated, again; she could easily free herself, draw back the curtains and leave. She doesn't. It is like a game, or a test. Whatever.

Time takes a cigarette, puts it in your mouth. Burns a finger, then another finger, then—

But she is still not ready to give up. She has to concentrate. Stefan comes back. They drink wine out of ordinary kitchen tumblers. They smoke cigarettes and talk of nothing, as if the pale blue leash did not exist, as if all kinds of things, listening to music, even laughing.

Then the others come, Stefan's friends, three of them. Renée knows them slightly, they are a few years older than her. They will play cards, that is the arrangement. "You can stay or you can go," says Stefan roughly, as if he had happened to establish that the sea is blue, for the sea is blue and she is sure to stay. She drinks more wine, smokes, lies down on the bed, listens to the music, the card game going on beyond the door in another room, time passes, dusk falls beyond the curtains, the sense of floating. The room, my friend, do not be afraid of the room.

TESTERS: you who do not know what a game is. Or tests.

You have to concentrate.

Renée knows it all.

Stefan is first.

It's about to fall apart.

The others are the others. It falls apart.

Renée undoes the leash, gets up, leaves Stefan's house, goes straight to Charlotta's house.

Charlotta has baked an apple pie, and they eat it with custard.

Renée tells Charlotte about Stefan and herself in a way that makes Charlotta phone Stefan immediately, to tell him that it's all over. Then she turns to Renée, giggling and fooling around, takes her to her mother's dressing table, and paints her face ivory with a flash of lightning on her forehead.

But what is it in Renée that makes people want to do something to her, Charlotta, too, by tenderly painting her into a space child? Charlotta would never paint herself like that. Never! Charlotta is solid and sunny and natural. Through Renée she can evoke something in herself that she does not dare to see directly.

What is *too much* in this story is that Stefan and Charlotta reunite a week or two later, spurred on by the fact that Renée has died. They work out their grief, talk it through, love, which they say to each other they are doing, holding hands, in other words somehow repeating the process that brought them together in the first place, the grieving for Stefan's dead dog, Cherry Bomb, the dog that had a pale-blue leash and was, allegorically speaking, trampled to death at a cocktail party.

1973, October, a few days before Renée's death: in the department store's fitting room; Renée takes out the pasty. In her mind's eye she sees the grayish-brown gloves with holes for cracked fingertips on the woman in the pasty stand. She blows up. "I haven't fucking got any more," insisting until she gets a discount. Her real purse is in her bag, not in the trouser pocket she dug into. Her handbag, yes, it was closed, and she could not be bothered to open it. She is wearing something red: some kind of athletic suit with jacket and pants.

The fifth mouthful tastes disgusting. She spits the fifth mouthful straight into the waste basket. She retches and flings away the remains of the pasty, now spilling over with rice and bits of meat, and it lands on the floor, rice and egg yolk, hard, on the green wall-to-wall carpeting.

She stands up and brushes crumbs off her suit.

She sees her face in the mirror. There is no music in her head, although the store reverberates with it. It is silent. She wets her palm and fingers with pasty-smelling spit, drags them through the short hair, over the crown of her head, until her hair is damp. She lowers her head a trifle. Her face seems especially oval, her eyes protruding, if she keeps her head lowered, extra large and dark. She raises her head, breathes in and out, in and out, in a rhythm of her own; now, her face close to the mirror, she exhales. The mirror mists over. The warmth and moisture from her breath strikes back into her own face. She sticks out her tongue. She licks the mist off the mirror in long swoops, forcing herself to go on licking despite the growing unpleasantness. She licks until she retches and spews into the waste basket, a mouthful. She sits down on the stool, puts her head between her knees, and presses her knees against her temples. Ten seconds.

Then the thunder starts again. She pricks up her ears.

1973, October, a few days before Renée's death: Rosa comes to Renée's basement. She sits down on the enormous beanbag chair, is surprised at losing her balance as the beanbag wraps itself around her, lands half-lying on the floor, has had one sherry too many. Both are embarrassed, not over the beanbag or the sherry, but because Rosa and Renée usually never meet in Renée's basement room. When necessary, Renée goes upstairs. It is also true that Gabby, in his capacity as financier of the sailing project, chauffeur, and wallet, has more to do with Renée's life than Rosa does.

Renée is busy painting her nails white. Rosa looks at the splayed fingers on the table. "Great," she says, "lovely," just as she usually compliments Renée on her red hair, white makeup, white satin shirt, which she nevertheless thought too expensive, much too expensive for Renée. "Great," says Rosa, not ingratiatingly. She means what she is saying; the main thing for Rosa, among other things the main thing, is that Renée is not and never has been slovenly in the way so many other teenagers are slovenly. Renée has style—that weird space outfit.

Rosa would like to ask about that.

She will have reason to regret that she does not.

In addition, not much coaxing would be necessary with Renée on this day, she's painting her nails white, painting herself carefully to catch sight of herself, for something fell apart earlier in the day, behind green curtains. Or? Afterthoughts, Stefan, she took off the necklace, with mixed feelings, and as soon as she had taken it off, she vomited, weakened, caught by detectives.

So there should be some basics now, Renée should be able to imagine being flung back into the world of infantilists, thoroughly and lengthily describing the shy starman somewhere in space who feels lonely and wants company and would like to descend to earth and get to know the people there, if it were not for the fact that he is afraid to "blow our minds," frighten us, frighten us to death with his space appearance.

Rosa scrambles into a better sitting position on the floor and straightens out the rug beside her, suddenly remembering that she is here to settle a dispute with Gabby up on the first floor; she had literally promised she would go and see what "her daughter was REALLY up to" because the department store has been in touch with Gabby. Renée was caught in the perfume department in a clumsy attempt to steal a bottle of Chanel No. 19, toilet water not perfume. Under normal circumstances Renée would never dream of stealing toilet water—it isn't hard to steal. Then they contacted Gabby, and so the shambles in the fitting room in the sports department came to light. GOOD GOD I MEAN NO NO what did they think of her, that she was a crazy cunt, tell me now if I'm sort of crazy, my hand in daddy's pocket where his wallet is, the buckles on those pumps go up, don't the staff get discounts so that they can wear proper shoes in this department store? I mean: the world is full of department stores.

You could blow up.

The bottle of toilet water annoys Renée. So many failures, one after another. What was happening, was she losing her strength? Removing the dog collar: a sign of loss? Washing yourself clean, be clean, new, white, glimmering, start again. And again. Start again and again and again.

It was such a clumsy attempt, a semiattempt at stealing. Naturally the store should just have let it go. Calling Gabby was a formality. Gabby drove Renée home, and on the way she made him laugh at her descriptions of the women in the perfume department, the same laugh she herself cultivated. I would not take toilet water, as if I don't know what I want. I took it simply to tease them, like a test, you have to concentrate. As soon as Gabby is back home, he goes to Rosa and asks her why she does not know what "her daughter is REALLY up to," at which Rosa, fortified with her third glass of sherry, pulls herself together and says that it is his business just as much as hers, and when did he last speak to Nina, *for instance.*

Nina is Gabby's weak point. They do not speak to each other. In Nina's eyes—as in Renée's eyes, but Gabby does not know that. That would destroy Gabby (the only thing that could console Gabby, if he knew, is that he is not a pig in the same ideological and political way for Renée). Renée hates Commies, Reds like Nina and her stencil-ink-smelling friends who bully Renée at school, less so since she's become the Space Child and found a home in the revolting Bracke gang, who are so noisy and important they can be hated, not directly as they hated Renée before, but with a touch of respect, somewhat like a partner you are prepared to argue with—in Nina's eyes, for some time back, Gabby has been the same as the pig on the other side of the desk in the handsome office building twelve floors up in a world where the air-conditioning works perfectly for half of one percent of the population, puff puff puffing cigars and deceiving decent people on the other side of the desk into signing disadvantageous contracts, dismissing the needy of the world with a cold hand . . . .

Nina and all other good people tramp the sizzling hot

streets, rattling their collection boxes; we must do something, it concerns us!

Rosa is proud of Nina, in the same way and for the same reason that she is proud of Renée: neither is a slovenly teenager dressed in T-shirts so short that their navels show. But Renée, now finished doing her nails, has also used her, Rosa's, Overcoat Enamel, which makes the polish dry at once, while she herself, Rosa, tries to stay elegantly seated, giggling, the sherry apparently gone to her head again, on this elegant seat on her daughter's enormous beanbag, without knowing what to say.

She asks Renée if things are going all right at school.

Renée looks at her from her superior position on the table, where she is seated cross-legged, rocking back and forth to the music, and Rosa has never seen such carefully black-framed eyes before, such white eye shadow sparkling on eyelids, such pale cheeks, and such brilliant red hair. Rosa again fumbles in her strange chains of thought: cannot get this person sitting cross-legged on the table aligned with someone else in an orange T-shirt and with unspeakable hair it was forbidden to touch, running strands between her front teeth, glittering with saliva.

"Hello. What's happening?"

Rosa realizes that she has said nothing again, that once again she has lost the thread, that yet again she has had one glass too many.

"Mommy." (Does she actually say Mommy, or does she say Rosa? Rosa will brood at length over that question in the weeks, months, years to follow, will perhaps never stop brooding over it, but in her mind she gradually decides on Mommy once a suitable time has passed; these are actually some of the last words Renée will ever say to Rosa, the last sentences of all, just between the two of them, to be exact.)

"Mommy," says Renée. "Have you seen that movie with Elizabeth Taylor, *A Place in the Sun*?"

Renée bursts into hysterical laughter, which excludes Rosa. It is the type of laughter discussed in pamphlets for parents who suspect their children are taking drugs and the pamphlets note that when parents hear it, they have good reason to be truly suspicious. But Rosa does not think in those terms, she merely feels hurt and excluded by Renée's laughter. On her way to losing her grip, heavens, she shouldn't have another sherry, not one single damn sherry more. That has to be it, the end, *fini!*

"You're just a little tipsy, Mom. Don't go over the top. Pull yourself together"—Rosa usually goes to Nina with her problems (and in Nina's room that was just what they called it: *problems*), never the other way around; she went to Nina's room, and here in Renée's room now, she begins to see the difference between her two daughters, the totally different, stranger-alien Renée room, bare and smelling differently, Chanel No. 5, makeup, sweat, menstruation, teenager, and Chanel No. 5, that strange mixture of hot-dog stand and perfume that is so confusing, compared with Nina's brightly lit stencil room, the numbers of dead on the walls, the collection boxes. We have to do something. *El pueblo unido amacer . . .* she was really truly proud of Nina. My daughter is aware of what happens in the world, she was able to say in her social world, making her daughter into a trump card. In her social world, elegantly seated in the social world, but cracking up there, too, recently quite obviously. While the other women, especially the sparkling Gunilla Pfalenqvist, becoming increasingly sparkling, self-confident, and aware in accordance with the times, without having to renounce their own elegance, still able to bewitch everyone present for whole evenings as she occasionally imagined she could, or was it a myth, was that also a myth, ALSO a myth she screams to herself as she thinks over and over again later on that evening, guaranteed recklessly drunk, sniveling, entangled in her own silk pantyhose, brand name Wolford, for there is no point in having tights which are not the Wolford brand, in the solitude of the bathroom, ALSO a myth, like the myth of rebellion in connection with her tedious marriage to an old school friend? As disheveled as Elizabeth Taylor in "Who's Afraid of Virginia Woolf," she will ask Gabby in the bed beside hers, in the best therapy language: *Gabriel, is there any point to our marriage?* With the difference that she will be talking to an empty pillow, since Gabby has long since left home to meet one of this flight attendants, who are not always flight attendants, but flight attendant is the collective term, JESUS, so Rosa does not bother with any of it, TOMORROW IT IS OVER, ENOUGH, total STOP. Never again never never never any more sherry but a nightcap, a sundowner, then Nina comes in, no, there are no longer any thoughts, she has no thoughts, has become a thoughtless person without *fuel:* she is so thirsty now. "Mommy, are you sitting there feeling sorry for yourself again?" "Pull yourself together." "Don't look on yourself as a victim." "Take an interest in something."

Rosa is truly proud of Nina.

But she is still in her other daughter's room, wondering what is really wrong with her, when, elegantly, in the social world, when she fails to enchant, or somehow simply cannot, simply cannot finish sentences she has started and speaks indistinctly and inarticulately with no drink whatsoever, getting involved in retelling long-winded jokes without ever getting to the point, to put it briefly, arranging herself painlessly increasingly within the framework of the filthy rich bourgeoisie, portrayed by Nina as loathsome, the epitome of her contempt and revulsion.

And now she is seated on her daughter's enormous beanbag and has lost every single thread.

There is not much more, apart from the fact that she is thirsty, that after she stops laughing, Renée starts reading an international sailing magazine, ignoring Rosa. But that makes Rosa, oh hell, that makes her, OH HELL, remember her whole life, so that when she closes the door of Renée's room and goes upstairs to the kitchen, where she secretly drinks during the times when she is secretly drinking and does nothing else, a vague but powerful feeling of utter abandonment comes over her. *Someone abandoning someone completely.* She needs sherry for the particulars of that feeling. Someone leaving someone. It is vague. But who is it? Renée? Rosa? Do not think it's unambiguous. For it is not unambiguous.

Renée stays cross-legged on the table like a yogi.

Quietly she feels her strength returning, purity, stillness, the complete part . . . particular. A faint Rosa smell, drink and "Diorissimo." She opens the window to get rid of it. Entirely. To be particular alone.

Suddenly, as her strength returns, she remembers a powerful image. When she was a wild creature in the forest. Had a knife, smelled of pine trees, of sweat and sap, hunted by fifteen rifles, *God*, how she likes the thought of being free and hunted in the forest.

■ ■ ■

1973, October, a few days before Renée's death: (She had a friend, Thomas. He ran after her in the summers, not like Lars-Magnus Lindbergh, because she hates Lars-Magnus Lindbergh. Once he beat her up. Usually, she was the one who hit. She bit him, she never abandoned the habit of biting, or ever wanted to abandon it. He had been a real friend, Thomas. They had done things together: played rockets, gone fishing, and drowned a cloth dinosaur from a row boat. Does she never think about Thomas? Is there nothing to link her now to Thomas, the only true friend? It isn't all that long ago. Don't they ever run into each other by The Three Blacksmiths statue and talk on these warm late autumn days? No, Renée does not meet Thomas during these days before her death. Does not even think about him. Why should she . . . does she know about the link between them? Is she aware of Julia, now seven? Hardly, it is not a topic of conversation, quite Out Of The Question.)

1973, October, Lars-Magnus Lindbergh's party. Renée sinks: Lars-Magnus Lindbergh is wearing his black wet suit. It is the only fancy dress at this fancy dress party. Even Renée has put on something quite ordinary. The drink is free and flowing. That is always a reason to go to a party. Renée has brought a waterproof tape recorder, yellow, encased in rubber, one of Gabby's products; a test model. She brought it along to play on the bus and out of doors, not to take with her on the Lindberghs' old mahogany tub, which is actually still moored by the jetty almost farthest in among the reeds. Renée, part of a noisy elite gang in a hot bus one Saturday afternoon, is taken to the Lindberghs' island across the bay, which she knows like the back of her hand but which now seems alien, in the

Lindberghs' latest, fast, shiny model, a fiberglass craft, by Klas Lindbergh, who has presumably been put in charge of chaperoning the party, but who is soon devoting himself to Charlotta's delights swirling blondly and freshly in the autumn wind, the cold hard wind sweeping around the boat taking the horrible upper-class young to the Lindberghs' huge mansion hovering hawklike over the bay on the highest hill of the largest island. From the Lindberghs' jetty, where she is sitting with her yellow tape recorder, Renée looks at everything that to her is utterly alien. The house on the hill far away on the other side of the bay is empty or has been rented out. Do they even own it any longer? Renée cannot remember, they own so much, she cannot remember everything. And they have acquired places out in the real archipelago as well, beyond the sound.

Time takes a cigarette. Puts it in your mouth. Burns a finger. Then another finger. Then . . . .

Cigarette.

She sees the boat in the reeds, jumps down on deck, bounces up and down, the timber gives way on the Lindberghs' shiny mahogany speedboat, once the most coveted object in the bay, now cast aside, lacking style, shabby and used, like the Lindberghs themselves.

There are eight chosen young people freely helping themselves from the Lindberghs' punch bowl and the Lindberghs' dishes of shrimp with toast and mayonnaise.

There are seven chosen young people after Charlotta disappeared with Klas Lindbergh, who still has some kind of bronze charm anyhow, charm or not: Charlotta is eager to get THAT over with very quickly. The thought of getting THAT over with has taken up her time ever since she broke with

Stefan after she learned what he'd done to Renée (owing to the circumstances, Stefan is not one of the chosen young people), who had got rid of THAT. Charlotta has even bought condoms—ribbed ones by mistake. On the bus she and Renée bet on whether you can feel the ribbing. Charlotta will never have a chance to report who won the bet. Actually, Renée dies, in just a few hours. Charlotta giggles in a way that indicates that perhaps she did not buy ribbed condoms by mistake. That it is a test; is she also a tester?

"Do you know what's special about you?" says Charlotta Pfalenqvist on the bus. "What's special about you," Charlotta Pfalenqvist goes on, "is that you have a cassette tape recorder on which you can't play ordinary cassettes."

"It's the wrong *standard,*" whispers Renée, drawing out the word so noticeably that some of the horrid upper-class girls sitting in front of them turn around and glance with envy at the understanding between Renée and Charlotta Pfalenqvist.

"And it's waterproof," Renée goes on. Her warm breath tickles Charlotta Pfalenqvist's marvelous ear with its ruby earring.

"No?" Charlotta Pfalenqvist raises her eyebrows, just as her mother Gunilla Pfalenqvist usually does, and smiles, just as Renée usually smiles, for Renée and Charlotta are aware that everyone on the bus is looking enviously at the two of them.

"Yes," says Renée. "Idiot. Why else do you think it's made of plastic?"

If at that moment Renée had known that she was going to die in a few hours' time, she might have railed a little at her fate; she might have preferred to see what was going to happen, about her and Charlotta Pfalenqvist.

Charlotta switches on the tape recorder and turns up the volume.

Your face, your race, the way that you talk
I kiss you, you're beautiful, I want you to walk
We've got five years

But there are no years left, no months.

Hours, minutes, that's all.

They are five chosen young people left after Lars-Magnus and Renée have gone out to sea in the Lindberghs' discarded mahogany tub. The wind is six on the Beaufort scale. The seas are high, their lights the only things visible in the darkness. The darkness at sea is not black but green and gray, and a few stars are shining in the sky. The green and gray are cold, the foam, the stiff wind and a slow, tingling awareness that they are going wrong, the fact that Lars-Magnus Lindbergh insists he knows the waters like no one else, except possibly Renée, now curled up on the bottom with her tape recorder which is still playing in the wind and the cold, and her growing irritation with Lars-Magnus Lindbergh, who is a bungler and an idiot.

Then they run aground. CLANG, rock bottom . . . into the green, gray windy darkness lit only by stars and their own bright lights.

But as yet Renée is still on land. She has gone back to the party, eaten shrimps on toast, tasted a glass of horrible punch, poured it into the sink, and left her open-faced sandwich the wrong side up on Tupsu Lindbergh's sofa.

■ ■ ■

She continued up to the first floor, where Charlotta is in one room with Klas Lindbergh but where the other room is empty. An empty room, Klas Lindbergh's brother's, whatever was his name? From there she looks out again. She can see farther from here than she can down from the jetty. The flagpoles, the roof ridges, and the forest she knows, . . . I want to, thinks Renée, Christ how I want to go . . . somewhere. And she imagines herself out at sea. She goes downstairs and out, then on the jetty and sees a suitable boat. Then Lars-Magnus Lindbergh comes and says that they have to take the old tub, the old boat, he says, the family's old boat. He is drunk. What the hell does he want to come for? In he jumps, starts her up, and off they go, heading straight for the Johanssons' sauna on the shore. But at the last moment they turn and steer through the sound and out to sea. Nor is the sauna any longer the Johanssons'. The Johanssons have bought the white villa and are moving in: they are building a grand sauna above the glass veranda, *with all conveniences.* The wood jetty on the shore no longer exists, either. The inlet is overgrown with reeds. The bottom of the bay has silted up on this side, it has not been dredged. No one is interested in dredging it, since no one is hardly ever down on the beach; somehow there is no time: Erkki messes about with mopeds in the garage.

But Renée and Lars-Magnus are no longer there.

They're out on the open sea.

CLANG, rock bottom, in the darkness. The engine stops. Lars-Magnus Lindbergh is screaming that he can't. Just stands there screaming while the lights go out, and yet he is the one wearing the wet suit.

"I can't, my hands are stiff!"

And Renée: "Wait now, idiot, let me." But her fingers are just as stiff, and she knows nothing about engines.

The boat comes free immediately. It is drifting in the wind and is carried on waves that are high. Renée realizes very quickly that there is not much they can do. And when she and Lars-Magnus Lindbergh together try to raise the engine to look at the propeller, she grasps something else besides—that it is useless, because it is so dark and they have no flashlight; that there is a hole in the boat, that the boat is leaking, and that the water slowly filling it must be coming from below.

"Bail!"

Lars-Magnus obeys like a sleepwalker.

"Nothing will happen. Bail now, you idiot, we're close to land."

All lies. Everything will fall apart.

Renée has only a vague idea of where they are. The boat may be drifting out to sea (it is actually drifting toward land. Lars-Magnus Lindbergh survives in his wet suit, is found unconscious but alive on the beach of a summer cottage. Clothes that might have belonged to Renée, who is lost, are not found until the spring on an islet).

She is fumbling with the distress flares.

Lars-Magnus is bailing.

Three flares light up the sky, one after another, the fourth and last fails, fails to rise. Then there is only deep silence.

At this stage the boat is full of water, waves crash over it.

Last of all they tried to cling to the foredeck: the tricky thing is that although events ought to go quickly, everything happens quite slowly. They had time to lift the orange life jackets from under the foredeck and to put them on, but not to fasten them, so that they loosen at once in the water, time for those flares—to prepare themselves, in other words, while the silence and darkness continue all around them.

They shout all the time. Their shouts are not heard.

Not in this story, either. The shriller the cries, the more silent it becomes.

Lars-Magnus Lindbergh knows one thing: *he is going to die.*

Renée and Lars-Magnus Lindbergh are clinging to the foredeck. There, somewhere, Lars-Magnus Lindbergh loses sight of Renée. She just disappears, swept off deck, sinks, is lost. Then Lars-Magnus Lindbergh is alone in the cold and the dark, drifting with the boat. Then there is no longer a boat. Lars-Magnus Lindbergh starts swimming. Dark. Empty. Then the buzz of an engine and helicopter blades, searchlights lighting up the sea . . . .

By then Renée is already dead. Sunk. Drowned.

Quite a distance away, under the stars.

Nothing but wind and gray there. And green darkness.

A yellow tape recorder somewhere in the water.

Lars-Magnus Lindbergh, numbed and unconscious, but alive, miraculously alive, is found on a shore fifteen minutes later, after sounds of helicopter rotors and motorboat engines, lights shattering the stillness and the whistling dark in which Renée has disappeared and is lost.

But, listen, somewhere, from outer space perhaps, this song begins to be heard, reproducing itself out there at sea in the autumn darkness and the hideous cold, sailing over the waves in the wind with Lars-Magnus Lindbergh totally weak and unconscious somewhere and the scuttled mahogany magnificence smashed to pieces on the rocks. And there, somewhere in the water, lies a waterproof yellow tape recorder, keeping the water out.

Didn't know what time it was the lights were low
I leaned back on my radio
Some cat was laying down some rock'n roll lotta soul, he said Then the loud sound did seem to fade
Came back like a slow voice on a wave of phase
That weren't no D.J. that was hazy cosmic jive

There's a starman waiting in the sky
He'd like to come and meet us
But he thinks he'd blow our minds
There's a starman waiting in the sky
He's told us not to blow it
Cause he knows it's all worth while
He told me:
Let the children lose it
Let the children use it
Let all the children boogie